Bound to the Billionaire

CHANTELLE SHAW
MAGGIE COX
CHRISTINA HOLLIS

MILLS & BOON

First Published in Great Britain 2016
By Mills & Boon, an imprint of HarperCollins*Publishers*
1 London Bridge Street, London, SE1 9GF

BOUND TO THE BILLIONAIRE © 2016 Harlequin Books S. A.

Captive In His Castle, *In Petrakis's Power* and *The Count's Prize* were first published in Great Britain by Harlequin (UK) Limited.

Captive In His Castle © 2013 Chantelle Shaw
In Petrakis's Power © 2013 Maggie Cox
The Count's Prize © 2012 Christina Hollis

ISBN: 978-0-263-92071-0

05-0716

Our policy is to use papers that are natural, renewable and recyclable products and made from wood grown in sustainable forests.The logging and manufacturing processes conform to the legal environmental regulations of the country of origin.

Printed and bound in Spain
by CPI, Barcelona

CAPTIVE IN HIS CASTLE

BY
CHANTELLE SHAW

Chantelle Shaw lives on the Kent coast, five minutes from the sea, and does much of her thinking about the characters in her books while walking on the beach. She's been an avid reader from an early age—her schoolfriends used to hide their books when she visited, but Chantelle would retreat into her own world and still writes stories in her head all the time. Chantelle has been blissfully married to her own tall, dark and very patient hero for over twenty years and has six children. She began to read Mills & Boon as a teenager, and throughout the years of being a stay-at-home mum to her brood found romantic fiction helped her to stay sane! She enjoys reading and writing about strong-willed, feisty women and even stronger-willed sexy heroes. Chantelle is at her happiest when writing. She is particularly inspired while cooking dinner, which unfortunately results in a lot of culinary disasters! She also loves gardening, walking and eating chocolate (followed by more walking!).

Catch up with Chantelle's latest news on her website: www.chantelleshaw.com.

CHAPTER ONE

'WHO THE HELL is Jess?'

Drago Cassari raked his fingers through the swathe of dark hair that had fallen forward onto his brow, concern and frustration etched onto his hard features as he stared at the motionless figure of his cousin lying in the bed in the intensive care unit. Angelo's face was grey against the white sheets. Only the almost imperceptible rise and fall of his chest indicated that he was still clinging to life, aided by the various tubes attached to his body, while the machine next to the bed recorded his vital signs.

At least he was now breathing unaided, and three days after he had been pulled from the wreckage of his car and rushed to the Venice-Mestre hospital there were indications that he was beginning to regain consciousness. He had even muttered something. Just one word. A name.

'Do you know who Angelo is referring to?' Drago turned his gaze on the two women who were standing at the end of the bed, clinging to each other and weeping. 'Is Jess a friend of Angelo's?'

His aunt Dorotea gave a sob. 'I don't know what his involvement with her is. You know how strangely he has been behaving lately. He hardly ever answered his phone when I called him. But I did manage to speak to him a few days before…' her voice shook '…before the accident, and he told me that he had given up his college course and was living with a woman called Jess Harper.'

'Then perhaps she is his mistress.' Drago was not overly surprised to hear that his cousin had dropped out of the business course he had been studying at a private London college. Angelo had been overindulged by his mother since his father's death when he had been a young boy, and he shied away from anything that approached hard work. Rather more surprising was the news that he had been living with a woman in England. Angelo was painfully lacking in self-confidence with the opposite sex, but it sounded as though he had overcome his shyness.

'Did he give you the address of where he was staying? I need to contact this woman and arrange for her to visit him.' Drago glanced across the bed to the expert neurologist who was in charge of his cousin's care. 'Do you think there is a chance that the sound of her voice might rouse Angelo?'

'It is possible,' the doctor replied cautiously. 'If your cousin has a close relationship with this woman then he might respond if she talks to him.'

Aunt Dorotea gave another sob. 'I'm not sure it would be a good idea to bring her here. I am afraid she is a bad influence on Angelo.'

Drago frowned. 'What do you mean? Surely if this Jess Harper can help to rouse him then it is imperative that she comes to Italy as soon as possible? Why do you think she is a bad influence?'

He controlled his impatience as his aunt collapsed onto a chair and wept so hard that her shoulders shook. His jaw clenched. He understood her agony. When he had first seen Angelo after he had undergone surgery to stem the bleed in his brain Drago had felt the acid burn of tears at the back of his throat. His cousin was just twenty-two, in many ways still a boy—although when *he* had been that age he had already become chairman of Cassa di Cassari, with a great weight of responsibility and expectation on his shoulders, he remembered. The deaths of his father and uncle, who had been killed in an avalanche while they were skiing, had thrust Drago into the cut-throat world of big business. He had also had to take care of his devastated mother and aunt, and he had assumed the role of a father figure to his then seven-year-old cousin.

Seeing Angelo like this tore at his insides. The waiting, the wondering if the young man would be left with permanent brain damage, was torture. Drago was a man of action, a man used to being in control of every situation, but for the past three days he had felt helpless. His aunt and his mother were distraught, and he wished he could comfort them and assure them that Angelo would recover. For the past fifteen years he had done his best to look after his family, and he hated the feeling that in this situation he was powerless. He had no magic wand to bring Angelo back to consciousness, but he had the name of a woman who might be able to help.

His mother was gently patting her sister-in-law's shoulder. 'Dorotea, you must tell Drago what Angelo has done, and why you are so worried about his involvement with the Englishwoman.'

Drago stared at his aunt. 'What *has* he done?'

For a few moments she did not answer, but at last she choked back her sobs. 'He has given this woman money…a lot of money. In fact all of the inheritance that his father left him,' Aunt Dorotea said in wavering voice. 'And that's not all. Jess Harper has a criminal record.'

'How do you know this?'

'A week ago Maurio Rochas, who used to be in charge of Angelo's trust fund and still acts as his financial adviser, phoned me. He was troubled because what he had to tell me was confidential information, but he felt I should know that Angelo had withdrawn his entire inheritance fund from the bank. When I spoke to Angelo I asked him what he had done with the money. He was very abrupt with me,' Aunt Dorotea explained in a hurt voice. 'It was most unlike him. But he finally admitted that he had lent his inheritance fund to this woman—Jess Harper—but he did not say why she needed the money, or when it would be repaid.'

Drago knew that the bulk of his cousin's inheritance was tied up in shares and other investments, but Angelo still had a huge fortune available to him—which he had apparently handed over to a woman who had a criminal record. It was not surprising Aunt Dorotea was concerned.

'Angelo was very cagey,' she continued. 'I felt he was hiding something from me. I was so worried that I phoned Maurio back to discuss the matter. Maurio admitted that out of concern for Angelo he had tried to find out more about this Englishwoman and had discovered that she was convicted of fraud some years ago.'

Drago swore softly and received a reproachful glance from his mother. *Dio!* He could not help feeling frustrated. Sometimes he wondered if his relatives would ever take charge of their own lives instead of relying on him to deal with their problems. He had encouraged his cousin to go to England to study, believing that it would do him good to be more independent. But it sounded as though Angelo had walked straight into trouble.

'What has the damned idiot done?' he muttered beneath his breath.

Unfortunately his aunt had excellent hearing.

'How can you blame Angelo? Especially when his life hangs in the balance?' she said tearfully. 'Perhaps this Jess Harper told Angelo some sob story that he fell for. You know what a soft heart he has. He is young, and I admit a little naïve. But I'm sure you remember how *you* were conned by that Russian woman years ago, Drago. Although of course that situation was a lot worse, because your actions almost forced Cassa di Cassari into bankruptcy.'

Drago gritted his teeth at his aunt's reminder of the most humiliating episode of his life. When he had been Angelo's age his judgement had been compromised by a woman's beautiful face and sexy body. He had fallen hard for the sensual promise in Natalia Yenka's dark eyes, and he had persuaded the board members of Cassa di Cassari—the luxury homeware company that had been founded by his great-grandfather—to make a huge investment in the Russian woman's business venture. But the venture had been a scam, and the catastrophic financial loss incurred by Cassa di Cassari had resulted in Drago only narrowly escaping a vote of no confidence from the board.

Since then he had worked hard to win back their support, and he was proud that under his leadership Cassa di Cassari had grown to be one of Italy's highest-grossing businesses, with a global export market. At the recent AGM he had announced that the company would be floated on the stockmarket for a record opening share price that would raise several billion pounds.

It had been Drago's crowning moment—one that he had striven for with ruthless determination—but neither the board members nor his family knew of the personal sacrifices he had made in the pursuit of success, or of the emptiness inside him.

He shook his head as if to dismiss his thoughts, although dark memories of his past lingered in the shadows of his mind. Focusing his attention once more on his cousin, he felt a sharp pain, as if a knife blade had been thrust between his ribs. He did not think his aunt would cope if she lost her only son. This desperate waiting and hoping was intolerable, and if there was even the slightest chance that hearing the Englishwoman's voice would bring Angelo back from the abyss then Drago was convinced that he must persuade her to come to the hospital.

'Where are you going?' his aunt asked tremulously as he swung away from the bed and strode across the room.

'To find Jess Harper. And when I do you can be sure I will demand some answers,' he replied grimly.

Struggling to carry her heavy toolbox and a bulging bag of groceries, Jess let herself into her flat and stooped to pick up the post from the doormat. There were two bills, and a letter which she recognised was from the bank. For a moment her heart lurched, before she remembered that her business account was no longer in the red and she did not have to worry about paying back a hefty overdraft. Old habits died hard, she thought ruefully. She wondered if the novelty of being financially solvent would ever wear off.

On her way down the hall she glanced into Angelo's room. It was still unusually tidy—which meant that he hadn't come back. Jess frowned. It was three days since he had disappeared, and since then he hadn't answered any of her calls. Should she be worried about him? He had probably moved on to another job, like so many of the casual labourers she employed did, she told herself.

But Angelo had been different from the other labourers who asked for work. Despite his assurances that he had experience as a decorator it had quickly become apparent that he did not know one end of a paintbrush from the other. Yet he was clearly intelligent and spoke perfect English, albeit with a strong foreign accent. He had explained that he was a homeless migrant. His gentle nature reminded Jess of her best friend Daniel, whom she had known at the children's home, and perhaps that was why she had impulsively offered him the spare room in her flat until he got on his feet. Angelo had been touchingly grateful and it just wasn't like him to leave without saying goodbye—especially as he had left his stuff, including his beloved guitar, behind.

Reporting him missing seemed like an overreaction, and although it was a long time since her troubled teenage years she still had an inherent mistrust of the police. But what if he'd had an accident and was lying in hospital with no one to visit him? Jess knew too well what it was like to feel utterly alone in the world, to know that no one cared.

If she hadn't heard from him by tomorrow she would notify the police, she decided as she dumped the bag of groceries on the kitchen worktop and dug out the frozen ready meal she'd bought for dinner. She'd missed lunch. Owing to a mix-up with paint colours, the job she was working on was behind schedule—which was why Angelo's disappearance was so inconvenient. He might not be the best painter in the world—in fact he was the worst she'd ever known—but to get the contract finished on time she needed all the help she could get.

The instructions on the box of pasta Bolognese said it cooked in six minutes. Jess's stomach rumbled. Six minutes sounded like an eternity when she was starving. Taking a screwdriver from her pocket, she pierced the film lid and shoved the meal into the microwave. At least it gave her enough time for a much-needed shower. A glance in the mirror revealed that she had white emulsion in her hair from where she had been painting a ceiling.

Pulling off her boots, she headed for the bathroom, stripped off her dungarees and shirt and stepped into the shower cubicle. One day, when she could afford to buy her own flat, the first thing she would do would be to install a power shower, she thought as the ferocious jet of water washed away the dust and grime of a hard day's work. For her birthday the previous week she had treated herself to a gorgeous luxury shower *crème*. The richly perfumed lather left her skin feeling satin-soft, and using a liberal amount of shampoo she managed to rinse the paint out of her hair.

Her team of workmen would tease her unmercifully if they found out that she had a girly side, she thought ruefully. Working in an all-male environment was tough, but so was Jess—her childhood had seen to that.

The sound of the doorbell was followed almost instantly by the ping of the microwave telling her that her food was ready. Pulling on her robe as the doorbell went again, she padded barefoot back to the kitchen. Why didn't whoever was ringing the doorbell give up and go away? she wondered irritably. The microwave meal smelled unpleasantly of molten plastic, but she was too hungry to care. She peeled back the film covering and cursed as the escaping steam burnt her fingers. The doorbell rang for a third time—a long, strident peal that Jess could not ignore—and it suddenly occurred to her that maybe Angelo had come back.

Drago snatched his finger from the doorbell and uttered a curse. Clearly no one was at home. He had broken the speed limit driving from the airport to Hampstead, which was where, he had learned from his aunt's lawyer, Jess Harper lived. According to Maurio Rochas the Englishwoman was a painter. Presumably she had a successful career to be able to afford to live in this attractive and affluent part of north-west London, Drago mused. He guessed that the Art Deco building had once been a magnificent house. It had been converted into six flats that must be highly sought after.

Maurio had not known any more information about the woman Angelo had been living with, and as yet the private investigator Drago had hired to run a check on her had not got back to him. But for now the question of why his cousin had given her money was unimportant. All that mattered was that he should persuade Jess Harper to visit Angelo. Hopefully the sound of her voice would rouse him from his unconscious state.

Where the hell *was* she? He wondered if she worked from a studio—maybe he could get the address from a neighbour. He did not have time to waste searching for her when Angelo's condition remained critical. Frustration surged through him and he pressed the doorbell again, even though he knew it was pointless. He was exhausted after spending the past three days and nights at the hospital, snatching the odd half-hour's sleep in the chair beside Angelo's bed.

His eyes felt gritty and he rubbed his hand across

them as images of his cousin flashed into his mind. Angelo had been a sensitive, serious little boy after his father's death, and he had hero-worshipped Drago. It was only during the nightmare of the last few days, while Angelo hovered between life and death, that Drago had acknowledged how deeply he cared for the young man he had helped to bring up.

There was no point waiting around when it was clear that Jess Harper wasn't here, he told himself. He was about to head back down the stairs when the door of the second-floor flat suddenly opened.

'Oh!' said a voice. 'I thought you were someone else.'

Drago spun round, and as he stared at the figure standing in the doorway his breath seemed to rush from his body. He felt a strange sensation, as if his ribcage had been crushed in a vice. There had only been one other occasion in his life when he had been so blown away by a woman, and then he had been an impressionable twenty-two-year-old. Now he was thirty-seven, highly sexually experienced—and, if he was honest, somewhat jaded from a relentless diet of meaningless affairs. But for a few crazy seconds he felt like a hormone-fuelled youth again.

His nostrils flared and he gave his head a slight shake, utterly nonplussed by his reaction. He had met hundreds of beautiful women in his life, and bedded more of them than he cared to think about, but this woman quite literally took his breath away. His eyes were drawn to the front of her white towelling robe, which was gaping slightly to reveal the pale upper slopes of her breasts. The realisation that she was probably naked beneath the robe heated his blood, and every nerve-ending in his body prickled with fierce sexual awareness.

Swallowing hard, Drago studied the woman's face. It was a perfect oval, and her delicate features looked as though they had been sculpted from fine porcelain. The high cheekbones gave her an elfin quality that was further accentuated by her slanting green eyes. Her long, damp, dark red hair contrasted starkly with her pale skin.

Something unfurled deep in his gut—a primitive hunger and an inexplicable sense of possessiveness that made him want to seize her in his arms and lay claim to her.

'Can I help you?'

Her voice was soft, with a slight huskiness that made his heart jolt. He found himself hoping that his aunt's lawyer had made a mistake with the address and this woman was not his cousin's mistress. The idea of Angelo making love to her incited a feeling of violent jealousy in him.

He gave himself a mental shake, irritated by his body's unwarranted response to her, and demanded abruptly, 'Are you Jess Harper?'

Her green eyes narrowed. 'Who wants to know?'

'My name is Drago Cassari. I understand that my cousin Angelo has been living here with you.'

'*Cousin!*' She sounded genuinely shocked. 'Angelo told me that he was alone and had no family.'

So he had the right address, and the right woman. Drago's jaw tightened as he struggled to dismiss the image that had come into his mind of tracing the perfect cupid's-bow shape of her lips with his tongue. As he walked towards her she retreated behind the half-open door and eyed him distrustfully.

'I was unaware that Angelo had any relatives. Do you have proof that you are his cousin?'

Irritated by her suspicious tone, he withdrew his mobile phone from his jacket and accessed a photograph stored in the phone's memory.

'This is a picture of me with Angelo and his mother, taken six months ago when we attended the opening of the new Cassa di Cassari store in Milan,' he explained, handing the phone to her.

She stared at the screen for several moments. 'It's definitely Angelo, although I've never seen him wearing a tuxedo before,' she said slowly. 'But…it doesn't make sense. I don't understand why he never mentioned his family.'

Drago did not think it strange that his cousin had kept details of his private life secret. The Cassaris were one of the wealthiest families in Italy and attracted huge media attention. Drago had been hounded by the paparazzi since he was a teenager. He had learned to choose his friends carefully, and had taught his cousin to do the same. Although if the information about Jess Harper having a criminal record was true, then perhaps Angelo had not been careful enough, he mused.

The confused expression on Jess Harper's face was surprisingly convincing.

'There's a Cassa di Cassari department store in Oxford Street that sells the most beautiful but incredibly expensive bedlinen and other household furnishings.' If she ever won the lottery, Jess had promised herself that she would shop exclusively at Cassa di Cassari. 'It had never occurred to me until now that Angelo has the same name—Cassari. I suppose it's just coincidence.' She looked at the photo of the shop-opening again and her frown deepened. 'I mean—Angelo can't have any connection to a world-famous brand-name—can he?'

Could she really not know? Drago found it difficult to believe that she was unaware of Angelo's identity.

'Our great-grandfather founded Cassa di Cassari shortly after the First World War. After our fathers were killed in an accident I inherited a seventy per cent stake of the company. Angelo owns a thirty per cent share.'

Drago's eyes narrowed when Jess Harper made a startled sound. Either she really had not known the true extent of his cousin's wealth or she was a good actress. Perhaps she was wishing she had 'borrowed' more money from Angelo, he thought cynically. But for now the question of how she had got her hands on Angelo's inheritance fund wasn't important. He simply wanted to get her to Italy as quickly as possible. There would be time for questions once his cousin had regained consciousness.

She thrust his phone at him. 'I don't understand what's going on, or why Angelo lied to me, but he isn't here. He left a couple of days ago without saying where he was going and I have no idea where he is. I'm afraid I can't help you.'

She began to close the door, but with lightning reaction Drago jammed his foot in the doorway.

'He's in hospital, fighting for his life.'

Jess froze. Her anger and incomprehension that Angelo had not been honest with her faded and she felt as if an ice cube had slithered down her spine. She was shocked to hear that he had a family and dumbstruck by the revelation that he was connected to the famous Cassa di Cassari luxury Italian homeware brand. The whole thing was unbelievable, and if it wasn't for the photo of him on Drago Cassari's phone she would have assumed it was a case of mistaken identity. But the news that Angelo was in hospital was more shocking than anything.

'Why…? I mean, is he ill?' She felt guilty that she had not reported Angelo missing. He was a nice guy, and she should have realised that he would not have moved out of her flat without saying goodbye.

'He was in a car accident. He suffered a serious head injury and has been unconscious for three days.'

Drago Cassari spoke in a controlled voice, but when Jess looked closely at him she saw lines of strain around his eyes.

She felt sick as she pictured Angelo the last time she had seen him, the evening before he had disappeared. She had cooked dinner—only omelettes, which was all her limited culinary skills could manage—and he had been flatteringly appreciative and afterwards helped with the washing up. She had been surprised to find he was gone the following morning, but she had assumed he was used to being alone, just as she was, and hadn't thought to inform her he was going away. As the days had passed she had started to worry, though—independent as he was, he was still young.

Drago Cassari's voice cut into her thoughts. 'I've come to ask if you will visit him in hospital. The longer he remains unconscious the more chance there is that he will have permanent brain damage.'

'He's that seriously hurt?' Jess swallowed as she imagined Angelo injured and unconscious. A memory flashed into her mind of seeing Daniel in Intensive Care after he had been knocked off his push-bike by a speeding car. He had looked so peaceful, as if he was asleep, but the nurse had said he was only being kept alive by the machine that was breathing for him and that he was showing no signs of brain activity. Jess had understood that Daniel was seriously injured but she hadn't expected him to die. He had only been sixteen. Even eight years later, thinking about it brought a lump to her throat.

Could Angelo die? The thought was too awful to contemplate, but from his cousin's grave expression it was clearly a possibility.

'Of course I'll visit him,' she said huskily. She had no idea why Angelo had told her he was alone and destitute, but the mystery of why he had lied wasn't important when his life was at risk.

She stared at the man who said he was Angelo's cousin and saw a faint resemblance between the two men. Both had olive skin and dark, almost black hair. But, unlike Angelo's untidy curls, Drago Cassari's hair was straight and sleek, cut short to reveal the chiselled bone structure of his features. And whilst Angelo could be described as boyishly attractive, with his soulful eyes and gentle smile, his older cousin was the most striking, *lethally* sexy man Jess had ever met.

His face was cruelly beautiful—hard and angular, with slashing cheekbones and eyes the colour of ebony beneath heavy brows. His jaw was square and his mouth unsmiling, yet the curve of his lips was innately sensual. Jess could not stop staring at his mouth—could not prevent herself from wondering what it would feel like to be kissed by him. She knew without understanding *how* she knew that his lips would be firm and he would demand total capitulation to his mastery.

Her wayward thoughts were so unexpected that she almost gasped out loud. Her gaze was drawn upwards to his eyes and she saw something flicker in their inky-dark depths that evoked a curious dragging ache deep in her pelvis. Shaken, she looked away from him and snatched a breath.

'Of course I'll come to the hospital,' she repeated. 'I'll just get some clothes on.'

As the words left her mouth she became acutely conscious that she was naked beneath her bathrobe. She stiffened as Drago Cassari subjected her to an intent scrutiny. She had the feeling that he was mentally stripping her, and she clutched the edges of the robe together, hoping he could not guess how fast her heart was beating.

The glitter in his dark eyes warned her that he was fully aware of his effect on her. She felt herself blush and wondered why she was behaving so strangely. She worked in an all-male environment and was regarded as 'one of the lads' by her team of workmen. Only once in her life had she been sexually attracted to a man, and the experience had left her with emotional scars that would never completely heal. Since then she had been too busy with her job to have time for relationships— and maybe too scared, she acknowledged honestly. She did not respond to men on a sexual level, and she was shocked by her reaction to a stranger—even if he *was* the sexiest man she had ever laid eyes on.

Drago Cassari wasn't a stranger; he was Angelo's cousin, she reminded herself. She felt ashamed for indulging in inappropriate thoughts about him when Angelo was in a critical condition. Taking a deep breath, she ignored the unsettling thought that she did not want to be alone with a man who exuded such raw sexual magnetism and pulled the door open fully to allow him to enter her flat.

'Do you want to come in and wait? It'll only take me a minute to change.'

'Thank you.' He stepped through the doorway and instantly seemed to dominate the narrow hall. He must be several inches over six feet tall, Jess estimated. The fact that he was dressed entirely in black—jeans, shirt and leather jacket—accentuated his height and powerful physique. Standing so close to him, she caught the sensual musk of his aftershave, and she felt a tingling sensation in her nipples as they hardened and rubbed against the towelling robe.

Horrified that she seemed powerless to control her reaction to him, she led the way down the hall and ushered him into the sitting room. 'If you would like to wait in here, I won't be long.'

'While you are getting ready I'll call the hospital for an update on Angelo's condition.' He glanced up from his phone. 'I hope your passport is valid.'

Halfway out of the room, Jess paused and gave him a bemused look. 'Why do I need my passport to visit a hospital? Where is Angelo, anyway? The Royal Free Hospital is the closest to here.' She hesitated. 'But I don't know where the accident happened. Was it locally?'

Drago had walked across the spacious sitting room to stand by the window. The view of the leafy suburb of Hampstead was charming. Glancing around the room, he was impressed with the excellent quality of the décor and furnishings, which reinforced his opinion that Jess Harper must have a lucrative career to be able to afford this stylish apartment.

He turned his head and it seemed to Jess his black eyes bored into her very soul. 'It happened in Italy,' he said flatly. 'On the highway between the airport and Venice. I assume Angelo was coming home, but he never made it. He's being cared for at a hospital in Mestre, which is on the mainland of Venice.'

His phone buzzed and he looked down at the screen.

'I've had a message to say that my plane has been re-
fuelled. Can you be ready to leave for the airport in
five minutes?'

CHAPTER TWO

'AIRPORT!' AS THE meaning of Drago Cassari's words slowly sank in Jess shook her head. *'I can't go to Venice!'*

In a minute she would wake up and find she'd been having a crazy dream, she thought dazedly. Maybe the six double-shot espressos she'd drunk during the day instead of eating a proper lunch were causing her to have strange hallucinations—because this could *not* be happening.

'Don't you care about Angelo? I thought you had a close relationship with him.'

Drago's harsh voice broke the silence, forcing Jess to accept that he was not a figment of her imagination.

'Of course I care that he's hurt,' she said quickly. 'But I wouldn't say that we have a close relationship, exactly. I've only known him since he started working for me about two months ago.'

'He *worked* for you?' It was Drago's turn to look puzzled. 'What kind of work? I was informed that you are a painter.' Into his mind flashed a startling image of his cousin posing for her. 'Did Angelo model for you?'

'Hardly,' Jess said drily. Crossing the room, she took a business card from the desk and handed it to him. 'I paint houses, Mr Cassari, not masterpieces.'

The card read 'T&J Decorators' and gave a phone number and a website address. Drago glanced at it and then looked back Jess, struck once again by her petite stature and fragile build. The notion that she was a manual labourer was ridiculous.

'Do you mean you are an interior designer for this decorating company? Or do you deal with office administration? I find it hard to believe that you actually paint walls for a living.'

Jess was irritated by the note of disdain she was sure she heard in his voice. 'I do some general decorating, but as a matter of fact I'm a trained chippie—a carpenter,' she explained when he frowned. 'I also act as site foreman and make sure that my workmen finish their contracts on time and follow safety procedures.'

His black brows lifted. 'It seems an unusual career choice for a woman.'

She was tempted to tell him that very few careers were available to someone who had flunked school and failed to gain any academic qualifications. She would have loved to train to be an interior designer, but most people working in the industry had an art degree, and she had more chance of flying to the moon than going to university.

'And you're saying that you employed Angelo as a decorator?' Now Drago's tone was sceptical. 'Why would he choose to work as a labourer when he belongs to one of the wealthiest families in Italy?'

'You tell me.' The situation was growing more bizarre by the minute, Jess thought. 'I took him on because I was short of staff. To be honest he was pretty hopeless at decorating, but he said he had no money and nowhere to live and I felt sorry for him. I told him he could stay with me until he could afford to rent his own place.'

Drago's expression became blatantly cynical. 'Why would you do that for someone you barely knew?'

'Because I know what it's like to reach rock-bottom.' Unbeknown to Jess her eyes darkened to deep jade as she recalled the despair she had once felt. There had been a time when she had felt she had nothing to live for—until her wonderful foster-parents had given her a home and a future.

She had sensed despair in Angelo and had wanted to help him as she had been helped by Margaret and Ted Robbins. But now she felt a fool. Why had he made up all that stuff about being poor and homeless when, according to Drago Cassari, Angelo came from a wealthy family?

She stared at Angelo's cousin, her mind reeling. 'How do you know about me?' she demanded, unsettled by his statement that he had been given information about her. It almost sounded as though he had asked someone to investigate her. The situation was so unreal that anything seemed possible.

He gave a noncommittal shrug. 'Angelo spoke about you to his mother, and obviously he gave her the address of where he was living in London.

'Oh…yes, I suppose he would have done.'

Drago studied Jess Harper speculatively for a few moments. He had no intention of revealing that he knew Angelo had given her money. He did not understand what was going on, and until he had more facts he did not want to give away too much. He checked his watch. 'We need to be going.'

'I'm sorry, but I can't go with you.' Jess bit her lip. She felt terrible about Angelo, but disappearing off to Italy simply wasn't an option. 'I have a business to run—we're behind schedule on our current contract and I can't—'

'He spoke your name.' Drago cut her off in a driven voice. His accent was suddenly very pronounced, as if he was struggling to control his emotions. 'This morning Angelo roused very briefly and he asked for you.'

He walked towards her, his midnight-dark eyes never leaving her face. 'You might be his best hope of recovery. Hearing your voice might be the key that will release him from his prison and bring him back to his family.'

Jess swallowed. 'Mr Cassari...'

'Drago,' he said huskily. 'You are Angelo's friend, so I think we should dispense with formalities.'

He halted in front of her and Jess had to tilt her head to look up at his face. She felt overwhelmed by his height and sheer physical presence. Her heart slammed against her ribs when he laid a finger lightly across her lips to prevent her from speaking.

'*Please*, Jess. Angelo needs you. *I* need you to come with me. I think of him as my brother, even my son—for since his father died I have tried to be a father to him.'

Dear heaven, how could she refuse such a heartfelt entreaty? The raw emotion in Drago's voice made Jess's heart ache. Only a few days ago she had listened to Angelo playing his guitar, but now he was fighting for his life. She thought of Daniel, who had never regained consciousness. Surely if there was a chance she could help Angelo she must try?

Her common sense argued that she would be crazy to agree to go away with a man she had never met before, but she was haunted by the image of Daniel the last time she had seen him. He had died a few hours after her visit. She hadn't been allowed to attend his funeral—the head of the care home had decided it would be too upsetting—and so she had never had a chance to say goodbye.

'All right,' she said shakily. 'I'll come. But I need to make some phone calls and arrange for someone to cover for me at work.'

Mike could take over as foreman while she was away. She trusted him, and knew he would push her team of decorators to get the contract finished. Thoughts raced through Jess's head. She was fiercely proud of T&J Decorators and hated the thought of leaving it even for a few days. Like most businesses in the construction industry, the company had suffered because of the economic recession, but thankfully the windfall of money she had recently received meant that T&J was now financially stable—as long as she kept working hard and securing new contracts.

'I can only be away for a couple of days,' she warned.

She glanced at Drago and felt a tiny flicker of unease when she found him watching her intently. He was so big and imposing, and there was a faintly predatory expression in his eyes that made her think of a lethal jungle cat preparing to make a kill—and she was the prey. But when she blinked and refocused on him she cursed herself for being over-imaginative. His smile was dangerously attractive but the only thing she had to worry about was her unexpected reaction to him.

'Thank you,' he murmured in the husky accent that sent a shiver across her skin. 'I hope that Angelo will respond when he hears your voice. When it is time for you to leave Italy I will arrange for you be flown home on my plane.'

Once the matter of Angelo's missing inheritance fund

had been resolved, Drago thought to himself. As Jess stepped away from him his eyes were drawn to the deep vee of her robe, which revealed the curve of her breasts, and he felt a sharp stab of desire in his gut as he imagined untying the belt around her slender waist and sliding his hand inside the towelling folds. The glimpse of her body evoked a picture in his mind of her lying beneath him, her milky-pale thighs entwined with his darker olive-toned limbs. Light and dark, soft and hard, fiery Latin male and cool English rose.

He met her startled gaze and was intrigued to see soft colour stain her cheeks. The mysterious alchemy of sexual attraction was impossible to explain, he mused. He recognised that she felt it as fiercely as he did, and under different circumstances he would have wasted no time in bedding her. But the circumstances could not be more wrong. His cousin was critically injured and, for all her apparent concern for Angelo, Jess Harper had a lot of explaining to do. For now, Drago was prepared to keep an open mind, but he could not risk his judgement being undermined by indulging in fantasies of her naked in his arms.

The sound of her voice dragged him from his uncomfortable thoughts. 'I'll get dressed, and if you don't mind quickly have my dinner,' she said as she hurried over to the door. 'I haven't eaten all day. It was ready when you arrived and it will only take a couple of seconds to reheat.'

'*Santa Madonna!* You mean that terrible smell is your evening meal?' Drago was genuinely horrified. 'I thought you had problems with the drains.'

Jess felt a spurt of annoyance at his arrogant tone. There had been plenty of times in the past when she hadn't been able to afford to buy even the cheapest supermarket budget food, and even though she now had money she was careful with it. She doubted Drago Cassari had ever known what it felt like to be so hungry that you felt sick, or so cold that your bones ached, as she had often been as a child.

'I take it you don't often dine on microwave meals?' she said drily.

His eyes narrowed at her sarcastic tone. 'Nor do I ever intend to. There's no time for you to eat now. We'll have dinner on the plane. Please hurry,' he added impatiently. 'While you are wasting time Angelo's condition may be worsening.'

By the time they landed at Marco Polo airport Jess was under no illusion about what kind of man Drago Cassari was. Powerful, compelling and utterly self-assured, he took control of every situation with quiet authority, and she'd noticed that everyone around him, from the airport staff to the crew on his private jet, treated him with a deference few men could command.

Maybe it was his wealth that set him apart from ordinary people and gave him an air of suave sophistication. She guessed he must be well-off. Let's face it, how many people had she ever met who owned their own plane? she thought wryly. When they had boarded his jet a uniformed steward had ushered her over to one of the opulent leather sofas in the cabin and offered her a glass of champagne. During the flight the dinner they had been served had been exquisite—the sort of food she imagined you would expect at a five-star restaurant. She felt as though she had entered a different world where she had no place, but in which Drago was completely at home.

Now, as they walked through the airport foyer, she

was conscious that her jeans were scruffy and her tee shirt, which had shrunk in the wash, revealed a strip of bare midriff when she moved. In contrast, Drago looked as if he had stepped from the pages of a glossy magazine, with his designer clothes and stunning good looks. The shadow of dark stubble on his jaw added to his potent sex appeal, and as he strode slightly ahead of her Jess noticed the interested glances he attracted from virtually every female he passed.

He was talking into his phone, which had been clamped to his ear for most of the flight from England, and although he spoke in Italian she guessed from his lowered brows that he was not happy. A cold hand of fear gripped her heart as she wondered if Angelo's condition was worse. *Please, God, don't let him die*, she offered up in silent prayer. Twenty-two was too young for anyone to leave this world—especially someone as sweet and gentle as Angelo. They had become good friends while they had been flatmates. But she was still reeling from the discovery that he came from a wealthy family and was related to this formidable man who had now halted in front of the airport doors and was waiting for her to catch up with him.

'Were you talking to someone at the hospital? Has something happened with Angelo?' she asked anxiously.

'There's no change,' Drago replied curtly.

He wondered if the concern in Jess's voice was genuine or whether she was simply adept at fooling people. During the flight he had tried to think about her objectively, bearing in mind that all he knew about her so far was that she had a criminal record and had either begged, borrowed or stolen a fortune from his cousin. But to his intense irritation he had been distracted by his physical reaction to her, and had found himself admiring her hair—which, now that it had dried, reminded him of the colour of autumn leaves: a glorious mixture of red, copper and gold, which rippled down her back and shimmered like raw silk.

He noted how her fashionable skinny jeans emphasised her slender figure and her long-sleeved tee shirt clung to her small breasts. With a rucksack over one shoulder and a guitar hanging from the other she looked as if she was going to a pop festival rather than to visit a hospital. Her clothes were totally inappropriate, he thought irritably, and he was certain she wasn't wearing a bra—although her breasts were pert enough that she did not need to.

Trying to ignore the flare of heat in his groin, he said, 'I've just heard from the head of my security team that the press have got wind of the accident. Probably one of the hospital staff tipped them off,' he growled angrily. 'The paparazzi are hanging around the hospital, and they must have heard that my plane just landed because there's a mob of reporters waiting outside the airport. Stick close to me. I'll make sure no one hassles you,' he reassured her when he saw her startled expression. 'My car is on its way to pick us up, and Fico, my bodyguard, will clear a path for us.'

'You have a bodyguard?' she said faintly.

He shrugged, drawing Jess's attention to his broad shoulders and a muscular physique that indicated he followed a punishing workout regime.

'I can take care of myself, but it's sensible to take precautions. I am well-known in Italy, and there have been a couple of kidnap attempts in the past. Many criminal gangs would love to get hold of me and demand a billion-pound ransom,' he told her.

He did not seem unduly worried, and looked amused

when she could not disguise her shock at his revelation that he was a billionaire.

'It's amazing what some people will do for money,' he murmured sardonically.

It was dark outside, but through the glass doors Jess could see a large crowd of shadowy figures moving around. 'Let me take your bag,' Drago ordered, lifting her rucksack from her shoulders. He looked surprised when he felt how light it was. 'There can't be much in here. I told you to bring clothes for a few days, in case Angelo doesn't immediately respond to your voice.'

It was only natural that he was concerned for his cousin, but *jeez*, he was bossy! Jess lifted her chin. 'I've brought everything I own that isn't covered in paint. I don't have many clothes.'

'Or any that fit properly, seemingly,' he drawled as he raked his eyes over her too-small tee shirt and lingered on her breasts.

To her horror Jess felt her nipples harden, and knew they must be clearly visible beneath her clingy top. She wished she had made a better search for one of the few bras she possessed, which had inconveniently disappeared from her underwear drawer. She rarely wore a bra because she felt more comfortable working without one, but she had not bargained on her body's embarrassing reaction to Drago. Against her will her gaze was drawn to his, and her heart jolted against her ribs when she saw the unmistakable glint of sexual awareness in his black eyes.

This could not be happening, she thought dazedly. A few hours ago it had just been an ordinary day—until a darkly handsome stranger had turned up at her flat. Now she had been whisked to Italy on a private jet to visit Angelo, who was not the penniless migrant he had led her to believe but a member of the hugely wealthy Cassari family. Even more disturbing was the way she reacted to Angelo's cousin. She hated how her body responded to Drago's virile masculinity. Not since she had dated Sebastian Loxley had she felt so unsettled by a man. The memory of her one brief love affair—although it could hardly be called that, because Seb had never loved her—served as a stark reminder of why she needed to ignore her dangerous attraction to Drago.

He was watching her from beneath hooded eyelids that hid his expression, so that she had no idea what he was thinking. Just then the door behind him opened, and as he turned his attention to the thickset man who appeared Jess released her breath on a shaky sigh.

The man spoke to Drago in rapid Italian. He replied in the same language and then glanced back at Jess. 'The car is outside. Let's get this over with,' he growled.

To Jess's shock he gripped her arm and pulled her close to his side. She was intensely conscious of his hard body pressed against hers, and the sensual musk of his aftershave swamped her senses. But then he opened the door and she was blinded by an explosion of bright flashing lights.

Despite the efforts of the bodyguard the reporters closed in on them like a pack of wolves, and a cacophony of voices shouting words she did not understand bombarded her ears. It seemed like a lifetime until they reached the black limousine waiting with its engine already running.

Drago pulled open the car door. 'Get in and we'll soon be away from this madness.' He swore when he saw her struggling to climb inside with the guitar still strapped to her back. '*Madonna!* Was it necessary to bring this with you?' he muttered as he tugged the strap over her shoulder. He pushed her into the seat and thrust the guitar onto her lap before sliding into the car after her. 'Are you expecting Angelo to wake at the sound of your strumming? I think you must have watched too many romantic films.'

'Hearing music might rouse him,' Jess snapped, infuriated by his sarcasm. 'The guitar isn't mine; it's Angelo's. I thought he would like to have it with him when he regains consciousness. You *must* know how much his guitar means to him?'

'I didn't know he could play an instrument,' Drago said bluntly.

'But he plays all the time, and he's a brilliant guitarist. He told me his dream is to play professionally.' She stared at him. 'How come you know so little about your cousin? You say you think of him as a brother, but you don't seem to know the first thing about him.'

Drago was annoyed by the implied criticism in her voice. 'Just because I was unaware of his hobby does not mean I'm not close to him.'

Jess shook her head. 'It's not just a hobby. Music is Angelo's passion.'

The limousine was now streaking along the highway, but the sound of the engine was barely discernible inside the car. The privacy glass separated them from the driver and bodyguard who were sitting in the front, and enclosed them in the rear in a dark, silent space that was shattered by Jess's fervent outburst. She tensed when Drago turned his head and subjected her to a slow appraisal.

'Passion?' he murmured, in the deep, accented voice that caressed her senses like rough velvet.

The word seemed to hover in the air between them. Jess's mouth felt dry and she wet her lips with the tip of her tongue as a shocking image flashed into her mind of Drago pushing her back against the leather seat and covering her mouth with his. It was utterly crazy, but she longed for him to kiss her with the heated passion she sensed burned within him. She pictured him running his hands over her body and sliding them beneath her tee shirt to caress her breasts and stroke her nipples that were as hard as pebbles from her erotic thoughts.

She shuddered, acutely conscious of the flood of heat between her legs. Dear heaven, what was happening to her? Even worse, he *knew* the effect he was having on her. The unnerving predatory expression that she had told herself she had imagined back at her flat had returned to his eyes, and she could almost taste the sexual tension simmering in the air between them.

Drago shrugged. 'I admit I did not know of Angelo's interest in music. What about you—are you a musician too?'

'No. Angelo taught me to play a couple of tunes on the guitar, but I'm not very good.'

He trapped her gaze and his voice took on a husky quality that caused the tiny hairs on Jess's body to stand on end.

'So—what is *your* passion, Jess?'

She swallowed, and searched her mind desperately for something to say—some way to break the spell he seemed to have cast on her. 'I…I make things from wood…sculptures and ornate carvings. I suppose you could say that is my passion. I love the feel of wood— its smoothness and the fact that it feels alive when I shape it. It's very tactile, and I love creating sculptures that invite people to touch them, stroke their polished surfaces—'

She broke off abruptly, embarrassed by her enthusiasm. Drago could not possibly understand how she poured all the painful emotions that were locked up inside her into her sculptures. Of all the wonderful things that Ted, her foster-father, had done for her, teaching her how to work with wood meant the most to her, because he had given her a way to express herself and unlocked an artistic talent that had given her a sense of self-worth.

She was relieved when Drago's phone rang. While he took the call she stared out of the window and watched the street lamps flash past in a blur as the car sped along the highway. A few minutes later the imposing modern building of the Venice-Mestre Hospital came into view. As they approached Jess saw dozens more reporters crowded around the entrance, and when the limousine halted outside the front doors camera flashbulbs lit up the interior of the car, throwing Drago's stern features into sharp relief.

'Do the press always hound you like this?' she asked him. She felt nervous about leaving the car, even with the reassuring presence of his huge bodyguard.

'The paparazzi often follow me—they have a relentless fascination with my love-life,' he said drily. 'But I will not allow them to upset my aunt and mother. I'll issue a statement about Angelo's accident in the morning and ask for my family to be given privacy while his condition remains critical. Hopefully that will make a few of them back off.'

When the driver opened the door Drago climbed out of the car first and turned to offer Jess his hand. The sound of loud, unintelligible voices hit her ears, and she instinctively ducked her head to avoid the flashlights. The crowd of reporters pushed forward and she stumbled—would have fallen but for the arm that Drago snaked around her waist. Half carrying her, he hurried her through the main doors of the hospital while the reporters were prevented from entering by several security guards.

'Are you all right?' he asked, glancing at her tense face.

'Yes, I'm fine.' No way was Jess going to admit that being in close proximity to his hard body had made her heart race. As she followed Drago along a corridor her heart began to pound for a different reason. She hated hospitals—hated the frightening clinical atmosphere and the smell of disinfectant that were such a painful reminder not only of Daniel, but of her own brief stay on a hospital ward when she was seventeen.

A nurse met them at the door of the intensive care ward, and while Drago spoke to her Jess struggled against a rising sense of panic. All her life she had learned to block out unhappy experiences—and there had been plenty of those during her childhood, both before and after she had gone into care—but being in the hospital brought back agonising memories that she had never been able to bury. She did not want to think about Daniel. And she did not dare think about Katie. Opening that particular Pandora's box was simply too painful.

Her instincts screamed at her to turn and run from the ward. But it was too late. Drago had halted and was opening a door which she saw led into a small private room. She glimpsed a figure lying on a bed surrounded by machinery which beeped and flashed sporadically.

'Maybe we shouldn't disturb Angelo now,' she said shakily. 'It's nearly midnight. Do the staff mind us being here outside of visiting hours?'

'Of course not.' Drago's dark brows rose in surprise. 'We can come whenever we want. Until this morning when I flew to London I hadn't left the ward since Angelo was admitted. As for disturbing him—that is the point of bringing you here,' he said sardonically. He glanced at her and frowned when he saw that her face was so white that the golden freckles on her nose and cheeks stood out. 'Did the reporters upset you? Why are you so pale?'

Jess fought the nauseous sensation that swept over her. 'I don't like hospitals,' she muttered.

'Does anyone?' Impatience crept into Drago's voice. His jaw tightened.

The past days he had spent at the hospital had evoked painful memories that would always haunt him. It had been a long time ago, he reminded himself. Life had moved on. He was thankful that Vittoria had found happiness with the man she had eventually married, and now she had a child. God knew she deserved to be happy after everything that had happened, the way he had let her down...

With an effort he forced his mind from the past and concentrated on the woman at his side. 'I can assure you that my aunt would rather not be here, keeping a vigil at her son's bedside.' He hesitated and deliberately lowered his voice so that only Jess could hear him. 'Angelo's mother is understandably distraught. You must forgive her if she is a little...abrupt.'

Jess did not understand what Drago meant, but there was no time to query his curious statement as he ushered her into the room. As she nervously approached the bed a horrible sense of dread and déjà-vu filled her. Angelo looked very different without his wild curls half-hiding his face. His skull was covered in bandages and his skin and lips were deathly pale. He reminded her of a waxwork figure: perfect in detail but lifeless, just as Daniel had been.

Hot tears suddenly burned her eyes. She rarely cried; experience had taught her that it was a pointless exercise. But for once she could not control her emotions. It seemed so cruel that a young man in the prime of his life might never open his eyes again or smile at the people he loved.

A movement from the other side of the room made Jess turn her head, and she saw a woman whom she guessed from her strained face and red-rimmed eyes to be Angelo's mother.

Overwhelmed by an instinctive need to express her sympathy, Jess murmured, 'I'm so sorry about Angelo.'

The woman stared at her, and then spoke to Drago in a torrent of Italian. Jess could not understand a word, but she sensed that her presence was not welcome. Remembering Drago's warning that his aunt was distraught, she wondered if she should leave and come back to visit Angelo later, but as she turned towards the door Drago placed a firm hand on her shoulder and pushed her forward.

'Aunt Dorotea, Jess has come to talk to Angelo in the hope that he will respond to her voice.' He looked steadily at his aunt. 'I'm sure you appreciate that she has rushed from England to visit him.'

His aunt continued to stare at Jess, with no hint of welcome on her rather haughty face. But then she said sharply, 'You are my son's girlfriend?'

'I am his *friend*,' Jess corrected her.

'So you are not his mistress?'

'No.' Jess frowned, puzzled by Angelo's mother's distinctly unfriendly attitude. She glanced questioningly at Drago. 'I could come back another time, if you think it would be better.'

He shook his head. 'I brought you here to talk to Angelo. Your name is the only word he has uttered, so perhaps he will respond to you.' He looked at his aunt. 'I want you to go home for a few hours. Fico is waiting to take you. You need to get some rest and have something to eat. You will not be any help to Angelo if you collapse,' he added, countering his aunt's attempt to argue.

Despite her obvious reluctance to leave her son, his Aunt Dorotea nodded as if she was used to her nephew taking charge. 'You will call me if there is any change?'

Drago's voice softened. 'Of course.'

He escorted his aunt from the room, leaving Jess alone with Angelo. She sat by the bed, watching him, just as she had done with Daniel when one of the care workers from the home had taken her to visit him. Angelo looked so young and defenceless. It was agonising to think that he might not survive. Her throat ached, but she swallowed her tears and leaned closer to take hold of his hand. It felt warm, and that filled her with hope.

'Hi, Angelo…' she said huskily. 'What have you done to yourself?' It was difficult to know what to say, but after a moment's hesitation she continued, 'The guys missed you when you didn't show up for work. Gaz said you make the best tea. We've nearly finished the Connaught Road job. I've just got to fit new skirting boards.'

She felt comfortable talking about work and kept up a flow of chatter, although her heart sank when Angelo did not make any kind of response.

A slight sound from behind her alerted her to the fact that Drago had come back to the room and was leaning against the wall, his arms crossed over his broad chest. Immediately Jess felt self-conscious. 'My coming here hasn't done any good,' she told him flatly. 'He hasn't shown the slightest flicker of reaction.'

'We can't expect a miracle. All we can do is keep

trying.' Drago walked over to the bed and stared at his cousin's motionless form. He knew it was stupid to feel disappointed that Angelo had shown no sign he had heard Jess. He had put too much faith in her. But, *Dio*, he was desperate—and he *had* hoped for a miracle, he acknowledged heavily.

'I overheard some of what you were saying to him,' he said abruptly. 'I admit I still find it hard to imagine that are you a decorator. You don't look the type to do manual work.'

She shrugged. 'I'm stronger than I look.'

Studying her slender figure, Drago was tempted to disagree. She seemed more upset by seeing Angelo than he had expected. Her delicate features looked almost pinched, and earlier he had watched her blinking back tears. Her eyes looked huge in her pale face and there was a vulnerability about her that was unexpected.

If it wasn't for the phone call he had received a few minutes ago from the private investigator he might have been taken in by her. But the confirmation that she *was* a petty crook who had been found guilty of fraud a few years ago increased his suspicion that she had used some underhand and possibly illegal means to get her grubby hands on his cousin's inheritance fund. If necessary he was prepared to use equally underhanded methods to get the money back, Drago thought grimly.

CHAPTER THREE

JESS DRAGGED HER eyes from Drago, wishing she did not find him so unnerving. He had removed his leather jacket and she could not help noticing how his black silk shirt moulded his broad chest and clung to the ridges of his abdominal muscles. The contrast between his strong, powerful body and his cousin's unconscious form emphasised the seriousness of Angelo's condition.

She leaned closer to the bed and touched Angelo's hand, which lay limply on top of the sheet. 'I'll carry on talking and perhaps I'll get through to him.'

'I think it's unlikely anything will happen tonight,' Drago said roughly.

He could not explain the fierce objection he felt to the sight of Jess holding his cousin's hand. She had denied that they were lovers, but who knew what methods she had used to persuade Angelo to give her his inheritance fund? He had brought her to the hospital in the hope that Angelo would respond to her voice, but after hearing the information the private investigator had dug up about her he was impatient to demand some answers.

He glanced at his watch and saw that it was past midnight. He could not remember the last time he had slept and his brain ached.

'I've arranged for a nurse to sit with Angelo for the

rest of the night. You will come home with me, so that you can sleep, and we'll return in the morning and try talking to him again.'

Jess stiffened. She disliked being in a hospital, with all the memories it evoked, but it was preferable to accompanying Drago to his home. The prospect of being alone with him made her heart lurch—although he might have a family, her mind pointed out.

'Are you married?' she asked abruptly. The speculative look he gave her made her feel uncomfortable, and she flushed.

'No. Why do you ask?'

'I just thought it wouldn't be fair to disturb your wife—and children if you have any.'

'Well, I don't.' His voice was suddenly terse.

'Even so, I don't mind staying here. I'll sleep in the chair if I need to. Or I could find a hotel. There must be a hotel near to the hospital.' Hopefully a budget one that wasn't too expensive, Jess thought to herself.

Drago shook his head. 'I have already asked my housekeeper to prepare a room for you.' Seeing that she wanted to continue the argument, he said in a softer tone, 'You are not going to reject my hospitality, are you, Jess? Having rushed you to Italy, the least I can do is offer you somewhere comfortable to stay.'

This was a man used to having his own way, Jess realised. Behind his persuasive smile and his sexy voice that brought her skin out in goosebumps she sensed an iron will. But in truth she was so tired that she could barely think straight. She had got up at six that morning—yesterday morning—she amended when she glanced at the clock on the wall and saw that she had been up for nearly nineteen hours. The idea of walking around a strange town looking for a hotel did not appeal.

'All right,' she murmured. 'I'll stay at your house for the rest of the night. Thank you.'

'Good.' Drago felt a spurt of satisfaction. Until he knew the truth about Jess Harper he wanted to know her whereabouts every second of the day and night, and while she was staying at his home she would be in his control.

They left the hospital by a back door to avoid the reporters still congregated at the main entrance. Jess leaned back against the seat and closed her eyes as the car sped away. Reaction to the events of the past few hours was setting in, and part of her still wondered if she was going to wake up and find her life was back to normal.

She must have dozed and woke with a start at the sound of Drago's voice.

'Wake up. We've crossed the bridge and we're about to swap the car for a boat.'

She was startled. Her lashes flew upwards and she saw that they had arrived at a marina.

'There are no roads on the islands that make up the historical city of Venice,' Drago explained as he led the way along a jetty and jumped aboard a motorboat.

Jess viewed the gap between the jetty and the boat nervously, having no wish to miss her footing and fall into the water. But as she hesitated Drago clamped his hands around her waist and lifted her down onto the deck. The brief contact with his body sent a tremor through her, but she assured herself that she was simply reacting to the cool night air after the stifling warmth of the car.

He must have noticed her shiver, because he pulled off his jacket and handed it to her, saying roughly, 'Here—put this round you.'

Not wanting to appear ungrateful, she draped the jacket over her shoulders. The leather was as soft as butter, and the silk lining still retained the heat from his body and the scent of his aftershave. Oh, *hell*, Jess thought ruefully, feeling her heart rate accelerate in response to his potent masculinity. He started the boat's engine and as they moved away from the jetty her sense of apprehension grew. It had been a mistake to come to Italy with Drago, and an even greater mistake to have allowed him to talk her into agreeing to stay at his home, but bar diving over the side and swimming back to shore she had no choice but to go with him.

Her thoughts were distracted by the breathtaking sight of Venice in the moonlight. The Grand Canal wound through the city like a long black ribbon dappled with silver moonbeams, while the water at its edges reflected the golden lights streaming from the windows of the houses that lined the two banks.

'What a beautiful building,' Jess murmured as the boat drew steadily towards a vast, elegant house which had four tiers of arched windows and several balconies. 'It looks like a medieval palace.'

'That's exactly what it is. It was built in the early fifteenth century by one of my ancestors and has belonged to the Cassari family since then.'

'You're kidding—right?' Her smile faded when she realised Drago was serious.

'The name Palazzo d'Inverno means Winter Palace—so named because traditionally the family lived here during the winter and spring, but spent the hot summer months at a house in the Italian Alps.' Drago steered the boat alongside a wooden jetty and looped a rope around a bollard before jumping out. 'Give me your hand,' he ordered.

It was a fair leap onto the jetty so Jess reluctantly obeyed, feeling a tingling sensation like an electrical shock shoot up her arm when his fingers closed around hers.

'Does Angelo live here?' she asked, staring up at the magnificent house rather than meet Drago's far too knowing gaze.

'He has an apartment in one of the wings, and my mother and aunt have accommodation in another wing.'

Jess fell silent as she followed Drago along the stone walkway that ran beside this part of the canal. He led her up a flight of steps and through a huge, ornately carved front door. 'I told the staff not to wait up,' he explained as he ushered her into the quiet house. 'They are all fond of Angelo and the past few days have been a strain for everyone.'

The entrance hall was vast, and their footsteps rang on the marble floor and on the sweeping staircase that wound up through the centre of the house.

'This is your room,' Drago announced at last, stopping at the far end of a long corridor. He opened the door and Jess could not restrain a startled gasp as she walked past him. The proportions of the room were breathtaking, and as she lifted her eyes to the ceiling high above she was amazed to see that it had been decorated with a series of frescoes depicting plump cherubs and figures that she guessed were characters from Roman mythology.

'Thank heavens I don't work as a decorator in Venice,' she murmured. 'How on earth did anyone get up there to paint such exquisite artwork?'

The bed was covered in a cobalt blue satin bedspread, and the floor-length curtains were made of the same rich material. Walking across the plush cream velvet carpet to the window, she stared down at the canal below and watched a gondola decorated with lanterns glide past.

'I don't understand why Angelo let me think he had no money or family,' she said flatly. 'Was it some kind of joke to him?' She felt angry and hurt that Angelo had played her for a fool, but she was more furious that she had allowed herself to be duped. God, if she had learned anything from Seb surely it was never to trust anyone.

'It doesn't make sense to me, either.'

Alerted by a curious nuance in Drago's tone, Jess spun round and found that he had come up silently behind her. Once again she was struck by his height and muscular physique, and as she lifted her eyes to his face she felt a flicker of unease at his grim expression.

'I can think of no possible reason why he would have made up a story that he was destitute,' he said in a hard voice. 'My cousin is inherently honest. But I suspect that *you* are a liar, Jess Harper.'

'Excuse me?' She wondered if she had heard him correctly. At the hospital, when he had persuaded her to stay at his house, he had exerted an easy charm, but there was no hint of friendliness now in eyes that were as hard as shards of obsidian. 'I'm not a liar,' she said angrily.

'In that case I assume you will tell me the truth about why you persuaded my cousin to give you a million pounds?'

Jess's jaw dropped. 'Angelo never gave me anything,' she stammered. 'In London he didn't have a penny, and if I hadn't paid for his food he would have starved.' She pushed her hair back from her face with a trembling hand, feeling that she was sinking ever deeper into a nightmare. 'This is crazy. I don't understand anything.

Why do you think Angelo gave me money—let alone such an incredible amount?'

'Because he told his mother he had done so,' Drago said coolly. 'My aunt was concerned when she learned from Angelo's financial adviser that he had withdrawn his entire inheritance fund from the bank. She asked him what he had done with the money and he said he had given it to you.'

Jess drew a sharp breath. 'But he *didn't*, I swear. I know nothing about any money.'

Drago's eyes narrowed. He had expected her to deny it, but he was surprised by how convincing she sounded. Did he want to believe her because he was intrigued by her fey beauty? taunted a voice inside his head.

Dismissing the unwelcome thought, he said harshly, 'I think you do. I also think you were fully aware of Angelo's identity. I admit the situation is not clear to me yet, but I'm convinced that you somehow conned him into giving you a fortune. I don't know how you did it, but I intend to find out—and I warn you that I will use every means available to me to make sure you repay the money.'

'This is outrageous,' Jess snapped, anger rapidly replacing her disbelief at Drago's shocking accusation. 'I don't have to listen to this…this fantasy story you've concocted.' She swung away from him and hurried over to the door, but his next words halted her in her tracks.

'It's not a fantasy that you were convicted of fraud a few years ago, is it?'

Shock ricocheted through Jess and the blood drained from her face. She did not hear Drago's footsteps on the thick carpet, and she flinched when he caught hold of her arm and jerked her round to face him.

'The private investigator I hired to look into your

background found evidence of your criminal record, so don't waste your time denying it.'

She shivered at the coldness in his black eyes. 'It wasn't what it seems,' she muttered.

He ignored her and continued ruthlessly, 'You were found guilty. It was only because you were seventeen at the time you committed the offence that you were ordered to carry out community service rather than receive a custodial sentence.'

Shame swept through Jess, even though she had nothing to feel ashamed of. The fraud charge had been a mistake, but no one had believed her. The evidence had been stacked against her—Seb had made sure of it, she thought bitterly. She had been found guilty of a crime she had unwittingly committed, set up by the man she had loved and who had told her he loved her.

The arrogant expression on Drago's face made her wish she could crawl away and hide. She cringed when she recalled how she'd thought she had sensed a sexual chemistry between them. Now she knew that he had been watching her so closely because he believed she was a common criminal, not because he was attracted to her.

'I know nothing about Angelo's missing money,' she insisted. 'It isn't fair to accuse me just because of something that happened years ago.'

To her surprise, Drago nodded. 'You're right—it's not up to me to find out the truth. That's the job of the police. And I am sure that when I hand you over to them tomorrow they will quickly establish whether you are innocent or guilty.' His brows rose at the sound of her swiftly indrawn breath. 'Now, why does the mention of the police cause you to look so worried, I wonder?' he drawled.

'It doesn't,' Jess lied.

She had nothing to hide, but the memory of when she had been arrested and the claustrophobic terror she had felt when she had been locked in a police cell made her tremble. On the rough estate where she had spent her early childhood the police had been mistrusted by many people, including her father, and she had grown up with an intrinsic wariness of authority.

Drago strolled over to the door. 'Well, you've got a few hours to come up with an explanation about Angelo's missing inheritance fund. *Buonanotte*, Jess. I'd try to get some sleep if I were you. You're going to need your wits about you tomorrow.'

Jess stared at the door as he closed it behind him, feeling another jolt of shock when she heard a key turn in the lock. *'Hey!'* Disbelief turned to anger as she tried the handle and found that it wouldn't move. She hammered on the solid oak. 'Let me out of here. You have no right to imprison me.'

'My cousin's missing a million pounds gives me every right' came the curt reply. 'By the way, you can make as much noise as you like—no one will hear you. My room is at the other end of the hall, and the staff quarters are on the other side of the house.'

If this was a crazy dream it would be helpful if she could wake up now, before she attempted her daring escape plan, Jess thought some twenty minutes later. But as she stood on the balcony outside her room the whisper of the cool night breeze on her face and the faint lapping sound of the water in the canal were very real. It was fortunate that her room was on the second storey of the house rather than the top floor, but the canal path below still looked a long way down and she almost lost her nerve.

But the prospect of being questioned by the police and having to try to convince them that she knew nothing about Angelo's missing money filled her with dread. Drago clearly thought she had conned his cousin out of his inheritance fund, and because of her criminal record the police were likely to share his suspicions. The only person who could clear her name was Angelo, but until he regained consciousness she once again stood accused of something she had not done.

The image of Drago's haughty expression flashed into her mind. How *dared* he imprison her in his house? Her spurt of temper steadied her nerves, and after checking that the sheets she had stripped from the bed and knotted together were tied securely to the balcony she climbed over the balustrade and began to inch down the makeshift rope. Thankfully it took her weight.

It was lucky she was so agile and had a head for heights. In her job she was used to climbing up and down scaffolding, but when she looked down and saw how far away the ground was she felt sick with terror. Deciding not to glance down again, she continued her cautious journey, buoyed by the thought that Drago Cassari was in for one hell of a surprise in the morning.

'Leaving us so soon, Miss Harper?' a familiar voice enquired smoothly.

Giving a startled cry, Jess lost her grip and fell. She closed her eyes, waiting to feel the impact of her body hitting the stone path, but instead two hands roughly grabbed hold of her and her fall was cushioned by Drago's broad chest.

'*Santa Madonna!* You crazy fool,' he growled as

he set her on her feet, fury blazing in his eyes as she swayed unsteadily.

Jess was so shocked she could not speak, but Drago had no problem voicing his feelings.

'You could have been killed.' He glanced up at the balcony above them and shuddered. 'I can only assume you *do* know more than you've admitted about Angelo's missing money as you were prepared to risk your life trying to get away from me.'

'I refuse to be held against my will by an *amateur sleuth* who has made a totally unfounded accusation against me,' Jess snapped.

Now that she was safely on the ground she could see how dangerous her escape attempt had been, and she felt sick when she imagined how badly injured she might have been if she had fallen. But it was Drago's fault that she had been forced to take such a risk. Her temper sizzled.

'I came to Italy because I wanted to try to help Angelo, but if you think I'm going to stick around and take your accusations and insults you'd better think again,' she said hotly. 'Instead of hounding me you should be asking yourself why your cousin seemed so worried and unhappy while he was in London. I could tell that something was troubling him, but he didn't confide in me—or in you, apparently. So much for your assertion that you think of him as your brother—it seems to me that you didn't think about him enough, because if you had you would have known that something was wrong.'

Drago's face darkened. 'You know nothing about my relationship with my cousin,' he growled.

He was infuriated by her criticism, but part of his anger was fuelled by guilt that there was some truth in what Jess said. He had been so busy running Cassa di

Cassari, and he had assumed that Angelo was doing well at college in London. It had been a relief to relinquish some of the responsibility he felt for his family, and although his aunt had been upset that Angelo hardly ever phoned home Drago had felt glad that his cousin was becoming independent. He'd had no idea that the young man had been unhappy—but he only had Jess's word on his cousin's state of mind, he thought grimly. And he didn't have any faith in the word of a woman who had been convicted of fraud.

'Where do you think you're going?' he demanded when she jerked away from him and swung her rucksack onto her back.

'Home.' Shaking back her glorious Titian hair, she flashed him a glittering glance from her green eyes. 'I've decided to forgo the pleasure of your hospitality,' she said with heavy irony. 'Just point me in the direction of the nearest airport and I'll be on my way.'

'The hell you will. You said you would stay until Angelo regained consciousness,' Drago reminded her.

'That was before I realised what an arrogant bully you are.'

Jess's voice rose, drawing the attention of a group of people who were walking across a nearby bridge over the canal. They were Americans, Drago realised when he overheard one of them speak in a distinctive accent. Many of the thousands of tourists who visited Venice each year preferred to come in the spring, to avoid the heat and the crowds who packed St Mark's Square in the summer months.

He saw Jess glance at the people, and caught the flash of relief on her face as she realised they spoke English. It was easy to read her mind. She had proved when she had climbed down from the balcony that she was sur-

prisingly resourceful and determined. There was only
one way Drago could think of to stop her from creating a scene, and before she had time to comprehend his
intention he pulled her into his arms and lowered his
head, muffling her startled cry with his lips.

As he had expected she instantly stiffened, and he
winced when her clenched fist made sharp contact
with his ribs. He should have known from her vibrant
hair and flashing green eyes that she was a hellcat, he
thought ruefully. But the feel of her lithe body squirm-
ing against his as she struggled to escape from his grasp
heated his blood and fired up his pride. He wasn't used
to women resisting him. Most women he met were a
little too keen for him to take them to bed—which perhaps explained his recent restlessness as he searched
for an elusive something that he did not even understand. It was a long time since he had felt the thrill of
the chase or had to persuade a woman to kiss him back,
but Jess had clamped her lips together in a tight line and
the challenge of drawing a response from her was too
strong to resist.

She had accused Drago of being a bully, but she had
not expected him to prove it by kissing her against her
will, Jess thought bitterly. She was furious that he had
chosen to use his superior size and strength to control
her. He was holding her so tightly that she could not
move and was unable to jab her fist into him again. Her
breasts were crushed against his chest, and the feel of
his warm body through his silk shirt, together with the
slight friction created as she struggled to pull herself
free, was making her nipples feel hot and hard.

Dear heaven, what was happening to her? When had
her determination to get away from him changed to desire? One minute she had been resisting him with all

her strength, but now a curious lassitude was stealing through her and her body was sinking into him, her soft curves melting against the hardness of his thighs.

Her mouth felt bruised from his savage assault, but the nature of the kiss was changing. His lips were no longer demanding her submission but gently coaxing a response from her that she found impossible to deny. His warm breath filled her mouth as she parted her lips, and she tasted him when he dipped his tongue into her moist interior. His gentleness was unexpected and utterly beguiling. Sexual desire was something she had been sure she would never experience again, but as Drago cupped her bottom and pulled her so close that her pelvis was in direct contact with the hard ridge of his arousal straining beneath his jeans liquid heat coursed through her veins. With a soft moan Jess slid her hands to his shoulders and kissed him with the fiery passion that had lain dormant inside her for so long.

'You see, honey, I told you they were just having a lovers' tiff.'

The voice of one of the American tourists broke the silence. His companions' laughter faded with the sound of their footsteps as they continued on their way. But the comment hurtled Jess back to reality and with a low cry she tore her mouth from Drago's. To her relief he let her go, and she had a feeling that he was as shocked as she was by the chemistry that had exploded between them. He raked a hand through his dark hair, sweeping it back from his brow, and the moonlight slanting across his face struck the sharp lines of his cheekbones and revealed his tense expression.

'That shouldn't have happened,' he said harshly.

Inexplicably, Jess felt hurt by his words. Of *course* the kiss had been a mistake, a moment of madness, but by pointing it out he made her feel cheap, and the self-disgust she had heard in his voice was a shameful reminder of his low opinion of her.

She wished she could think of something sarcastic to say, but she had never been clever with words. Drago was staring at her as if he couldn't believe he had kissed her, and the disdainful curl of his lip was the final humiliation. She had to leave—now, before she felt any worse. She was furious with herself for responding to his kiss with such shameful enthusiasm.

The path running beside the canal did not continue past the end of the *palazzo*, and the American tourists had now had to retrace their steps back across the bridge. That meant the bridge was her only route of escape. But as she headed towards it Drago stepped in front of her, blocking her way.

'Come back to the house,' he ordered.

'You must be kidding.' Frantic to get away from him, she ran out along the jetty to where his boat was moored, realising as she did so how stupid the action was. She didn't know how to start the boat. As she glanced over her shoulder and saw him following she knew she was trapped. 'Leave me alone.' She held out a hand to ward him off.

'*Dio*, I'm not going to hurt you.' Drago's voice grew sharp. 'Jess—be careful!'

But his words were too late. In the dark, she hadn't realised how close she was to the end of the jetty, and with a cry she slipped and plunged into the inky depths of the canal.

CHAPTER FOUR

JESS WAS SUFFOCATING. Water filled her mouth and nose as she sank deeper. The water was so cold that her limbs, her brain, felt numb. An instinct for survival kicked in and she began to scrabble desperately against the blackness engulfing her. Her backpack was weighing her down. In panic she tore her arms free from the straps.

And then miraculously something jerked her back to the surface and she was able to drag oxygen into her lungs.

'I can't swim!' she gasped, terrified that she would sink back down again.

'It's all right. I've got you. *Santa Madre!* Stop flapping like a stranded fish and let me pull you out.'

Strong hands hauled her up and dumped her onto the jetty. Choking up the foul-tasting water she had swallowed, Jess collapsed in a heap, shudders running through her as her terror gradually receded. Pushing her tangled wet hair out of her eyes she glared at Drago. 'Of course I was damned well flapping—I thought I was going to drown.'

'You can thank me for saving you later,' he said drily. He frowned when her teeth began to chatter. The water in the canal was cold, but he assessed that the shivers racking her body were more likely due to shock. Without another word he bent and lifted her into his arms, taking no notice of her protests.

'What about my rucksack? It's still in the canal.'

'And there it will stay—unless you want to dive back in and retrieve it.'

'I told you. I can't swim.' Jess stared at Drago's implacable face with a rising sense of frustration. 'My passport is in that bag.'

'Then it's lucky you won't need it for a while,' he drawled. 'Not until Angelo has regained consciousness and the matter of his missing money has been resolved.'

A new feeling of panic swept through Jess at the prospect of being Drago's prisoner. 'You can't force me to stay,' she muttered, struggling to speak when she was shivering so hard she felt as though her bones would snap.

'I don't see how you can leave without your passport,' was his laconic reply—which ignited Jess's temper so that she renewed her efforts to force him to put her down. Drago simply tightened his hold on her and growled, 'Keep still. You've already got me wet enough. *Dio*, you're as slippery as an eel.'

Charming. That was twice in the space of a few minutes that he'd likened her to a fish! Jess knew she should continue to struggle, but she felt so tired and cold, and being carried in Drago's strong arms was dangerously seductive. Besides, where could she go now that her rucksack, containing her clothes, money and passport, was at the bottom of the canal? In a game of chess Drago would have her at checkmate, she acknowledged wearily.

He strode into the house and carried her up two flights of stairs as if she weighed nothing. Shouldering a door, he walked into a room that Jess guessed was the master suite. The elegant sitting room was decorated in shades of cream and gold and furnished with burgundy velvet sofas, and exquisite patterned rugs on the floor. But Jess only had a glimpse of the room as Drago continued on through a set of double doors into the bedroom.

Her eyes were immediately drawn to an enormous four-poster bed with gold damask drapes. The room, in particular the bed, was designed for seduction, she thought, as she took in the exotic décor of burgundy silk wallpaper. The satin bedspread was in the same rich shade.

With a renewed sense of panic she tried again to struggle out of his arms. 'Why have you brought me here? I'd like to go back to my room.'

'Not a hope. I'm not going to hang around under your balcony waiting to catch you when you take another leap out of the window.'

'I didn't leap out. It was a carefully planned escape, which I wouldn't have needed to attempt if you hadn't locked me in,' Jess snapped, stung by his scathing tone. 'And I wouldn't have fallen if you hadn't startled me. What are you doing?' she demanded when he carried her into the *en suite* bathroom and set her down in the shower cubicle. She gasped when he activated the shower and she was hit by a deluge of warm water. Her jeans and tee shirt were already wet from where she had fallen into the canal, but within seconds of standing beneath the spray her clothes were plastered to her body.

'Do you need any help getting undressed?'

'No!' She glared at Drago, incensed by his mocking smile. Following his gaze, she glanced down and was horrified to see that her thin shirt had become almost transparent and the hard points of her nipples were

plainly visible through the sodden material. 'Go to hell,' she muttered, hating him—but hating her body more, for its traitorous response to his virile sex appeal.

Unexpectedly, the stricken look in Jess's eyes caused Drago a pang of remorse. Beneath her defiance she looked young and scared, and the realisation that she might be frightened of him made him uncomfortable. *Dio*, the idea of frightening a woman was abhorrent to him. He had behaved like a brute tonight, he acknowledged heavily. His concern for his cousin and the fact that he'd had barely any sleep in seventy-two hours had clouded his judgement. Although he suspected that Jess knew more about Angelo's missing inheritance fund than she was letting on, nothing had been proved—and he could not forget how convincing she had sounded when she had protested her innocence.

'Remain under the shower until you've warmed up,' he said roughly. 'I'll find something for you to wear to sleep in.'

Ten minutes later, when Jess cautiously peered around the shower screen, she was relieved to find she was alone. A pile of towels had been left for her, and a man's white shirt that she guessed belonged to Drago. He had been right about the shower warming her up—she had a feeling he was right about most things, she thought ruefully. But at least she had stopped shivering and her hair no longer smelled of canal water.

The shirt was so big on her that it reached halfway down her thighs. After blasting her hair with the dryer hanging on the wall, she acknowledged that she could not remain in the bathroom for ever.

The first thing she noticed when she opened the door was that Drago had changed out of his damp clothes into a navy blue silk robe that revealed an expanse of broad, tanned chest overlaid with whorls of dark hair.

'Feeling better?' he queried when Jess edged into the bedroom.

She nodded, her heart jolting against her ribs as he walked over to her and handed her a glass.

'Drink this—a shot of brandy will warm your insides.'

'No, thanks. I never touch spirits.' She jerked back from him, blanching as she smelled the alcohol.

'I'm not trying to poison you,' he said drily.

'I'm sorry.' She flushed as she realised how rude she must seem. 'I loathe alcohol. Even the smell of it reminds me…'

'Reminds you of what?' Drago prompted, puzzled by her strange reaction.

'Nothing.' Jess bit her lip when she realised Drago was waiting for her to answer. 'My dad used to drink…a lot,' she muttered. 'He was an alcoholic. He drank rum, mainly, although he wasn't fussy. He'd drink anything. Our house used to stink of alcohol.'

Drago hesitated, struggling for the first time in his life to know what to say. Jess's voice had been expressionless, but he sensed that she kept a tight hold on her emotions. 'You said your father *used* to drink?' he said after a moment. 'Does that mean he is no longer an alcoholic?'

'He's dead. He died when I was eleven.'

'That must have been hard for you—to lose your father when you were so young.'

She shrugged. 'To be honest he wasn't a great dad. I don't remember him ever being sober, and he used to spend all his money on drink so there was never much to eat at home.' Once again her tone was matter-of-fact, but her eyes had darkened to a deep jade colour and held a faintly haunted expression.

'What about your mother? She didn't drink too, did she?'

'I don't think so. She died when I was a baby and I have no memory of her.'

Drago frowned. Why was he interested? he asked himself. He shouldn't give a damn about Jess's background. But he could not dismiss the image of her as an undernourished, uncared-for child. 'Who brought you up after your father died?'

'I went into a children's home, which wasn't so bad. At least I had dinner every day.' Her wry smile turned into a yawn. 'Sorry, but I'm shattered. It's been an eventful day,' she said pointedly.

'Then get into bed.' He pulled back the covers and gave her a querying look when she did not move.

Jess stared at the gold silk sheets and her heart began to pound. Surely Drago was not expecting her to sleep with him? The idea was outrageous, and yet... An image flashed into her mind of lying in that bed and feeling the sensual silk against her naked flesh. Like a film playing inside her head, she pictured Drago lying next to her, his tanned torso so dark in contrast to her paleness, his wiry chest hairs feeling faintly abrasive against her breasts as he lowered himself onto her.

Dear heaven. She drew an audible breath. Where had her shocking thoughts come from? She darted a glance at him and her heart missed a beat when she saw the predatory hunger in his eyes. The realisation that she had not imagined the sexual chemistry between them was frankly terrifying.

'No way am I going to sleep with you,' she said jerk-

ily. 'Was that why you wanted me to drink brandy—to make me more amenable?'

'Amenable!' Drago gave a harsh laugh. 'I swear you don't know the meaning of the word.'

He did not know what angered him most—her accusation that he had planned to seduce her or the fear he glimpsed in her eyes. *Dio*, she made him feel like a monster, when in fact he'd had the patience of a saint tonight.

'For your information, I have never had to get a woman drunk to persuade her to sleep with me.'

His gaze narrowed on her flushed face. She looked a whole lot better than she had when he had pulled her from the canal: no longer a drowned rat but a red-haired sexpot with her soft lips slightly parted and the swift rise and fall of her breasts betraying her agitation. But it was not fear that made the pulse at the base of her neck beat erratically—he knew women too well, and he recognised the subtle signals her body was sending him.

'I would not need to ply you with alcohol to get you into bed, would I, *cara*?' he taunted softly. 'From your response when I kissed you earlier I got the impression that I could take you any time I liked.' Ignoring her fierce denial, he continued ruthlessly, 'But someone with a conviction for fraud is not my ideal mistress. I have no intention of sharing a bed with you. The only reason I suggested you should sleep here is because you stripped the sheets from *your* bed to use in your juvenile escape attempt, and I'm not going to disturb the housemaid and ask her to prepare another bed for you. I'll sleep in my dressing room for what's left of tonight.'

As he strode past Jess on his way to his dressing room her dumbstruck expression awarded Drago some satisfaction. She was the craziest, most irritating woman he had ever met, he assured himself. But when he stretched

out on the sofa bed sleep eluded him despite his tiredness, and his body ached with sexual frustration as he
remembered how soft her lips had felt beneath his.

The sound of someone calling her name dragged Jess
from a deep sleep, and she was vaguely aware of something lightly brushing her face. She blinked blearily as
Drago's hard-boned face filled her vision, and she was
instantly awake and acutely aware of him.

God, he was gorgeous, she thought ruefully. His casual clothes of yesterday had been replaced with a dark
suit and crisp white shirt that contrasted starkly with
his olive-toned skin. He had evidently shaved, for his
jaw was smooth and she inhaled the subtle scent of san-
dalwood cologne.

His sensual mouth was unsmiling, and as her memory of all the previous day's events returned a sense of
dread gripped her. 'Is there any news about Angelo?'

'His condition is unchanged,' he informed her in a
clipped tone. 'When you've got up and had something
to eat we'll go to the hospital. I still believe you are the
best hope of rousing him.'

With an effort Drago moved away from the bed before he gave in to temptation and joined Jess between
the sheets. She reminded him of a sleepy kitten, curled
up beneath the covers, her tawny hair spread across the
pillows and her cat-like green eyes watching him from
beneath long silky lashes.

He had woken earlier, feeling better for a few hours'
uninterrupted sleep, and more in control of himself.
He'd hardly been able to believe that he had allowed a
skinny redhead with an attitude problem to provoke him
into losing his cool. But when he had leaned across the
bed, intending to wake Jess, he had been riveted by her

beautiful face. Unable to resist, he had run his finger lightly down her sleep-flushed cheek and discovered that her skin was as velvet-soft as a peach. Her lips had been slightly parted, and he'd felt a fierce longing to cover them with his own.

Cursing silently, he walked over to the window and pulled back the curtains to allow the bright April sunshine to flood the room. 'From now on you will sleep in the bedroom adjacent to mine. It does not have a balcony, so I'm afraid you won't be able to try another escape trick,' he said sardonically. 'I have also arranged for some clothes to be delivered for you as yours are at the bottom of the canal.'

Jess decided not to point out that she considered it entirely *his* fault she had lost all her belongings. He had not mentioned his threat of the previous night to hand her over to the police and she deemed it better not to antagonise him. Once Angelo had regained consciousness and explained that he had not given her his inheritance money Drago would owe her a grovelling apology, but for now, bearing in mind that she did not have a passport, she realised she had no choice but to remain in Venice with him.

'Thank you,' she murmured. 'If you give me the bill for the clothes I will, of course, pay you what I owe.'

She sounded genuine, and she looked so goddamned innocent. Drago's eyes narrowed. Were his suspicions about her wrong? How could they be when the evidence was stacked against her? Angelo had told Aunt Dorotea he had given Jess his inheritance fund, and the private investigator had confirmed that she had a criminal record for fraud. She might look as though butter wouldn't melt in her mouth but he was not fooled by her, he assured himself.

'It isn't necessary for you to pay for them. The clothes belong to me.'

Her eyes widened. 'Well, either I'm going to look pretty silly, wearing clothes designed for a six-foot man, or you're a cross-dresser.'

For a few seconds Drago could think of nothing to say in response to her startling statement, but then his lips twitched and he threw back his head and laughed. 'I promise you I don't have a penchant for dressing up in women's clothes and stiletto heels.'

He watched Jess's mouth curve into a smile and realised she had been teasing him. It was a novelty. He was not used to women with a sense of humour; most of the women he knew took themselves far too seriously. It felt strange to laugh, he mused. Even before Angelo's accident there had rarely seemed anything to laugh about recently. The responsibility of running a business empire and taking care of his family weighed heavily on him. Although he made time to play squash and work out in his private gym, and he enjoyed an active sex life with numerous mistresses, his life was dictated by work and duty and he could not remember the last time anyone had made him smile.

'The clothes are from the Cassa di Cassari collection,' he explained. 'Clothing is a new venture that the company is expanding into, and we have employed the top Italian fashion designer Torre Umberto. The new line won't be available in the shops until next month, but Torre has sent some samples over for you to wear.'

His phone rang, breaking the curious connection he had briefly felt with Jess. He headed a global business empire which demanded his constant attention. He was distracted enough, worrying about his cousin, and he definitely did not have time to be distracted by a sassy redhead whose sweet smile made his guts ache, Drago reminded himself.

'When you're ready, the maid will show you the way to the dining room,' he told her abruptly before he headed out of the door.

They had been at the hospital for hours, but still Angelo showed no sign of regaining consciousness. Jess stood up from her chair next to the bed, needing to stretch her legs. The small room felt claustrophobic, and although the blind at the window was pulled down the bright sunshine beating against the glass increased the stifling atmosphere.

As she walked over to the water dispenser and filled a plastic cup she was aware of two pairs of eyes following her. Angelo's mother was no friendlier today than she had been last night and had not spoken a word to her. The poor woman was devastated, Jess reminded herself. But she also knew that the vibes of distrust from Drago's aunt were due to her belief that Jess had conned her son out of his inheritance fund. When Angelo woke up he was going to have a hell of a lot of explaining to do, she thought heavily.

Dorotea turned her attention back to her son, but Jess was conscious that Drago's gaze was still focused on her, and she self-consciously ran a hand over the cream jersey-silk skirt that she had discovered, along with a selection of other outfits, in the wardrobe of her room at the Palazzo d'Inverno.

The last time she had worn a skirt had been years ago, on one of the rare occasions when she had attended school, she thought wryly. She lived in jeans or work overalls, and she felt overdressed in the skirt and the delicate white blouse she had teamed with it. The tan

leather belt around her waist matched the three-inch
stiletto-heeled shoes. The elegant outfit had called for
her to try to tame her thick hair, and she had swept it
up into a loose knot on top of her head.

Staring at her reflection in the mirror before she had
left her bedroom, she had been stunned by the transfor-
mation. She had always thought of her body as shapeless and too thin, but the beautifully designed skirt
suited her slim figure, and the blouse was cleverly cut
so that her small bust looked fuller. For the first time in
years—since she was seventeen, in fact, and had worn
a new dress to go out to dinner with her boss, Sebastian
Loxley—she felt like an attractive woman. The glitter of
sexual awareness in Drago's eyes when she had walked
into the dining room at the *palazzo* had sent a thrill of
feminine pride through her. He had not commented on
her appearance, but she had been aware of him glancing
at her several times as they had eaten breakfast—just
as she was aware of him watching her now.

'I need some air,' he announced abruptly. The metal
feet of his chair scraped loudly on the floor as he stood
up. His eyes met Jess's, but his expression was unreadable. 'We'll go and get a coffee. You need a break,' he
insisted when she opened her mouth to argue. 'You have
talked to Angelo and sung to him—' he glanced briefly
at the guitar standing by the bed '—almost constantly
for four hours.'

'I came to try to help,' she replied huskily, feeling
herself blush. She had sung a couple of pop ballads
that Angelo had taught her to play on the guitar while
Drago had gone to make a phone call, and she felt embarrassed that he must have been just outside the door
and had heard her.

'Hopefully he will regain consciousness soon, and if

he does it will be no small thanks to you,' Drago said roughly.

He could not help but be impressed by Jess's efforts to rouse his cousin. She had barely moved from his bed-side since they had arrived at the hospital that morning, and she had talked to him until her throat sounded dry. The question of whether they were lovers returned to taunt him. She had denied it, had said that they were simply friends, but she was so goddamned beautiful and it was easy to believe she had seduced shy, inexperienced Angelo with her sex-kitten sensuality and persuaded him to give her a fortune.

Drago's jaw clenched. She had taken his breath away when she had joined him for breakfast at the *palazzo* that morning, dressed in clothes that had drawn his gaze to her slender but shapely figure. The scruffy tomboy had turned into an elegant woman, but beneath her new sophistication he recognised her inherently sensual nature, and his appetite for food had deserted him as he'd fantasised about having hot, hard sex with her on the dining table.

Frowning at the inappropriateness of his thoughts when his cousin was in a critical condition, Drago was unaware of how forbidding he looked as he escorted Jess to the hospital cafeteria. He ordered two coffees and carried them over to the empty table she had found.

She seemed distracted as she added three spoons of sugar to her coffee, prompting him to ask, 'Is something wrong?'

'I wish my phone wasn't at the bottom of the canal,' she said ruefully. 'I'd like to call Mike, my foreman, to make sure the job we've been working on will be finished on time. Clients hate delays, and it's important that the company maintains a good reputation.' Jess pushed a stray tendril of hair back from her face. 'Do the doctors have any idea of when Angelo might regain consciousness? I want to stay if it is deemed that hearing my voice might help rouse him, but I have a responsibility to my team of decorators in London. If I don't finalise our next contract they won't have any work.'

Drago sipped his unsweetened black coffee, relishing the hit of caffeine, and gave her a speculative look. 'I understand that your decorating business was facing bankruptcy until a few months ago?'

'How do you know that?' Her startled expression turned to anger. 'I suppose the investigator you hired to spy on me told you?'

He did not deny it. 'I know you paid twenty thousand pounds into the company account to clear its debts and overdraft. I can't help thinking how remarkably convenient it was that you suddenly acquired a large sum of money just in time to save the business from financial meltdown.'

As his meaning became clear, Jess felt sick. 'If you think I got the money from Angelo, you're wrong.'

'So where *did* it come from? And perhaps you can also explain how you live in a luxury apartment with a rental value far higher than you could afford on a decorator's wage.'

Jess was stunned at how much he knew about her personal life, and felt violated by the intrusion.

'I don't have to explain anything to you,' she said angrily. 'But as a matter of fact the money I used to bail out T&J Decorators was left to me.'

Drago looked disbelieving. 'You're saying you received an inheritance? Who from? You told me your alcoholic father spent all his money on drink.'

'Yeah, *he* certainly never gave me anything—not

even affection,' Jess said bitterly. 'Have you any idea what it's like to be the only child in the class not to be dressed in clean clothes? Or the only one not to go on a school trip because your dad was too drunk to sign the permission form?' She clamped her lips together, startled by her outburst. Her childhood was something she *never* spoke about. 'Of course you don't know. You were born into a wealthy, loving family.'

She swallowed. 'I didn't know what it felt like to be part of a family until I was seventeen, when I went to stay with a wonderful couple who had experience of helping troubled teenagers. Ted and Margaret changed my life in so many ways. Sadly they are both dead now, and six months ago I learned that I was a beneficiary in Margaret's will.'

The raw emotion in Jess's voice tugged on Drago's insides. He was shocked by her revelations about her childhood and felt uncomfortable that his questioning of her had forced her to talk about a subject she clearly found painful. She could be making up a sob story to gain his sympathy, his mind pointed out. But the haunted expression in her eyes was too real to be an act.

'As for how I afford to live in an expensive property,' she continued, 'I have an arrangement with a property developer who allows me to live in properties he owns rent-free. In return I carry out renovation work and decorate them to a high standard. As soon as the work is finished on the flat I'm currently living in I'll move out, and the developer will lease it to paying tenants.'

Jess glared at Drago. 'You are wrong about me,' she said fiercely. 'And when Angelo wakes up and tells you where his money is I'll expect an apology from you.'

His coldly arrogant expression did not soften. 'I'm not wrong about your criminal record. It is an undeniable fact that you were convicted of fraud, and in light of that I think my suspicion that you know what has happened to my cousin's inheritance is understandable.'

'I was seventeen, for God's sake, and very naïve.' Jess bit her lip. 'I was set up and I didn't understand that I was committing a crime.'

'Set up by whom?'

The rank disbelief in Drago's tone made Jess's heart sink. She had no chance of convincing him of her innocence when she had been found guilty by a jury, she acknowledged bleakly. The injustice of what had happened still burned inside her. But at the same time as the court case seven years ago, she had had to make a monumental decision that had left her feeling numb and strangely distanced from other events in her life.

'Explain what you mean about being set up,' Drago demanded.

'What's the point?' She tore her eyes from his hard-boned face, hating the way her body responded to him. 'You have already judged me. The only person who can exonerate me is Angelo.'

The strident ring of his phone made them both jump. Drago frowned when he saw the hospital consultant's number flash on the caller display, and he quickly answered. After a terse conversation in Italian he ended the call and stared across the table at Jess.

'Angelo has just regained consciousness—and he has asked for you.'

CHAPTER FIVE

THEY WERE MET at the door of the intensive care unit by a smartly dressed woman whom Drago hurriedly introduced as his mother. Luisa Cassari subjected Jess to a sharp stare, which became speculative as she turned her gaze on her son.

'I thought the new Cassari clothing range wasn't going to be launched in stores until May, but I see Miss Harper is already wearing pieces from the collection.'

Drago met his mother's enquiry coolly. 'It was necessary to provide Jess with something to wear after she lost all her belongings.'

Her brows rose as she glanced back at Jess. 'How did you lose your things?'

'Um…I fell into the canal.' Jess felt her face burning. 'It's a long story,' she mumbled.

'And an intriguing one, I'm sure.'

There followed a rapid conversation in Italian between mother and son, and Jess was surprised to see that Drago looked faintly uncomfortable.

'We should be concentrating on Angelo,' he told his mother, reverting back to English and speaking in a firm tone that caused Luisa to compress her lips. But she made no further comment as Drago placed his hand on Jess's shoulder and pushed her towards the bed.

Aunt Dorotea was gripping Angelo's hand while tears streamed down her face.

Drago spoke to the doctor who was standing nearby. 'What's happened?'

'He came round a few minutes ago and asked for his mother. He was lucid, and the signs are good that he is emerging from the coma.' The doctor looked at Jess. 'He also murmured *your* name. I think it would help if he heard your voice.'

Supremely conscious that everyone in the room was watching her, Jess leaned over the bed and said softly, 'Hi, Angelo. It's great to have you back.'

His eyelids fluttered and slowly opened. 'Jess?'

'Yeah, it's me.' Tears clogged her throat so that her voiced emerged as a croaky whisper. She felt weak with relief that Angelo was back from the brink.

His eyes had closed, but now they opened again. 'What happened to me?'

After darting a questioning glance at the doctor, Jess said gently, 'You had a car accident. Do you remember?'

Angelo's brow furrowed. 'No,' he said at last. 'I needed to tell Drago something…but I don't remember what it was.' He focused unsteadily on Jess and managed a faint smile. 'I know that we are friends.' His smile faded. 'But I don't remember how I know you. I don't remember anything…except that I had to see Drago urgently.'

'I'm here,' Drago said gruffly, struggling to control his emotions. 'Take it easy, Angelo. I'm sure your memory will come back soon.'

Angelo turned his head on the pillow and smiled at his mother. *'Ciao, Mamma.'*

Aunt Dorotea promptly burst into tears again, and

as she leaned across the bed to kiss her son Drago indicated that Jess should step back.

'Aren't you going to ask him about his inheritance money?' she demanded in a fierce whisper, while the doctor and nursing staff crowded around the bed.

'He's hardly in a fit state. You heard what he said. He doesn't remember anything at the moment. I need to have a word with the doctor about Angelo's memory loss.'

Drago followed the consultant out of the room, and when he returned a few minutes later his expression was grim. Angelo had fallen into a peaceful sleep, and Drago spoke in a low voice.

'The consultant says that amnesia after a head injury is fairly common, but he can't predict how long it will last. There are some other issues that he is more concerned about—particularly the serious break to Angelo's left leg, which will require surgery.' His aunt gasped, and he put his arm around her shoulders. 'Try not to worry,' he told her gently. 'The doctor says he will be fine, and he is sure that in time his memory will return. A brain scan will tell us more. But for now we must be patient, and not excite or upset Angelo in any way that could hinder his recovery.'

He looked at Jess as he made this last statement, the hard expression in his black eyes warning her not to say anything until they had moved away from Angelo's bedside. Holding open the door, he waited for her to precede him out into the corridor.

'The consultant believes you could be the key to Angelo regaining his memory,' he told her. 'The fact that he remembers you, but not the accident, means that the amnesia is patchy, and if you keep talking to him you may jog his memory into returning fully.'

But until his memory did return *she* was still under suspicion from Drago and the other members of Angelo's family, who believed she had persuaded him to give her a fortune, Jess realised heavily. 'It could take days, or even weeks before he regains his memory.' A note of panic crept into her voice. 'You can't possibly expect me to stay in Venice indefinitely.'

'That's exactly what I expect,' Drago said coolly. 'Angelo's mind is trapped at a point in time when he believes you are his friend. When his memory eventually returns he may be able to explain why he told his mother that he gave you his inheritance fund and the truth of the matter will be revealed. But until then you will stay at the Palazzo d'Inverno as my guest.'

'As your prisoner, you mean,' she said angrily. 'Guests aren't usually locked in their room. Much as I want to help, I can't abandon my business.' She felt bad about leaving Angelo, but her team of workmen relied on her. 'I'm sorry, but I have to go back to London.'

Drago's dark brows lifted in the arrogant expression Jess was becoming familiar with. 'How do you intend to do that without a passport or money?'

'I suppose I'll have to go to the British Embassy and report that I've lost my passport.' In truth she did not have a clue how she was going to get home, but she did not want him to guess she was worried.

'You don't even have money to pay for a taxi to the airport, much less an air ticket to London,' he pointed out. 'You should be grateful that I have offered you somewhere to stay.'

The mockery in his voice ignited Jess's temper. 'Grateful? I'd rather take my chances in a pit of rattle-snakes than stay with you.' Her voice rose as she forgot that they were standing outside Angelo's room, within earshot of Drago's mother and aunt, not to mention half a dozen medical staff. Fury flashed in her green eyes. 'You are a dictatorial, egotistical—' She broke off and gave a startled gasp when his arm shot around her waist and he dragged her hard up against him. Too late she realised that she had pushed him beyond the limits of his patience.

'And *you* have viper's tongue,' Drago growled, before he silenced her by bringing his mouth down on hers in a punishing kiss designed to prove his dominance.

Determined not to respond, Jess clamped her lips together, but her senses were swamped by the tantalising scent of his aftershave and the feel of his smooth cheek brushing against hers. His warm breath filled her mouth as he teased her lips apart with his tongue, probing insistently until with a low moan she sank against him, a prisoner to his masterful passion. But he was as much a slave to the explosive sexual chemistry that burned like a white-hot flame between them as she was, she realised, when he cupped her bottom and pulled her into the cradle of his thighs, so that she was intensely aware of his powerful erection.

His breathing was ragged when he finally tore his mouth from hers, and the savage glitter in his eyes echoed the harshness of his voice. '*Madonna*, I think you must be a witch. You are driving me crazy.' His lip curled with self-disgust. 'My cousin has serious injuries, the extent of which are not fully known, yet all I can think about is how goddamned beautiful you are and how badly I want you.'

Jess was shaken to hear him admit he was attracted to her. But rather than feeling triumphant that a man as gorgeous and sexy as Drago desired her she was afraid of where their mutual awareness might lead, and terri-

fied that she would be unable to resist him if he kissed
her again.

'Let me go,' she pleaded huskily. 'If you help me get
to England I'll repay you the cost of my flight, and I
promise I'll come back to visit Angelo.'

He gave a harsh laugh. 'I'm not letting you out of
my sight until I find out what happened to my cousin's
inheritance.'

The door to Angelo's room suddenly opened, making them spring apart. But not quickly enough to escape Drago's mother's keen scrutiny. Jess's mouth felt
swollen and her breasts ached with a sweet heaviness. A
glance downwards revealed that her nipples were plainly
visible, jutting beneath the fine material of her blouse.
She hastily crossed her arms in front of her, blushing
furiously when Luisa stared at her and then at her son.

'Angelo would like to see you,' she said to Jess. 'If
you are not busy?' she added, in a tone as dry as a desert.

'I'll come and sit with him,' she mumbled. She felt
humiliated by the look of disdain in Luisa Cassari's
eyes, but Drago seemed indifferent to his mother's disapproval. He was reading a message he had received on
his phone and then glanced briefly at Jess.

'I need to go to the office for a couple of hours. When
you have spent some time with Angelo my bodyguard
will take you back to the *palazzo*.'

As he spoke the stocky man who had met them at the
airport the previous day walked down the corridor towards them. Fico planted himself outside Angelo's room
and crossed his arms over his massive chest.

'He doesn't speak a word of English,' Drago murmured. 'And he is under strict orders to escort you from
the hospital straight to my house.'

Anger surged through her. 'In other words he's my jailer?'

He gave a laconic shrug of his broad shoulders. 'Don't be so melodramatic. I'll see you at dinner tonight.'

'I can't wait,' Jess muttered sarcastically. As she turned away from him and marched into Angelo's room she was unaware of a flare of amusement and grudging admiration in Drago's eyes.

Much later that night, Drago strode through the Palazzo d'Inverno, his solitary footsteps echoing hollowly on the marble staircase. It was not the first time he had instructed the household staff not to wait up for him, nor the first time he had missed dinner because he'd had to deal with a crisis at work.

No doubt Jess would have been glad of his absence this evening, he mused. She had already left the hospital with Fico by the time he had arrived to visit his cousin and meet with Angelo's medical team. The young man's injuries were serious, and he faced a long road back to recovery, but thank God he had not suffered brain damage. The brain scan had revealed severe bruising, and there was the worry of his memory loss, but there was every reason to hope that the amnesia would be short-lived. Once Angelo's memory had returned hopefully he would shed some light on the matter of his missing inheritance fund and confirm if he had given the money to Jess—something she strenuously denied.

Madonna! How had she crept into his mind again? Drago asked himself angrily. He had accused her of being a witch. Perhaps she really was a sorceress and had cast a spell on him? Even during the emergency board meeting he'd chaired to discuss a problem that had arisen with a new project in China he had struggled to keep his thoughts from wandering to the sassy, sexy redhead who was currently a guest or a prisoner at his home, depending on your viewpoint.

Jess had made her feelings very clear, he thought wryly. She had antagonised him until he had kissed her, but when she had kissed him back his anger had turned to scorching desire. For the rest of the day he had been able to taste her on his lips, and the lingering scent of her perfume still tormented him. Guilt assailed him that Jess dominated his thoughts, but he was relieved to know for certain that she and his cousin were not lovers. Angelo had given him a curious look when Drago had asked him about his relationship with Jess, but had explained that they were simply friends.

The chef had left a platter of cold meats and salad in the fridge for him. Drago carried his supper up to his room, his footsteps slowing as he walked past Jess's bedroom and saw light filtering beneath the door. Ignoring the temptation to check if she was awake, he carried on into his suite of rooms, flicked on the TV and forced himself to eat even though he had no appetite—at least not for food, he acknowledged, aware of a tightening sensation in his groin as an image of Jess lying naked on his bed flooded his mind.

Muttering a curse, he put down the plate and headed into the *en suite* bathroom, hoping that a shower would help to relieve his tension.

Jess felt too wound up to sleep. She lay in bed, staring up at the ceiling which, like in the first room she had occupied, before her ill-fated attempt to climb down from the balcony, was decorated with elaborate artwork. But even though the fresco depicting the goddess Aphrodite was beautiful she was bored with studying it—just as she was bored with watching television when all the programmes were in Italian.

Her mind returned to wondering why Drago had not returned to the *palazzo* for dinner. Not that she had wanted to spend time with him, and she certainly hadn't changed into a gorgeous green silk dress from the Cassa di Cassari collection because she had hoped to impress him, but she had felt strangely lonely sitting on her own at the huge polished dining table. And that really did not make sense, because after growing up in the children's home constantly surrounded by other kids she liked her own company.

Drago had probably gone to visit a girlfriend. It was inconceivable that a man as devastatingly handsome and sexy as he was did not have a lover—or maybe more than one. Good luck to them, she thought as she sat up and thumped her pillows. Any woman who took him on would have to cope with his arrogant and bossy nature.

A sudden crash, followed by a shout, shattered the silence. The sounds had been loud, even through the walls that separated her room from Drago's, and the deathly quiet that followed seemed ominous to Jess's overactive imagination. Curiosity got the better of her and she slid out of bed.

The door to Drago's suite was shut. She knocked, but received no answer, and after a moment's hesitation she turned the handle and found that the door was unlocked. Her bare feet made no sound on the carpet as she crossed the sitting room. The door leading to his bedroom was ajar, and as she cautiously peeped round it she inhaled an overwhelmingly strong scent of aftershave.

Just then he emerged from the *en suite* bathroom,

and the sight of his blood-soaked chest caused her to give a sharp cry.

'*Santa Madre!*' He stopped dead, clearly shocked to see her. 'What are you doing, flitting around the house as noiselessly as a wraith?'

'I heard a crash...' Jess could not tear her eyes from what she now realised was a blood-stained towel wrapped around the hand that he was holding against his chest. 'What have you done?'

He glanced down at his front and said wryly, 'It's not as bad as it looks. I cut my hand on some glass and it's made a bloody mess—literally. I knocked a bottle of cologne into the sink and then compounded my clumsiness by trying to pick up the shards of glass. The damned cut won't stop bleeding. Can you look in the bathroom cabinet for a bandage?' He gave her an intent look when she hesitated. 'Does the sight of blood bother you?'

No way was Jess going to admit that it was not the blood that bothered her but the sight of Drago's naked, olive-skinned chest as he shrugged off his stained shirt. Her gaze was drawn to the hard ridges of his abdominal muscles, and followed the path of wiry black hair that arrowed down his torso and disappeared beneath the waistband of his trousers.

She swallowed, and replied in a faintly strained voice, 'No. When I was a kid I regularly used to patch my dad up after he'd had some accident or other while he was drunk. Once he fell through a neighbour's greenhouse and was cut to ribbons.'

Drago frowned. 'How old were you when that happened?'

She shrugged. 'Eight or so. Sit down while I dress the wound,' she bade him, when she had followed him into the bathroom and found a medical box in the cupboard.

He sat on the edge of the bath and unwound the towel to reveal a deep cut across his palm. 'I've kept pressure on it and elevated my hand. The bleeding seems to be easing.'

'I don't think it needs stitching,' Jess said after she had inspected the wound. 'You're lucky.'

'*Sì.*' He could not disguise the weariness in his voice. 'I don't fancy another trip to the hospital tonight.'

She threw him a quick look. 'Is that where you've been? I wondered why you weren't at dinner.'

'Why, *cara*, you almost sound as though you missed me,' he drawled.

'Of course I didn't. Why would I miss my jailer?' Aware that she was blushing, she concentrated on her task. 'At least the cut will have been sterilised by the cologne,' she murmured as she began to bandage his hand. 'It smells like a sultan's harem in here.'

'Are you speaking from personal experience?'

Drago subjected her to a leisurely inspection that for some reason made her feel hot and shivery at the same time.

'I'm sure you would be a sultan's favourite concubine, with your creamy skin and fiery hair,' he said softly.

Startled by the sudden change in his voice, from teasing to husky and achingly sensual, Jess caught her breath. Her eyes flew to his, and saw the undisguised hunger in his glittering stare. 'Of course I've never been in a harem,' she choked. 'I would never be a man's plaything. I believe in equality between men and women.'

Nothing on earth would make her confess her secret fantasy of being swept into the arms of a handsome, powerful man and being seduced on silken sheets. In the fantasy she fought against his dominance at first, but she could not resist the skilful touch of his hands and mouth as he aroused her and tormented her until she begged for him to possess her.

Her dream lover had never had a face—until now. She darted a glance at Drago's chiselled features and felt her stomach dip. He was all her fantasies rolled into one, she acknowledged ruefully. His hard-boned masculine beauty was made even sexier by the shadow of dark stubble on his jaw. She stared at his mouth, remembering how it had felt on hers when he had kissed her, and unconsciously she wet her lips with the tip of her tongue, as if she could recapture the taste of him.

The atmosphere in the bathroom altered subtly and the sexual tension was almost palpable. Drago was conscious of the slow thud of his heart, and even more aware of the throbbing ache in his groin, the urgent drumbeat of desire flooding through his veins. It had started with the brush of Jess's fingers on his skin as she'd wrapped the bandage around his hand. The contrast of her pale fingers against his darkly tanned flesh had made him imagine her naked in his arms, her smooth white limbs entwined with his hair-roughened thighs.

But in all honesty it had started before that—when she had appeared in his room looking utterly delectable, wearing a nightgown from the Cassa di Cassari collection that was little more than a wisp of white silk and lace. She was an intriguing mixture of virginal innocence and sensual siren, with her crushed-berry lips and those startling green cat's eyes.

As she leaned over him to tend to his hand he breathed in the delicate rose-scented fragrance of her skin, and the brush of her silky hair against his bare shoulder inflamed his senses. From the first moment he had seen her in London he had felt a primitive hunger to possess her and claim her as his woman. He was no Neanderthal; he was a twenty-first century guy who believed in equality between the sexes as much as she did. But his desire for her was a pagan force he had no control over.

He had never wanted any woman the way he wanted Jess, Drago acknowledged. The gentle concern in her eyes as she tied the bandage on his hand called to something deep inside him. Since the death of his father he had been the carer and protector of his family, always strong and in control. Tonight that control was slipping away from him. He was not thinking about his suspicion that she was involved with his cousin's missing inheritance fund, or that she had once been convicted of fraud. All he could think of was that her glorious red-gold hair felt like silk when he brushed it back from her face, and her rose-flushed cheek was velvet-soft beneath his fingertips.

Driven purely by instinct, he threaded his fingers through her hair and drew her head towards him. He was still sitting on the edge of the bath, and her petite stature meant that her face was level with his and her lips were tantalisingly close. She did not resist or pull away, but he could hear the catch of her breath and see the pulse at the base of her throat beating frantically. For a few seconds they remained poised while anticipation built to an intolerable level. Their eyes locked and held, until with a harsh groan Drago slanted his mouth over hers and kissed her with slow deliberation that quickly flared into a firestorm of passion.

Drago's tongue probed expertly between Jess's lips to coax them apart—although in truth he did not need to do much coaxing, she acknowledged ruefully. From the moment he had captured her mouth she had been lost, and with no thought in her head to deny him she parted her lips and heard him give a low groan as he explored her inner sweetness.

He was the man of her fantasies. The only man she had ever allowed to breach her defences since Seb. The memory of that disastrous relationship made her stiffen and question what she was doing. Drago had openly stated that he mistrusted her. Why, then, was she allowing him to kiss her? And why was she responding to him?

Because she could not help herself, whispered a little voice inside her head. Because the very first time she had seen him she had felt that she belonged in some deep and fundamental way to him. Her sensible self knew it was ridiculous; she did not need to belong to anyone, and she knew how dangerous it was to want to be cared for. She had fallen for Seb because she had been lonely and desperate to be loved. But he had abused her trust and she had vowed never to risk her heart again.

Drago finally broke the kiss and Jess knew she should pull out of his arms and end the madness. She knew it, but she could not do it. He trailed his lips over her cheek, her throat, and she shivered with pleasure when he found the sensitive place behind her ear.

'*Cara*, you are so beautiful,' he said raggedly, and his deeply sensual voice made her shiver again with a fierce, sharp need that started low in her belly and radiated through her so that every nerve-ending on her body felt acutely sensitive.

He captured the pulse throbbing at the base of her throat and then brushed his mouth along her collarbone. Her heart stopped when he slid the strap of her nightgown over her shoulder. Her breasts ached with a sweet heaviness, and when he brushed his fingers over the swollen peaks of her nipples, straining beneath the silk, she jerked as if an electrical current had shot through her.

He gave a husky laugh, but there was no amusement in eyes that were as black as jet and glittering with predatory intent. 'I know. It's the same for me too. The wanting. The hunger clawing in my gut.'

His jaw tightened and Jess sensed he was fighting an internal battle with himself, as if he resented his desire for her.

'When you opened the door of your flat in London I took one look at you and knew I had to have you,' he admitted in a driven tone.

'Drago…' Jess gave a keening cry when he tugged her nightgown lower and bared one of her breasts.

He stared at her, tension in every sculpted line of his face, his skin stretched tight over his sharp cheekbones. 'No games,' he said harshly. 'If you don't want this then go—now.'

He did not try to persuade her to stay with words and promises that they both knew would be false, and Jess was glad of that. She had been fooled by promises once before and her heart had been broken as a consequence. She was not a vulnerable seventeen-year-old any more, she reminded herself. She had grown up and discarded her silly dreams. Sexual desire was a perfectly natural feeling, and there was nothing wrong with wanting to give in to its demands. As long as she remembered to keep her head screwed on her heart would be in no danger.

CHAPTER SIX

'WE BARELY KNOW each other.' An instinct for self-protection made Jess cling to the last shreds of her sanity and offer a valid reason why she should walk away from Drago. 'And what you think you know about me isn't the truth,' she added, unable to hide the bitterness in her voice.

'Maybe it isn't.' As he uttered the words, Drago accepted that he did not know what to think about her.

He had evidence that she had been convicted of fraud, but it had happened a long time ago, when she had been a teenager. A mistake in her past did not mean she was inherently untrustworthy, his mind argued. *Madonna*, was he making excuses for her because he needed to justify his desire for her? He still did not understand what her true involvement with his cousin was, but she had fiercely denied knowing anything about Angelo's missing inheritance fund.

He did not know what to believe, and right now—shocking though it was to admit it—he did not care about his cousin, or the money, or anything that had happened in Jess's past. All he cared about was that she was half-naked and so exquisitely lovely that simply looking at her made him harder than he had ever been in his life. His hand actually shook as he reached out and slid the other strap of her nightgown down her arm, until her small, firm breasts with their dusky pink nipples were revealed to his hungry gaze.

'It's true we don't know many details about each other, but from the moment we met we were both aware of the chemistry that exists between us. No other woman has ever made me feel this out of control,' Drago admitted roughly. 'Say something, damn it,' he growled, feeling his blood pound through his veins when she simply stared at him with her stunning green eyes. Witch's eyes, trapping him in her spell.

He didn't care. Nothing mattered but the feel of her silken skin as he clasped her shoulders and pulled her to him. Nothing mattered but the honeyed taste of her as he lowered his head and captured her mouth in a potent kiss that demanded a response she gave so willingly that he could not restrain a husky groan when he felt her lips part obediently, allowing him to thrust his tongue between them.

Jess's heart thudded hard against her ribs when Drago suddenly stood up from the edge of the bath and scooped her into his arms as if she was a rag doll. She felt as boneless as one, she thought ruefully. One kiss was all it had taken to turn the sharp-tongued firebrand Jess Harper she prided herself on being into a trembling mass of nervous excitement. Drago was going to make love to her, and she was not going to stop him.

He carried her through to his bedroom. As her gaze fell on the four-poster bed, with its opulent gold silk drapes and sheets, the dull ache in the pit of her stomach became an insistent throb and she was conscious of molten warmth between her thighs. He placed her on the bed and stared down at her with a brooding intensity in his black eyes that was just as arousing as if he had touched her.

'I want to make love to you slowly—indulge in leisurely foreplay and prolong the pleasure until one of us begs for release,' he bit out. 'But I am so turned on that there isn't a chance in hell of that happening, *mia bella*.'

His taut voice revealed that he was hanging onto his self-control with supreme effort. Amazed that she could have such an effect on him, Jess touched the nerve jumping in his cheek. Her heart leapt when he turned his head so that his mouth grazed her fingers.

'I want you too,' she whispered.

It was what Drago wanted to hear, and his body reacted predictably. But the faint hesitancy he heard in her voice made him hold back from ripping off her nightgown and pushing her legs apart so that he could take her hard and fast, as the blood pounding in his veins urged him to do. She was not behaving as he had expected her to. His previous sexual encounters had always been with experienced women, who knew how to please him and were not shy about stating what pleased them. But Jess was clearly waiting for him to take the lead.

She looked incredibly sexy, stretched out on the bed with her fiery hair spread over the pillows, her small, pale breasts with their tightly puckered pink nipples practically begging for the ministrations of his tongue. And yet at the same time he sensed an innocence about her that made him think that she had not had many lovers.

Why the idea should make him want to grin he did not know, but as he smiled at her and watched her lips curve in a tentative response he felt a curious tug on his insides, and he forced himself to relax and slow the pace a little.

'Show me how much you want me,' he murmured as he bent his head and slanted his mouth over hers. Her immediate response stoked his desire, and he groaned and deepened the kiss until he felt tremors run through her body and realised that he was shaking too.

He heard the faint catch of her breath when he stroked her breasts, and the soft moan she gave as he flicked his thumb-pads across her nipples made him want to drag her beneath him and seek the release he craved. She was so sweetly responsive, and yet he sensed she was surprised by his caresses, as if the sensations she felt when he kissed her and touched her body were new to her.

From then on Drago forgot his own needs and concentrated on arousing Jess. He breathed in the delicate fragrance of her skin as he kissed her throat, the creamy slopes of her breasts, and finally closed his lips around one taut, dusky peak and then its twin. Her nightgown was bunched up around her waist, and he pushed it over her hips and placed his hand over the slight mound of her womanhood, hidden from his gaze beneath the fragile barrier of white lace knickers. She gave an involuntary movement and tried to clamp her legs together, but released her breath on a shivery sigh when he gently eased her thighs apart and slid his fingers beneath her panties. With delicate precision he dipped a finger into her moist opening and felt her buck her hips as he probed deeper into her honeyed sweetness.

Jess trembled as Drago continued his intimate exploration. She had never experienced such intense pleasure as he was eliciting, with his wickedly inventive fingers and with his mouth as he bent his head to her breasts and lashed her swollen nipples with his tongue. Sex with Seb had been very different, she thought ruefully. The few times she had slept with him he had seemed far more intent on his own pleasure than hers, but she had been so besotted with him that she'd felt grateful for any small sign of affection from him.

She was jolted from her thoughts of the past when Drago stood up from the bed and stripped off the rest of his clothes. Black silk boxers followed his trousers to the floor, and the sight of his naked, hugely aroused body stole her breath.

Feeling a little nervous now, she circled her lips with the tip of her tongue in an unknowingly provocative gesture and blurted out, 'Oh, heavens.'

Drago gave a ragged laugh. '*Cara*, if you continue to look at me like you are doing I think I'll explode.' His voice thickened. 'It has to be now, *mia bella*. I can't wait any longer.'

As he knelt above her, his dark eyes glittering with the intensity of his desire, Jess's heart rate quickened and the slight fear she'd felt that he was too big and powerful for her to cope with faded. She had never been so aroused, so *desperate* to ease the aching need that throbbed in every pore of her body.

His skin felt warm beneath her palms as she slid her hands over his chest and felt the faint abrasion of his chest hair. She loved the feeling of closeness to another human being. It was something she had rarely experienced. She did not remember her father ever hugging her as a child, and at the children's home the staff had been kind but never affectionate.

All Drago was offering was sex, she reminded herself. And that was all she wanted too—the satiation of this feverish yearning that blotted out all other thoughts and left her mindless with desire. Her heart thudded when he pulled her knickers down her legs and pushed her thighs apart. The deliberation of his actions increased her excitement and she whimpered when he touched her intimately again, the sensations he aroused as he found the most sensitive part of her making her arch her hips in urgent invitation.

The solid ridge of his erection jabbed her belly, but when she curled her fingers around his swollen manhood he made a harsh sound.

'Not this time, *cara*,' he growled as he pressed forward and entered her with a deep thrust that drove the breath from her lungs. Feeling her sudden tension, he stilled and stared into her eyes, a look of puzzlement in his. 'Did I hurt you?' His voice was rough with concern. 'I did not expect you to be so tight.'

She flushed. 'It's been a while,' she admitted, suddenly fearful that he would be disappointed by her.

'If it is uncomfortable for you we'll stop.'

'No!' Feeling him begin to withdraw, she clutched hold of him and wrapped her legs around his hips. 'I don't want to stop.'

Drago closed his eyes, struggling for control as his body reacted to the mind-blowing delight of feeling her vaginal muscles grip him in a velvet embrace. As Jess slowly relaxed he could not resist sinking deeper into her, and his buttocks clenched as he fought against the hot tide of pleasure that was threatening to overwhelm him.

'I'm not going to stop,' he assured her as he withdrew a little and she made a husky protest. If he was honest he did not think he *could* stop when his body was so tight and hot and hard, he acknowledged ruefully. 'See?' He thrust into her again—once, twice—each stroke harder and faster than the last as he set a rhythm that drove them both higher.

'Oh…' Jess gasped as he slid his hands beneath her bottom and tilted her so that the tip of his steel-hard arousal hit an especially sensitive spot deep within her. Waves of pleasure ripped through her as he plunged between her trembling thighs with an urgency that told her his control was close to breaking. Her breath came in short, sharp gasps, and she gripped the silk sheet beneath her, her fingers clawing at it as her excitement built to an intolerable level.

Nothing had prepared her for the ecstasy of her first ever orgasm. It overwhelmed her. Shock waves of incredible sensation pounded her and she shuddered with convulsive pleasure. Almost simultaneously she felt a tremor run through Drago's big body and he gave a harsh groan. The sound of it was somehow more shocking than anything that had gone before. The fact that this powerful man had come apart in her arms filled Jess with fierce tenderness, so that she curled her arms around his neck and stroked his hair as he laid his head on her breasts.

In the lull after the storm only the sound of their breathing gradually slowing broke the intense quiet, and in those moments when they were still joined it seemed to Jess that they were the only two people in a private, magical world.

Early next morning—so early that the light filtering through the crack in the curtains was a pale, iridescent glimmer—Jess lay still, pretending to be asleep, although in fact she was studying Drago from beneath her lashes.

He was lying on his back, staring up at the drapes of

the four-poster bed. His hard-as-granite profile was not encouraging and her heart sank. Of course she had not expected to wake in his arms, or for him to kiss her tenderly as the new day dawned. She was stupid—falling into his bed last night had proved that—but she harboured no illusions that the passion they'd shared had been anything more than mind-blowing sex.

So why were tears blurring her vision? Why was she wishing with all her heart that he would pull her close and stroke her hair? She had been starved of affection all her life, so why did his indifference hurt so much?

Perhaps he sensed that she was awake, because he turned his head on the pillows. She blinked hard to dispel her tears. Pride was her faithful ally. No way was she going to act like a whipped puppy.

'Before you say anything, I'd like to agree. Last night was a mistake that should not have happened,' she said quickly. 'And it would definitely be best to forget about it.'

He frowned. 'How can you agree with me when I haven't made a comment? Can you read my mind?'

'I don't need to. You look…' Her heart lurched as she stared at his face. He looked gorgeous and incredibly sexy, with his silky hair falling onto his brow and dark stubble shading his jaw. She could not prevent the slight catch in her voice as she muttered, 'You look angry.'

Drago gave her a quizzical look. 'Well, it's true that I am angry—with myself. And I admit I *did* make a mistake last night. But I don't regret what happened between us and I definitely won't forget making love to you any time soon.'

The sultry gleam in his eyes sent a quiver of response through Jess. 'Then what mistake did you make?' she asked uncertainly.

'I forgot to use a condom.' His jaw tightened. 'I have no excuse other than that you have such an effect on me that I temporarily lost my sanity. I wanted you so badly I simply didn't think about protection. It was crass and irresponsible of me, and I apologise. I also want to assure you that I am healthy. I don't make a habit of having unprotected sex,' he said roughly.

Drago's self-respect had taken a hard knock when he had realised how stupid he had been. He had broken one of his golden rules. *Dio*, after what had happened with Vittoria he had always been so careful to avoid an unplanned pregnancy. He hoped that Jess took care of herself and used some method of contraception, but the knowledge that he had failed to act responsibly was a matter of bitter regret.

His frown deepened when he noticed how pale she looked this morning. In contrast to her white cheeks her lips were reddened and slightly swollen, and the faint bruises on her shoulders were shameful evidence that in his impatience to make love to her the previous night his touch had been too rough.

Guilt roughened his voice. 'I trust you will inform me if there are any consequences?'

'There won't be any,' Jess said in a quick, sharp voice.

She was painfully aware that her reply was based on wishful thinking rather than certainty. Her heart hammered against her ribs as the enormity of what she had done sank in, and she jerked upright, belatedly realising that she was naked. It was a bit late to feel self-conscious after she had spent a night of wild passion with Drago, she thought ruefully. But she could feel his gaze lingering on her breasts and she hastily pulled the sheet around her, wincing as the silk grazed nipples that felt ultra-sensitive from where he had kissed and sucked them.

She closed her eyes as memories of having sex with him flooded her mind. Not only had she behaved shamelessly, but she had been criminally stupid to forget about contraception. Dear heaven, how could she have taken such a risk again, when she had bitter experience of the consequences of having unprotected sex? Surely history would not repeat itself? Some women tried for years to fall pregnant. The odds of it happening to her again as a result of this one night must be a million to one, she tried to reassure herself.

Drago relaxed a little when he realised that Jess must be protected. She had sounded absolutely sure there was no risk she could have conceived. It did not change the fact that he was a damned fool, though. He could not believe he had allowed his desire for her to override his common sense. Even more disturbing was the fact that he was still not thinking logically. His mind was enjoying an erotic image of pushing her back against the pillows and tugging the sheet away from her body. Impossibly, he was even more turned on than he had been last night.

But she was sitting stiffly, hugging her knees, and her tension was palpable. He wondered if she regretted sleeping with him. She had been eager enough at the time, and afterwards she had curled up against him and fallen asleep almost instantly. God knew what she had dreamed about that had caused her to cry out in her sleep, he thought, frowning as he recalled the harrowing sobs that had racked her slender frame.

'Who is Daniel?' he asked abruptly. 'You called out the name during the night and you seemed to be upset,' he explained when she stared at him.

She bit her lip. 'He was a friend…my best friend. We grew up together in the children's home.' Her voice grew husky. 'He died when he was sixteen. He was hit by a car and suffered a serious head injury. He was on life support…but he never regained consciousness.'

Instinctively Drago reached for her hand and gave it a gentle squeeze. 'I'm sorry,' he said gruffly.

'I suppose seeing Angelo in the hospital brought back memories of the last time I saw Daniel. He looked like he was asleep and I kept thinking he would wake up.' Her throat moved as she swallowed hard. 'But the nurse said there was no hope. I'm so relieved that Angelo has regained consciousness.'

The raw emotion in her voice tugged on Drago's insides. Jess had known more than her fair share of pain in her young life, he thought heavily. He understood now why she had looked so pale when she had walked into the intensive care unit and seen Angelo in a coma. He felt guilty that he had not been more understanding, but he had not known about her past. He knew very little about her, he acknowledged, merely the small pieces presented to him by his private investigator.

Infuriated that he could not think straight when she was so close to him, and his senses were inflamed by the scent of her, he threw back the sheet and got out of bed. Making love to her last night had been an aberration he was determined not to repeat. Pulling on his robe, he headed for the bathroom, but paused in the doorway and glanced back at her.

'I have to go to the office this morning. Fico will take you to visit Angelo and I'll meet you at the hospital later.' He hesitated, still troubled by the memory of her distress during the night. 'You called out another name in your sleep. Was Katie also a friend from the children's home?'

A haunted expression flared in her eyes. 'Katie? I…I don't know anyone with that name. I've no idea what I was dreaming about.'

Drago stared at her for a few moments, noting how she avoided meeting his gaze. Why was she lying? he wondered as he closed the bathroom door and stepped into the shower. He felt frustrated that he knew so little about her. Jess's strange reaction was another puzzle to add to the intrigue surrounding her.

CHAPTER SEVEN

'SIX WEEKS WITH my leg in traction,' Angelo groaned. 'I think I'll go mad. If only my memory would come back. I feel as though my brain is surrounded by a grey mist.' He stared frustratedly at Jess, who was sitting beside his bed, helping herself to grapes from the fruit bowl. 'I don't understand why I was living in London and not Venice.'

'Drago said you had enrolled at a college to study business. Do you remember being at college?'

'No. And although you've told me I worked for your decorating company I have no recollection of it.' He frowned. 'To be honest, painting walls is not something I can imagine myself doing. Was I good at it?'

'Not very,' Jess admitted with a grimace.

'In that case why did you employ me?'

'You told me you were destitute and I wanted to help you.'

Angelo shook his head, as if the action would clear the fog from his mind. 'I lived with you, didn't I? In a big house surrounded by lots of trees? You cooked omelettes for dinner.'

Jess felt a flicker of excitement. 'You stayed at my flat for a few weeks. I made dinner for us the night before you disappeared. Can you remember where you were going, or why?'

'I'm sure it had something to do with Drago, but I just don't know what.'

'It's all right. Your memory will come back soon.' Jess squeezed Angelo's hand reassuringly. She hesitated for a moment. 'I suppose you don't remember why you withdrew a huge sum of money from your bank account, or who you gave it to?'

His brow furrowed. 'Money?'

'Yes, your inheritance fund—' Jess broke off when a noise from behind her alerted her to the fact that someone had entered the private hospital room.

'I'm sure Angelo will remember everything in good time,' Drago said smoothly as he walked towards the bed.

He smiled at his cousin, but Jess sensed his anger, and when he glanced at her his black eyes were as hard as jet.

'I think you should get some rest now.' He spoke gently to Angelo. 'The nurse tells me you have been playing your guitar?'

'It's strange that I can remember some things.' Angelo sighed. 'Why do I get the feeling that there is some mystery surrounding me? Something that I was going to tell you just before the accident?'

'Try to relax. Jess has been here with you all day and I'm afraid she has overtired you.'

Bristling, Jess followed Drago out of the room. 'Thanks a lot,' she snapped as soon as he had closed the door. 'I didn't overtire him. He slept on and off during the day. I stayed because you said that talking to him might trigger his memory.'

'Perhaps you have another motive?' he said darkly. 'I

don't want you to mention Angelo's missing inheritance fund in case you put ideas into his head.'

Nonplussed, she stared at him—and then wished she hadn't when she felt a coiling sensation in the pit of her stomach. Dressed in a pale grey suit teamed with a navy blue shirt, he looked incredibly sexy, and she could not help remembering him last night, naked and aroused as he had positioned himself over her.

'What sort of ideas?' she mumbled, thankful that he did not know what ideas were in *her* mind.

'Ideas such as he didn't give you a fortune. He's in a vulnerable state at the moment, and likely to believe anything you tell him.'

Drago's arrogant expression ignited Jess's temper like a flame set to tinder.

'For the last blasted time—I know nothing about Angelo's missing money,' she hissed.

She felt unbelievably hurt that although he had slept with her he clearly did not trust her. What had she expected? she asked herself miserably. He regarded her as good enough to have sex with but he did not respect her, and by falling into his bed so wantonly she had lost respect for herself.

'Where are you going?' he demanded.

'Anywhere so long as it's a long way away from you.' She marched along the corridor without having a clue where she was heading.

'The exit is in the other direction.' Drago caught hold of her arm and swung her round to face him, feeling a stab of guilt when he saw tears shimmering in her eyes. 'I've had a difficult day,' he owned gruffly. 'I appreciate that you've given up a whole day to spend it with Angelo. Shall we go back to the *palazzo*…?'

'You mean you're giving me a *choice* of whether or not to return to my prison?' she said sarcastically.

'*Madonna!*' He raked a hand through his hair and glared at her in exasperation. 'You would test the patience of a saint. If you hate my home so much we'll go to a restaurant and get something to eat. Who knows? Perhaps a good meal will improve your temper.'

The restaurant was not scarily sophisticated, as Jess had feared, but a charming little place tucked away down a side street with tables set out on the terrace overlooking a narrow canal. The waiters were quietly attentive and seemed to know Drago.

'Trattoria Marisa is the place I come to when I want to chill out,' he admitted. He did not reveal that he never brought the women he dated here. In truth he did not know why he had brought Jess to the restaurant which he regarded as a sanctuary away from the stresses of his hectic life.

'What did the waiter say to you?' she asked curiously. 'And why did he keep looking at me?'

'He said that you are very beautiful and I am very lucky,' he said drily. He met her startled gaze and his mouth curved into a sudden smile. 'I agreed with him. You look stunning in that dress.'

Flustered, Jess glanced down at the white silk dress covered with a pattern of pink roses. Like all the clothes from the Cassa di Cassari collection it was pretty and elegant and made her feel very feminine. She studied the menu, which was in Italian and could have been written in hieroglyphics for all the sense it made.

'You had better order for me,' she murmured, and was even more disconcerted when Drago moved his chair closer to hers and patiently translated the choice of dishes. She found it hard to concentrate on what he was saying when she was achingly aware of the sensual musk of his aftershave. Her eyes seemed to have a magnetic attraction to his mouth. If he turned his head their lips would almost touch.

Her breath caught in her throat as he trapped her gaze, and she felt his warm breath feather across her lips. *Kiss me*, she willed him. She wanted him to so badly that she trembled, and her disappointment when he drew his head back from her felt like a knife through her heart.

His eyes darkened, and he gave a ragged laugh as he moved his chair back around the table. 'Sexual frustration is hell, isn't it, *mia bella*? You are driving me insane.'

Thankfully the waiter returned with the wine list and Jess did not have to reply.

The food served at Trattoria Marisa had been excellent as always, Drago mused later as he sipped his coffee. He had declined dessert but Jess had opted for an exotic concoction of chocolate ice-cream and whipped cream, which she had eaten with undisguised enjoyment. Had she any idea how much he was turned on by seeing the tip of her pink tongue lick the last morsel of cream from her spoon? he wondered with wry self-derision.

'Explain how you were set up to be accused of fraud,' he said abruptly.

Jess stiffened and gave him a rueful glance. 'I don't suppose you'll believe me.'

'Try me.'

She sighed. 'In a way I suppose it started with Daniel dying. He was the closest thing I had to a brother and I missed him terribly. I had to leave the children's home when I was sixteen. My social worker helped me find a bedsit and I got a job as a waitress in a café.'

She watched a gondola glide along the canal, her expression unknowingly wistful.

'I was lonely and grieving for Daniel. The highlight of my day was when a handsome businessman would come in to the café for his regular coffee. He would chat to me and ask me how I was, and he sounded as though he really cared. His name was Sebastian Loxley. He told me he had just set up an internet company selling tickets for pop concerts and festivals, and he needed someone to work in the office. I couldn't believe it when he offered me the job. I was such a naïve fool,' Jess said bitterly. 'Seb must have found it so amusing to seduce me. I fell desperately in love with him, and when he invited me out to dinner on my seventeenth birthday and then took me back to his flat—well, let's just say he didn't have to try very hard to get me into his bed.'

'*Santa Madre!* You were a child,' Drago said harshly.

She shrugged. 'Not in legal terms. Unfortunately the law does little to protect vulnerable young adults. At my new job I faithfully followed the instructions I was given by Seb. Every time I took a credit card payment I made a separate record of the card details, including the security code, and passed the information on to Seb's accountant because apparently it was needed for tax purposes. I didn't question what I was doing.'

She blushed with embarrassment.

'I was bullied at school, so I didn't go very often, and I left without any qualifications. I didn't understand about credit cards, and I had no idea that Marcus, the so-called accountant, ran an illegal business cloning cards, or that he paid Seb for the information I was passing to him. Eventually the police discovered the cloning scam, but Marcus must have had a tip-off and he disappeared abroad before they could arrest him. The trail led back to Seb's company and to me.'

Drago swore beneath his breath. 'Go on,' he encouraged when Jess hesitated.

'I was stunned when Seb told the police he was unaware of what I had been doing. I thought he would explain that he had instructed me to pass on the card details, but instead he put all the blame on me. The police believed him and decided that I had been working with Marcus. I was arrested. At the trial, Seb gave evidence against me.' Her voice shook. 'I thought he loved me. He'd even said we'd get married one day. But it was all lies. He didn't care about me. He didn't even want...'

'He didn't want what?' Drago prompted. He felt a curious pain in his gut when he saw the misery in her eyes. The feisty Jess he had come to know looked crushed. The idea that she had been preyed on by an unscrupulous crook when she had been so young filled him with rage, and a longing to smash his fist into Sebastian Loxley's face.

Jess shook her head. 'It doesn't matter,' she said dully. Seb's scathing response when she had told him she was pregnant with his baby was too painful to talk about. She glanced at Drago, searching for some sign that he believed her story, but his hard features were unreadable.

'What happened after the court case?'

'I felt I had hit rock-bottom,' she said huskily. 'I had no job, nowhere to live, and no self-respect. I met my social worker from the children's home, and she arranged for me to stay with a couple who'd had experience fostering troubled teenagers.' A soft smile lit her face. 'Ted and Margaret were wonderful people. It's no exaggeration to say that they changed my life. For the first time ever I felt part of a family. Ted ran a decorating business and he took me on as an apprentice. I discovered a natural talent for woodwork, and I went to college and trained in carpentry before Ted took me on as a business partner. The T and J in the company name stands for Ted and Jess.'

Jess broke off as a waiter came up to the table to offer them more coffee. The interruption gave Drago the opportunity to mull over everything she had told him. He did not even question whether he believed her story. The emotion in her voice when she had spoken of how she had been so cruelly betrayed by the man she had loved had been too raw to be an act. But the question of whether or not he trusted her still remained. Until his cousin's memory returned there was no possibility of discovering if Jess knew what had happened to Angelo's missing inheritance fund, Drago acknowledged frustratedly.

As they were about to leave the restaurant a gondola drew up alongside the terrace. Like most Venetians, Drago was unimpressed by a mode of transport used almost exclusively by tourists, but after catching the hopeful look in Jess's eyes he called to the gondolier to assist her into the boat.

Dusk was falling, and the sun was a fiery orb sinking below the horizon, streaking the sky with gold and pink and casting golden shadows on the elegant buildings which lined the canal.

'It's so beautiful,' Jess breathed.

It was also incredibly romantic, sitting beside Drago in the gondola, but it was doubtful he thought so, she acknowledged ruefully. He had given no indication that he believed she had unwittingly been involved in the fraud scam when she had worked for Seb. She wondered why she cared about his opinion of her. She wasn't dishonest, and when Angelo regained his memory he would explain what he had done with his inheritance fund and Drago would realise he had misjudged her. But what if Angelo never recovered from his amnesia? she thought anxiously. The truth about his missing money might never be uncovered and Drago would always think the worst of her.

He could not force her to stay in Venice for ever, she reminded herself. But in order to return to England she would first have to organise a new passport, and to do that she needed her bank card, which was also in her rucksack at the bottom of the canal. Everything seemed complicated, and sleeping with Drago last night had confused the situation even more. She must have been mad. It was no excuse that her common sense had been obliterated by the firestorm of passion that had ignited between her and Drago. No excuse at all…

She darted him a glance, and her heart missed a beat when her eyes met his brooding gaze. The evening air was cool, and he frowned when he saw her shiver.

'Here—take this,' he said as he slipped off his jacket and draped it around her shoulders.

'Thank you.' Was that breathy, seductive whisper really her voice?

The silk lining of the jacket retained the warmth of his body and felt sensuous against her bare arms. She wished it was his arms around her rather than the jacket, and recalled with shocking clarity how wonderful his naked body had felt when he had pulled her beneath him and made love to her. Desperate to banish her traitorous thoughts, she closed her eyes. But images remained of Drago's bronzed chest, overlaid with the whorls of dark hair that had scraped the sensitive tips of her breasts when he had lowered himself onto her.

'I still want you, too,' his deep, gravelly voice whispered in her ear, and his breath feathered her cheek. Her lashes flew open and, startled, she caught her breath when she saw the hunger in his eyes that glittered like polished jet.

'I don't...'

'Yes, *cara*, you do.' He captured her denial with his lips and banished it with a kiss that was fiercely passionate yet held an underlying gentleness that was unexpected and utterly beguiling.

Jess lost her battle with herself. The pleasure of having Drago's mouth move over hers was impossible to resist, and when he traced his tongue over the tight line of her clamped lips she gave a little moan and parted them so that the kiss became intensely erotic.

Lost in the magic he was creating, Jess stared at him helplessly when at last he lifted his head. 'If it's any consolation, I don't know what the hell is going on either,' he told her roughly. 'This was not meant to happen.'

Drago's taut voice revealed his frustration. He disliked public displays of affection and could not believe that he had kissed Jess on a gondola in the middle of Venice's main waterway. At least the gondolier had discreetly averted his gaze, and when they drew up by the Palazzo d'Inverno he handed the man a large tip.

Jess walked ahead of Drago into the *palazzo*, her stiletto heels tapping on the marble floor, echoing the staccato beat of her heart.

He caught up with her as she reached the stairs. 'What would you like to do for the rest of the evening? I have a selection of English DVDs if you want to watch a film.'

She tore her eyes from the sensual curve of his mouth that only a few moments ago had decimated her ability to think, and knew that she dared not spend another minute alone with him. 'If you don't mind, I'd like to go straight to bed.'

His sudden grin stole her breath. Without his usual arrogant expression he looked almost boyish and heart-stoppingly sexy.

'Excellent idea,' he murmured.

She flushed with mortification when she realised he had taken her words as an invitation, but her frantic, 'I meant *alone*,' was muffled against his shoulder as he scooped her into his arms and strode up the stairs. 'Drago—we can't,' she whispered when he reached his suite of rooms and carried her through to the bedroom. 'Last night was a mistake.'

He tumbled her onto the bed and came down on top of her so that she felt the hard proof of his arousal nudge her thigh. Threading his fingers through her hair, he stared into her eyes, the amusement fading from his.

'Last night was inevitable from the moment we met,' he said harshly.

It was the truth. She had taken one look at him and fallen in lust—not love, Jess quickly assured herself. No way would she risk her heart with *him*. But no other man had ever made her feel this way. He kissed her mouth, her cheeks, her eyelids—light, delicate kisses that melted the last vestiges of her resistance. His fingers tugged open the buttons running down the front of her dress and he gave a low murmur of approval when he pushed the material aside and discovered that she was not wearing a bra.

'*Bellisima,*' he said thickly as he cupped her small

breasts in his hands and anointed one dusky peak and then the other with his lips.

She caught fire, arching her slender body to meet his mouth and eagerly helping him to remove her dress and knickers. This was not the time for words; their need was too urgent. Drago stripped with a clumsy haste that was strangely touching, and after taking a condom from the bedside drawer and sliding it over the proud jut of his arousal he moved over her.

Jess caught her breath as he entered her. He filled her, completed her, and she wrapped her legs around him and held on tightly to his shoulders as he possessed her with deep, measured strokes, driving her higher. As her body trembled with the exquisite ripples of orgasm her heart soared, and when Drago groaned with the power of his own release she felt a fierce tenderness and the strangest sense that their souls had joined.

The crowds of tourists in St Mark's Square had thinned in the early evening and the restaurants became busier. Sitting beneath the striped awning of a café on the edge of the square, her elbow propped on the table and her hand cupping her chin, Jess had a clear view of the ornate and incredibly beautiful Basilica.

'I think I'm in love,' she murmured. Beside her she felt Drago stiffen, and when she glanced at him and saw his startled frown she laughed. 'Not with you. With Venice.'

'Ah.' His relief was evident in his smile.

For some reason Jess felt a little pang of regret that he wanted nothing more from her than sex. *Don't be an idiot*, she told herself sternly. She knew their affair was based purely on their physical attraction to one another.

Their sex-life was amazing, but inevitably the fiery passion they shared would burn out.

'At the weekend we can climb to the top of the Campanile again, if you like,' he offered. 'I know how much you enjoyed the views over the city. Or I'll take you to see the Doge's Palace. The interior is impressive, and filled with stunning artworks. And of course you can't visit Venice without walking over the Bridge of Sighs.'

'It's such a romantic name. I wonder why it's called that?'

'The popular explanation is rather less romantic than the name suggests. The bridge used to lead to the state prison, and crossing it would often be a prisoner's last view of Venice.'

Jess sighed. 'I feel guilty sightseeing when Angelo is stuck in hospital.'

'You have visited him every day for the past few weeks, and I know how much he appreciates your company. Angelo would not begrudge you some free time,' Drago insisted.

'But I shouldn't have free time. I should be at home, running my business.' Jess chewed her bottom lip with her teeth—something she unconsciously did when she was anxious. 'I know that when I phoned Mike he said everything is fine, and that he had secured a new contract for T&J Decorators to refurbish a commercial property, but I need to go back and take charge. My company means everything to me. It's the only thing I've ever succeeded at,' she admitted ruefully.

'Once Angelo's memory has returned you will be free to leave.'

Drago's smile was full of easy charm but his tone was uncompromising, and Jess's spirits plummeted with the realisation that he still suspected she had some involvement with his cousin's missing inheritance fund. And in truth she *was* still his prisoner, for she never went anywhere without either him or his bodyguard Fico to accompany her. On a couple of occasions during the first week of her stay she had attempted to slip away from the bodyguard. It had crossed her mind that if she explained her situation to one of the nurses at the hospital they might help her. But none that she had met spoke English, Fico had followed her doggedly, and she still had the problem of no passport or money.

Jess pushed away the uncomfortable thought that she had not tried harder to leave Venice because she was captivated by her affair with Drago. His hunger for her showed no sign of abating. But aside from their mutual desire for one another a sense of companionship, even friendship, had unexpectedly developed between them. He had given her several guided tours of Venice, and Jess loved wandering around the city with him, exploring the narrow streets and the many charming *piazzas*. She visited Angelo every day while Drago was at work. Usually he met her at the hospital in the evening, and after spending some time with his cousin they would return to the *palazzo* or go for dinner at a restaurant— the Trattoria Marisa being their favourite place to eat.

'How was Angelo today?'

'He still has a bad headache.' She frowned as her thoughts returned to Angelo. 'It has lasted for three days now, and your aunt is very concerned.'

Dorotea had admitted as much. After spending endless days cooped up with her in the small hospital room Angelo's mother had thawed slightly towards Jess, and had even thanked her for her efforts to help her son. Drago's mother was also friendlier, but once or twice Jess had been aware of Luisa's speculative glance, and she had a feeling that Luisa knew she was sleeping with her son.

'I'll speak to the consultant about him—' Drago broke off and smiled at a small child who had toddled over from where his parents were sitting at a nearby table.

The little boy was about two years old, Jess estimated, and utterly adorable, with a halo of blond curls and big blue eyes. He seemed to be intrigued by Drago, and grinned as he waved the sticky ice-cream cone he was holding.

'*No*, Josh!' The child's mother hurried over just as the toddler smeared ice-cream over Drago's superbly tailored trousers. 'I'm so sorry...' she said in English.

Drago interrupted her frantic apology with a laugh. 'Don't worry. He's an angelic-looking child,' he said, in a soft tone that captured Jess's attention.

'He can be a little terror,' the woman said ruefully. She glanced at Jess. 'You know what they're like at two—into everything.'

She nodded at the woman and smiled back, trying to ignore the knife-blade that sliced through her heart. What had Katie been like at two years old? she wondered. Had she been 'into everything'? She would never know, and the reminder of all she had lost was an ache inside her that never went away.

The woman picked up the little boy and carried him back to her table. 'Cute kid,' Drago commented as he attempted to clean his trousers with a napkin.

'I've noticed that Italians really seem to love children,' Jess said musingly. 'Have you never wanted to marry and have children?'

'I'm happy with my life the way it is.'

Puzzled by the sudden curtness in his voice, Jess

studied him curiously. 'You were so gentle with that little boy. I think you would make a great father.'

'*Madonna!* Can we drop the subject?' he snapped. 'My personal life is not up for discussion.'

Jess felt a flare of irritation at his arrogant tone. 'Why not?' she demanded. 'I've told you things about me and what happened with Seb. Why don't you want to talk about yourself?'

He made no response, and the hard gleam in his eyes warned her to back off, but Jess refused to be dismissed. She knew she meant nothing to Drago, but the reminder that he only wanted a sexual relationship with her hurt more than it should.

'Maybe you're hiding some terrible secret?' she taunted.

'Don't be ridiculous.'

His mouth tightened, and to Jess's surprise he seemed uncomfortable. She sensed there was something in his past that he wanted to keep hidden. Was it a woman? He had a reputation as a playboy, but perhaps he'd once had a relationship that had been important to him. The idea evoked a sharp stab of jealousy inside her.

'Have you ever been in love?' she blurted out.

His eyes narrowed and his impatience was tangible, but after a few moments he shrugged and admitted tautly, 'Once. A long time ago.'

Jess caught her breath. 'What happened?'

'Nothing happened. The relationship ended and I grew up. It was an educational experience,' he said, with heavy irony that made Jess even more intrigued. It sounded as though he had been hurt, and she guessed he had not wanted his relationship with the woman he had loved to end. She longed to ask him more questions, but he did not give her the opportunity as he glanced at his watch and stood up.

'I'm going to the hospital to talk to the doctor about Angelo's headaches,' he said abruptly. 'Fico will take you back to the *palazzo*. The party is due to start at eight o'clock tonight.' He made an effort to lighten his tone. 'I'm sure you will want to spend some time getting ready. I appreciate that you have agreed to act as my hostess. This dinner party is an annual event attended by senior management staff from Cassa di Cassari's worldwide operation. My mother and aunt usually attend, but this year they naturally wish to devote their time to Angelo.'

'No problem,' Jess said in a fiercely bright voice.

She was determined not to let him see how hurt she felt by his refusal to talk about himself, and equally determined to hide the fact that she was feeling nervous about her role as hostess at the party. Drago had assured her that most of the guests would be able to speak English, but what on earth did a decorator have in common with high-flying businessmen and company executives from the world famous Cassa di Cassari? she thought anxiously.

As she stood up she was overcome by an unpleasant sensation that the pavement beneath her feet was tilting, and she gripped the edge of the table.

'What's the matter?' Drago asked, frowning as he watched the rosy pink flush on her cheeks fade so that she looked ashen.

'I just feel a bit dizzy. It'll pass in a minute.'

He looked unconvinced. 'I hope you're not coming down with something. You felt dizzy when you got up this morning.'

'It's nothing.' Jess dismissed his concern, not revealing that she had waited until he had left for work before she had rushed to the bathroom to be sick the last two mornings. 'Maybe I've had too much sun. It's much hotter here in Venice than in London, and I'm not used to the heat.' That had to be the explanation, she assured herself.

'With your delicate colouring you need to wear a hat.' Drago smoothed a tendril of her fiery gold hair back from her face and could not resist dropping a light kiss on her soft mouth. 'I adore your freckles, *cara*. Especially the ones that look like gold-dust scattered over your breasts,' he murmured, his voice dropping to a sexy whisper that sent a little shiver of response down Jess's spine.

One look from his glittering black gaze was all it took to make her melt, she acknowledged wryly. As she picked up her bag the magazine she had bought at the hospital slid out and fell on the floor. Drago bent to pick it up, but instead of handing it to her he stared at the front cover and his expression darkened.

'Why do you read such trash? Gossip magazines print utter rubbish,' he said tersely, flicking through the pages with a look of arrogant disdain on his face that irked Jess.

'I suppose you think I should only read highbrow novels by classical authors such as…' She frantically searched her mind for an author she had heard of whom he would deem suitable. 'Dickens.' It was the only name she could come up with. 'Actually, I bought that magazine because it mainly has photos of celebrities' houses, and I'm interested in interior design. I can't read it because I don't understand Italian. But don't think that I read literary stuff at home, because I don't. Unlike you, I wasn't born into a wealthy family and I don't have the advantage of a good education.'

Jess could not hide the tremor in her voice. Drago

was highly intelligent and had an extensive knowledge of many subjects. She felt embarrassed by her lack of education, and he clearly thought she was a brainless bimbo. 'At least I'm not a snob, who criticises other people for their tastes,' she finished hotly.

Drago raked a hand through his hair. 'I wasn't trying to insult you. *Dio*, you are such a firebrand.'

His exasperation faded and he felt an unexpected tug of tenderness when he saw the glimmer of tears in her eyes. He was unwilling to explain that the photograph of a beautiful socialite on the front cover of the magazine was an unwelcome reminder of his past. Nor could he explain to Jess that watching the little boy in the café had evoked an ache in his gut. Some things were best left buried. He had never before felt inclined to talk about his past to any of his lovers, and there was no reason why he should do so with Jess, he told himself.

He gave a frustrated sigh when he saw Fico's burly figure heading towards them across the square. What he wanted to do was take Jess back to the *palazzo* and make love to her but, as always, duty to his family prevailed. He was concerned about his cousin, and had promised his aunt that he would speak to the consultant and find out whether Angelo's headaches were an indication of something more serious.

CHAPTER EIGHT

WHERE WAS DRAGO? Jess glanced at the clock for the hundredth time, and her tension escalated when she saw that it was ten to eight. Any minute now the party guests would begin to arrive, expecting to be greeted by their host. Instead they would be met by a hostess whose social skills were sadly inadequate, she thought, feeling another stab of nervousness at the prospect of the evening ahead. Fortunately Drago's butler Francesco was his usual unflappable self, and had informed her that the household staff had completed all the preparations for the party.

Leaving her bedroom, which she had never actually slept in during her stay at the *palazzo* but used as a dressing room, she walked back to the master suite and felt weak with relief when Drago strolled into the sitting room from his bedroom.

'There you are!' Her relief gave way to anger as she watched him calmly adjust his cufflinks as if he had all the time in the world. 'Where have you been? I've been worried sick.'

His brows lifted. 'Why, *cara*, I didn't know you cared,' he drawled.

'I meant I was worried you wouldn't get back in time.' She fell silent, puzzled by his attitude, and by the strange feeling that he was avoiding her gaze. 'Were you delayed at the hospital? How is Angelo?'

'He's fine.' Perhaps realising that he had sounded curt, Drago finally looked at her. 'We'll talk about him later,' he said obliquely.

He smiled suddenly, and Jess felt a familiar knee-jerk reaction as he roamed his eyes over her.

His voice softened. 'You look amazing, *mia bella*. The dress is perfect for you.'

She flushed, feeling stupidly shy. 'It's a beautiful dress. I've never worn anything like it before.'

The full-length royal blue satin gown that Jess had discovered in her room when she had gone to change for the party was exquisite; the deceptively simple design flattered her slender figure and the crystal studded shoulder straps and narrow belt gave the dress extra glamour. One of the maids had helped her with her hair, and had swept it up into a sleek chignon. Three-inch sliver stiletto sandals gave her additional height, and when Jess had studied her reflection in the mirror she had been shocked to see herself looking so elegant.

'Is the dress from the Cassa di Cassari range of clothes?'

'No. I asked the designer Torre Umberto to make it especially for you. This will be a perfect accessory for the dress.'

As he walked towards her Drago took something from his pocket. Jess gasped when he held it up and she saw that it was a strand of glittering diamonds interspersed with square-cut sapphires.

'I don't think I should wear it. Supposing I lose it?' she said nervously. A little shiver ran through her when she felt his warm breath on the back of her neck as he fastened the necklace around her throat.

'Of course you won't lose it.' He turned her towards the mirror and she caught her breath at the sight of the diamonds sparkling with fiery brilliance against her skin.

'I feel like I've stepped into the pages of a fairy tale,' she whispered, staring at the reflection of the beautiful woman whom she hardly recognised as herself, and the dark, dangerously attractive man standing behind her. She gave another shiver when Drago bent his head and trailed his lips down the length of her slender white neck. In the mirror she watched his eyes glitter with a look she knew so well, and his hunger for her made her insides melt.

He turned her to face him, but instead of kissing her, as she longed for him to do, he stepped away from her and ran a hand through his hair.

'Jess…we need to talk.'

Puzzled that he seemed uncharacteristically ill at ease, she said quietly, 'What about?'

He cursed at the sound of a knock on the door, and strode across the room to open it. After a brief conversation with the butler he glanced back at her, his frustration that they had been interrupted revealed in his taut voice. 'Francesco says that some of the guests have arrived. We had better go down and greet them.'

Her foster-mother had had a habit of quoting proverbs, and one in particular—*You can't make a silk purse out of a sow's ear*—had never seemed more appropriate, Jess brooded later in the evening. Thanks to the *haute couture* dress she was wearing she did not look out of place among the glamorous women party guests. But it had quickly become apparent that she did not fit into Drago's rarefied world of the sophisticated super-rich.

Dinner had been a nightmare; she hadn't known which cutlery to use for each course, and she'd managed to knock over a glass of wine belonging to the guest sitting next to her. One of the waiters had calmly mopped up the mess, but she'd felt everyone's eyes on her and wanted to die of embarrassment.

The fact that she did not speak Italian had not proved a problem, as most of the guests spoke English, but while they'd discussed a range of subjects including politics, current affairs and the arts, Jess had struggled to find something to say. She knew nothing about opera, she had never skied in Aspen—or anywhere else for that matter—and enquiries about her chosen career were met with surprise followed by an awkward silence when she revealed that she ran a decorating company.

It would have been better if Drago had hosted the party on his own, she thought dismally. And from the way he had avoided her all evening it seemed he thought so too. While cocktails had been served he had mingled with his guests and hardly spoken a word to her. Now, during dinner, although he was sitting opposite her, he focused his attention on the two beautiful women seated on either side of him and paid her scant attention. As coffee and *petit-fours* were served he lapsed into a brooding silence, and his grim expression deterred anyone from approaching him.

'Of course I'm not surprised that our host looks so dour,' the woman sitting next to Jess commented in an undertone.

'What do you mean?' She cast a sideways glance towards the elegant wife of Drago's chief financial officer, who had introduced herself as Theresa Petronelli.

'I imagine any man would find it hard to see pictures of his ex-fiancée, her husband and two children looking the epitome of the perfect family on the front page of a top-selling magazine. It must be a kick in the teeth for Drago—and a painful reminder of what he lost.'

Shock ran though Jess. 'Are you saying he was once engaged to be married?'

'To the lovely Vittoria—who I have to say looks simply stunning in this week's edition of *Vita* magazine,' Theresa confirmed. 'Drago was engaged to her years ago, and Vittoria's parents' organised a lavish wedding. Then out of the blue the relationship ended. There were rumours that Vittoria was rushed into hospital, but no one from the family would say what was wrong with her, or whether her illness had anything to do with the ending of their relationship. The paparazzi hounded Drago for his side of the story but he remained tight-lipped about what had happened.

'I've often wondered if he was more upset by the split than he let on,' Theresa confided. 'Vittoria's father is a count. She is very beautiful and gracious, and would have been the perfect wife for Drago, but a couple of years ago she married a Swiss banker and she has just given birth to their second child.'

It was *Vita* magazine that had fallen out of her bag earlier, Jess thought. She hadn't understood why Drago had seemed in such a bad mood when he had flicked through the pages, but from what Theresa had said he had clearly been dismayed to see pictures of his ex-fiancée who was now happily married to someone else.

Presumably Vittoria was the woman he had once been in love with. Was he still in love with her? she wondered. For some strange reason the thought caused a sharp pain in her chest, as if she had been stabbed in the heart. Her eyes were drawn across the table to him, and she stiffened when she discovered that he was watching her with a curious intensity.

He leaned forward suddenly, his dark gaze trapping hers. 'Are you enjoying the party?'

Hurt by his indifference towards her all evening, she saw no reason why she should be tactful. 'Not really. I feel out of my depth among all these posh people. The kind of party I'm used to is a barbecue in the rain, burnt sausages and my team of workmen having a competition to see how much beer they can drink. I don't belong here.' She looked away from him, cursing the silly tears that stung her eyes as she added silently, *with you.*

Drago frowned. 'That's not true. Of course you belong here. You are my guest.'

'I'm your prisoner, suspected of something I have not done,' Jess said fiercely, thankful that Theresa Petronelli was chatting to another guest and not listening to her conversation with Drago.

He gave her a sardonic look. 'I'm sure that someone as resourceful as you could have left Italy if you had really wanted to. Which makes me think that perhaps you wanted to stay with me,' he drawled.

'Of course I wanted to leave,' she snapped, outraged by his suggestion. 'But thanks to you my passport is at the bottom of the canal.'

'Thanks to me? I had nothing to do with your crazy climb down from a second-floor balcony—except to save you when you fell. You're kidding yourself, *cara.* You stayed because you love the way I make you feel,' he stated, in his deep, sexy voice that caressed her senses like crushed velvet.

She stared at him and felt her stomach dip. He looked incredibly handsome in a dinner suit and white silk shirt. The candles on the table cast a flickering light that accentuated the hard angles and planes of his chiselled features, and his dark hair had fallen onto his brow. Jess longed to run her fingers through it.

She'd stayed because she had fallen in love with him.

Jess swallowed as the shocking realisation hit her and quickly lowered her eyelashes, terrified that he might be able to read her thoughts. She cautiously examined the idea and gave a silent groan at her stupidity. Images flashed into her mind of walking hand in hand with him through the streets of Venice, of the candlelit dinners they'd had at Trattoria Marisa, where he was always able to relax after a hectic day at work and they'd talk about nothing in particular, in the way that lovers do. And underlying their easy companionship was the simmering sexual attraction which ignited the moment he took her in his arms and always culminated in him making love to her with hungry passion and an unexpected tenderness that somehow eased the loneliness inside her.

To her relief one of the guests stood up and proposed a toast to Cassa di Cassari's chairman. This apparently signified the end of the party, and Jess took advantage of the bustle of people getting up from the table and preparing to leave to slip upstairs. Out of habit she went straight to Drago's suite, but as she walked into his bedroom she stopped and stared at herself in the mirror. She looked lovely in the fairy-tale dress, but she didn't look like the Jess Harper who ran a decorating business and was more used to wearing painting overalls. It was time to end the madness. She had thought she could have an affair with Drago without her emotions getting involved, but now that she had committed the ultimate folly of falling for him she had to end her relationship with him.

The headache that had started earlier had developed

into a thudding sensation in her skull and she felt nauseous again. Maybe she had picked up a virus and that was why she had felt sapped of energy for the last few days. Releasing her hair from the chignon lessened the pain in her head a little, and after running a brush through her hair she unfastened the diamond necklace, wondering where she should put it. It must be worth a fortune. She guessed Drago probably stored it in a safe, but for now she decided to slip it into his bedside drawer.

His passport was lying on top of some papers. She carefully placed the necklace in the drawer, her attention still on the passport—which, to her surprise, was an English one, not an Italian passport. Curiosity got the better of her. After a moment's hesitation she opened it—and a bolt of shock ran though her. It was impossible! Her passport had been in the rucksack that was now at the bottom of the canal. Staring at the photo of herself, she felt utterly confused.

The click of the door being closed made her swing round. Clutching the passport, she said helplessly, 'I don't understand. Why is my passport in your drawer?'

'I removed it from your bag when you first arrived at the *palazzo*.' Drago gave a laconic shrug. 'It seemed the best way to ensure you stayed in Italy until I was ready for you to leave.'

'But you know I've been worrying about how I can get a replacement.' Jess's temper ignited. 'How dare you deceive me?' She gave a bitter laugh. 'But why am I surprised? I should be used to men lying to me. You're just the same as Seb—devious and controlling...' Her voice cracked as the realisation of Drago's lack of trust in her sank in. How stupid she had been to believe that they had become friends as well as lovers while she had been in Venice. To her horror, she felt a tear slide down her cheek. Angrily she dashed it away. Pride was all she had, and she lifted her chin and glared at him. 'You have accused me unjustly and treated me unfairly. I know nothing about your cousin's missing money—'

She broke off as Drago strode across the room towards her, his eyes blazing with an expression she could not define.

'I *know*,' he said roughly. 'Angelo has regained his memory and he remembers everything. That's why I was delayed at the hospital.'

It was one shock too many. Jess sank down weakly onto the bed. 'You mean he remembers what he did with his inheritance fund? Why didn't you say something earlier instead of avoiding me at the party?' she demanded, unable to hide the tremor in her voice.

Drago exhaled slowly. He prided himself on his good judgement, and was rarely wrong, but he had been very wrong about Jess and had no idea how he was going to make amends for the way he had jumped to conclusions about her.

'I'm sorry,' he said roughly. 'I did not know what to say to you. I have so many things to apologise for that I don't know where to begin. 'Angelo invested his money in a gold mine,' he continued after a moment. 'It sounds crazy, I know,' he said when he saw the startled look on Jess's face. 'Apparently while he was at college in London he met some people who told him about an investment opportunity at a mine on the west coast of Australia. The owners had proof that there was a lot of gold underground, and were looking for investors to put up funds to start mining it. Angelo was convinced that the investment was sound, and was assured that once the mine was running he would triple his investment, so he went ahead without first discussing it with me.

'A few months later he discovered that he had been duped. The whole thing turned out to be a scam run by confidence tricksters. Instead of asking for my help, Angelo was so ashamed that he'd been fooled that he felt he couldn't come home. He *was* literally destitute, but thankfully you gave him a job and somewhere to live. He admits he dreaded telling me what he had done,' Drago said heavily. 'He says he felt I was too controlling, and he wanted to prove that he could succeed in business to impress me.' He grimaced. 'All these years I have taken care of him and tried to be a father figure to him. I had no idea he resented me.'

Jess heard the hurt in his voice and could not help but feel sympathetic. 'I'm sure he doesn't resent you,' she said softly. 'He just needs to find his own way in life.'

'He doesn't want a position in Cassa di Cassari. He wants to be a professional musician,' Drago muttered. 'I wish he'd told me about the investment scam. It would have saved a lot of trouble. When Aunt Dorotea revealed that she knew he had withdrawn all his money from the bank he panicked and told her he had lent it to an English friend—Jess Harper. Naturally my aunt was worried, and asked me to find out more about you.'

'And when you learned that I had been found guilty of fraud you believed I had somehow conned the money from Angelo,' Jess said dully. She stiffened as Drago sat down next to her on the bed. The musky scent of his aftershave teased her senses and she resented her fierce awareness of him. She felt ashamed that, even knowing he had a low opinion of her, she had fallen into his bed willingly.

Drago glanced at Jess's white face and his gut clenched with guilt at the way he had treated her. 'Eventually Angelo decided he had to own up to what he had done. But on his way here to see me he was involved in the car accident. I was instantly suspicious of you because I have had experience of being conned,' he explained grimly. 'When I was a similar age to Angelo I was thrust into the role of chairman of Cassa di Cassari, after my father and uncle died. I was young, and determined to prove myself a worthy successor to my father. I was impressed by an investment opportunity in Russia—although if I'm totally honest I was more impressed by the exotic and very beautiful Russian woman who persuaded me to put a huge amount of Cassa di Cassari's money into her company,' he admitted with wry self-derision. 'Natalia must have found it very amusing to seduce me, but when she disappeared with several million pounds of the company's money the board members were rather less than impressed.

'I cursed myself for being a gullible fool and worked like a dog to regain the board's support. I'd learned a valuable lesson and was more careful about who I trusted. I admit that discovering you had a criminal record made me suspicious of you. But when I met you at your flat—' He broke off and shook his head at the memory of their first meeting. 'You blew me away,' he said thickly. 'I took one look at you and was smitten. I felt violently jealous that you might be my cousin's lover. It was easy to believe that Angelo had been conned by a beautiful woman, as had once happened to me. But within a very short time I began to wonder if I had misjudged you. You were so kind to Angelo, and spent hours at the hospital trying to jog his memory. Rather than seeming worried about what he might remember, you were adamant that he would exonerate you—which he did, completely, when I visited him tonight.'

Looking into Jess's eyes, Drago said strongly, 'I believe the Loxley guy set you up, and that you are innocent of the crime you were convicted of. Soon after I brought you to the *palazzo* I started to have doubts that you knew anything about Angelo's missing money.' Catching her doubtful expression, he grimaced. 'I understand why you might not believe me.'

'You hid my passport,' she said sharply. 'Why would you have done that if you trusted me?'

He looked away from her and said, in a strangely muted voice, 'There was a reason why I wanted you to stay that had nothing to do with my cousin.'

Jess frowned; puzzled by his sudden tension evident in the rigid line of his jaw. 'What reason?'

Drago had asked himself the same question numerous times and still did not have a clear answer. He did not understand what his feelings were for Jess. All he knew was that he had never felt this way about any of his previous mistresses. He had tried to convince himself that his fascination with her was simply because they had great sex, but deep down he knew it was something more than that. He was not ready to examine his emotions, but now his hand had been forced—and if he did not want Jess to catch the next flight to London he knew he would have to lower his barriers.

He looked into her green eyes and saw her confusion. 'I didn't want to lose you,' he admitted quietly. 'I still don't.'

The huskiness in Drago's voice made Jess's heart flip. Was he saying that their relationship meant something to him? That *she* meant something to him?

She swallowed. 'I don't understand. Angelo's memory has returned, and you know I had nothing to do with his missing money.' She cast a rueful look at the passport in her hand. 'Why shouldn't I go home?'

'You know why, *cara*. You feel it too.'

It was the one thing Drago was sure of. This inexplicable thing that was happening to him, that made him think about her at inconvenient times and made him want to be with her all the time—he was certain that Jess felt the same way. He had seen evidence of it in the way her face lit up whenever she saw him, and in her sleepy, sexy smile when she woke in his arms every morning. She was so beautiful. Simply looking at her made his insides ache. He knew that if he touched her he wouldn't be able to stop, and his hand was unsteady as he threaded his fingers into her glorious autumn-gold hair and tilted her face to his.

'I have never desired any woman the way I desire you, *mia bella*.' He gently traced his thumb-pad over the curve of her lower lip. 'I would like our relationship to continue.'

Jess's heart was beating so fast that she was sure he must feel it when he placed his hand just below her breast. She was stunned by Drago's revelation that he did not want their affair to end yet. He had not promised commitment of any kind, she reminded herself, but the voice of caution inside her head was drowned out by the thunderous beat of her heart. Drago wanted her, and she did not care for how long.

Reality poked its nose into her fairy tale. How could she continue this affair with him when she needed to return to London to run her decorating business? She was sure that Drago would soon tire of a long-distance relationship. What if he suggested that she move to Venice? She would be a fool to give up her business for the sake of an affair with him that doubtless would end after a few months—yet the thought of leaving him and never seeing him again ripped her apart.

Jess's thoughts were reeling. She wanted to ask Drago what he meant when he said he wanted their relationship to continue, and how exactly their affair would work, but she was afraid of his reply. If he asked her to give up her life in London she was scared she might be tempted to agree.

Feeling too restless and worked up to remain sitting next to him, she jumped up from the bed. The room spun and she felt dizzy again—as she had after she'd ridden on a carousel years ago, when her social worker had taken her to a fairground. She felt hot and cold at the same time, there was a peculiar roaring noise in her ears, and she heard Drago calling her name as she fell into blackness.

CHAPTER NINE

THE ROOM WAS no longer spinning. Cautiously Jess turned her head and met Drago's tense gaze.

'Lie still. The doctor is on his way.'

She immediately jerked upright—and gagged as a wave of nausea swept over her.

'*Dio!* Do you ever do as you are told?' Concern over-rode the impatience in his voice as he eased her back down onto the pillows.

'My dress will get creased if I lie down in it,' she argued, although she did not try to move again for the simple reason that she was afraid she would be sick. 'I don't need a doctor.'

His answer was uncompromising. 'Of course you do. You passed out, you're as white as death, and you've been suffering from dizzy spells.'

It was easier to let Drago take control, Jess decided wearily. And in truth she felt awful.

The doctor arrived a few minutes later. A softly spoken man, with grey hair and a reassuringly calm manner, he checked her blood pressure, asked various questions and took a blood sample which he said he would test to see if she was anaemic.

'It is a fairly common problem with young women as iron is lost during menstruation each month—especially if they do not eat properly because of the fashion to be thin,' he said, with a meaningful glance at Jess's slender figure.

'I eat well. I can't help being naturally skinny,' she muttered.

Her mind was focused on the first part of the doctor's statement and she did a frantic calculation. Her period was only a couple of days late. There was no need to panic, she told herself. No need for the sick dread that had settled in the pit of her stomach when she remembered how she had woken the last two mornings feeling horribly sick. The possibility that she could be pregnant was too terrifying to contemplate. She could *not* have conceived by accident a second time, she assured herself. Lightning couldn't strike twice. She was convinced that she must be suffering from a gastric virus.

'Where do you think you're going?' Drago demanded as he walked back into the room after the doctor had departed.

'To my room.' Jess shot a glance at him and felt her heart give a familiar flip as she recalled the conversation they'd had before she had fainted. She was no wiser as to what sort of relationship he wanted with her, but tonight she felt too weak and vulnerable to press him for an explanation. 'I think it will be better if I sleep alone. I'm sure I've picked up a stomach bug, and I don't want to disturb you if I'm ill during the night.'

He shook his head and, ignoring her protest, lifted her and deposited her back on the bed. 'I'm not risking you being alone in case you faint again. Hopefully the doctor will have some answers as to what is wrong with you tomorrow, but tonight you're sleeping in here, where I can keep an eye on you. *Madonna!*' Drago's patience evaporated as she slid off the mattress. 'You are the most stubborn, infuriating woman—'

'I need to take my dress off.'

Without another word he turned her round and ran the zip down her spine. It was ridiculous to feel shy when she had spent every night of the past weeks in his bed, Jess thought wryly. But she could not prevent a soft flush spreading across her cheeks as Drago slid the straps over her shoulders and tugged the dress down until it pooled at her feet.

Her breasts had felt ultra-sensitive recently, and her nipples were as hard as pebbles. Drago's eyes narrowed and Jess found herself holding her breath, willing him to take her in his arms and make the world go away. When he made love to her she could pretend that it was more than just good sex, and that maybe he really *did* want more than a casual affair with her. To her disappointment he moved away, and a moment later handed her one of his shirts.

'You'd better wear this to sleep in,' he said, without giving an explanation of why he wanted her to cover up when she usually slept naked. 'Would you like a drink? I'll ask Francesco to bring a pot of tea, if you like.'

For some inexplicable reason his gentle concern made Jess feel like bursting into tears, and only by biting down hard on her lip was she able to control her emotions.

'I don't want anything, thanks. I'm very tired.' *Drained* would be a better description, she thought as she climbed into bed. The silk sheets were deliciously cool, and she closed her eyes and gave a deep sigh that, unbeknown to her, increased Drago's concern.

Jess looked ethereally fragile, lying in the huge bed, with her fiery hair so bright in contrast to her pale face, he thought grimly. Until the doctor could come up with an explanation of what was wrong with her he was not going to let her set foot outside the *palazzo*—not to go back to London and her job as a decorator. He still had difficulty imagining her climbing ladders and painting walls for a living. Not because he thought that being a decorator was demeaning, but because her petite, slender figure was not suited to a physically demanding job.

As he joined her in the bed his body reacted predictably to the feel of her small, round bottom pressed up against him. He was thankful he had persuaded her to wear his shirt. She would tempt a saint, let alone a mortal man who was painfully aroused, he thought ruefully. The steady sound of her breathing told him that she had fallen asleep. Hopefully she would feel better after a restful night, so long as she did not have another of her disturbing dreams or weep silently in her sleep as she sometimes did. When he had asked her more about the dreams she had insisted she did not remember, but he sensed that she had not told him the whole truth, and he felt frustrated that she clearly did not trust him enough to confide in him.

Jess opened her eyes to find sunshine flooding the bedroom. Frowning, she glanced at the clock and was shocked to see that it was ten a.m. She had never slept so late in her life, but the long sleep must have done her good because she did not feel sick this morning. The panic she'd felt the previous night when she'd realised her period was a couple of days late seemed a silly overreaction. In fact she often felt nauseous and overemotional just before her monthly period, and she wouldn't be surprised if it started today.

'How are you feeling?'

Drago's deep voice made her jump, and she turned her head to see him sitting in an armchair. Dressed in immaculately tailored beige chinos and a black polo shirt, his silky hair falling onto his brow and his square jaw bearing a faint shadow of dark stubble, he was so incredibly handsome that her heart performed its usual somersault. At first glance he appeared relaxed, with his long legs stretched out in front of him, his elbows resting on the arms of the chair and his fingers linked together. But closer inspection revealed the tense line of his jaw, and his black eyes were as hard as jet and curiously expressionless.

'I feel fine,' Jess assured him. 'I don't know why I fainted last night. Maybe I am a bit anaemic, as the doctor suggested.'

'Santa Madre!' He leapt to his feet with the violent force of a volcanic eruption. 'You can stop the pretence that you don't know what is wrong with you. I know you are pregnant with my child,' he said savagely. 'Why didn't you tell me?'

Scalding fury coursed through Drago's veins. Ever since he had received the phone call from the doctor an hour ago rage had been building inside him like steam in a pressure cooker, and now he exploded. Why had Jess kept her pregnancy a secret? Memories of the nightmare scenario that had happened eight years ago returned to haunt him. He would never forget Vittoria's terrified face—or the blood. There had been so much blood. He closed his eyes in an attempt to blot out the images, and when he opened them again he focused grimly on Jess.

'Tell me—were you planning to keep my child a secret from me for ever?' he demanded bitterly. He watched the colour drain from her face until she was even paler than she had been the previous night. 'Are

you going to faint? Put your head between your knees.'
His voice roughened with concern as he strode over to
the bed and tangled his fingers in her bright hair, holding her head down so that the blood rushed back to her
brain.

'I'm all right.' Jess drew a shuddering breath, conscious of the painful thud of her heart as it jerked erratically against her ribcage. Her head was still spinning
as she lifted her eyes to Drago. Intense shock made her
skin feel clammy and strangled her vocal cords, so that
her voice emerged as a shaky whisper. 'I'm not pregnant. I can't be.'

Drago frowned. Jess shocked reaction was clearly
genuine, and his anger faded with the realisation that
she had been unaware that she was expecting his baby.

'We both know we took a risk once and had unprotected sex the first night we slept together,' he said in a
softer tone. 'Dr Marellis phoned earlier this morning,
while you were still asleep, and confirmed that your
blood test gave a positive result for pregnancy.'

Jess's mouth felt parched. 'He had no right to give
you confidential information about me.'

'Eduardo is an old family friend. Presumably he
believed I had a right to know that you are carrying
my child, and he congratulated me on my impending
fatherhood.'

Jess shook her head, as if she could somehow dismiss his words. *It couldn't be true*, she thought frantically. But why would Drago lie? Maybe the doctor was
wrong about the test result? She knew she was clutching
at a very fragile straw. A blood test to detect pregnancy
was almost one hundred per cent likely to be accurate.

'I swear I didn't know,' she said numbly. 'I'm only a
few days late and I didn't think anything of it.'

That wasn't absolutely true, she admitted silently. The nausea she had been experiencing in recent days had seemed frighteningly familiar, but she had been too scared to think about a possible cause. It had been easier to ignore her suspicions. But now she could not hide from the devastating truth. She had conceived Drago's child—and from his furious expression he was no more pleased by the news than Seb had been when she had told him she was expecting *his* baby.

Jess began to tremble as reaction set in. She was going to have a baby. It was something she had assumed would never happen again. The trauma she had experienced as a teenager had left mental scars, and the memory of that terrible time, the desperate decision she had made, caused her to clench her fingers until her knuckles were white.

There was no doubt that she would go ahead with the pregnancy. Her acceptance of that fact was instant and resolute. But she had to face the bleak reality that her situation was no better than it had been years ago, when she was seventeen. She was older, and she had a job, she reminded herself. At least she had the means to support a child—although how she would manage to work as a decorator when she was heavily pregnant or with a newborn baby in tow was a problem she would have to face along with many others.

Caught up in her thoughts, she gave a start when Drago moved to stand by the window. His hard-boned profile looked so intimidating. She bit her lip. If only things had been different. If only they were lovers in the true sense of the word, and instead of standing stiffly on the other side of the room he had taken her in his arms and told her he was overjoyed that his child was developing inside her. Poor baby, she thought, and her heart splintered. She squeezed her eyes shut to prevent the sudden stinging tears from falling as she was overwhelmed by guilt. Two mistakes, two unplanned pregnancies, and two little lives affected by her stupidity.

'What are you thinking?' Drago turned back to face Jess, resenting the urgent, shaming desire that kicked in his gut as he studied her delicate beauty and the vibrant hair that fell past her shoulders in a rippling stream of red-gold silk. How could he be fantasising about making love to her when she looked so fragile that she might snap? he asked himself angrily. His only consideration should be for the child she was carrying inside her.

She gave a helpless shrug. 'I'm thinking about how I'll manage as a single mother. As long as I stay fit and healthy there's no reason why I shouldn't carry on working full-time until just before the baby is due. And afterwards—well, babies sleep a lot for the first few months, and I'm sure I'll be able to take the pram on site—'

She broke off as Drago growled something in Italian. She guessed it was probably lucky she did not understand.

'If you think I would allow you to take my child onto a building site you are even crazier than I believed when I caught you climbing down from the balcony of your room,' he said harshly.

Her pale cheeks flushed with temper at his bossiness. 'I don't work on building sites. I decorate houses. I don't build them. I realise it won't be ideal to take the baby with me, but how else do you expect me to manage? I'll have to work to support the baby.'

'No, you will not. As my wife you will not want for anything. I will provide more than adequately for you and my child.'

Jess stiffened, sure that she could not have heard Drago correctly. 'What do you mean, as your wife?' she asked unsteadily.

'Naturally I will marry you,' he stated, in a coolly arrogant tone. His brows rose when she made a choked sound. 'It is the obvious solution.'

'Not to me, it isn't.' She bit her lip. 'Last night you said you wanted our relationship to continue, but you had no intention of marrying me, did you?' she said shrewdly.

'That was different. Last night I did not know that you are carrying my heir,' he replied bluntly.

'Your *heir*!' She quickly looked down at her fingers, which she had unknowingly been twisting together, determined not to let him see how much his comment hurt. Of course the only reason he was considering marrying her was for the sake of his child. 'I'm expecting your baby, Drago—a tiny new human being that in a few months' time will take his or her first breath of life. It's rather too early to be planning the baby's role as CEO of Cassa de Cassari.'

Jess's description of the new life developing inside her touched a chord deep inside Drago and brought home to him as nothing else had the astounding, amazing reality that in a few months from now she would give birth to his child. Her pregnancy was unplanned and totally unexpected. She had seemed so certain she could not have conceived the first time they had slept together. But now, with irrefutable proof that she had not been protected, he was trying to come to terms with how he felt.

Immediately after his telephone conversation with the doctor he had been stunned—and, if he was honest, dismayed. His life was already busy enough, without the additional responsibilities that having a child would bring. But, like it or not, Jess's pregnancy was a reality he needed to deal with. She was carrying the Cassari heir and he had a duty towards her and the child. His decision to marry her was not only driven by a sense of duty, Drago acknowledged. Now that his shock was fading he felt excited, somewhat overwhelmed, but ultimately delighted by the prospect that he was going to be a father.

The doctor had confirmed that the baby was due in January. As long as all went well with Jess's pregnancy, Drago reminded himself. His euphoria faded as memories of Vittoria's pregnancy returned to haunt him. He would always feel guilty that he had not paid her enough attention or taken proper care of her. He would not make the same mistake again, he vowed. Jess would receive the best medical care.

Her talk of working during her pregnancy sent a shaft of fear through him. She was so hot-headed and independent. He could not risk her deciding to go back to England to run her decorating company. The only practical solution, whereby he could keep a close eye on her during her pregnancy *and* be a full-time father to his child once it was born, was to persuade her to marry him.

'I'm not thinking of the baby's possible future role within the company. After what happened with Angelo I will not put the pressure of expectation on my child,' he said ruefully. 'But this baby will be a member of the Cassari family, and he or she has a right to grow up here at the *palazzo*. It is also our child's right to be loved and cared for by both its parents. Surely, after growing up in a children's home, you must agree that the best thing we can do for our child is to provide a stable family unit?'

Shaken by the fervour in his voice, Jess felt a lump form in her throat. All her life she had longed to be part of a family, and of course she wanted that security for her baby. But it had not crossed her mind that Drago would want his child, let alone that he would suggest they should marry. She knew he was not talking about the sort of marriage that featured in romantic films and fairy tales. He had not mentioned love. Was it foolish to want to be loved? she thought painfully. Was it selfish to wish that she mattered to someone?

'We can give the baby security without getting married,' she said quietly. 'We could lead separate lives but still share parenting responsibilities.'

'You mean we could go to court and argue over access rights and which of us the child will spend Christmases and birthdays with?' Drago's voice deepened. 'Is that the best we can offer the little person we have created, who shares your blood and mine, *cara*?'

Jess bit her lip. She wondered if Drago had deliberately played on her ragged emotions with his evocative words. He did not know that she had once made the hardest decision a mother could make so that her child would have the best possible life. Now she was being asked to make another difficult decision—this time to marry a man who did not love her for the sake of the child she carried.

The strident ring of his phone shattered the tense silence that had fallen between them. Muttering a curse, Drago glanced at the caller display and frowned. 'It's Dorotea. I'd better speak to her.'

After a brief conversation in Italian he ended the call and glanced at Jess. 'Angelo is to undergo more surgery on his leg this morning. My aunt wants me to go to the hospital, but I told her I have something important to deal with here.'

'I think you should go,' Jess said quickly. 'Your family need you. Dorotea must be so worried.'

'I'm not leaving you while we have issues to resolve,' Drago told her fiercely. 'You, and the child you are carrying, are the most important things right now. I have asked you to marry me and I need your answer, Jess.'

The huskiness in his voice tugged on Jess's emotions, and she swallowed the lump in her throat. Part of her wanted to accept Drago's proposal. He had sounded as though he meant it when he'd said she was important to him, but she reminded herself that it was the baby he cared about—not her. The idea of giving up her life in London, her independence, and agreeing to marry a man who did not love her was not a decision she could make lightly, and the fact that she was in love with Drago made that decision even harder.

She lifted her eyes to his handsome face and knew she needed to be alone while she considered her options. 'I want some time on my own to think,' she said quietly. 'Marriage is an enormous step, and I need to be sure in my mind that it is the right thing to do.'

Something in her voice made Drago control his frustration. It was true that marriage was a big step, he acknowledged. Yet strangely he did not find the prospect of giving up his playboy lifestyle and committing himself to a long-term relationship with Jess unwelcome. She was the mother of his child, and for that reason the decision to marry her was an easy one to make.

He wanted to stay with her and try to allay her doubts, but she had asked to be alone and he had to respect her request. 'You're right. I should go to the hospital and try to keep Aunt Dorotea calm,' he said abruptly. 'God knows, she has suffered enough stress lately.' He walked over to the bed and stared down at Jess. 'We'll continue this conversation later.' He leaned over her and captured her mouth in a brief, hard kiss. 'But I warn you, *cara*, I will do everything I possibly can to persuade you to be my wife.'

Hours later Jess could still feel the imprint of Drago's lips on hers. He would not have to try very hard to persuade her to marry him, she acknowledged ruefully. One kiss turned her to putty in his hands—which was why she was glad she had insisted on him giving her time to think about his proposal.

The *palazzo*'s gardens were an oasis of green tranquillity in the heart of Venice. Usually she loved to sit beside the ornamental pool and watch the goldfish dart beneath the water lilies, but as the afternoon slipped towards evening her thoughts were still confused and she found no sense of peace in her beautiful surroundings. She knew that for the baby's sake the sensible option would be to accept a marriage of convenience with her child's father, but her heart ached at the prospect of being Drago's unwanted wife. Would it be possible to sustain a relationship built solely on passion? Jess feared not. And when Drago's desire for her faded would he seek his pleasure elsewhere? Oh, she was sure he would be discreet, but the idea of him having affairs with other women was unbearable.

'Francesco tells me you have been out here for most of the day. I hope you kept out of the sun?'

Jess whipped her head round at the sound of Drago's voice, and her heart lurched as she watched him striding across the garden towards her. What chance did her heart stand when he was so impossibly gorgeous? she thought wryly. As he sat down on the bench beside her she tore her eyes from him and pretended to study the fish in the pool.

'How is Angelo?'

'The surgery went well, and now that the plaster cast has been removed from his leg the consultant is hopeful that he can be discharged from hospital in a week or so.'

'Good...that's great news. I'm sure he's pleased.' She didn't know what to say to him, and sticking to the topic of his cousin's recovery seemed a safe option.

'Jess...' Drago could not hide the faint impatience in his voice. 'Much as I care about my cousin, my only interest right now is whether you have reached a decision.' He slid his hand beneath her chin and tilted her face so that he could look into her troubled green eyes. 'I can see you still have doubts. Talk to me, *cara*, and tell me what is holding you back.'

'I don't belong in your world,' she muttered, voicing one of her biggest worries. 'Aren't you concerned that I won't be a suitable wife for you? I proved at the party last night that I am a hopeless hostess.' She flushed as she remembered her awkward attempts to talk to the guests and her clumsiness at the dinner table.

Drago frowned. 'That's not true. Many people remarked on how charming you were, and how much they enjoyed chatting with you.'

Jess wasn't convinced. 'You can't get away from the fact that I am the daughter of a drunk, not a member of the Italian aristocracy. Theresa Petronelli told me you were once engaged to a woman called Vittoria whose father is a count. I know she is very beautiful and sophisticated because she featured on the front cover of that magazine that you saw when we were in St Mark's Square.'

He shrugged, but beneath his casual air Jess sensed sudden tension. 'It's no secret that at one time Vittoria and I planned to marry. But it didn't happen. She ended our engagement and now she is happily married to another man. I'll be honest and admit that until I received the phone call from Dr Marellis this morning I had no great desire to marry,' he said bluntly. 'But knowing that you are expecting my baby has changed everything. I don't want my child to be born illegitimate. I know it is not considered important these days, but to me it matters a great deal that my child will bear my name.'

He grimaced when he saw the doubtful expression in Jess's eyes. 'I know you don't have happy memories of your father, but I swear to you that I will not be like him.' He took her cold hands in his strong, warm ones. 'I will love our child with all my heart,' he promised, 'and I will be the best father I can possibly be.' He would not fail at this second chance to be a father, Drago vowed silently. He would not fail this child.

Jess stared at their linked hands through eyes blurred with tears. Perhaps pregnancy was making her feel emotional. She hadn't cried since… She drew a swift breath as she was bombarded with memories that still had the power to make her weep.

Seven years ago, after Seb had made it clear that he wanted nothing to do with the child she had conceived by him, she hadn't known what to do. She had felt alone and scared. But now, with Drago, she did not have to fear the future. He had promised to take care of her and the baby, and as the full implications of his offer to marry her sank in she felt an overwhelming sense of relief. There was no need for her to worry about how she would manage to bring up a child on her own, and no need for her to make a terrible choice like the one she had made seven years ago.

'I suppose you will want me to sign a prenuptial agreement?' she muttered. 'It makes sense for you to protect your assets should we decide to…to divorce.'

She caught her bottom lip with her teeth as he slid his hand beneath her chin and gently forced her to meet his steady gaze.

'I'm not planning for us to divorce. I am prepared to make a lifelong commitment to you as well as to our child.' Drago stood up and drew her to her feet, his midnight-dark eyes focused intently on her face. 'What is your answer, Jess?'

All that mattered was the baby, she reminded herself fiercely. So she would have a husband who did not love her? Well, there were many worse things in life. Drago's avowal that he viewed marriage to her as a lifelong commitment gave her some measure of reassurance, but even so her heart was hammering hard against her ribs and she found it difficult to breathe as she said unsteadily, 'All right…I'll marry you.'

CHAPTER TEN

'AT THE END of this month! Why do you want us to get married so quickly?'

Her expression tense, Jess twisted the enormous diamond solitaire ring on her finger. For the past week she had tried to ignore the reservations she still had about accepting Drago's proposal, but when he had slid the engagement ring onto her finger a few moments ago she had been gripped by panic. She had always known he was powerful and commanding, but the speed with which he was organising everything and taking over her life was frightening. Her common sense told her she was doing the right thing for the baby, but Drago's determination to rush ahead with the wedding, and the way he bulldozed any objections she voiced, made her feel trapped.

He shrugged. 'What reason is there to wait? You are expecting my baby and I want to make you my wife as soon as possible.'

'But what if…?' Jess's voice faltered. 'I'm very early in my pregnancy. What if something goes wrong and there *is* no baby? We will have married for no reason.'

Drago's expression was hidden beneath his heavy lids. 'Nothing will go wrong,' he stated with fierce conviction, as if he dared fate to argue with him. 'The doc-

tor said after he examined you this morning that you
are fit and healthy—although you need to put on a bit of
weight. From now on I am going to make sure you eat
properly,' he added in a warning tone. 'You also need to
get plenty of rest—especially in the early months while
the baby is developing. I don't want you to do too much,
or feel stressed. That's why it is best for us to have the
wedding soon. And you won't have to worry about the
arrangements. I'll take care of everything.'

Drago was certainly taking his duties as a prospec-
tive father seriously, Jess thought with a sigh. It was
rather nice to receive so much attention from him after
a lifetime of fending for herself, but she knew his only
concern was for the baby—which meant that while she
was pregnant he was concerned for her well-being too.
Of course she was glad that he was going to be a devoted
father. After her own miserable experiences, growing
up with her alcoholic father and then in the children's
home, she was relieved that her baby would have a very
different childhood from the one she'd had. But it would
be nice if Drago cared for *her* a little, rather than regarding her as an incubator, she thought wistfully.

From the sound of it she was not going to have much
say regarding what sort of wedding she would like. She
could imagine his reaction if she told him she had always dreamed of getting married on a white sandy
beach, barefoot, with flowers in her hair. The huge,
blindingly brilliant diamond engagement ring was an
indication that the wedding would have no expense
spared, and she assumed that the guest list would be
made up of his sophisticated friends.

'Are you ready to go down to dinner? You're not feeling sick again, are you?' Drago frowned when he saw

how pale Jess was. 'I thought morning sickness was called that for a reason,' he said drily.

'It can happen at any time of the day. I used to—' She stopped abruptly.

'Used to what?' he demanded, puzzled by her sudden, palpable tension.

'I…I used to have a friend who was sick at all times of the day when she was pregnant.' Jess could feel herself blushing. She was not a natural liar, and she could tell from the speculative look Drago gave her that he was not convinced by her explanation. To her relief he did not pursue the matter.

'I can arrange for your dinner to be served up here, if you would prefer it?'

'No, I feel fine. Besides, I want to see Angelo on his first evening home from the hospital. He's going to be surprised when he hears about us.'

'My cousin is delighted—as are my mother and aunt.'

'You mean you've told them already?'

Ever since she had agreed to marry Drago, Jess had suffered badly from pregnancy sickness and had not left his wing of the *palazzo* or seen Luisa and Dorotea. She had assumed that he would wait until she was with him to announce their engagement, but clearly that had not been the case. He was like a steamroller, driving forcefully towards his goal—which in this case was marriage to the mother of his child, Jess thought dismally. Once again she felt a sense of panic that she was trapped and powerless against his formidable strength of will.

'Of course I informed my family of our intention to marry,' he said coolly. 'They are all delighted about the baby.' He hesitated, and to Jess's surprise streaks of colour flared along his sharp cheekbones. 'My family are under the impression that our marriage is a love-match.'

The expression in his dark eyes was faintly challenging. 'I don't want them to be disappointed.'

Jess could not hide her confusion. 'I don't understand. Are you saying that they think we are...' she stumbled over the words '...in love? Why don't you tell them that we're marrying for the baby's sake?'

'It is precisely for the baby's sake that I haven't explained the nature of our relationship.' When Jess frowned, Drago continued coolly. 'Babies do not stay babies for very long. They grow up fast. And children are very perceptive. Do you want our child to have the pressure of knowing that we married purely for their sake? If it is believed by everyone that we married for love then there will be no risk of our child feeling that we sacrificed our happiness for him or her.'

Jess bit her lip. Did Drago feel that by marrying her he was sacrificing his happiness? If so, how on earth were they going to give a convincing performance that they were in love? she wondered.

He drew back the cuff of his dinner jacket and glanced at the gold Rolex on his wrist. 'We should go down for dinner. Before we go, I want to say how beautiful you look, *mia bella*,' he murmured, his eyes darkening as he studied her. The emerald silk strapless dress revealed her slim white shoulders, she had piled her hair into a loose knot on top of her head and, unbeknown to Jess, she looked so exquisitely lovely that desire corkscrewed through Drago.

Still smarting from the idea that he viewed marriage to her as a sacrifice, she stalked over to the door with her head held high, and said coolly, 'Presumably we don't have to start the pretence that we are in love until we are in front of your family? Although, to be honest, I'm not sure I'm that good an actress.'

'Perhaps this will help you get into character.' He caught up with her and spun her round, stifling her angry protest with his mouth as he lowered his head and claimed her lips in a searing kiss that left her trembling and breathless.

It was over far too quickly, and to compound Jess's shame Drago had to unfurl her fingers from the lapels of his jacket as he stepped away from her.

'Keep responding to me like that and you'll even convince *me* that I'm the love of your life, *cara*,' he mocked gently, and without giving her a chance to reply he put his hand in the small of her back and steered her out of the room.

Jess's face still felt hot when Drago ushered her into the dining room. Running her tongue over her lips, she felt their slight puffiness and knew she must look as though she had been thoroughly kissed by her fiancé.

Seeing Angelo, balanced on crutches and looking drawn but otherwise remarkably well, provided a welcome distraction—although his greeting, 'Here are the two lovebirds,' brought another flush to her cheeks.

Aunt Dorotea rushed up and enveloped her in a hug. Angelo's mother was convinced that Jess had been responsible for her son regaining his memory and she congratulated the newly engaged couple effusively. Drago's mother was more reserved with her congratulations, and not for the first time Jess was conscious of Luisa studying her speculatively.

After dinner she cornered Jess in the conservatory. 'I'm surprised by your choice of engagement ring,' she murmured, lifting Jess's hand and studying the enormous diamond. 'This bauble seems a little too ostentatious for your tastes.'

'I didn't choose it,' Jess admitted. 'Drago…surprised me when he gave it to me. And I think it's absolutely lovely,' she lied.

For some strange reason she found that she did not want to be disloyal to Drago. Luisa had been right to guess that the ring wasn't her taste, but she certainly didn't want to risk hurting Drago's feelings by saying so.

Luisa looked at her closely. 'So you really do love him?' she murmured. For the first time that evening she smiled warmly at Jess, who had gone bright red. 'I am very happy for both of you.' Her voice became serious. 'May I offer you a word of advice? I adore my son, but Drago is strong-willed—like his father—and you may find it necessary to stand up to him from time to time.' She smiled again. 'But don't let him know I told you that.'

Jess was still reeling because Luisa had guessed how she felt about Drago. 'I won't,' she promised. 'I'm strong-willed myself, and we've already had a few clashes,' she said ruefully.

'It won't do him any harm. Vittoria was too soft-natured for him, and had they married they would not have been happy. But I was sorry their relationship ended so tragically. It took Drago a long time to get over what happened. I expect he has told you—' Luisa broke off as Drago entered the conservatory.

'I've been looking for you,' he said as he walked over to them and slid his arm around Jess's waist. 'I missed you, *tesoro*.'

His velvet-soft voice, and the gentle look in his eyes as he stared down at her caused Jess's heart to lurch. His performance as an adoring fiancé was very convincing, and she had to remind herself sternly that it was an act for his family's benefit. But she wished he had not interrupted her conversation with his mother, for she was none the wiser about why his engagement to Vittoria had ended.

Did he still love the beautiful socialite? she wondered later as she followed him into the bedroom. He had sounded regretful when he had explained that Vittoria had been the one to break off their engagement. What had Drago's mother meant when she'd said his engagement to Vittoria had ended 'tragically'?

Frustrated that there was so much she did not know about the man she was to marry in two weeks' time, Jess watched him shrug off his dinner jacket and begin to unfasten his shirt buttons, revealing inch by inch the muscular bronzed chest covered with whorls of dark hair that arrowed over his flat abdomen and disappeared beneath the waistband of his trousers. His devastating good looks took her breath away, and a different kind of frustration unfurled in the pit of her stomach.

He glanced over at her, and Jess glimpsed a predatory hunger in his eyes which was quickly masked beneath the sweep of his thick lashes. But the glittering look lifted her spirits, because it was proof that Drago's desire for her had not faded. They had been drawn together by their fierce sexual attraction to each other, and it was likely that desire was all he would ever feel for her, she acknowledged sadly. But it was better than nothing, and life had taught Jess to settle for what she could get and not wish for the moon.

'Did I mention how gorgeous you look in that dress?' Drago murmured.

'You told me before we went down to dinner,' she reminded him.

Rosy pink colour flared on her cheeks, and Drago knew she was remembering him kissing her. She had goaded him so that he had lost his self-control and punished her with a searing kiss, but his anger had quickly turned to desire and he had spent the evening in a state of uncomfortable semi-arousal.

She was a work of art—so slender and fine-boned that she reminded him of a delicate porcelain figurine. But her bare shoulders were satin-soft beneath his fingers as he traced the line of her collarbone, and the pulse jerking at the base of her throat was evidence that she was a warm, responsive woman, not a cold statue. Her eyes glowed emerald-bright and her mouth was a soft pink temptation that he could not resist. He felt his body stir, and his need for her pounded an urgent drumbeat through his veins.

He cupped her face in his hands, but a frown drew his brows together when he noticed the purple shadows beneath her eyes. She looked infinitely fragile. His frown deepened. What was he thinking of, putting his own selfish need for sexual fulfilment before her well-being? And not only *her* well-being, but that of the child in her belly. How could he consider making love to her during these crucial early days of her pregnancy? Drago asked himself angrily. He knew better than most how precarious was the tiny life she carried.

Ignoring the ache of frustration in his gut, he dropped his hands from her shoulders. 'You should get to bed. You look all in,' he murmured. 'Here.' He took one of his shirts from a drawer and handed it to her. The look of disappointment in her eyes tested his resolve, and Drago knew there was no way he would be able to keep his hands off her if he had to lie next to her delectable body all night. 'I need to read a report that won't keep. I don't want to disturb you, so I'll sleep in my dressing room tonight.'

'There's no need for you to do that,' Jess mumbled, taken aback by his sudden change from sensual lover to enigmatic stranger. So much for her belief that there would at least be passion in their marriage, if not love, she thought bleakly. Drago was in such a hurry to get away from her that he was already walking through the door leading to his dressing room.

He turned back to her, his expression serious. 'It is important for the baby's development that you sleep well. But every night you have dreams that upset you, and you speak of someone called Katie.' He waited for Jess to make a response, and when she remained silent frustration surged through him. He sensed there was something in her past that she was keeping secret, but he could not force her to confide in him, he acknowledged heavily. 'I'll check with Dr Marellis if it is harmful to experience disturbing dreams during pregnancy,' he said gruffly. '*Buonanotte*, Jess.'

I'll check with Dr Marellis was a phrase Drago repeated often during the following days, and his obsessive concern for her health drove Jess mad. He consulted an array of health care books, monitored every aspect of her pregnancy, and fretted about her bouts of morning sickness, which grew worse daily and left her feeling weak and drained.

'How can you be sure it is normal to be so sick?' he demanded when she tried to reassure him. She almost let slip that this was not her first experience of morning sickness. But the idea of talking about her first pregnancy was too painful to contemplate when the wound in her heart was so deep and raw.

Even when Drago was abroad she still felt stifled by him, Jess brooded, three days before their wedding was due to take place. He had explained that his business trip to Germany was unavoidable. She had refrained from admitting that she would be glad to have a few days to herself. But her hopes of having some time alone, so that she could come to terms with the dramatic changes in her life and especially her feelings about her pregnancy, had been dashed by Drago's constant phone calls.

'Yes, I ate breakfast,' she told him patiently. 'No, I haven't been sick this morning.'

'Why not?' His voice sounded sharp over the phone. 'Why would the sickness suddenly stop?'

'I don't know. I'm just glad to have kept my food down for once,' Jess muttered. Really, there was no pleasing him, she thought irritably. According to Drago, she was either too sick or not sick enough.

'Yes—that's good, of course. Perhaps you'll start to put on weight rather than lose it. But I'll call Eduardo Marellis and arrange for him to come to the *palazzo* and check that your pregnancy is progressing as it should.'

'There's no need. I only saw him four days ago.'

'It's better to be safe,' Drago said in the uncompromising voice Jess knew so well. 'I don't want you to do too much today. In fact why don't you spend the morning in bed?'

It was on the tip of Jess's tongue to tell him that being in bed on her own wasn't much fun, but pride kept her quiet. Drago had slept in his dressing room every night since he had announced their engagement to his family, and she was determined to hide how hurt she felt and how much she missed him. It wasn't just the sex; it was the feeling of closeness to him that she longed for—because then she could fool herself that he cared for her a little.

When he ended the phone call she wandered over

to the window and stared out at the view of the Grand Canal, which was busy with the boats and water taxis that provided the main mode of transport through the city. Venice attracted thousands of tourists in the summer, but Jess had lived her whole life in London and was used to busy streets. She was also used to being independent and going out when and where she pleased, but Drago had insisted that she did not leave the *palazzo* without being accompanied by his bodyguard Fico.

She felt as if she was imprisoned in a gilded cage, she thought heavily. She missed her freedom, and with her wedding only days away she felt trapped. Marrying Drago was undoubtedly the best thing she could do for the baby. Their child would enjoy a privileged lifestyle that she could not possibly give if she was a single mother. But she was struggling to come to terms emotionally with being pregnant for a second time, and the guilt she had buried for so long was a permanent ache in her heart.

If only she could just have a few hours to herself to think—without Fico or the other household staff hovering around her. She grimaced as she remembered her crazy attempt to climb down from the balcony the first night Drago had brought her to the *palazzo*. She was not going to do anything as stupid as that again, but there was no reason why she shouldn't slip away by herself for a couple of hours. Drago need never find out.

'*What do you mean, she's not here?*' Drago roared, venting his fury on the hapless maid who had hurried downstairs to tell him that Signorina Harper was not anywhere in the *palazzo* or the garden.

Dropping his briefcase on the marble floor of the entrance hall, he thrust his fingers through his hair and discovered that his hand was shaking. Fear was rapidly replacing the anger that had blazed in him when he had received a phone call from Fico to tell him that Jess had apparently disappeared.

Thank God he had decided to cut his trip to Germany short and had already been at Marco Polo airport when he had spoken to Fico. Drago glared at the bodyguard, who had just returned from St Mark's Square, which was one of Jess's favourite haunts.

'No sign of her,' Fico said gruffly. 'But the place is packed with tourists and I could have missed her if she's in a café. I've left three members of the security team to continue searching—'

Puzzled by the bodyguard's abrupt silence, Drago followed his gaze and spun round to see Jess walking up the front steps of the *palazzo*. Relief caused his knees to sag, but incensed by the effect she had on him, and the unpalatable fact that she weakened and unmanned him, he strode forward to meet her.

'Where the *hell* have you been?' he demanded, his voice taut with fury. 'Why did you go out without Fico when I expressly forbade you to? Why did you disobey me?'

Several hours of walking about in the hot sunshine had left Jess feeling exhausted, but as she was subjected to Drago's verbal attack she forgot her tiredness and her temper simmered.

'You *forbade* me! I *disobeyed* you! Listen to yourself, Drago. They are not the words of a husband to his wife—at least not in any marriage I want to be part of. Why shouldn't I go out on my own? I only went to Murano to visit the glassblowers' workshops. What harm is there in that?'

She suddenly became aware that they were not alone.

Several of the staff had been drawn to the hall by the sound of raised voices, and Fico was shifting from foot to foot, looking as though he would rather be anywhere but witnessing her argument with Drago.

'I am *not* going to stand here and allow you to *harangue* me in front of the staff,' she muttered, and she raced towards the staircase.

'Come back here.' Drago was beside her in an instant, and kept pace with her as she marched up the stairs.

When they reached the landing he scooped her into his arms and, ignoring her furious protest, strode into the suite of rooms they had shared since she had arrived at the *palazzo*.

'I'll tell you what harm there is in you jaunting off alone,' he growled, as he carried her through to the bedroom and dropped her onto the bed so hard that she bounced on the mattress. Before she could even think of trying to get up he leaned over her, imprisoning her against the satin bed cover. 'I am one of the wealthiest men in Italy. I attract a lot of media attention. And now that you are my fiancée, so do you,' he told her bitingly. 'Ever since a photo of us leaving Trattoria Marisa was published on the front page of several newspapers you have been at risk of being kidnapped by criminal gangs who would demand a huge ransom for your release. *That* is why Fico sticks to your side like glue.'

Jess swallowed, shaken not just by his words but by the intensity in his black eyes that told her the threat of kidnap was a very real and frightening possibility. 'I didn't think,' she whispered.

'It seems to be a persistent theme with you,' he said sardonically. He jerked away from her as if he could not bear to be near her. 'And I see you're not wearing your engagement ring again.'

Anger burned like acid in Drago's gut as he stared at her, sprawled on the bed, with her glorious hair spread across the satin bedspread. Wearing a simple white sundress that had rucked up to reveal her slim thighs, she was a beguiling mixture of innocence and earthy sensuality, and the idea that she would have attracted much male interest while she wandered around Venice filled him with rage.

'Did you go out without your ring so that you could flirt with other men?' he demanded savagely. 'Do I need to remind you that you are carrying *my* child?'

Stunned to see streaks of colour run along Drago's cheekbones, Jess shook her head. That could *not* be jealousy she had heard in his voice, she told herself. 'Of course I didn't go out to meet other men. And being sick constantly is enough of a reminder that I'm pregnant,' she said drily. 'I'm not used to wearing jewellery, and I find my ring a bit cumbersome for everyday wear, so I thought I would just put it on for social events.'

Realising the effort Jess was making to be tactful about the engagement ring that he had already guessed she did not like, Drago felt his anger fade. Most women he knew would love to own a diamond the size of a rock, but Jess was different from any other woman he'd ever met, he acknowledged wryly.

'Have you any idea how worried I was when Fico told me you had disappeared?' he asked raggedly. '*Dio*, I was scared. you had had an accident, or been taken ill.' He closed his eyes as memories of rushing to the hospital with Vittoria flooded his mind. 'Why did you go off like that?'

Jess bit her lip, overcome with guilt that her irresponsible behaviour had caused Drago to look so haggard. She knew how concerned he was for the baby.

'I needed some space. I'm used to being independent,' she mumbled. 'It has struck me in the last couple of days that Italy is going to be my home once we are married. I love Venice, but I miss London,' she admitted. 'You probably find it hard to understand, but I *like* running T&J Decorators, and I miss Mike and Gaz and the other guys I used to work with. I don't have a life of my own or friends in Venice. I especially miss my workshop and being able to do my wood-carving. You're smothering me,' she said in low tone. 'I understand that your interest—obsession, even—with my pregnancy is because you are concerned for the baby. But I'm not an invalid. Pregnancy is a perfectly natural state.'

'Unless something goes wrong,' Drago said harshly. 'I have witnessed how devastating the consequences can be if there is a problem during pregnancy. If I have been obsessive, it is because I want to do everything possible to take care of you and the baby.'

His jaw clenched and his voice roughened with emotion as he stated flatly, 'It is something that I bitterly regret I did not do for my first child.'

CHAPTER ELEVEN

SHOCK RAN THROUGH Jess as she absorbed Drago's statement. 'What do you mean?' she said unsteadily. 'What child?'

He exhaled slowly. 'While I was engaged to Vittoria she fell pregnant, but she did not tell anyone—including me.' Noticing Jess's confused expression, he said heavily, 'I'd better start from the beginning. I first met Vittoria when we were children. Our families were friends, and as we grew up we often used to meet at social events. My ill-fated love affair with Natalia, the exotic Russian woman who conned me and Cassa di Cassari out of a fortune, was humiliating, and I vowed that in future I would use my head and not my heart in relationships,' he explained grimly. 'I felt it was my duty to marry and produce an heir. Vittoria was beautiful and charming, and her family connections to Italian nobility made me decide that she would be the perfect wife.'

'It sounds a coldly clinical way to choose a wife,' Jess said, taken aback by his lack of emotion. 'Didn't you love her?'

'I cared for her and respected her.' Drago hesitated. 'But I did not love her as I should have done. A few years before I had been crazily in love with Natalia,' he admitted roughly. 'I met her while I was still grieving for my father, and I completely lost my heart to her.'

Jess nodded. 'I can understand that. I fell desperately in love with Seb when I was very vulnerable after my friend Daniel died.'

'Discovering how Natalia had betrayed me hurt like hell,' Drago continued. 'I never wanted to feel pain like that again. So it seemed eminently sensible to marry a woman I liked who shared my goals. Vittoria seemed to accept that I needed to devote time to running Cassa di Cassari.' He grimaced. 'It shames me to say that I did not devote the same amount of time to my relationship with her. I was unaware that she suffered badly from nerves and illogical fears and had, among other things, a phobia of hospitals.'

Drago strode restlessly around the room, his mind bombarded by memories that still haunted him. 'I had no idea that Vittoria had conceived my child. She showed no signs, and she said nothing until she started to bleed heavily. Only then did she admit that she was four months pregnant. Poor Vittoria was petrified,' he said raggedly. 'Initially it was thought that she was suffering a miscarriage, but she haemorrhaged severely and was rushed to hospital—where she was found to have a condition called placenta preavia. It is a complication during pregnancy, but in extreme cases it can lead to the death of the mother and the baby. Because Vittoria had not been for any prenatal checks her condition went undetected until she started to bleed. She almost lost her life.' His throat moved as he swallowed hard. 'And tragically she lost the baby.'

'I'm sorry,' Jess whispered, her heart aching for him and his ex-fiancée. 'To lose a child during pregnancy must be agonising.'

'I blamed myself.'

She shook her head. 'You could not have prevented what happened to Vittoria. You said yourself she suffered a rare complication with her pregnancy.'

'If I had paid her more attention she might have told me sooner that she was pregnant and I would have persuaded her to see a doctor,' Drago said, his voice raw with guilt. 'If I had taken better care of her then her condition would have been detected and her pregnancy would have been closely monitored. I did not realise how much I wanted a child until my baby died,' he confessed huskily. 'Vittoria was heartbroken, and I certainly did not blame her when she decided that she no longer wished to marry me. I felt I had failed her *and* our unborn child.'

He looked at Jess, his eyes blazing with emotion. 'That is why I am determined to do everything I can to ensure that the child you are carrying is born safely. I want this baby very much, but I don't know how you feel, Jess.' He frowned. 'You seem…distant. I get the feeling that you are unhappy about being pregnant and that maybe you do not want our baby.'

It was his words "our baby" that wrecked Jess. Unlike during her first pregnancy, she was not alone this time. This baby had a father who clearly would be devoted to his child. The knowledge made her glad, but also desperately sad that she had been unable to be a mother to her first child.

'Of course I want our baby,' she told Drago thickly. Tears blinded her and she felt a pain inside as though her heart had cracked. *'You have no idea how much I want to be a mother.'*

The storm had been building for a long time, and

now it broke. She buried her face in her hands and her shoulders shook as sobs tore through her slender frame.

'Jess?' Shaken to the core to see her sobbing so uncontrollably, Drago strode over to the bed and lifted her into his arms. '*Cara*, don't cry. I'm sorry I upset you. I just wasn't sure how you felt about being pregnant.'

Once again he had misjudged her, he thought grimly. There was so much about this woman he was about to marry that he did not understand—so many secrets that she kept from him. He could only hope that one day she would learn to trust him. For now all he could do was cradle her in his lap and wrap his arms tightly around her while she wept.

It was a long time before Jess regained a fragile hold on her emotions. She had never allowed herself to cry like that before, and now she felt drained. Glancing at Drago from beneath her lashes, she felt her heart clench when she saw the bleak expression in his eyes. She wondered if he was thinking about the baby he and his fiancée had lost. He was clearly still haunted by the tragedy, and he must have found it hard to talk about the circumstances that had led to the ending of his engagement to Vittoria.

Jess was touched that he obviously trusted her enough to confide in her about his painful memories. Trust was an important element in a relationship. She knew Drago was curious about the dreams that troubled her and caused her to cry out in her sleep. He had asked her several times who Katie was, and lately she had been tempted to tell him. But something held her back. Her troubled childhood and teenage years had left her wary of revealing her feelings, and deep down she was afraid that Drago would judge her badly for what she had done. She could not bear to see disgust or condemnation in his eyes. No one could understand the utter devastation she had felt when she had given her child away, and it was just too agonising for her to talk about.

She closed her eyes, as if she could banish the heartbreaking memories of her past, and slowly became aware of how comforting it felt to be held close to Drago's chest, listening to the steady beat of his heart beneath her ear. She could feel the warmth of his body through his silk shirt, and the scent of his aftershave teased her senses.

He was stroking her hair, threading his fingers through its length in a rhythmic motion that was soothing but also sensual. A tremor ran through her as he cupped her chin and tilted her face to his dark gaze. Jess's heart missed a beat when he gently brushed away the tears from her cheeks. Something was unfurling inside her, and she knew from the sultry gleam in his eyes that he felt it too. Desire beat a slow but insistent drum in her veins.

'*Cara?*' His breath whispered across her lips before he covered them with his own and kissed her long and sweet and with increasing passion until she trembled. 'Do you want this?' he asked in a voice roughened with need as he trailed his mouth down her throat.

'Yes,' she said honestly. 'But do you?' She gave him a troubled look. 'You haven't touched me since you found out I'm pregnant. I thought…I assumed you no longer found me attractive.'

Drago lay back on the bed, still holding her in his arms, and rolled over so that she was beneath him. 'Does this feel like I'm not turned on by you?' he said wryly as the solid ridge of his arousal straining beneath his trousers pushed against her pelvis. 'I have not dared sleep in the same bed as you because I knew I wouldn't be able to resist making love to you.' He frowned. 'I read that sex in the early days of pregnancy carries a small risk of causing a miscarriage.'

'Well, Dr Marellis told me that it was perfectly safe to make love while I'm pregnant,' Jess murmured. She caught her breath when Drago slid his hand beneath her tee shirt and skimmed it over her ribcage to curl his fingers possessively around one breast.

'In that case, do you think it's okay for me to do this…?' he said softly, smiling at her reaction when he stroked his thumb-pad across her nipple and it immediately hardened.

'Perfectly okay,' she gasped as he whipped her tee shirt over her head and closed his mouth around the taut peaks he had exposed. Pregnancy had made her breasts incredibly sensitive, and starbursts of pleasure shot through her as he flicked his tongue across one nipple and then its twin. After weeks of being denied him she was instantly aroused, and she gave a tiny embarrassed laugh when he tugged off her skirt and panties and dipped his finger into her honeyed sweetness.

Eagerly she helped him strip, and when he stretched his bronzed, naked body next to her she clung to him and tried to pull him on top of her.

'Not yet, *tesoro*,' he said softly and, moving down the bed, he eased her legs apart and lowered his head so that his mouth found the sensitive heart of her femininity.

Jess whimpered with delight at his skilled foreplay and the dedication with which he used his tongue to bring her to the edge of heaven. After her emotional breakdown she needed him to restore her, and she trembled with desire when the fierce glitter in his eyes told her the moment had come. But instead of entering her he rolled onto his back, taking her with him, and lifted her above him.

'This way you're in control,' he murmured, and groaned as she slowly took his swollen length inside her. 'I always knew that with those amazing green eyes you had to be a sorceress,' he said thickly.

And then there were no more words—just the sound of their quickening breaths and moans of pleasure as together they set a driving rhythm that quickly took them higher and higher, until with a sharp cry Jess shuddered with the sweet ecstasy of her climax. Seconds later Drago lost his battle to hold back the tidal wave of his need for this one unique woman, and he buried his face in Jess's fragrant hair as his big body shook with the force of his release.

She was the mother of his child, and soon she would be his wife. Those two things brought Drago a level of contentment he had not expected, and he felt a curious tug on his heart as he placed his hand possessively on Jess's flat stomach. Her pregnancy was unplanned but he had no regrets. He wanted his baby, and he wanted to marry his flame-haired firebrand.

He tensed as the realisation hit him. But after a moment he relaxed, and his mouth curved into a smile when he saw that Jess had fallen asleep with her head resting on his shoulder. She was so beautiful she made his insides ache. But as he watched a tear seeped from beneath her lashes and slid down her cheek, and she whispered a name. *Katie.*

They married in a small, pretty church tucked away down a narrow side street that few tourists had discovered. Jess was surprised, for she had expected the wedding to take place in a register office, and she was even more surprised when Drago's mother met her at the door of the church and handed her an exquisite bouquet of cream roses.

'I had no idea that my son is such an incurable romantic,' Luisa said drily. 'He said to tell you that he chose these to complement your dress.'

Jess swallowed the lump that had formed in her throat. 'They're perfect.' Her ivory silk wedding dress was a fairy-tale creation that had been made for her by the designer Torre Umberto. The fluid lines of the gown suited her slender figure, and the crystal-covered bodice sparkled in the sunshine of a Venetian summer's day.

But the biggest surprise came when she walked into the church with Fico, who was to give her away, and saw Mike, Gaz and the rest of her workforce from T&J Decorators gathered in the pews.

'Drago arrange for your friends to come,' Fico told her in a gruff whisper. 'He say it make you happy.'

As she reached the altar and lifted her eyes to Drago's handsome face Jess knew she was happier than she had ever been in her life—and the thought terrified her. In all the bleak years of her childhood she had not imagined happiness like this, and she felt she did not deserve it.

Drago did not love her, she reminded herself. He was only marrying her because she was expecting his baby. But the gentle expression in his eyes as he took her hand and the marriage service began filled her with hope that they could make their marriage work.

Remember how Seb betrayed you, she told herself sternly. She had fooled herself into believing that he cared for her, and the legacy of that mistake would haunt her for ever. But she could not prevent the frantic leap of her heart when Drago slid a gold wedding band onto her finger and followed it with an exquisite emerald and diamond ring in the shape of a flower.

'The solitaire ring was too big and showy for you,' he murmured. 'This suits your small hand much better, and the emeralds match the colour of your eyes.'

Emerging from the church as man and wife, they boarded a gondola decorated with roses, and as Drago kissed her and the wedding guests cheered Jess decided that fairy tales could come true after all.

The reception at the Palazzo d'Inverno was an informal affair, and she was able to spend time chatting with the guys from T&J Decorators. Mike, who had acted as foreman in her absence, had now taken over running the business.

'I'm glad things have worked out for you, Jess,' he told her. 'But me and the lads miss you. If you ever get bored of swanning around in a palace I'll always find you some work. You're one of the best chippies in the trade.'

'Thanks, but being a mother is the only job I'm going to want for a long time,' Jess replied, her eyes softening as she imagined holding her baby in her arms.

'I enjoyed meeting your friends,' Drago said later, as they drove across the bridge linking Venice to the mainland. They were on their way to his house in the Italian Alps, where they were to spend their honeymoon. 'Remind me of the name of the guy covered in tattoos?'

'You mean Stan the Van? He does most of the driving to job sites.'

'And the guy with spiky pink hair and a missing front tooth?'

Jess grinned. 'He's called Sharky because he's Australian and has a scar that he says is from where he was bitten by a shark, but no one believes him.' She hesitated. 'I know they're a bit rough round the edges, but they're great guys and they have been like a family to me.'

Drago glanced at her and felt again that curious tug on his insides as he thought how beautiful she looked in her wedding dress. 'Now you are a member of the Cassari family,' he said gently. 'But we'll go to London often, so that you can visit your friends. I own a penthouse in Park Lane.'

The address of his London apartment was a reminder that they came from different worlds, Jess thought ruefully. She couldn't help feeling worried again that she would not fit into his sophisticated lifestyle with his glamorous friends.

'By the way, Sebastian Loxley is in prison.'

She shot him a startled look. 'How do you know?'

'I hired someone to track him down.' Drago gave a grim smile. 'I wanted to have a…let's call it a *discussion*,' he said in a dangerous voice, 'about the way he treated you. But for now he's out of my reach—serving eight years for credit card fraud.'

'I'm glad,' Jess said shakily. 'At least while he's in prison he can't hurt anyone else.'

Tired after the hectic day, she slept for much of the three-hour drive to the north of Italy, and woke to find the car was winding up a steep road surrounded by mountains.

'Welcome to Casa Rosa,' Drago said as he pulled up on the driveway of a picturesque alpine lodge.

The lower slopes of the mountains were grassy meadows, but the highest peaks of the Alps were still covered in snow that reflected the fiery brilliance of the setting sun.

'I've never been this close to mountains before,' Jess murmured in an awed voice as she looked around at the breathtaking scenery.

'In the winter even the lower slopes are covered in snow.' Drago smiled at her. 'After the baby is born I'll teach you to ski, if you like.'

Jess gave him a puzzled look. 'But who would look after the baby while we were skiing?'

'We will employ a nanny. You'll need help with the baby. Although I intend to cut down my work commitments, I'll still need to spend time running the company.'

While he was speaking Drago led the way into the house—a charming lodge with low ceilings, wood-panelled walls and stripped-pine floorboards scattered with colourful rugs.

But Jess did not notice the quaint charm of the house as she said fiercely, 'I don't want a nanny. I'm perfectly capable of taking care of my baby.'

Seeing the light of battle in her eyes, Drago held back from telling her that he planned to hire a nanny so that he and Jess could enjoy some time together. Much as he was looking forward to being a father, he intended to be a very attentive husband. 'We'll discuss it another time,' he murmured. 'For now, I think you should go to bed. You must be tired after a busy day.'

'I slept in the car,' Jess reminded him, 'and I'm not at all tired.' Her heart missed a beat when he cupped her chin in his hand and tilted her face to his.

'Good. I'm not tired either.' His deep voice seemed to wrap around her like a cloak of crushed velvet. 'So, what do you think that two people who are on their honeymoon and who are not tired should do, *cara*?'

His mouth was tantalisingly close to hers. Jess licked

her suddenly dry lips and watched his eyes blaze with feral hunger. 'I think they should go to bed,' she answered huskily.

'How can our marriage be anything but a success when we are clearly on the same wavelength?'

His sexy smile stole her breath. And then he kissed her and the world went away.

The master bedroom had a wall of glass that gave stunning views of the mountains. In the purple softness of dusk Drago removed her wedding dress and the tiny wisps of lacy underwear, and Jess helped him out of his grey wedding suit, her fingers clumsy with impatience as she undid his shirt buttons.

'My wife,' he said softly, testing the words.

They sounded good. Better than good. They sounded like the most beautiful words Drago had ever heard. But he wasn't ready to share his deepest thoughts with her when they were so new to him, and so he told her instead how beautiful she was as he kissed her mouth and her breasts, and the sweetly sensitive place between her thighs. And when she cried his name he lifted himself above her and sank his powerful erection into her slick heat so that they became one.

He made love to her with passion and an underlying tenderness that touched Jess's soul. And in the aftermath of their mutual pleasure, when he gathered her close to his chest and they watched the stars pinprick the night sky, she knew that he had captured her heart and would hold it prisoner for all time.

CHAPTER TWELVE

'DO YOU REALLY use the hot tub in winter?' Jess asked the next day, as she and Drago relaxed in the frothing water of the tub, which was positioned on the terrace and afforded a stunning view of the surrounding mountains. 'It must be freezing, running back to the house through the snow in a towel.'

His eyes glinted wickedly. 'There are ways to quickly restore body heat,' he assured her. 'I'll give you a demonstration later.' He climbed out of the hot tub and pulled on a bathrobe. 'But first I have a surprise for you.'

'I feel bad that I haven't given you a wedding present,' Jess murmured as she wrapped a towel around her and followed him back to the house.

'In a few months you will give me a child, and that's the only gift I want.'

His words were a timely reminder that she was only here at this beautiful mountain retreat as his wife because she had conceived his baby. Jess pushed the thought away when she saw a large wooden chest on the floor of the sitting room.

'My wood-carvings!' she said in delight.

'I had all your tools and the carvings that you kept in your workshop sent over from London,' Drago explained. 'I'm having a room prepared at the *palazzo* for you to use as a studio.'

Jess had opened the storage trunk and was on her knees searching through it.

Drago took out an exquisite carving of an eagle and inspected it with a growing sense of incredulity. 'Your work is amazing. The detail on this eagle's wings is astounding.' As he studied a carving of a lion, which was perfect in every detail, he recognised that Jess had a very special talent. 'Each piece must take hours to complete. Have you had any formal training in art?'

'No. I would have loved to study art at college,' she revealed wistfully, 'but when I left school I needed to work to support myself.'

Drago picked up another sculpture of a young child. The detail on the face was so perfect that the small wooden figure was uncannily lifelike. He was puzzled as he watched Jess take other figurines from the chest. There were seven in all, clearly of the same little girl at different stages of her life—from a tiny baby lying in a carved crib to a child standing on skis, smiling joyfully.

'These figurines are so beautiful, *cara*. Who is the child?' Drago stared intently at the wooden figure he was holding and then at Jess. 'She looks a little like you.'

'Do you think so?'

A tremor shook her voice, and the expression in her eyes was so bleak and full of pain that Drago drew a sharp breath.

'Jess, what's wrong? Why are you crying?'

He stretched out a hand to her, but she turned away and began to place the carvings back in the box. 'I'm not crying, and nothing is wrong.' She stood up and gave him a fiercely bright smile. 'Everything is wonderful,' Jess insisted.

But Drago sensed she was keeping something from him, and once again frustration surged through him that she did not feel able to reveal the secrets that he could tell haunted her.

'The weather is too nice for us to stay indoors. Let's go for a walk higher in the mountains.'

Beneath the request Drago caught an almost desperate plea in her voice. He was tempted to shake her, to *force* her to open up to him and explain the cause of the tears that she sought to hide from him. It was not surprising that Jess had trust issues after the diabolical way she had been treated by the lowlife scum who had seduced her when she had been a vulnerable teenager, he reminded himself, but surely she knew he was nothing like Sebastian Loxley?

Her lack of trust in him was tearing him apart, and with a savage oath he caught hold of her shoulder and spun her round to face him. 'Who is Katie?' he demanded urgently.

His instincts told him that the name Jess cried out in her sleep, a person she denied she knew, was the cause of the raw anguish in her eyes. He glanced at the wooden figurine he was still holding and somehow knew it had a connection to Katie. The little wooden child had been carved with such infinite care, such *love*.

He stared at Jess, and his gut clenched when he saw her fearful expression. *'Tesoro,'* he said thickly, 'do you really think I could ever hurt you?'

She swallowed and shook her head. 'No,' she whispered.

Drago released his breath slowly. 'Tell me about Katie, *cara*. Who is she?'

In the silent room the ticking of the cuckoo clock on the mantelpiece echoed the painful thud of Jess's heart.

She felt as though she was standing on the edge of a precipice, but when she looked into Drago's dark eyes she knew suddenly that he would catch her if she fell, that she would always be safe with him. She thought of their wedding the previous day. He had gone to so much effort to make the day special for her, and when he had looked into her eyes while they had made their vows his tender expression had reassured her that she could have faith in him.

'You're holding her,' she said huskily. She gazed at the wooden figurine in his hand. 'Katie is my daughter.'

More shocked than he had ever been in his life, Drago forced himself to speak calmly. 'You have a child? Where is she? And who is her father?' His eyes narrowed on Jess's white face and the truth hit him as if he had been punched in the stomach. 'It's Loxley, isn't it?'

'He didn't want to know when I told him I was pregnant.' Jess's voice was a thread of sound. 'I was seventeen, alone, and terrified about the court case I was facing for the fraud charge. My social worker suggested that it might be best for the baby to be adopted and… and I agreed, because I didn't know how I would cope.'

Jess closed her eyes and so did not see the conflicting emotions that crossed Drago's face: anger at the man who had hurt her so badly, and a depth of compassion for Jess that made him pull her into his arms and simply hold her tight.

He stroked her hair, and the gentle caress calmed Jess a little. 'The baby was born on the fifth of April,' she said quietly, wanting to tell him everything now—needing to let out the pain she had lived with for so long. 'She was such a pretty thing. I'd never seen anything so perfect. I called her Katie because it was the prettiest name I could think of, and I took her home because I loved her more than anything in the world and I wanted to keep her.'

Tears slipped down her cheeks. 'I was living with Ted and Margaret by then, and they were so supportive. But I had no job or money. I loved my beautiful baby, but I knew that she needed more than I could give her. The couple who wanted to adopt her had tried for a baby for ten years and they were desperate to have Katie. They promised they would love her and give her the happy and safe childhood that I hadn't had. When she was three weeks old I cuddled her and kissed her one last time, and told her that I would never, ever forget her.'

The tears were falling harder now, and as Drago pulled her close she clung to him and her shoulders shook. 'And then I gave her to the social worker and that was the last time I saw my baby.'

'It's all right, *tesoro*, it's all right. Let the tears fall.' Drago did not know what to say. There were no words that would help. So he simply held Jess tight and laid a cheek that was wet with his own tears against her hair.

'Once a year Katie's adoptive parents send me a photo of her,' Jess continued after a moment in a choked voice. 'They moved to Canada when she was a year old, and they live in a beautiful house in the mountains where Katie is learning to ski. She has a pony, and for her seventh birthday her parents gave her a puppy. They adore Katie, and I can see from the photos that she is happy. She knows she is adopted, and when she is eighteen she can decide if she wants to meet me. Every year I carve a new figure of her in the hope that if we do ever meet I will be able to show her that even though we were apart she was always in my heart.'

'Why didn't you tell me about her before?' Drago said quietly.

'I was afraid to,' she admitted. 'I was scared you would think badly of me because I gave my baby away, and maybe you would think I wouldn't be a good mother to our child.'

He shook his head. 'How could I think badly of you? I think you are incredible. Your decision to allow Katie to be adopted was utterly selfless. You put her best interests before your own happiness.'

He dropped his arms to his sides as an agonising realisation became clear to him. 'That is the reason you agreed to marry me, isn't it?' Drago said hoarsely. His throat felt as if he had swallowed broken glass. 'You chose what you believed to be best for our child over what you wanted—which was the freedom to return to your friends in London.'

'That's not true,' Jess said shakily, stunned by the raw emotion in his voice.

'It *is* true. You admitted the day you went on your own to Murano that you felt smothered and missed your independence. You didn't tell me about Katie because you didn't trust me—and I understand, *cara*, I understand why you find it hard to trust, but I hoped I had shown that you could trust me.'

He brushed a hand across his eyes and grimaced when he felt his wet lashes. His heart was being shredded and he was in agony. 'After what happened with Loxley it's not surprising that you felt you had no option but to accept my proposal rather than struggle to bring up a child on your own. And so you chose to sacrifice your personal happiness and marry me.'

His voice deepened. 'You once accused me of keeping you a prisoner, but now I am offering you your freedom. If you want to go back to England, you and the baby, I won't stop you. All I insist is that you will allow me to support you both financially. And of course I will want to visit our child often. But I have to tell you…' He took a harsh breath and felt his lungs burn. 'I have to tell you that the thought of living without you kills me.'

Drago looked into Jess's eyes, uncaring that there were tears on his face, unable to hide any longer how he felt for her.

'I love you, Jess. I didn't ask you to marry me just because of the baby. The truth is I want you in my life, always and for ever. But I was a coward and I didn't want to admit how I felt, so I used your pregnancy as an excuse to force you to marry me.'

He swallowed as he saw a tear slide down her cheek. 'Say something,' he pleaded.

'You really love me?' Jess was afraid to believe him—afraid to believe in the happiness that was slowly unfurling inside her.

'I adore you. I desired you the second I laid eyes on you, and I think I fell in love with you when I caught you trying to escape from the *palazzo* by climbing down from a second-floor balcony.' Drago's patience snapped, and with a groan he pulled her into his arms and threaded his hands through her vibrant hair. 'Jess, *ti amo*! Please say you'll stay with me and let me love you and take care of you and our baby.'

Jess looked into his eyes and saw the intensity of his emotions, and she finally believed.

'I will,' she said softly. 'I love you with all my heart. You stormed into my life, and from that day I knew that you were the only man I would ever love.' She heard him catch his breath when he saw her love for him blaze in her green eyes. 'I would trust you with my life.'

'*Tesoro...*' Drago's voice cracked, but there was no need for words when he kissed her with such tender passion, such love, that Jess felt her heart would burst with happiness.

'My heart is your willing prisoner,' she whispered against his lips, 'and I never want you to set it free.'

'I've thrown away the key,' he promised as he swept her up and carried her to the bedroom, where he undressed them both and worshipped her body with loving caresses until she gasped his name.

He made love to her with exquisite care, and afterwards, as they lay content in each other's arms, he pressed his lips to her stomach, where his child lay, and told her that he was the happiest man in the world.

EPILOGUE

THE BABY WAS due in early January, but on Christmas Day, after a short labour, Jess gave birth to a son. They named him Daniel, and when she held him in her arms for the first time Jess felt a sense of peace that helped to heal the ache in her heart. She would always love and miss her daughter, but she knew that Katie was happy and adored by her adoptive parents. With Drago's reassurance she had gradually came to terms with the devastating decision she had had to make when she had been a teenager.

'At least we'll never forget his birthday,' Drago said ruefully as he cradled his son in his arms and fell instantly and irrevocably in love with the tiny dark-haired infant.

His stress levels had gone through the roof when Jess had woken him at dawn and calmly informed him that her waters had broken. For a man used to being in control of every situation he had been riven with anxiety and frustration that he could do nothing to take away the pain of childbirth.

'You were amazing,' he told Jess, love and admiration blazing in his eyes. 'You *are* amazing. Have you any idea how much I love you, *mio amore*?'

'Show me,' she invited softly.

And he did. With a kiss that held tenderness and passion and the promise of a deep and abiding love that would last a lifetime.

* * * * *

IN PETRAKIS'S POWER

BY
MAGGIE COX

The day **Maggie Cox** saw the film version of *Wuthering Heights*, with a beautiful Merle Oberon and a very handsome Laurence Olivier, was the day she became hooked on romance. From that day onwards she spent a lot of time dreaming up her own romances, secretly hoping that one day she might become published and get paid for doing what she loved most! Now that her dream is being realised, she wakes up every morning and counts her blessings. She is married to a gorgeous man and is the mother of two wonderful sons. Her two other great passions in life—besides her family and reading/writing—are music and films.

CHAPTER ONE

'TICKETS, PLEASE.'

Having just dropped down into her seat after a mad dash to catch the train, flustered and hot, Natalie Carr delved into her voluminous red leather bag and unzipped an inside compartment to retrieve her ticket. The discovery that it was nowhere to be seen was akin to the jolting shock of tumbling down an entire flight of stairs. With her heartbeat hammering in her chest, she raised her head to proffer an apologetic smile to the guard.

'Sorry…I know it's here somewhere…'

But it wasn't. Desperately trying to recall her last-minute trip to the ladies' before running onto the platform to catch the train, she had a horrible feeling that after checking her seat number she'd left the ticket, in its official first-class sleeve, on the glass shelf beneath the mirror, when she'd paused to retouch her lipstick.

Feeling slightly queasy as a further search through her bag failed to yield it, she exhaled a frustrated sigh. 'I'm afraid it looks like I've lost my ticket. I stopped off at the ladies' just before boarding the train and I think I might have accidentally left it in there. If the train weren't already moving I'd go back and look for it.'

'I'm sorry, miss, but I'm afraid that unless you pay for another ticket you'll have to get off at the next stop. You'll also have to pay for the fare there.'

The officious tone used by the florid and grey-haired train guard conveyed unequivocally that he wouldn't be open to any pleas for understanding. Natalie wished that she'd had the presence of mind to bring some extra cash with her, but she hadn't. Her father had sent her the ticket out of the blue, along with an unsettling note that had practically begged her not to 'desert him' in his 'hour of need', and it had sent her into a spin. Consequently, she'd absent-mindedly grabbed a purse that contained only some loose change instead of the wallet that housed her credit card.

'But I can't get off at the next stop. It's very important that I get to London today. Could you take my name and address and let me send you the money for the ticket when I get back home?'

'I'm afraid it's company policy that—'

'I'll pay for the lady's ticket. Was it a return?'

For the first time she noticed the only other passenger in the compartment. He was sitting in a seat at a table on the opposite side of the aisle. Even though she'd flown into a panic at losing her ticket, she couldn't believe she hadn't noticed him straight away. If the arresting scent of his expensive cologne didn't immediately distinguish him as a man of substantial means and impeccable good taste, the flawless dark grey pinstriped suit that looked as if it came straight out of an Armani showroom certainly did.

Even without those compelling assets, his appearance

was striking. Along with blond hair that had a fetching kink in it, skin that was sun-kissed and golden, and light sapphire eyes that could surely corner the market in sizzling intensity, a dimple in his chin set a provocative seal on the man's undoubted sex appeal. Staring back into that sculpted visage was like having a private viewing of the most sublime portrait by one of the great masters.

A wave of heat that felt shockingly and disturbingly intimate made Natalie clench every muscle in her body. If she hadn't already been on her guard, she certainly was now. She didn't know this man from Adam, *or* his motive for offering to pay for her ticket, and she quickly reminded herself that the newspapers were full of stomach-churning stories about gullible women being duped by supposedly 'respectable' men.

'That's a very kind offer but I couldn't possibly accept it…I don't even know you.'

In a cultured voice, with a trace of an accent she couldn't quite place, the stranger replied, 'Let me get the matter of a replacement ticket out of the way. Then I will introduce myself.'

'But I can't let you pay for my ticket…I really can't.'

'You have already stated that it is very important you get to London today. Is it wise to refuse help when it is offered?'

There was no doubt she was in a fix and the handsome stranger knew it. But Natalie still resisted. 'Yes, I do need to get to London. But you don't know me and I don't know you.'

'You are wary of trusting me, perhaps?'

His somewhat amused smile made her feel even more gauche than she felt already.

'Do you want a ticket or not, madam?' The guard was understandably exasperated with her procrastination.

'I don't think I—'

'The lady would most definitely like a ticket. Thank you,' the stranger immediately interjected.

Her protest had clearly landed on deaf ears. Not only did he have the chiselled good looks of a modern-day Adonis, the timbre of the man's voice was like burnished oak—smoky, compelling, and undeniably sexy. Natalie found her previous resolve to be careful dangerously weakening.

'Okay...if you're sure?'

Her need to get to London was paramount, and it overrode her reservations. Besides, her instinct told her the man was being utterly genuine and didn't pose any kind of threat. She prayed it was a good instinct. Meanwhile the train guard was staring at them in obvious bewilderment, as though wondering why this handsome, well-heeled male passenger would *insist* on paying for a complete stranger's ticket. After all, with her bohemian clothing, casually dried long brown hair with now fading blonde highlights, and not much make-up to speak of, she knew she wasn't the kind of 'high-maintenance' woman who would attract a man as well-groomed and wealthy as the golden-haired male sitting opposite her. But if the smoky-coloured pencil she'd used to underline her big grey eyes with helped create the illusion that she was more attractive than she was, then at that moment Natalie was grateful for the ruse. For she knew she had no choice but to accept the man's kindness. It was vital that she met up with her dad.

She could hardly shake the memory of his distressed tone when she'd rung him to confirm that she'd received the train ticket and once again he'd reiterated his urgent need to see her. It was so unlike him to admit to a human need, and it suggested he was just as fallible and fragile as anyone else—she had guessed all along that he was. Once, long ago, she had heard her mother angrily accuse him of being incapable of loving or needing anyone. His business and the drive to expand his bank account was the real love of his life, she'd cried, and Natalie didn't doubt his obsessive single-mindedness had been a huge factor in their break-up.

When, after their divorce, her mother made the decision to return to Hampshire, where she had spent much of her youth, Natalie, then sixteen, had elected to go with her. As much as she'd loved her dad, and known him to be charming and affable, Natalie had also known he was far too unreliable and unpredictable to share a home with. But in recent years, after visiting him as often as she could manage, she'd become convinced that in his heart he knew money was no substitute for not having someone he loved close by.

From time to time she'd seen loneliness and regret in his eyes at being separated from his family. His tendency to try to compensate for the pain it caused him by regularly entertaining the company of young attractive women was clearly not helping to make him any happier. Several of her visits over the past two years had confirmed that. He seemed disgruntled with everything…

even the phenomenally successful chain of small bijou hotels that had made him his fortune.

'I just need a single,' she told the arresting stranger, who didn't seem remotely perturbed that she'd taken so long to make up her mind about whether to accept his offer or not. 'And it doesn't have to be in first class. My dad sent me the ticket, but I'm quite happy to travel as I usually do in second.'

She couldn't disguise her awkwardness and embarrassment as she watched the man hand his credit card over to the guard. She felt even more awkward when he deliberately ignored her assertion and went ahead and requested a first-class ticket. Natalie hoped to God he believed her explanation about her dad sending her the ticket. After all, she was sure she didn't resemble a typical first-class passenger.

Trust her dad to unwittingly add to her discomfort by making such a needlessly overblown gesture. He always travelled first class himself, which was why he'd automatically paid for his daughter to do the same. Now she really wished he hadn't.

When the satisfied train guard had sorted out the necessary ticket, then wished them both an enjoyable journey, the impeccably dressed stranger handed it over to her and smiled. Natalie was very glad that the compartment was occupied by just the two of them right then, because if anyone else had witnessed the man's astonishing act of chivalry she would have wanted the floor to open up and swallow her.

Accepting the ticket as her face flooded with heat, she prayed her see-sawing emotions would very soon calm down. 'This is so kind of you…thank you…thank you so much.'

'It is my pleasure.'

'Will you write down your name and address for me so that I can send you what I owe you?' She was already rummaging in her voluminous red leather tote for a pen and notepad.

'We will have plenty of time for that. Why don't we sort it out when we get to London?'

Lost for words, and somewhat exhausted by her growing tension, Natalie lowered her bag onto the seat next to her by the window and exhaled a heavy sigh.

With a disarming smile, her companion suggested, 'Why don't we help ease any awkwardness between us by introducing ourselves?'

'All right, then. My name is Natalie.'

It was a mystery to her why she didn't give him her full name. The thought that it was because she was momentarily dazzled by his good looks hardly pleased her. What did she think she was playing at? How often had she groaned at a friend who seemed to lose every ounce of common sense whenever a fit, handsome man engaged her in conversation and became convinced he must think her the most beautiful girl in the world? Such embarrassing silliness was not for her. She'd rather stay single for the rest of her natural life than delude herself that she was something that she wasn't.…

'And I am Ludovic…but my family and friends call me Ludo.'

She frowned, 'Ludovic? How unusual.'

'It's a family name.' Beneath his immaculate tailoring the fair-haired Adonis's broad shoulders lifted and fell as if the matter was of little concern. 'And Natalie? Is that a name you inherited?'

'No. Actually, it was the name of my mum's best friend at school. She sadly died when she was a teenager and my mum called me Natalie as a tribute to her.'

'That was a nice gesture. If you don't mind my saying, there's something about you that suggests you are not wholly English…am I right?'

'I'm half-Greek. My mother was born and raised in Crete, although when she was seventeen she came to the UK to work.'

'What about your father?'

'He's English…from London.'

The enigmatic Ludo raised an amused sandy-coloured eyebrow. 'So you have the heat of the Mediterranean in your blood, along with the icy temperatures of the Thames? How intriguing.'

'That's certainly a novel way of putting it.' Struggling hard not to display her pique at the comment, and wondering at the same time how she could convey without offending him that she really craved some quiet time to herself before reaching London, Natalie frowned.

'I see I have offended you,' her enigmatic fellow passenger murmured, low-voiced. 'Forgive me. That was definitely not my intention.'

'Not at all. I just—I just have a lot of thinking to do before my meeting.'

'This meeting in London is work-related?'

Her lips briefly curved in a smile. 'I told you that my dad sent me the train ticket? Well, I'm going to meet him. I haven't seen him for about three months, and when we last spoke I sensed he was extremely worried about something... I just hope it's not his health. He's already suffered one heart attack as it is.' She shivered at the memory.

'I'm sorry. Does he live in the city?'

'Yes...he does.'

'But you live in Hampshire?'

'Yes...in a small village called Stillwater with my mum. Do you know it?'

'Indeed I do. I have a house that's about five miles from there in a place called Winter Lake.'

'Oh!' Winter Lake was known to be one of the most exclusive little enclaves in Hampshire. The locals referred to it as 'Billionaire's Row'. Natalie's initial assessment that Ludovic was a man of means had been spot-on, and she didn't know why but it made her feel strangely uneasy.

Leaning forward a little, he rested his hand on the arm of his seat and she briefly noticed the thick gold ring with an onyx setting he wore on his little finger. It might be some kind of family heirloom. But she was quickly distracted from the observation by his stunning sapphire gaze.

'I presume your parents must be divorced if you live with your mother?' he deduced.

'Yes, they are. In any case, tonight I'll be staying at my dad's place...we have a lot of catching up to do.'

'You are close...you and your father?'

The unexpected question took her aback. Staring into the fathomless, long-lashed blue eyes, for a long moment Natalie didn't know how to answer him. Or how much she might safely tell him.

'We definitely were when I was younger. After my parents divorced it was…well, it was very difficult for a while. It's got much better in the last couple of years, though. Anyway, he's the only dad I have, and I do care about him—which is why I'm anxious to get to London and find out what's been troubling him.'

'I can tell that you are a devoted and kind daughter. Your father is a very fortunate man indeed to have you worry about him.'

'I *endeavour* to be kind and devoted. Though, to be frank, there are times when it isn't easy. He can be rather unpredictable and not always easy to understand.' She couldn't help reddening at the confession. What on earth was she doing, admitting such a personal thing to a total stranger? To divert her anxiety she asked, 'Are you a father? I mean, do you have children?'

When she saw the wry quirk of his beautifully sculpted mouth she immediately regretted it, surmising that she'd transgressed some unspoken boundary.

'No. It is my view that children need a steady and stable environment, and right now my life is far too demanding and busy to provide that.'

'Presumably you'd have to be in a steady relationship too?'

Ludo's magnetically blue eyes flashed a little, as though he was amused, but Natalie guessed he was in no hurry to enlighten her as to his romantic status. Why should he be? After all, she was just some nondescript girl he had spontaneously assisted because she'd stupidly left her train ticket in the ladies' room before boarding the train.

'Indeed.'

His short reply was intriguingly enigmatic. Feeling suddenly awkward at the thought of engaging in further conversation, Natalie stifled a helpless yawn and immediately seized on it as the escape route she was subconsciously searching for.

'I think I'll close my eyes for a while, if you don't mind. I went out to dinner last night with a friend, to help celebrate her birthday, and didn't get in until late. The lack of sleep has suddenly caught up with me.'

'Go ahead. Try and get some rest. In any case I have some work to catch up on.' Ludo gestured towards the slim silver laptop that was open on the table in front of him. 'We will talk later.'

It sounded strangely like a promise.

With the memory of his smoky, arresting voice drifting tantalisingly through her mind like the most delicious warm breeze, Natalie leaned back in her luxurious seat, shut her eyes and promptly fell asleep…

In the generous landscaped garden of her childhood London home she squealed with excitement as her dad laughingly spun her round and round.

'Stop, Daddy, stop! You're making me dizzy!' she cried.

As she spun, she glimpsed tantalising snatches of blue summer sky, and the sun on her face filled her with such a sense of well-being that she could have hugged herself. In the background the air was suffused with the lilting chorus of enchanting birdsong. The idyll was

*briefly interrupted by her mother calling out to them
that tea was ready.*

The poignant dream ended as abruptly as it had
begun. Natalie felt distraught at not being able to summon it back immediately. When she was little, she'd
truly believed that life was wonderful. She'd felt safe
and secure and her parents had always seemed so happy
together.

A short while after the memory of her dream started
to fade, the muted sound of the doors opening stirred
her awake just in time to see a uniformed member of
staff enter the compartment with a refreshment trolley.
She was a young, slim woman, with neatly tied back
auburn hair and a cheery smile.

'Would you like something to eat or drink, sir?' She
addressed Ludo.

With a gently amused lift of his eyebrows, he turned
his head towards Natalie.

'I see that you have returned to the land of the living. Are you ready for some coffee and a sandwich?'
he asked. 'It's almost lunchtime.'

'Is it, really?' Feeling a little groggy, she straightened
in her seat and automatically checked her watch. She
was stunned to realise that she'd been asleep for almost
an hour. 'A cup of coffee would be great,' she said, digging into her purse for some change.

'Put your money away,' her companion ordered,
frowning. 'I will get this. How do you take your coffee? Black or white?'

'White with one sugar, please.'

'What about a sandwich?' He turned to the uniformed assistant, 'May I see a menu?' he asked.

When the girl handed a copy of said menu over to him, he passed it straight to Natalie. About to tell him that she wasn't hungry, she felt her stomach betray her with an audible growl. Feeling her face flame red, she glanced down at the list displayed in slim gold lettering on the leaflet in front of her.

'I'll have a ham and Dijon mustard sandwich on wholemeal bread, please. Thank you.'

'Make that two of those, and a black coffee along with the white one.' He gave the assistant their order, then waited until she'd arranged their drinks and sandwiches on the table and departed before speaking again. 'You sounded a little disturbed when you were dozing,' he commented.

Natalie froze. Remembering her dream, and thinking that she must have inadvertently cried out at the very real sensation of her dad spinning her round and round, she answered, 'Do you mean I was talking in my sleep?'

'No. You were, however, gently snoring,' he teased.

Now she really *did* wish the floor would open up and swallow her. As the train powered through the lush green countryside she hardly registered the sublime views because she was so incensed.

'I don't snore. I've never snored in my life,' she retorted defensively. Seeing that Ludo was still smiling, she added uncertainly, 'At least…not that I know of.'

'Your boyfriend is probably too polite to tell you.' He grinned, taking a careful sip of his steaming black coffee.

Her heart thudded hard at the implication. Not remotely amused, she stared fixedly back at the perfectly sculpted profile on the other side of the aisle. 'I don't have a boyfriend. And even if I had you shouldn't assume that we would—' Her impassioned little speech tailed off beneath the disturbing beam of Ludo's electric blue eyes.

'Sleep together?' he drawled softly.

Anxious not to come across as hopelessly inexperienced and naive to someone who was clearly an accomplished and polished man of the world and about as far out of her reach socially as the earth was from the planet Jupiter, Natalie bit into her sandwich and quickly stirred some sugar into her coffee.

'This is good,' she murmured. 'I didn't realise how hungry I was. But then I suppose it's because I didn't have any breakfast this morning.'

'You should always endeavour to eat breakfast.'

'That's what my mum says.'

'You told me earlier that she was from Crete?'

The less tricky question alleviated her previous embarrassment a little. Even though she had only visited the country a couple of times, she'd grown up on her mother's enchanting tales of her childhood homeland, and she would happily talk about Greece until the cows came home. 'That's right. Have you been there?'

'I have. It is a very beautiful island.'

'I've only been there a couple of times but I'd love to go again.' Her grey eyes shone. 'But somehow or other, time passes and work and other commitments inevitably get in the way.'

'You must have a demanding career?'

Natalie smiled. 'It's hardly a career, but I'm extremely glad that I chose it. My mum and I run a small but busy bed and breakfast together.'

'And what do you enjoy most about the enterprise? The day-to-day practicalities, such as greeting guests, making beds and cooking meals? Or do you perhaps like running the business side of things?'

Privately she confessed to being inspired to do what she did because her dad had run an extremely successful hotel business. As she'd grown older she'd picked up some useful tips from him along the way, in spite of the eventual dissolution of her parents' marriage.

'A bit of both, really,' she replied. 'But it's my mum that does most of the meeting and greeting. She's the most sublime hostess and cook, and the guests just adore her. Taking care of the business side of things and making sure that everything runs smoothly is my responsibility. I suppose it comes more naturally to me than to her.'

Ludo's compelling sapphire-coloured eyes crinkled at the corners. 'So…you like being in charge?'

The comment instigated an unsettling sensation of vague embarrassment. Did he perhaps think that she was boasting? 'Does that make me sound bossy and controlling?' she quizzed him.

Her handsome companion shook his head, 'Not at all. Why be defensive about an ability to take charge when a situation calls for it…especially in business? A going concern could hardly be successful if someone didn't take the reins. In my view it is a very admirable and desirable asset.'

'Thanks.' Even as she shyly acknowledged the unexpected compliment it suddenly dawned on Natalie that Ludo had revealed very little about himself. Yet he had somehow got her to divulge quite a lot about her own life.

Was he a psychologist, perhaps? Judging by his extremely confident manner and expensive clothing, whatever profession he was in it must earn him a fortune. She realised that she really *wanted* to know a bit more about him. What sentient woman wouldn't be interested in such a rivetingly attractive man? Maybe it was time she turned the tables and asked *him* some questions.

'Do you mind if I ask you what *you* do for a living?' she ventured.

Ludo blinked. Then he stared straight ahead of him for seemingly interminable seconds, before finally turning his head and gifting her with one of his magnetically compelling smiles. Her heart jumped as she found her glance irretrievably captured and taken hostage.

'My business is diverse. I have interests in many different things, Natalie.'

'So you run a business?'

He shrugged disconcertingly. Why was he being so cagey? Did he think she was hitting on him because he was wealthy? The very idea made her squirm—especially when he had displayed such rare kindness in paying for her train ticket. Not one in a thousand people would have been so generous towards a complete stranger, she was sure.

'I would rather not spoil this unexpectedly enjoyable train journey with you by discussing what I do,' he explained. 'Besides…I would much rather talk about you.'

'I've already told you what I do.'

'But what you do, Natalie, is not who you are. I would like to know a little bit more about your life…the things that interest you and why.'

She flushed. Such a bold and unexpected declaration briefly struck her dumb, and coupled with the admission that he was enjoying travelling with her, it made her feel strangely weak with pleasure. The last time she could recall feeling a similar pleasure was when she'd had her first kiss from a boy at school she'd had a massive crush on. Her interest in him hadn't lasted for more than a few months, but she'd never forgotten the tingle of fierce excitement the kiss had given her. It had been tender and innocently explorative, and she remembered it fondly.

Threading her fingers through her long, gently mussed hair, she lowered her gaze and immediately felt strangely bereft of Ludo's crystalline blue glance. What would a kiss from *his* lips feel like? It certainly wouldn't be like an inexperienced schoolboy's.

Disturbed by the thought, she drew in a steadying breath. 'If you mean my favourite pastimes or hobbies, I'm sure if I told you what they were you'd think them quite ordinary and boring.'

'Try me,' he invited with a smile.

Natalie almost said out loud, *When you look at me like that I can't think of a single thing I like except the dimples in your carved cheekbones when you smile.*

Shocked by the intensity of heat that washed through her at the private admission, she briefly glanced away to compose herself. 'I enjoy simple pleasures, like reading and going to the cinema. I just love watching a good film that takes me away from the worries and concerns of my own life and transports me into the story of someone else's…especially if it's uplifting. I also love listening to music and taking long walks in the countryside or on the beach.'

'I find none of those interests either boring or ordinary,' Ludo replied, the edges of his finely sculpted lips nudging the wryest of smiles. 'Besides, sometimes the most ordinary things in life—the things we may take for granted—can be the best. Don't you agree? I only wish I had more time to enjoy some of the pleasures that you mention myself.'

'Why can't you free up some time so that you can? Do you have to be so busy *all* of the time?'

Frowning deeply, he seemed to consider the question for an unsettlingly long time. His perusal of Natalie while he was mulling over her question bordered on intense. Flustered, she averted her gaze to check the time on her watch.

'We'll soon be arriving in London,' she announced, reaching over to the window seat for her bag and delving into it for a pen and something to write on. 'Do you think you could give me your full name and address now, so I can send you the money for my ticket?'

'We might as well wait until we disembark.'

He bit into his sandwich, as if certain she wouldn't give him an argument. She wanted to insist, but in the end decided not to. What difference could it possibly make to take his address now or later, as long as she got it? 'Never a borrower or a lender be,' her mother had always told her. 'And always pay your debts.'

Instead of adding any further comment, Natalie fell into a reflective silence. Observing that she wasn't eating her lunch, Ludo frowned, and the gesture brought two deep furrows to his otherwise silkily smooth brow.

'Finish your food,' he advised. 'If you haven't had any breakfast you'll need it. Especially if you face a difficult meeting with your father.'

'Difficult?'

'I mean emotional. If his health has deteriorated then your discussion will not be easy for either of you.'

The comment made a jolt of fear scissor through her heart. She was genuinely afraid that her dad's urgent need to see her was to tell her he'd received a serious diagnosis from the doctor. They'd had their ups and downs over the years but she still adored him, and would hate for him to be taken from her when he had only just turned sixty.

'You're right. No doubt it will be emotional.' She gave him a self-conscious smile and chewed thoughtfully on her sandwich.

'I'm sure that whatever happens the two of you will find great reassurance in each other's company.'

The sudden ring of Ludo's mobile instantly commanded his attention. After a brief acknowledgement to the caller, he covered the speaker with his hand and turned back to Natalie.

'I'm afraid I need to take this call. I'm going to step outside into the corridor for a few minutes.'

As he rose to his feet she was taken aback to see how tall he was…at least six foot two, she mused. The impressive physique beneath the flawless Italian tailoring hinted at an athletically lean and muscular build, and she couldn't help staring up at him in admiration. Concerned that she might resemble a besotted teenager, staring open-mouthed at a pop idol, she forced herself to relax and nod her head in acknowledgement.

'Please, go ahead.'

As the automatic twin doors of the compartment swished open Ludo turned to her for a moment and, with a disconcerting twinkle in his eye, said, 'Whatever you do, don't run away, Natalie…will you?'

CHAPTER TWO

'I ASSUME THAT all the papers are ready?'

Even as he asked the question Ludo rapidly assessed the detailed information he'd been given, turning it over in his mind with the usual rapier-like thoroughness that enabled him to dive into every corner and crevice of a situation all at once and miss nothing.

At the other end of the line, his personal assistant Nick confirmed that everything was as it should be. Rubbing a hand round his clean-shaven, chiselled jaw, Ludo enquired 'And you've scheduled the meeting for tomorrow, as I asked?'

'Yes, I have. I told the client that he and his lawyer should come to the office at ten forty-five, just as you instructed.'

'And you've obviously notified Godrich, my own man?'

'Of course.'

'Good. It sounds like you've taken care of everything. I'll see you back at the office some time this afternoon to give the papers a final once-over. Bye for now.'

When he'd concluded the call Ludo leant his back against the panelled wall of the train corridor, trying in vain to calm the uncharacteristic nerves that were fluttering like a swarm of intoxicated butterflies in the pit of his stomach. It wasn't the call or its contents that had perturbed him. Finalising deals and acquiring potentially lucrative businesses that had fallen on hard times was meat and drink to him, and he was famed for quickly turning his new acquisitions into veins of easily flowing gold. It was how he had made his fortune.

No, the reason for his current disquiet was his engaging fellow passenger. How could a mere slip of a girl, with the reed-slim figure of a prima ballerina, long brown hair and big grey eyes like twin sunlit pools, electrify him as if he'd been plugged into the National Grid?

He shook his head. She wasn't anything like the voluptuous blondes and redheads that he was usually attracted to, and yet there was something irresistibly engaging about her. In fact, from the moment Ludo had heard the sound of her soft voice she had all but seduced him… Even more surprising than that, what were the odds that she should turn out to be half-Greek? The synchronicity stunned him.

Distractedly staring down at several missed messages on his phone, he impatiently flicked off the screen and gazed out of the window at the scenery that was hurtling by instead. The mixture of old and new industrial buildings and the now familiar twenty-first-century constructions rising high into the skyline heralded the fact that they were fast approaching the city. It was time he made up his mind about whether or not he wanted to act on the intense attraction that had gripped him and decide what to do about it. It was clear that the lovely Natalie was in earnest about reimbursing him for her train ticket, but he was naturally wary of giving his home address to strangers…however charming and pretty.

Although she'd transfixed him from the moment she'd stepped breathlessly into the first-class compartment and he'd scented the subtle but arresting tones of her mandarin and rose perfume, it wasn't in his nature to make snap decisions. While he was a great believer in following strong impulses in his business life, he wasn't so quick to apply the same method to his romantic liaisons. Sexual desire could be dangerously misleading, he'd found. It might be tempting as far as satisfying his healthy libido, but not if it turned into a headache he could well do without.

Sadly, he'd had a few of those in his time. He didn't mind treating his dates to beautiful *haute couture* clothing or exquisite jewellery from time to time, but Ludo had discovered to his cost that the fairer sex always wanted so much more than he was willing to give. More often than not, top of the list of what they wanted was a proposal of marriage. Even his vast wealth couldn't cushion him from the disagreeable inevitability of another broken relationship because the woman concerned had developed certain expectations of him…expectations that he definitely wasn't ready to fulfil. No matter *how* much his beloved family reminded him that it was about time he settled down with someone.

His mother's greatest desire was to become a grandmother. At thirty-six, and her only son, Ludo seemed to be constantly disappointing her because he wasn't

any closer to fulfilling her wish. She was desperate for
him to meet a suitable girl—'suitable' meaning someone who she and his father approved of. But it wasn't
easy to meet genuinely caring and loving women who
desired a relationship and children more than wealth and
position, he'd found. And when his wealth and reputation preceded him it was apt to attract the very kind of
shallow, ambitious women he should avoid.

Frankly, Ludo was heartily tired of that particular
unhappy merry-go-round. The truth was, in his heart
he yearned to find a soulmate—if such a creature even
existed—someone warm and intelligent, with a good
sense of humour and a genuinely kind disposition. He
returned his thoughts to Natalie. If he embarked on a
relationship with her and she should learn that he was
as rich as a modern-day Croesus and counted some of
the most influential business people in Europe as his
friends, then he would never be sure that she was dat-
ing him for himself and *not* his money. Already he'd
inadvertently let slip that he lived in the affluent area of
Winter Lake. But then she must surely guess he wasn't
short of money if he was travelling first class and could
spontaneously pay for her ticket?

Regarding the ticket she'd lost, she'd told him that her
father had sent it to her. Was *he* a wealthy man? Surely
he must be. If that was the case then the pretty Natalie must have been used to a certain level of comfort
before her parents had divorced. Would she be holding
out for someone equally wealthy—if not more so—in
a relationship?

Frowning, Ludo quickly decided it would make sense

to ask for her phone number if he wanted to see her again, rather than give her his address. That way *he* would be the one in control of the situation, and if he should glean at any time that she was a gold-digger then he would drop her like a hot potato. Meanwhile, they could meet up for a drink while she was in London under the perfectly legitimate excuse of his allowing her to settle her debt. If after that things progressed satisfactorily between them, then Ludo would be only too happy to supply more personal information, such as his full address.

Feeling satisfied with his decision, he exhaled a sigh, briefly tunnelled his fingers through his floppily perfect hair, and slipped his mobile into the silk-lined pocket of his jacket. Before depressing the button that opened the automatic doors into the first-class compartment he stole a surreptitious glance through the glass at the slender, doe-eyed brunette who was gazing out of the window with her chin in her hand, as if daydreaming. His lips automatically curved into a smile. He couldn't help anticipating her willing agreement to meet up with him for a date. What reason could she possibly have *not* to?

'I don't understand. You're saying you want to meet me for a drink?'

Blinking in disbelief at the imposing Adonis who was surveying her with a wry twist of his carved lips as they stood together on the busy station platform, Natalie convinced herself she must have become hard of hearing. Ludo's surprising suggestion sounded very much as if he was inviting her out on a date. But why on earth would he do such a thing? It just didn't make sense. Perhaps she'd simply got the wrong end of the stick.

Practically every other woman who'd disembarked from the train was stealing covetous glances over her shoulder at the handsome and stylishly dressed man standing in front of her as she hurried by, she noticed. No doubt they were privately wondering why a girl as unremarkable as herself should capture his attention for so much as a second. Her heart skipped one or two anxious beats.

'Yes, I do,' he replied.

His jaw firmed and his blue eyes shimmered enigmatically. For Natalie, meeting such an arresting glance was like standing in the eye of a sultry tropical storm—it shook her as the wind shook a fragile sapling, threatening to uproot it. She held her voluminous red leather bag over her chest, as though it were some kind of protective shield, and couldn't help frowning. Instead of sending her self-esteem soaring, Ludo's suggestion that they meet up for a drink had had the opposite effect on her confidence. It hardly helped that in faded jeans and a floral print gypsy-style blouse she felt singularly dowdy next to him in his expensive Italian tailoring.

'Why?' she asked. 'I only asked for your address so that I can send you the money for my train fare. You've already indicated that you're a very busy man, so why would you go to all the trouble of meeting up with me instead of simply letting me post you a cheque?'

Her companion shook his head bemusedly, as if he couldn't fathom what must be, to him, a very untypical response. Natalie guessed he wasn't used to women turning him down for anything.

'Aside from allowing you to personally pay me back for the ticket, I'd like to see you again, Natalie,' he stated seriously. 'Did such a possibility not occur to you? After all, you indicated to me on the train that you were a free agent...remember?'

Unfortunately, she had. She'd confessed she didn't have a boyfriend when Ludo had assumed that if she had he must be too polite to tell her that she snored in her sleep. She blushed so hard at the memory that her delicate skin felt as if she stood bare inches from a roaring fire.

Adjusting her bag, she endeavoured to meet the steady, unwavering gaze that was so uncomfortably searing her. 'Are *you* a free agent?' she challenged. 'For all I know you could be married with six children.'

He tipped back his head and released a short, heartfelt laugh. Never before had the sound of a man's amusement brushed so sensually over her nerve-endings—as though he had stroked down her bare skin with the softest, most delicate feather. Out of the blue, a powerful ache to see him again infiltrated her blood and wouldn't be ignored...even if he *did* inhabit an entirely different stratosphere from her.

'I can assure you that I am neither married nor the father of six children. I told you before that I've been far too busy for that. Don't you believe me?'

Ludo's expression had become serious once more. Conscious of the now diminishing crowd leaving the train, and realising with relief that they were no longer the focus of unwanted interest, Natalie shrugged.

'All I'll say is that I hope you're telling me the truth. Honesty is really important to me. All right, then. When do you want us to meet?'

'How long do you think you'll be in London?'

'Probably a couple of days at most…that is unless my dad needs me around for longer.' Once again she was unable to control the tremor of fear in her voice at the thought that her father might be seriously ill. To stop from dwelling on the subject, and to prevent any uncomfortable quizzing from Ludo, she smiled and added quickly, 'I'll just have to wait and see, won't I?'

'If you are only going to be staying in town for a couple of days, that doesn't give us very much time. That being the case, I think we should meet up tomorrow evening, don't you?' There was an unexpected glint of satisfied expectation in his eyes. 'I can book us a table at Claridges. What time would suit you best?'

'The restaurant, you mean? I thought you said we were only meeting for a drink?'

'Don't you eat in the evenings?'

'Of course, but—'

'What time?'

'Eight o'clock?'

'Eight o'clock it is, then. Let me have your mobile number so I can ring you if I'm going to be delayed.'

Her brow puckering, Natalie was thoughtful. 'Okay, I'll give it to you. But don't forget it might be me who's delayed or can't make it if my dad isn't well…in which case you'd better let me have *your* number.'

With another one of his enigmatic smiles, Ludo acquiesced unhesitatingly.

She'd never got used to a doorman letting her into the rather grand Victorian building where her father's luxurious flat was situated. It made her feel like an audacious usurper pretending to be someone important.

The contrast between how her parents lived was like night and day. Her mother was a conscientious and devoted home-maker who enjoyed the simple and natural things in life, while her father was a real hedonist who loved material things perhaps a little *too* much. Although undoubtedly hard-working, he had a tendency to be quite reckless with his money.

Now, as she found herself travelling up to the topmost floor in the lift, Natalie refused to dwell on that. Instead she found herself growing more and more uneasy at what he might be going to tell her.

When Bill Carr opened the door to greet her, straight away his appearance seemed to confirm her worst suspicions. She was shocked at how much he'd aged since she'd last seen him. It had only been three months, but the change in him was so marked it might as well have been three years. He was a tall, handsome, distinguished-looking man, with a penchant for traditionally tailored Savile Row suits, and his still abundant silver-grey hair was always impeccably cut and styled...*but not today.* Today it was messy and in dire need of attention. His white shirt was crumpled and unironed and his pinstriped trousers looked as if he'd slept in them.

With alarm Natalie noticed that he carried a crystal

tumbler that appeared to have a generous amount of whisky in it. The reek of alcohol when he opened his mouth to greet her confirmed it.

'Natalie! Thank God you're here, sweetheart. I was going out of my mind, thinking that you weren't going to come.'

He flung an arm round her and pulled her head down onto his chest. Natalie dropped her bag to the ground and did her utmost to relax. Instinct told her that whatever had made her father seek solace in strong drink must be more serious than she'd thought.

Lifting her head she endeavoured to make her smile reassuring. 'I'd never have let you down, Dad.' Reaching up, she planted an affectionate kiss on his unshaven cheek as the faintest whiff of his favourite aftershave mingled with the incongruous and far less appealing smell of whisky.

'Did you have a good journey?' he asked, reaching over her shoulder to push the door shut behind her.

'I did, thanks. It was really nice to travel first class, but you shouldn't have gone to such unnecessary expense, Dad.'

Even as she spoke Natalie couldn't help but recall her meeting with Ludo, and the fact that he'd stumped up the money for her ticket when he'd heard her explain to the guard that she'd lost hers. His name was short for Ludovic, he'd told her. For a few seconds she lost herself in a helpless delicious reverie. The name was perfect. She really liked it...*she liked it a lot*. There was an air of mystery about the sound of it...a bit like its owner. They hadn't exchanged surnames but every second of their time together on the train was indelibly imprinted on her mind, never to be forgotten. Particularly his cultured, sexy voice and those extraordinarily beautiful sapphire-blue eyes of his. Her heart jumped when she nervously recalled her agreement to meet him for dinner tomorrow…

'I've always wanted to give you the best of everything, sweetheart…and that didn't change when your mother and I split up. Is she well, by the way?'

Her father's curiously intense expression catapulted her back to the present, and Natalie saw the pain that he still carried over the break-up with his wife. Her mouth dried uncomfortably as she privately empathised with the loss that clearly still haunted him.

'Yes, she's very well. She asked me to tell you that she hopes you're doing well too.'

He grimaced and shrugged. 'She's a good woman, your mother. The best woman I ever knew. It's a crying shame I didn't appreciate her more when we were together. As to your comment that she hopes I'm doing well… It near kills me to have to admit this, darling, but I'm afraid I'm not doing very well at all. Come into the kitchen and let me get you a cup of tea, then I'll explain what's been going on.'

The admission confirmed her increasingly anxious suspicions, but it still tore at Natalie's insides to hear him say it. Feeling suddenly drained, she followed his tall, rangy frame into his modern stainless-steel kitchen, watched him accidentally splash water over his crumpled sleeve as he filled the kettle at the tap—was she imagining it, or was his hand shaking a little?—and plugged it into the wall socket. He collected his whisky glass before dropping wearily down onto a nearby stool.

'What is it, Dad? Have you been having pains in your chest again? Is that why you wanted to see me so urgently? Please tell me.'

Her father imbibed a generous slug of whisky, then slammed his glass noisily back down on the counter, rubbing the back of his hand across his eyes. Communication was suspended for several disturbing moments as he looked to be struggling to gather his thoughts. 'For once it's not my health that's at stake, here, Nat. It's my livelihood.' His mouth shaped a rueful grimace.

Outside, from the busy street below, came the jarring sound of a car horn honking. Natalie flinched in shock. Drawing in a steadying breath, she saw that her dad was perfectly serious in his confession.

'Has something gone wrong with the business? Is it to do with a downturn in profits? I know the country's going through a tough time economically at the moment, but you can weather the storm, Dad...you always do.'

Bill Carr looked grim. 'The hotel chain hasn't made any profit for nearly two years, my love...largely because I haven't kept up with essential refurbishment and modernisation. And I can no longer afford to keep on staff of the calibre that helped make it such a success in the first place. It's so like you to blame it on the economy, but that just isn't the case.'

'Then if it's not that *why* can't you afford to modernise or keep good staff? You've always told me that the business has made you a fortune.'

'That's perfectly true. It *did* make a fortune. But

sadly I haven't been able to hold on to it. I've lost almost everything, Natalie…and I'm afraid I'm being forced to sell the business at a loss to try and recoup some money and pay off the vast amount of debt I've accrued.'

Natalie's insides lurched as though she'd just narrowly escaped plunging down a disused elevator shaft. 'It's really that bad?' she murmured, hardly knowing what to say.

Her father pushed to his feet, despondently shaking his head. 'I've made such a mess of my life,' he told her, 'and I suppose because I've been so reckless and irresponsible the chickens have come home to roost, as they say. I deserve it. I was blessed with everything a man could wish for—a beautiful wife, a lovely daughter and work that I loved… But I threw it all away because I became more interested in seeking pleasure than keeping a proper eye on the business.'

'You mean women and drink?'

'And the rest. It's not hard to understand why I had a heart attack.'

Needing to offer him some comfort and reassurance, even though she was shocked and slightly dazed at what 'the rest' might refer to, Natalie urgently caught hold of his hand and folded it between her own.

'That doesn't mean you're going to have another one, Dad. Things will get better, I promise you. First of all, you've got to stop blaming yourself for what you did in the past and forgive yourself. Then you have to vow that you won't hurt yourself in that way ever again— that you'll look after yourself, move on, and deal with what's going on right now. You said you're being forced to sell the business at a loss…to whom?'

'A man who's known in the world of mergers and acquisitions as "the Alchemist" because he can turn dirt into diamonds at the drop of a hat it seems. A Greek billionaire named Petrakis. It's a cliché, I know, but he really did make me an offer I couldn't refuse. At least I know he's got the money. That's something, I suppose. The thing is I need cash in the bank as soon as possible, Nat. The bank wants the money from the sale in my account tomorrow, after we complete, or else they'll make me bankrupt.'

'Don't you have any other assets? What about this flat? Presumably you own it outright?'

Again her father shook his head. 'Mortgaged up to the hilt, I'm afraid.' Noting the shock in her eyes, he freed his hand from hers, winced, and started to rub his chest.

Natalie's own heart started to race with concern. 'Are you all right, Dad? Should I call a doctor?'

'I'm fine. I probably just need to rest a bit and stop drinking so much whisky. Perhaps you'd make me a cup of tea instead?'

'Of course I will. Why don't you go and put your feet up on the couch in the living room and I'll bring it in to you?'

His answer to her suggestion was to impel her close into his chest and plant a fond kiss on the top of her head. When she glanced up to examine his suddenly pale features, his warm smile was unstintingly loving and proud.

'You're a good girl, Natalie…the best daughter in the world. I regret not telling you that more often.'

'You and Mum might have parted, but I always knew that you loved me.' Gently, she stepped out of the circle of his arms.

'It does my heart good to hear you say that. I don't want to take advantage, but perhaps you won't mind me asking another favour of you?'

Her throat thick with emotion, Natalie smiled back at him. 'Ask away. You know that I'll do anything I can to help.'

'I want you to come with me to this meeting I've got with Petrakis and his lawyers tomorrow. Just for a little moral support. Will you?'

Instinctively she knew it would probably be one of the hardest things she'd ever done, watching her father sign away the business he'd worked so hard to build all these years to some fat-cat Greek billionaire who didn't have a clue about how much it meant to him, or care that the sale might be breaking his heart…

'Of course I will.' She lightly touched her palm to his cheek. 'Now, go and put your feet up, like I said. I'll make that cup of tea and bring it in to you.'

Her father's once broad shoulders were stooped as he turned to exit the room. Natalie had never felt remotely violent towards anyone before, but she did now as she thought of the Greek billionaire known as 'the Alchemist' who was buying his business from him for a song when he could no doubt well afford to purchase it for far more and at least give her dad a fighting chance to get back on his feet again…

CHAPTER THREE

IF NATALIE HAD had a restless night, then her father had had a worse one. Several times she'd heard him get up to pace the hallway outside their bedrooms, and once when he'd omitted to close his door she'd heard the sound of violent retching coming from his bathroom. It had so frightened her that she'd raced straight into his room and banged urgently on the en-suite door. He had pleaded with her to let him sort himself out, telling her that it had happened before, that he knew how to deal with it, and Natalie had reluctantly returned to her room, heavy of heart and scared out of her wits in case he should have a seizure or a fit during the night.

After not much more than three hours' sleep she'd woken bleary-eyed and exhausted to find blinding sunshine beaming straight at her through the uncovered window, where she'd forgotten to roll down the blinds.

After checking that her dad was awake, she stumbled into the kitchen to make a large pot of strong black coffee. She rustled up some toast and marmalade and called out to him to come to the table.

The dazzlingly bright sunshine wasn't exactly a good friend to Bill Carr that morning, Natalie observed anxiously. The complexion that she'd judged as a little pasty yesterday looked ashen grey and sickly today. He made a feeble attempt at eating the toast she'd made, but didn't hesitate to down two large mugs of coffee.

Afterwards, he wiped the back of his trembling hand across his mouth, grimaced and said, 'I suppose you could say I'm ready for anything now.'

The weak smile he added to that statement all but broke Natalie's heart.

'You won't have to face this alone, Dad. I'll be with you every step of the way…I promise.'

'I know, darling. And, whilst I know I hardly deserve to have your support at all, I honestly appreciate it and one day soon I'll make it up to you…that's *my* promise to you.'

'You don't need to make it up to me. We're family, remember? All I want is for you to be well and happy. Now, remind me what time we have to be at this Petrakis's office?'

'Ten forty-five.'

'Okay. After I shower and dress I'll phone a cab to pick us up. Where is the office we're going to?'

'Westminster.'

'Not far away, then. Well, you'd better go and get ready, too. Do you need anything ironed?'

Getting to his feet and digging his hands deep into the capacious pockets of his dressing gown, her father seemed completely nonplussed by the question.

Taking in a consciously deep breath to calm her disquiet, Natalie asked, 'Do you want me to come with you and check?'

'No, darling, it's fine. I'm wearing my best Savile Row suit, and my one ironed shirt has been hanging in the wardrobe ready ever since I got the call that the meeting was today.'

'Good.' Giving him an approving smile, Natalie stole a brief glance at the fashionably utilitarian stainless-steel clock on the wall. 'We'd better get our skates on, then. We don't want to be late.'

'For the execution, you mean?' His grimace, clearly tinged with bitterness and regret, had never looked more pained. Yet the comment also contained a hint of ironic humour.

'I know it must be hard for you to contemplate letting go of the business that you put your heart and soul into to building,' she sympathised, 'but maybe this could be an exciting new start for you. An opportunity to put your energies into something else…something a little less taxing that you could manage more easily. Even the direst situations can have a silver lining.'

'And how am I going to start another business if I have barely a penny to my name?'

'Is running a business the only way you can earn a living?'

'That's all I know how to do.' Exhaling a leaden sigh, her father drove his fingers exasperatedly through his already mussed silver hair.

Struggling with her personal sense of frustration at not being able to find an instant solution that would cheer him and give him some hope, Natalie dropped her hands to hips clad in the pyjama bottoms and T-shirt she'd borrowed from him to wear to bed and thought hard.

'What if we ask this Petrakis if he could extend some humanitarian understanding and pay you a reasonable sum for the business? After all, if you say he has a reputation for being able to turn dirt into diamonds then surely he must know that he's bound to make another fortune from your hotel chain? What would it hurt for him to pay you a fairer price?'

'Sweetheart...I don't mean this unkindly, but you know very little about men like Petrakis. How do you think he acquired his considerable fortune? It wasn't from taking a humanitarian approach to making money! Whatever you say to him, however impassioned or eloquent your argument, it would be like water off a duck's back.'

Natalie's grey eyes flashed angrily. 'And that's how the business world measures success these days, is it? Someone is only thought of as successful if he's single-mindedly ruthless in his dealings and doesn't give a fig about the psychological damage he might cause to anyone—not even a fellow entrepreneur who's down on his luck—just as long as he can get what he wants?'

Breathing hard, she knew how much she already despised the Greek billionaire even though she hadn't even set eyes on him yet. But there was also something else on her mind. If this meeting with Petrakis was too devastating for her dad—and she'd certainly be able to tell if it was—then she couldn't abandon him later on tonight to go and have dinner with the enigmatic Ludo. Even though she'd barely been able to cease thinking

about the man since meeting him on the train yesterday...

'Apparently that is the case. But don't distress yourself by being angry on my behalf, love. I know I asked
you to come with me for moral support, but this isn't
your battle. It's mine. Now, I think we'd better go and
get ourselves ready.'

Giving a resigned shrug, her father turned on his
heel. With a heavy tread he made his way down the var-
nished wood-panelled hall to his bedroom, as if carrying the weight of the world on his shoulders.

'Ludovic...how are you? Traffic's bloody awful out
there today. Everything's moving at a snail's pace.'

Ludo had been staring out of the window of his plush
Westminster office, hardly registering anything on the
road outside because his mind was fixed on one thought
and one thought only. Tonight he was meeting the exquisite Natalie for dinner. He closed his eyes. For just a
few short seconds he could imagine himself becoming
entranced by the still, crystal-clear lake of her gaze all
over again, and could conjure up the alluring scent of
her perfume as easily as if she were standing right next
to him. It was impossible to recall the last time he'd had
this sense of excited anticipation fluttering in the pit of
his stomach at the prospect of seeing a woman again...if
it had *ever* happened at all. So, when the booming voice
of his public-school-educated lawyer Stephen Godrich
unexpectedly rang out behind him he was so immersed
in his daydream that he almost jumped out of his skin.

With a wry smile he pivoted, immediately steering

his mind back into work mode. There would be time for more fantasies about the lovely Natalie later, after they'd met for dinner, Ludo was sure.

Automatically stepping forward to shake the other man's hand, he privately noted that the buttons on the bespoke suit jacket he wore had about as much hope of meeting over his ever-expanding girth as Ludo had of winning the Men's Final at Wimbledon… An impossibility, of course, seeing as polo was his sport of choice, and not tennis.

'Hello, Stephen. You're looking well…in fact so well I fear I must be paying you too much,' he joked.

The other man's pebble-sized blue eyes, almost consumed by the generous flesh that surrounded them, flickered with momentary alarm. Quickly recovering, he drew out a large checked handkerchief from his trouser pocket and proceeded to mop the perspiration that glazed his brow.

'Being an inveterate lover of fine dining definitely has its price, my friend,' he remarked, smiling. 'I know I should be more self-disciplined, but we all have our little peccadillos, don't we? Anyway…do you mind if I ask if your client has arrived yet?'

Glancing down at the platinum Rolex that encircled his tanned wrist, Ludo frowned. 'I'm afraid not. It looks like he may well be late. While we're waiting for him I'll get Jane to make us some coffee.'

'Splendid idea. A few choice biscuits wouldn't go amiss either, if you have some,' the lawyer added hopefully.

Already at the door on his way out to Reception,

Ludo raised a hand in acknowledgement, thinking that if the man would only cut down on his sugar intake his handmade suits might fit him a whole lot better.

Ludo and his trusted representative Amelia Redmond—who had put the bid in for the once prestigious hotel chain on his behalf—sat at the polished table in the boardroom along with Stephen Godrich and Ludo's affable and highly professional assistant Nick. The younger man was re-reading some documentation in front of him and his olive-skinned brow was furrowed in concentration. Why it should suddenly occur to him at that precise moment that Nick's family came from Crete, he didn't know. Except that he'd been thinking about Natalie again, and he recalled her telling him that her mother had grown up there.

Suddenly impatient to have this meeting over and done with—even though the purchase of this particular hospitality business was a genuine coup—he had a strong urge to take some time out from work to go for a swim at his private health club. Not for the first time he recalled the surprising question Natalie had posed to him on the train. 'Do you have to be so busy *all* of the time?' she'd asked.

Ludo frowned. His family had raised him with a bulldog work ethic second to none, and he'd more than reaped the rewards of his tenacity and hard work. Yet there was still a perverse sense of not being deserving enough running through his veins that didn't always allow him to enjoy those rewards. Somewhere along the line he'd forgotten that a body needed rest and relaxation from time to time to recharge its batteries. Lord knew he could easily afford to take a year off or more if he wanted to. But to do what? And, more to the point, with *whom*?

Straightening the cuffs of his pristine cobalt shirt, he glanced up, intuiting the entrance of his diminutive middle-aged secretary Jane a moment before she appeared in the doorway.

'Mr Carr is here, along with his daughter and his solicitor Mr Nichols,' she announced gravely, as was her habit. 'Shall I show them in?'

'Please do. Have you asked them what refreshments they'd like?'

'I have.'

At the back of his mind Ludo was wondering why Bill Carr had brought his daughter along to the meeting. Neither Nick nor the ultra-efficient Amelia Redmond had informed him that she had any shares in the business, and the last thing he wanted to deal with today was some unforeseen complication that affected the deal. The look on Nick's face told him that he was equally puzzled by the daughter's attendance. As Jane held the door wide, so that the trio in reception could enter, Ludo was the first to rise to his feet to greet them.

When he registered that the pretty brunette who came in with the two men was Natalie he honestly thought his heart was going to jump clear out of his chest.

He stared. Natalie was the *daughter* of the hotel chain's owner, Bill Carr? Was fate playing some kind of outlandish joke on him? The wide-eyed liquid-silver glance that mirrored his own profound sense of shock instantly had him hypnotised, and he couldn't help but murmur her name beneath his breath. It was impossible to deny the instantaneous jolt of almost violent attraction that zigzagged through him at seeing her again.

The faded jeans that hugged her long slim legs and the cerise satin tunic she wore were in direct contrast to everyone else's ultra formal attire. Yet he couldn't help thinking that the ensemble was utterly charming and refreshing. But, as much as he was secretly delighted to see her, Ludo knew potentially that this was one of the worst situations he could have wished for. Already he could sense that she was on her guard, but not by so much as a flicker of an eyelid did she indicate that she'd met him before. Clearly it was going to be hard for her to trust him after realising that *he* was the man about to buy her father's business—and not at the best price either. She must know he was selling it at a substantial loss to Ludo.

Steering his glance deliberately over to the two men, in a bid to buy more time and think what to do, he asked, 'Which one of you is Bill Carr?'

He couldn't help his tone sounding on edge. In truth, Natalie's unexpected appearance, plus the astonishing fact that her father should turn out to be the businessman whose hotel chain he was purchasing, had seriously shaken him. As Ludo endeavoured to win back his equilibrium, the rangy, almost gaunt-looking man in a traditional grey pinstriped suit stepped forward to shake his hand.

'I am. This is my solicitor, Edward Nichols, and my daughter Natalie.'

Sadly, she *didn't* step forward to shake Ludo's hand.

Instead, her beautiful grey eyes flashed a warning, as if to tell him that under the circumstances it would be unwise to acknowledge her personally. At that moment, he couldn't help but agree.

'I presume you must be Mr Petrakis?' Bill Carr finished.

'That's right,' Ludo responded, adding quickly, 'Why don't we all sit down? I understand that my secretary is seeing to some refreshments, but in the meantime allow me to introduce you to my colleagues.'

The introductions over, he reached for the glass of water on the leather blotter in front of him and took a cooling sip. Somehow he had to endeavour to compose himself and not let anyone see that the sight of Natalie had almost robbed him of the power of speech—never mind his ability to present himself with his usually inimitable self-assurance. After Jane had brought coffee and biscuits, then shut the door behind her, Ludo seized the opportunity to hand over the formalities of the deal to Amelia and Nick. While they outlined the offer he had proposed, Bill Carr and his solicitor listened intently, every so often asking questions and jotting down notes.

Due to the uncharacteristic guilt that assailed him because he was buying her father's business, the back of Ludo's neck prickled uncomfortably every time he inadvertently caught Natalie's eye.

He tried hard to recall everything she'd told him about the man when they'd spoken on the train yesterday. *'He can be rather unpredictable and not always easy to understand,'* she'd confided. Ludo wondered if that had anything to do with what he chose to spend his money on. His assistant Nick had uncovered a story in the business community about the man having a reputation for being reckless with his money. The story went that he regularly indulged in various costly habits...not all of them entirely wholesome. No doubt that was why he found himself in the painful position he was in now, having to sell his business for less than half its value to meet the debt those expensive habits had incurred...

Ludo's two assistants brought their outlining of the deal to a concise and professional conclusion. Then his solicitor confirmed the conditions of the sum being offered, to make sure that Bill Carr was fully aware of every aspect of the deal. All that remained after that was for the deal to be signed and witnessed and the money transferred to his bank account.

As Ludo's solicitor Stephen Godrich pushed the necessary document across the table for the man's signature, Natalie stopped them all in their tracks with a stunning question. 'Mr Petrakis...do you think that the amount you're offering my father for his business is entirely fair?'

Mr Petrakis? Ludo almost smiled at her deliberate formality. But immediately after his initial amused reaction he registered the less than flattering implication behind the soft-voiced enquiry.

'Fair?' He frowned, turning the full force of his sapphire-blue gaze on her lightly flushed face.

'Yes—fair. You must know that you're getting what is one of the most innovative and successful hotel chains in the UK for practically peanuts! You're a very wealthy man, I hear. Surely you can afford to pay a less insulting amount to a man whose ingenuity and hard work created the business in the first place, so he might invest some of it in another entrepreneurial venture and make his living?'

As Natalie's little speech came to an end it was as though a bomb had exploded. As if in fear of igniting another, no one moved a muscle or so much as rustled a piece of paper. They were all in shock.

Going by her pink cheeks and over-bright eyes, so was Natalie. As for himself, for a heart-pounding few moments Ludo was genuinely at a loss as to know how to answer. But then his well-honed instinct for self-preservation thankfully kicked in, along with the first stirrings of genuine fury.

Leaning towards her across the table, he linked his hands together to anchor himself. 'You consider what I am paying your father for his business *insulting,* do you?'

'Yes, I do.'

'Have you asked him how many other people put in tenders for it? If not, why don't you do that now? Go on—ask him.'

The man sitting next to her slid a long, bony-fingered hand across his daughter's.

'I know you mean well, love, but the fact is no one other than Mr Petrakis is interested in buying the hotel chain. No doubt he is a realist about making money in business—as *I* am. The current market is in a slump, and I'm actually grateful that someone has made me an offer. The hotel chain isn't the roaring success it once was, Natalie. Whoever buys it is going to have to invest a substantial amount of money to bring it up to scratch again and make it profitable. Maybe that's the point you need to realise.'

Natalie bit her lip, and her answering glance up at him was verging on sorrowful. 'But this whole thing has so badly affected your health, Dad. You know it has. What are you going to do for a living if you can't get another business venture off the ground? That's the only reason I want more money for you.'

Hearing the devotion and concern in her voice, Ludo couldn't help admiring her—even though her unbelievable accusation had temporarily embarrassed him. It wasn't hard to see that Natalie Carr was a naturally caring woman who clearly adored her father and quickly forgave him for any poor decisions or mistakes he'd made—even if those poor decisions and mistakes hurt *her.* All in all, it made the idea of a liaison with her even more attractive, and Ludo wasn't above using whatever means he had at his disposal to persuade her that it was a good idea. But first he had a little more business to attend to.

'As indisputably tragic as your story is, Mr Carr, I now have to ask you… Do you wish to complete the deal and have this money paid into your account today? Or, after hearing of your charming daughter's admirable concern for your welfare, have you changed your mind?'

As he came to the end of his question Ludo deliberately raised a wry eyebrow at Natalie, as if to demonstrate that he hadn't become a very rich man by being soft-hearted and swayed by every sob story that came his way. As much as he wanted to bed her, he wouldn't go back on the principles that had made him his fortune. Not for *anyone*…

CHAPTER FOUR

THE DEAL WAS signed. And, although Natalie refused to meet Ludo's enigmatic glance as she, her father and his solicitor started to file out of the traditionally furnished office, with its leaded diamond-shaped windowpanes and lingering scent of beeswax, she couldn't help regretting that the much anticipated dinner date with him tonight wasn't going to happen after all.

How could it after he'd so coldly refused her heartfelt plea to help her father by increasing his offer for the hotel chain? It was evident that making money was far more important to him than helping his fellow man. *Good riddance*, she thought, deliberately averting her gaze as she swept past him. But just the same her heart hammered hard as the warmth from his body mingled with the alluring scent of his aftershave and disturbingly reached out to arouse her.

'Natalie?'

To her astonishment he lightly wrapped his hand round her slender-boned wrist.

'I'd like a word with you, if I may?'

Before she could register anything but the sensation of his warm grip against her flesh and the glittering cobalt blue of his eyes he removed his hand and turned to address his waiting colleagues.

'I need some time alone with Ms Carr.' There was a definite tone of command in his voice and immediately they all stood up and filed out behind Natalie's dad and his solicitor.

Before Ludo could shut the door behind them Bill Carr returned, to plant himself in the doorway, a perturbed expression on his long lean face.

'May I ask why you want to talk to my daughter alone? If you're angry that she was a little outspoken on my behalf, please don't take it personally. I'm sure she meant no offence, Mr Petrakis,' he apologised.

Natalie found it hard to quell her annoyance that her father was being so meek. For God's sake—he almost sounded subservient! One thing she was sure of: *she* wouldn't be following suit…

'Don't worry, Mr Carr. Although your daughter's outburst was somewhat ill-advised, you can rest assured that I did not take it personally. I simply want to have a quiet word with her in private—if she is in agreement?'

Beginning to feel like a piece of property being bartered, Natalie bristled. Folding her arms across the cerise blouse she'd thrown into her tote at the last minute, she made herself meet Ludo's wry glance head-on, without giving in to the urge to demonstrate her annoyance and deliberately look away.

'Whatever it is you want to say to me, Mr Petrakis, you had better make it quick. I want to get to the bank before it closes.'

'No doubt to check that your father's money has gone

into his account?' Ludo commented coolly, lifting a lightly mocking eyebrow.

How she refrained from slapping his smooth, sculpted cheek Natalie didn't know.

'My father's money is nothing to do with me. Believe it or not, I do have my own bank account.'

He grinned disconcertingly. 'I'm very glad to hear it. Why don't you come and sit down for a minute so we can talk?'

Turning towards her father, thinking he must be wondering what on earth was going on between the two of them, she just about managed a reassuring smile. 'I'm sure this won't take long, Dad. Will you wait for me outside?'

'I'll meet you in the coffee shop across the road. Goodbye, Mr Petrakis.'

'It has been a pleasure doing business with you, Mr Carr.'

As soon as Natalie's puzzled dad had closed the door behind him she could no longer stem her irritation at the handsome Greek. 'What on *earth* can you possibly have to say to me after what you've just done? Whatever it is, I'm not sure I want to hear it. Unless you want me to convey to my dad your sincere apologies for being so heartlessly mercenary, I'd rather not waste any more time today hoping that a man who is deaf, dumb and blind to pleas for understanding will change his mind and be more compassionate. I think I'd rather put the whole thing down to bitter experience and be on my way.'

The expression on Ludo's face suddenly reflected a

severe winter frost. 'Your indignant attitude beggars belief. What just went on between your father and me was a business transaction—pure and simple. If you can't see that then you are more naive than I thought. It is clear that you have *no* idea about the vagaries of buying and selling, not to mention the effect of current market forces. If perhaps not the most successful businessman in the world, your father is at least a pragmatist and he does understand these things. I am sure he realises how fortunate he is to have had me make an offer for his business at all. It is not as though he was exactly overrun with them... At least now he will be able to pay off some of his debts.'

Natalie was shocked. 'How do *you* know about his debts?'

'I make it a point to investigate the credentials of anyone who hopes to sell me anything, Natalie.' Emitting a weary-sounding sigh, Ludo rubbed his hand round his lean, cut-glass jaw. 'I am genuinely sorry that your father has got himself into such a mess financially, but that does not mean I should be responsible for helping to get him out of it. I too have business interests to maintain.'

'I'm sure you do.'

Even though his chastising reply had irked and irritated her, Natalie had to admit that she had no right to berate him when her father had brought this whole unfortunate situation down on himself. He was right. Ludo *wasn't* responsible for her father's inability to hold on to his once successful business because he'd become distracted by his propensity for acquiring more and more unhelpful bad habits. Should she really be angry at Ludo because he hadn't agreed to pay more for the hotel chain? After all, she knew for a fact that he wasn't a mean man. Hadn't he spontaneously paid for her rail ticket yesterday?

Curling some long strands of drifting hair agitatedly round her ear, she inhaled a steadying breath. No matter how much she tried to square it with herself, it was still hard to understand why a businessman as wealthy as Ludo couldn't extend a little more understanding and kindness towards a fellow entrepreneur when he was in trouble. Weren't the newspapers and the media always banging on about the need for businesses to be more ethical these days rather than solely profit-driven?

'Was that all you wanted to say to me?' she asked, perversely wishing that he would talk to her about far more interesting and perhaps *personal* things rather than business—just so that she could hear the sound of pleasure in his voice and store it in her memory.

Almost as if he'd read her mind, Ludo's deliberately slow, answering smile made her shiver. Inside Natalie's lace bra her nipples prickled hotly, just as if he had run his fingertips over them…

Gravel-voiced he replied, 'No. It isn't. Did you forget that you agreed to meet me for dinner tonight?'

'No…I didn't forget. But that was before I knew that you were the man buying my father's business.'

'What does that have to do with us meeting for dinner?'

Natalie's grey eyes widened in surprise that he should even have to ask. 'How do you think my dad would feel if he found out I'd gone out to dinner with you? He'd feel betrayed. He's already been through more than he can take without me adding to his problems.'

'It sounds like you don't believe that your own needs should be met, Natalie. Why is that, I wonder?'

'What needs are we talking about?'

Her face burned, because even as she posed the question she knew *exactly* what he meant. It was undeniable that Ludo Petrakis aroused her. He aroused her more than any other man she'd ever been attracted to before… And what took her breath away was that, going by the licentiously seductive look in his incredible blue eyes, he seemed to be having similar feelings. But it didn't make the situation any less awkward or uncomfortable.

Yes, her dad had made some very foolish errors concerning his business, and consequently lost everything he'd worked so hard for, but Natalie didn't want to appear as though she was deliberately punishing him by seeing Ludo. Somehow she had to find the strength to walk away from the man, no matter *how* much her senses clamoured for her to see him again.

She tossed her head in a bid to demonstrate that the particular needs he'd alluded to meant nothing in comparison to the more pressing one she still had on her mind. 'The only needs I have at the moment are for my father to recover from this crippling setback and return to full health so he can find the energy and the will to start over again. By the way—not that you'll care—did your investigations tell you that as well as losing his business he's about to lose his home, too? Anyway, the reason I have to get to the bank is not to check that your money's gone into his account but to get some money out to pay you back for the ticket you bought me on the train. Fortunately I have discovered that there's an emergency code I can use to get some cash from my account.'

'Forget about that. It's not important. As far as I'm concerned you don't owe me anything. Rather than have you pay me back for the ticket I'd much prefer to take you to dinner tonight and start to get to know you a little.'

Even though it was flattering that Ludo was being so persistent, Natalie couldn't help but frown.

'Didn't you hear what I said? I'm sorry, but I can't risk upsetting my dad by seeing you again. You might assume that he's taking it all rather well under the circumstances, but he's most definitely *not* coping.' She stroked a not quite steady hand down over her tunic. 'Look, I really do have to go now. But before I do there's one more thing I want to ask. Why didn't you tell me you were Greek when we met on the train? Especially after I told you that my mother came from Crete?'

In his mind, Ludo confronted a familiar wall that he was still reluctant to climb. He was proud of his heritage, but it had been three years since he'd last visited his homeland…three years since his beloved older brother Theo had perished in a boating accident off the coast of the private island that Ludo owned. It had been the darkest time of his life, and the aftermath of the tragic event had seen him spiralling into a pit of despair that he'd feared he might never get out of.

Instead of staying home to grieve with his family he'd left quite soon after the funeral, hoping to find relief from his despondency by increasing his international business interests, travelling everywhere round the globe *except* for his beloved Greece... His parents couldn't understand why he wouldn't come home. Whenever he spoke to his mother on the phone she'd plead and cry for him to return. But as far as Ludo was concerned he had disappointed her on two unforgivable counts, so he wouldn't. Not only had he been unable to provide her with evidence of a healthy romantic relationship and the prospect of a grandchild, worse— *much* worse than that—his brother had died holidaying on the beautiful island paradise that Ludo had bought himself, as a reward for attaining the success he'd so often dreamed of as a boy, ultimately so that his parents might see that he was as good and successful a man as Theo. Now they would never see that.

Momentarily glancing away from the beautiful clear grey eyes that were so avidly studying him, he endeavoured to keep his tone matter-of-fact. 'At the time I was more interested in finding out about you, Natalie. Don't women often make the complaint that men talk too much about themselves?'

'I don't know about that. I just thought you'd have been pleased to tell me where you came from.'

'Why *is* that? So we might have exchanged personal anecdotes and stories about our shared heritage?' Ludo heard a spike of irritation in his voice that he couldn't hide because he'd been inadvertently pushed into a corner. He hadn't spoken about his country of birth or what had happened to drive him away from it to anyone... not even trusted friends. If he wanted things to progress with Natalie he was probably going to have to talk about it now, whether he liked it or not. 'Sometimes a man in my position is apt to crave anonymity,' he continued. 'Whether that's about where he comes from or who he is. Besides, do you really think our only point of connection is the fact that each of us has a parent who is Greek?'

'Yesterday I might have thought so, if you'd admitted it.' Hugging her arms across her chest, Natalie frowned. 'But since then things have unfolded to connect us in a way I never could have imagined. When I walked into that room today and saw that it was you—the man I'd met on the train—I was lost for words. It was such a shock. Anyway, going back to yesterday, you helped me out by paying for my ticket and, whether you want me to or not, it matters to *me* that I pay you back.'

'If that's the case then perhaps you will start to see the sense in meeting me tonight after all?' Ludo interjected smoothly.

'I can't.'

'You mean you won't?'

'I mean I can't. Why won't you listen to what I'm saying?'

Pressing the pads of his fingertips against his brow, he lightly shook his head. 'I'm listening, Natalie, but perhaps I'm not giving you the response you're looking for because *you* are not giving me the one that *I* want.'

Her eyes flashed with irritation. 'And no doubt you always get what you want?'

She released an exasperated sigh and her lithe figure moved purposefully back towards the door. His heart thudding at the realisation that the opportunity to see her again might disappear from right under his nose unless he took action, Ludo thought fast. As an idea presented itself he mentally grabbed at it, as though it might vanish in the next instant unless he expressed it. The idea was perhaps a little preposterous, but it made a strange kind of sense. Ludo decided to take the plunge and go with it.

'Perhaps you won't be in such a hurry to leave if I tell you that I have a deal in mind that I'd like to talk to you about? A deal that would benefit your father as well as yourself,' he asserted calmly.

Riveted, she immediately pulled her hand away from the brass doorknob and turned to face him. 'What kind of a deal?'

Pacing a little, to help arrange his thoughts, Ludo took his time in answering. It had suddenly dawned on him that what he was about to propose would benefit *him* too. The concept didn't seem at all preposterous any more. In fact it might potentially be the solution he'd secretly longed for—a way out that might bring him some peace at last.

He stopped pacing to settle his gaze on the beautiful, inquisitive face in front of him. 'The deal I'm offering you is that I will increase what I paid for your father's business by half the amount again if you agree to come with me to Greece and play the role of my fiancée.'

Natalie turned as still as a statue, her stunned expression suggesting she wasn't entirely sure she'd heard him right. Her next words confirmed it. 'Would you mind repeating what you just said? I'm afraid I might have imagined it.'

'You didn't imagine it.' Willingly, he repeated his proposition.

'You really will increase the money you paid for the business if I travel to Greece with you and pretend to be your fiancée? Why would you want me to do such a bizarre thing?'

Shrugging a shoulder, Ludo sighed. 'It will perhaps not be as bizarre as you might think when I tell you my reasons,' he remarked.

'Go on, then.' Moistening her lips, she patiently waited for him to continue.

'My parents—in particular my mother—have long hoped that I will bring someone home that I am serious about. Someone who will help give them hope that they might one day have a grandchild.'

Noting the brief flash of alarm in Natalie's candid gaze, Ludo forced himself to press on regardless. He told himself she wouldn't still be standing there listening if the idea was absolutely abhorrent to her.

'Unfortunately I have not had a long-term relationship in a long time and, frankly, they are becoming despondent that I ever will. The situation has become sadly compounded by my only brother's death three years ago in a boating accident. Now I am their only son and heir. Unfortunately I have not been home since the funeral. I did not want to return until I could give them hope that the future was brighter than they had perhaps envisaged. I know it is a pretence, Natalie, but the intention behind it is a kind one. I promise you that if you can convincingly act the part of my fiancée while we are in Greece, when we return to the UK I will make sure you are richly rewarded.'

'But even if I should agree to the pretence, how hurt will your parents be when they find out that the whole thing was a lie? They must be broken-hearted as it is to have lost their son. Nothing you can do for me or give me would make up for how terrible I'd feel about deceiving them.'

'The fact that you care so much about that aspect of the deal assures me that you are the right woman to ask this favour of, Natalie. I will be forever in your debt if you do this for me.'

She looked to be thinking hard for a moment. 'And how do I explain to my father that I am going away with you to Greece for—for how long?'

'At least three to four weeks, *paidi mou*.'

The soft pink hue that tinted her cheeks at his use of the Greek endearment momentarily distracted him, because it brought a lustre to her eyes that was nothing less than magical and gave him an irresistible glimpse of how she might look if he were to try and seduce her... prettily flushed and aroused. A little buzz of pleasurable heat ricocheted through his insides. He suddenly became even more determined to have Natalie masquerade as his fiancée... Especially as—in the hope of convincing his parents—he fully intended to play the part of devoted fiancé to the hilt.

'You can tell him that I have offered you the chance to learn the ropes of good financial dealing with an expert,' he asserted with a teasing smile. 'I am sure he will see the benefits of such an opportunity. If you take it, and learn what I consider to be the essential skills for success in business, your father will need to have no worries about your financial future, because you will know exactly how to go about securing it.'

As he came to the end of this speech Natalie moved across the room to a burgundy-coloured wing-backed armchair and slowly sank down into it. When she glanced up again to meet his eyes, Ludo experienced a private moment of undeniable triumph and relief, because suddenly he knew she was giving the offer serious consideration.

CHAPTER FIVE

WAS SHE CRAZY to consider Ludo's incredible suggestion that she go with him to Greece and assume the identity of his fiancée? It would fulfil her longed-for desire to visit Greece again, but the most important aspect of the deal he was proposing was that he'd promised to increase what he had paid to her father for his business.

Half the amount again would allow her dad to keep his flat and not be forced to sell it. The fact that he could keep his home would go a long way, Natalie believed, to helping him make a new start. Not only that, it might give his health a real boost too. This deal Ludo was proposing was too important to dismiss, she realised. How could she live with herself if she didn't take it and her dad's health and self-esteem sank even lower because he'd lost all hope in making things better for himself?

But now, as she let her gaze roam over the strikingly handsome man silently observing her, with his chiselled good looks and piercing blue eyes, a nervous cartwheel flipped in the pit of her stomach. Could she really contemplate playing the part of his fiancée? Would she be strong enough to pull it off without letting her feelings get involved? Being in close proximity with Ludo in

Greece and pretending to be his fiancée would surely mean holding hands, kissing and touching, perhaps *intimately...*

Natalie didn't allow her thoughts to venture any further, because they had already induced a powerful wave of heat that made her body feel as if it were near to bursting into flames. Lifting the heavy swathe of long hair off the back of her neck in a bid to help cool her temperature, she noticed that Ludo's previously confident expression had altered. Now his glance was more contemplative, as if he wasn't entirely sure that her response would be the one he hoped for. If that were true, Natalie wondered how such an amazingly successful and attractive man could ever be plagued by doubt of any kind. It didn't make sense.

'Well?'

He was levelling his gaze upon her a little more intently, and she got the impression his patience was wearing thin.

'Are you going to give me an answer to what I have proposed? Is it to be yes or no, Natalie?'

Sucking in a breath, she pushed to her feet. 'You make it sound so simple...to just say yes or no.'

'Are you saying it's more complicated?'

'Where emotions are involved no situation is ever going to be straightforward.'

'Why should emotions be involved?' Frowning in puzzlement, Ludo dug his hand into his trouser pocket. 'Are you worrying about your father and his reaction when he learns you're going to come to Greece with me? I shouldn't imagine it will be a problem, considering I have offered to increase the amount I paid him.'

Her heartbeat accelerating, Natalie felt herself redden. 'Actually, it's not my father I was worrying about. I don't have any doubt he'll be more than pleased with your new offer for the business, and as for me going to Greece with you—he'll accept it if he knows it's what I want, too. I was just wondering how, if I should go with you, I'm going to cope with playing your fiancée when we've only just met and I hardly know you? Aren't engaged couples supposed to behave as though they're crazy about each other?'

Ludo's amused smile emphasised his even white teeth and sexy, sun-kissed tan. She caught her breath.

'Do you think you will find it difficult to pretend that you're crazy about me, *paidi mou*? Most women I know tell me I am quite a catch. Some have even called me "irresistible"… Shall we put the theory to the test?'

Before Natalie realised his intention he walked right up to her and encircled her waist. Being up close and personal with his body as he pulled her towards him, smelling the alluring musky aftershave he wore, made her knees come very close to folding even before he embraced her. A stunned gasp left her throat as he lowered his head and kissed her. As soon as his lips made contact she opened her mouth and he expertly inserted his smooth, silken tongue inside to make the kiss even more intimate.

Every thought in her head vanished except the one that registered the fierce addictive pleasure of his taste and the sexy heated brand of his skin against hers. It felt as though a torch had ignited an unforgettable flame in her blood that no other man before or after him could ever hope to compete with… In the silence of her mind a renegade response came. *Okay…I'll cope. It can't be that difficult.*

She enjoyed the kiss so much she was genuinely disappointed when Ludo eased the delightful pressure on her lips. Lifting his head to gaze down at her, he moved his hands from her waist to rest them lightly on her hips. Up close, his stunning sapphire eyes were matchlessly blue, like a sunlit Mediterranean sea in midafternoon. Even his dark blond lashes were impossibly lavish. It didn't matter if he were rich or poor, Natalie decided. The man's physical assets were simply amazing.

'Hmm…' He smiled. 'That was nice.'

She hoped he wouldn't want a more detailed assessment from her on how *she* felt about the kiss. She might just have to tell him she'd like to try another one, just to make sure she hadn't imagined the spine-tingling pleasure it had given her.

'Can I take it that the idea of playing my fiancée is not as repellent as you might have thought initially?' he teased softly.

Natalie couldn't help but be honest. 'I'm sure you know that you're far from repellent. But it still doesn't make it easy for me to pretend I'm something that I'm not. I feel very uneasy about deceiving anyone, even in a good cause. Especially your parents.'

Reaching towards her, Ludo moved some silken strands of hair away from her face and gently stroked his hand down over her cheekbone. 'Because you are naturally such a thoughtful person I know they won't have a problem accepting you as my girlfriend,' he asserted confidently.

'A girlfriend is one thing…I could cope with that. But introducing me as your fiancée is much more serious, don't you think?'

Removing his hand from her cheek, he expelled a heavy sigh. The quirk at the corner of his exquisitely carved mouth suggested some exasperation. 'Think of it as a harmless game of "Let's Pretend". Believe me when I say that you are not hurting anybody. After all, you will be getting what you want for your father, remember? That and an opportunity to visit your mother's country…something you told me you'd love to do again.'

Stepping away from him so that she might think straight, Natalie knew she had to make a decision. She sent up a silent prayer that it was the right one.

'All right, then. I'll do as you ask and go to Greece with you. But if when I'm there it becomes in any way difficult or untenable for me to keep up the charade of being your fiancée then do you agree I can go home, no questions asked?'

Somewhat reluctantly Ludo nodded his head. 'I will not be happy about it, but I will agree so long as you remember I am paying your father a great deal of money for his business. You at least owe me the courtesy of staying with me until I tell you I am satisfied.'

'Satisfied?' The hot colour started at the tips of Natalie's toes and travelled in an all-consuming heatwave right up to her scalp. The word *satisfied* had many connotations, so why did she have to focus on the sexual one first? Transfixed by Ludo's shimmering blue gaze, she didn't have to search very hard for the answer.

'Yes—satisfied that you have acted the part of my fiancée to the very best of your ability and played it as convincingly as possible.'

'I'm no actress. I can only do the best I can. All right, then.' Briefly withdrawing her gaze, she glanced down at the polished wooden floor to help regain her equilibrium, because her heart was thudding alarmingly at the daunting prospect of what she was agreeing to do. 'You'd better tell me when you're intending to travel.'

'As far as I'm concerned, the sooner the better. Could you be ready to go in a week's time?'

'That *is* soon. I'll need to arrange help at the B&B for my mum while I'm away. I hope a week will be enough time for me to organise things.'

'You have already intimated to me that you are a good organiser, Natalie. I'm sure a week will give you plenty of time. You should be ready to leave next Monday, when I intend us to travel on an early-morning flight. As we will be departing from Heathrow you should probably arrange to stay with your father the night before.'

'I'm sure that won't be a problem.'

'I'm sure it won't.' With a mocking glint in his eye, Ludo drolly echoed her comment. 'Especially when he learns that I am not as uncharitable and hard-hearted as you both first suspected.'

'I never meant to deliberately insult you by what I said. I was just upset, as any loving daughter would be, at the prospect of my dad struggling to get by after paying all his debts. It seemed so unfair that after being forced to sell his business after so many dedicated years of hard work the proceeds wouldn't even leave him enough to live on.'

Even though she had felt entirely justified, Natalie was still embarrassed at being reminded of her accusatory outburst at the meeting.

Flushing, she glanced briefly down at her watch and declared, 'I really do have to go now—but there's just one more thing I need to say before I leave.' Her teeth nibbled anxiously at her lip. 'I'm really sorry to hear about your brother. Such a dreadful loss must have been devastating for you and your family…I really feel for you all.'

A shadow seemed to move across Ludo's bright blue irises, momentarily darkening them. 'Devastating is not a big enough word,' he murmured, awkwardly dragging his fingers through his thick fair hair. 'But I appreciate your sympathy.'

'Well, I think it's time I left. Presumably you'll ring me when you have the flight times?'

'You can count on it.' Moving with her towards the door, Ludo lightly touched her arm. 'But I won't just be contacting you then. I'm going to ring you during the week—preferably in the evenings, when I'm not working. I think it's quite important that we get to know each other a little before our trip, don't you?'

'Talking to each other on the phone is hardly the best way to get to know someone, but I suppose it will have to do if we can't see each other.'

'As much as I would like to, it's impossible for me

to free up any time to see you this week, Natalie. For now, phone calls will have to suffice.'

Meeting his enigmatic gaze, she could do no more than shrug in agreement, even though in truth she was disappointed. It was a mystery to her how Ludo had got under her skin so quickly. She'd never experienced such a tangible sense of connection with a man before, and everything that she believed about herself had been turned on its head.

'Okay. I'll expect your calls later on in the week, then,' she murmured.

'Good. By the way, when we arrive in Rhodes the weather should be seasonally hot. Bring plenty of suitable clothing and sun-cream,' he suggested.

The sociable smile that accompanied his words was far warmer than she'd expected after the sorrow he'd just expressed about the loss of his brother, and Natalie was already nursing a secret hope that he might talk about his sibling more fully during their time together in Greece. There was so much about this complex, surprising man that she longed to discover.

'I will.'

She couldn't help feeling shy all of a sudden, and curled her palm round the brass doorknob, then swept out of the office into the reception area—only to be confronted by the curious glances of Ludo's colleagues.

After giving her father the good news that Ludo had increased the sum he had paid for the business, and hearing that he was much more optimistic about his future because of it, the following day Natalie returned home to Hampshire. Trepidation, hope and great doubt accompanied her.

First and foremost, she could hardly believe that she'd agreed to go to Greece with Ludo in just a week's time and endeavour to convince his parents that they were engaged. Surely they would know immediately that an unremarkable girl like her was the least likely woman he would choose as a fiancée? For a start, she was a million miles away from the perfect-looking women who adorned the arms of rich and powerful men like their son in the glossy magazines.

But the following evening when Ludo phoned, trepidation and doubt instantly fled to be replaced by a totally unexpected wild optimism and hope. All it took was hearing the sound of his rich baritone voice.

Without preamble he announced, 'It's me—Ludo.'

About to take a bath, Natalie grasped the white bathsheet she'd wrapped round her torso to make it more secure, just as if he'd suddenly appeared in the room and his arresting cobalt gaze was resting on her semi-naked form. Dropping down onto the bed, she sent up a fervent prayer that her voice wouldn't betray how strongly his call had affected her. Despite agreeing to go to Greece with him, it felt somehow surreal that the handsome businessman should call her personally.

'Hi,' she answered, the nerves she'd hoped she'd banished already alarmingly evident. 'How are you?'

'Tired and very much in need of a holiday.'

The surprisingly unguarded reply took Natalie aback and filled her with concern. 'Well, thankfully you don't

have too long to wait before you get away…just a few
more days.'

'Presumably I don't need to check you *are* still coming with me?'

With thudding heart, Natalie said quickly, 'No, you
don't need to check. When I give my word I keep it.'

'Good. Do you have a pen and paper at hand? I want
to give you some flight details.'

When she'd written them down she asked, 'Is that
all?'

'No.' She heard a disconcerting smile in his voice.

'I'd like to talk to you some more. What have you
been doing with yourself today?'

Sighing, Natalie smoothed her hand down over the
soft towelling nap of the bathsheet. Not that it remotely
mattered, but if Ludo intended talking for much longer
then her bathwater would be turning unpleasantly cold.

'What have I been doing? Helping to organise some
help in the B&B while I'm away, and also seeing to
some rather tedious administration, I'm afraid. But
thankfully it was alleviated by my mum's baking. Just
after three she brought me in some homemade scones
and jam with a cup of tea. No one in the world makes
scones as melt-in-the-mouth and tasty as she does!'

'You have an extremely sexy voice, Natalie. I can't
be the only man who's ever told you that.'

Dumbfounded, Natalie automatically shook her head,
as if Ludo was indeed in the room. The only thing she
could conjure up right then wasn't an answer but a mental picture of him smiling at her. The sculpted planes
of his tanned cheekbones, chiselled jaw and intense

sapphire-coloured eyes were more than enough to drive away any intelligible reply.

'Natalie? Are you still there?'

'Yes, I'm still here. But I ran a bath just before you rang and it must be getting cold. I'm afraid I'll have to go.'

On her feet, she carried her mobile to the slightly ajar bathroom door and anxiously bit down on her lip as she waited for his reply. The comment he'd made about her having a sexy voice had unravelled her.

'Well, then, you must go and take your bath. But know this… I don't think I'm going to be able to sleep at all tonight, since I will have in my mind the arresting image of you naked, soaking in a bath of scented bubbles. I hope when I ring again tomorrow night you'll end the conversation on a far less provocative note? Goodnight, Natalie. Sleep well.'

By the time Natalie had roused herself from the trance she'd fallen into, her bathwater and the scented bath foam she'd poured into it were too cold to contemplate immersing herself in. Resigning herself to going without, she pulled out the plug and once again got lost in thoughts of Ludo as she watched the water spiralling urgently down into the drain…

It had been a far from easy journey to his homeland for Ludo. The inner turmoil of his thoughts had made it impossible for him to relax.

The private plane he'd chartered was the epitome of the luxury he'd long come to expect when he travelled. As far as that was concerned there had been nothing to complain about. The cabin crew had been ultra-professional and attentive, and the flight had been smooth without any disconcerting turbulence. But even though the sight of Natalie at the airport, in a pretty multicoloured maxi-dress, with her shining hair, had quickened his pulse, it had still been difficult to raise his spirits.

Ludo had immensely enjoyed and indeed looked forward to the nightly telephone conversations he'd had with Natalie, but when she'd sat beside him on the plane, every now and then attempting to engage him in light conversation, he hadn't found it easy to respond in the same cheerful fashion he'd been able to adopt on the phone. In fact his mood had deteriorated more and more the closer they'd got to their destination.

The phone conversation he'd had with his mother earlier that morning had been a double-edged sword. While it had been a joy to hear her voice, and to be able to relate some good news to her, it didn't assuage the onerous weight of guilt and pain that still dogged him over his brother's death. Clearly overwhelmed and excited about the prospect of seeing Ludo again after three long years, his mother had had an emotion in her voice that had almost made it hard for him to breathe, let alone speak. There had been no words of reprimand or blame to make him feel guiltier than he was already, and somehow that had made the prospect of seeing her and his father again even more difficult.

Naturally they'd wanted to send a car to bring him and Natalie back to their spacious villa, but Ludo had carefully and respectfully declined the offer. He'd told her that he and Natalie were going to stay at his own waterside villa and take a valuable day's rest before they drove out to see them. Even though his absence had been a prolonged one, he'd need a little more time to acclimatise himself to the fact that he was home again, as well as time to take stock.

His mother had naturally been curious about Natalie. 'What's she like?' she'd asked excitedly. 'Are you happy with her, my son?'

All Ludo had told her was that Natalie was a 'charming, good-natured girl' and that he was sure they would love her. He'd deliberately squashed down the wave of remorse that had crashed through him because he was inventing a scenario that wasn't true.

For some strange, inexplicable reason, at the back of his mind the tentative hope had surfaced that some good might come of being with Natalie despite his deception. He hadn't just enjoyed their nightly phone conversations, he had started to *rely* on them. She'd always been so reassuring, and if he'd had a bad day his spirits had been buoyed by the idea of talking to her. He'd never experienced such a strong connection to a woman before. And the memory of the sexy, ardent kiss that he'd shared with her back in his office a week ago had definitely got him believing that having her with him in Greece might help alleviate some of the stress that would inevitably come his way.

But he also knew it would take more than one kiss or a reassuring conversation to ease the grief and anxiety he was feeling about returning home again.

Finally, just before they'd reached the cosmopolitan

Greek island they were heading for, Natalie had shaken him out of his morose mood with an unexpected comment.

'As you know, I'm not undertaking this trip purely because I'm in love with the idea of going to Greece, or because I need a holiday. I'm doing it because you offered me a deal that was impossible to refuse. While I'm not exactly looking forward to playing your fiancée, I respect the fact that you paid my father a much more realistic price for his business than you initially offered. And because of that I fully intend to honour my part of the bargain. However, it's a little off-putting that you don't seem to want to talk to me. If it's because you're having second thoughts about bringing me with you, I want you to know that I'm perfectly willing to get on the next flight home just as soon as it can be arranged.'

It was as though she'd dashed a bucket full of ice water in his face. For one thing, it didn't do his ego a whole lot of good to hear her confess that she wasn't looking forward to playing his fiancée and was willing to go home if he'd changed his mind. Turning in his seat, he studied the troubled but defiant expression on the lovely face before him with a stab of remorse.

'That is most definitely *not* what I'd prefer, *paidi mou*. Forgive me for not being a more amiable companion. It is nothing to do with my not wanting to be with you. It is purely a private dilemma that has been preoccupying me.'

Folding her hands in her lap across the pretty colourful fabric of her dress, Natalie lifted her huge grey eyes to his. 'Is that dilemma to do with returning to

Greece for the first time since your brother died? The last thing I want to do is distress you by asking you to talk about it, but don't you think it would help us both if you opened up a little? I'm sure it's going to seem very strange to your parents if I haven't got a clue about what your brother was like or how you felt about him.'

Ludo stared. What she said was perfectly true. He now saw that he hadn't given his impromptu plan nearly enough consideration. As painful and uncomfortable as it might be, he had no choice but to talk to Natalie about Theo.

Linking his hands together, he felt his heart race a little as he attempted to marshal his thoughts. 'Very well, then. I will tell you something of my brother Theo. Where do I begin? He was a giant of a man—our very own Rhodes Colossus... Not just in build—he was six foot four—but in character and heart too. Ever since he went to medical school to train as a doctor he knew he wanted to specialise in taking care of children.' He allowed himself a briefly strained smile. 'So that's what he did. He became a paediatrician. At the clinics he attended, or on the wards, the kids just loved him. More than that, when he told them he would make them better they totally believed him…as did their parents. More often than not he was able to keep that heartfelt promise. Pretty soon his services were in demand not just in Greece but all over Europe.'

Natalie's answering smile was unreserved and encouraging. 'It sounds as though he was quite a man. You and your parents must have been so proud of him.'

'Everyone was. He might have been my brother, but it was a privilege to know him, let alone be related to him.'

'Was he married? Did he have children of his own?'

The flush of pink that Ludo realised was a given whenever she was remotely embarrassed or self-conscious was very much in evidence again.

'No.' He hefted a sigh. 'He used to tell us all he was married to his work. He may not have been a father biologically, but he was father to many children when they were in his care.'

'I wish I'd been able to meet him.'

'If you had, you would never have given me a second glance.' The painfully wry comment was expressed before Ludo had a chance to check it.

Natalie's perfectly arched brows lifted in bewilderment. 'Why would you say that? You must know you have many appealing qualities—and I'm not referring to your wealth.'

'My brother was admired for his kind and unselfish nature as well as his desire to help heal children afflicted by illness or disability. Compared to him, my own achievements are a lot less worthy and nowhere near in the same league.'

'I can't believe you mean that. Not everyone has the skill of creating wealth like you do, Ludo—wealth that no doubt helps create jobs and opportunity—and I'm sure a lot of people wish they had. I don't doubt your family is as proud of you as of the son they sadly lost.'

'My parents will tell you they are, but my brother was a tough act to follow. He was a son in a million... irreplaceable.'

Natalie fell silent. The sadness in her eyes took Ludo aback. He regretted being so candid with her. He had never craved anyone's sympathy and never would, yet her unstinting kindness undid him.

Quickly searching for a new topic to divert her, he said, 'I should have asked you this before, but how did your parents take the news you were coming on this trip with me?'

He was disturbed by the idea that she might have put herself in an awkward position with her family. He didn't want them to give her a hard time over it. No doubt it would taint the experience for her if they did. Where he came from family were the number one priority, and he completely understood Natalie's devotion to her own. Clearly she didn't want to worry or shame them by taking off with a man they didn't even know. Even her father had only met him that one time in his office, and the occasion would hardly have let him warm to Ludo in any way.

As he silently observed her, Ludo felt his heartbeat quicken at the increasing evidence of her thoughtful and caring nature. It didn't hurt that she was rather beautiful too... To his surprise, the dour mood that had plagued him since the start of the trip lightened.

'My dad was very worried at first,' Natalie confessed. 'When I told him you'd substantially increased what you paid for the business he feared you'd only done it to try and blackmail me into becoming your lover.'

Her porcelain cheeks suddenly acquired the most radiant shade of pink Ludo had ever seen. But, surprisingly, he found he wasn't offended by the idea that her father had feared he was blackmailing his daughter, because he understood the older man's natural concern. It would surely take a hard-hearted father *not* to be concerned. Ludo was pleased that Natalie had frankly admitted it, because it gave him the opportunity to set her straight.

'I have been known to be ruthless in my bid to seal a deal, but I am no blackmailer, Natalie. Besides, does your father really think I'd need to resort to that in order to make you my lover?' Gently touching her lips with his fingertips, he was intrigued to know her response. 'I wouldn't, would I, Natalie?'

CHAPTER SIX

HER EYES WIDENED to incandescent twin full moons.

'Of course you wouldn't. I'm quite capable of making up my own mind about whether I take a man as a lover or not, without being coerced by the promise of money or—or whatever.'

Frowning and pursing her lips, she let her long hair slip silkily round her face, as though to shield her from closer scrutiny, and it made Ludo want to brush it back for her with his fingers. He would have done exactly that had she not started talking again.

'I told him I thought that despite your wealth and position you were most likely a decent man. I told him you'd suggested that if I spent some time with you in Greece I could benefit from learning important business skills that would help me in the future.'

'And you didn't mention that I'd asked you to assume the role of my fiancée?'

Hectic colour once again suffused her features. 'No…I thought it best not to mention that part.'

'I'm not sure whether I should take your declaration about me as being "most likely" a "decent man" as a compliment or not. The way you said it leaves me with the feeling that perhaps you doubt it.'

'I don't.'

In her haste to reassure him Natalie automatically laid her hand over his. Never before had the simple touch of a woman's hand inflamed Ludo to the point of wanting to haul her onto his lap and make love to her there and then, but that was what he felt at the sensation of her cool soft skin against his and the alluring drift of her pretty perfume.

'Even though you said you didn't want me to pay you back,' she continued, 'I haven't forgotten your generosity in paying for my train fare. Not many people would have been so quick to help out a complete stranger, and that absolutely illustrates how decent you are.'

The tension in his shoulders started to ease. He wouldn't normally care what a woman thought of his character if he was contemplating taking her to bed, but with Natalie he found he definitely craved her good opinion. The nightly phone calls they'd shared had played a big part in changing his attitude, especially when she'd talked about being concerned for family and friends, even the guests who stayed at the bed and breakfast. Her store of kindness knew no limits, it seemed.

'I confess to being reassured. What about your mother? What did she think of you going to Greece with me?' he asked interestedly. 'Did you tell her who I was, *glykia mou*?'

'Yes, I did.'

'And what did she say?'

To Ludo's great disappointment, she withdrew the

slim hand that still lay over his and lightly shrugged a shoulder.

'She told me to be careful…then she told me to tell you that she was very sorry to hear about your brother. She'd heard of him, you see. She told me about his reputation for being an incredible paediatrician and that the Greek community held him in the highest regard.'

Learning that Natalie's mother was Greek had been one thing. But discovering that she'd heard of his brother as well as of his shocking demise was deeply unsettling. He was also disturbed that she'd advised her beautiful daughter to 'be careful'. She could only mean one thing. Presumably, in her eyes, Ludo wasn't held in the same high regard as his brother had been. *No change there, then.* His lighter mood evaporated like ice beneath a burning sun.

'Hopefully that will reassure her that you are in good hands,' he commented dryly, 'even though it sounds like she mistrusts me. Why else would she warn you to be careful?'

'Every mother who cares about her grown-up daughter worries about who they're associating with… especially when it comes to men.'

'Well, my beautiful Natalie, I will do my best to allay her fears and send you home completely intact.'

Smiling ruefully, he signalled to the male flight attendant standing nearby and without hesitation ordered a glass of Remy Martin brandy.

On their arrival at his stunning waterside villa, Ludo's housekeeper Allena and her husband Christos came out to greet them. As he found himself embraced by two of the warmest hugs he'd had in a very long time Ludo was almost overcome by the couple's genuine pleasure at seeing him again. It made him realise just how much he'd missed their familiar faces and unreserved regard.

They were a little more politely restrained when he introduced them to Natalie, but their smiles couldn't hide their pleasure and curiosity. *He didn't doubt they'd heard on the grapevine that he was bringing his fiancée home.* As a wave of guilt descended yet again, he filed it away irritably and refused to think about it. Wasn't it enough that he'd fulfilled his parents' wishes and come home?

After Allena had told him that she'd prepared something special for their dinner that night, and that there were cool drinks waiting for them out on the terrace, Christos lifted their luggage from the car and he and his wife transported it into the villa to dispatch it to their rooms. Relieved that he could have Natalie to himself for a while, in the privacy of his own home, Ludo guided her through the open-plan living room out onto the large terrace to take in the view. He couldn't deny the sense of pride it gave him to know that she would adore it.

The shimmering azure sea glinting in the midafternoon sun just a few feet from the door was like a sheet of sparkling glass it was so still and perfect. And the warm scented breeze that blew in to caress her skin was infused with the most heavenly scent of bougainvillaea. With delight Natalie saw that the radiant red and pink flowers were generously draped over every dazzling white wall in sight. It was hard to believe she hadn't wandered into a dream. For a long time she had yearned to come back to Greece, and to find herself here in this breathtaking idyll with a man as handsome and charismatic as Ludo Petrakis made the experience seem even more like the most incredible fantasy.

'What a gorgeous view! It's just wonderful! It's even more stunning than I'd hoped it would be,' she breathed, letting her hands rest on the sun-warmed railing of the stone-pillared balustrade.

Her companion smiled fleetingly. 'Many people call it the Jewel of the Aegean.'

'It must be,' Natalie concurred.

Ludo shook his head. 'Personally, I think that title should go to *my* island.'

'What do you mean, *your* island?' She wasn't sure why, but underneath her ribs Natalie's heart bumped a little faster. It was already racing due to Ludo's enigmatic smile. Her only regret was that she wished his smiles weren't quite so rare...

'It is called Margaritari, which is the Greek word for pearl.'

'That's beautiful. And this island? It's somewhere that you're particularly fond of?'

His chiselled profile was facing out to sea as she asked him this, and a sudden breeze lifted some dark golden strands from his hair and blew them across his forehead. As Natalie stared, mesmerised, a muscle flinched in the side of his carved cheekbone and he went very still.

'I was so enamoured of it that I bought it. Sadly, I

am not so enamoured of it any more, since my brother died there in the boating accident.'

As she reeled from the shocking admission Ludo left her side to make his way to a cane chair positioned next to a slatted wooden table and sat down.

'I hardly know what to say.' Immediately she moved to the other side of the table, so that she could see his expression. 'What a devastating blow for the accident to have happened on the waters of your own island.'

It was almost unbearable to think of Ludo being consumed not only by grief but also by guilt. Did he blame himself for the accident? Was that why he sometimes looked so troubled and didn't believe he was as well regarded as his brother Theo had been?

'It was…it *is*.' He didn't bother to try and disguise the painful emotion that gripped him. It was written all over his face. 'I had often urged him to take a holiday and make free with the island for as long as he wanted. It is so private there that only people I personally invite are allowed to stay. It is a magical place, and I'd hoped it would work its magic on him and help him relax. He rarely took time off from his work and my parents often expressed their concern that he looked so tired.'

Restless again, Ludo shot to his feet and strode round the table. He stopped directly in front of Natalie, and the look in his diamond-chipped blue eyes was so full of torment it made her catch her breath.

'He finally took up the offer and went to stay there. One day he took a boat out and it capsized. It was hard to understand how it had happened… Theo was a good sailor. But I found out afterwards that there were strong gusts of wind that day. Apparently they must have caught the mast and turned the boat over before he could do anything about it. He was a good swimmer, but the coroner told us that if he had been particularly fatigued his reactions would have been slow, and that's why he had been dragged under the boat and drowned.'

'Ludo, I'm so sorry…really I am.'

'A thing like that…a loss so grievous…the pain of it never goes away.'

It was a purely humanitarian instinct to offer comfort that made Natalie bridge the short distance between them and embrace him. At first she sensed his body turn rigid as the trunk of an oak, immovable, with no give or softness in it whatsoever. Her stomach sank to her boots as she thought she'd done the wrong thing. But before she could retreat self-consciously Ludo captured her shoulders and crushed her lips beneath his in a searing, passionate kiss that stole her breath and rendered her limbs weak as a new-born babe's.

The leap of unexpected raw desire that shot through her in response was like a lightning bolt appearing out of a cloudless blue summer sky. She emitted a hungry groan that she could scarce believe was her. It was coupled with a delicious languorous ache that suddenly stole over her like a fever, and Natalie couldn't help but kiss him back with equal ardour, loving the feel of his hard, honed body beneath her explorative fingers so much that she didn't at first register his palm spreading over her breast or sense that he was aroused.

Stunned that she'd let things progress quite so far, she immediately started to draw away. But Ludo held her fast, lifting his head to gaze down at her with a sensual, rueful smile that made her heart thump hard.

'Where do you think you are going?'

The commanding tenor of his captivating voice made it impossible for her to move.

'I shouldn't have done that.' Even though she'd intended to withdraw, his languorous sexy gaze continued to transfix her.

With his hands now resting lightly on her hips, Ludo made no concession to the comment other than to subject her to a provocative study of her eyes and lips.

'You did absolutely the right thing, *paidi mou.* Make no mistake about that. I was in a dark place and your warm, very welcome embrace brought me out into the light.'

'Then I don't regret it.' Proffering a tentative smile, Natalie found she could neither move nor look away, and didn't wish that she could.

'That pleases me very much.' His hand reached out to capture a long strand of her glossy brown hair and he wound it round and round his fingers, as though mesmerised by the treasure he'd found.

If his housekeeper hadn't appeared on the patio just then Natalie wondered how long he would have kept her there, just playing with her hair and staring at her as if he'd like to do so much more…

'Excuse me, Mr Petrakis.' Allena's charming faltering English was no doubt in deference to his guest. 'Your rooms are ready.'

'*Efharisto,* Allena,' Ludo replied, reluctantly freeing the coil of hair he'd captured and stepping round to Natalie's side.

Feeling her face grow hot at being caught out in what could have been a highly awkward situation, she turned slowly. Her lips still ached and throbbed from the passionate kisses she'd exchanged with Ludo, and the expensive musky cologne he used that smelled of pure sex clung to her skin, as though to ensure she would never forget the encounter. Just in time she remembered there was no need for any awkwardness or embarrassment as she was supposed to be Ludo's fiancée. But the inflammatory thought didn't help to cool the heat that still tumbled like an unstoppable raging river through her bloodstream...

'Come.'

Placing his hand beneath her elbow, the man at her side led her back into the pleasantly cool villa and up a flight of white marble stairs. Determinedly holding on to the fact that Allena had said 'rooms', and not 'room', Natalie tried not to feel so tense. Even though she found herself intensely attracted to Ludo, it was still overwhelming to imagine being in his bed. For one thing, her experience of such a scenario was extremely limited. In fact one might legitimately say it was non-existent. No wonder she was tense. And if that weren't enough to contend with tomorrow she would be introduced to his parents as his intended bride-to-be! What if they saw immediately that she was merely putting on an act and she was no such thing?

'This room is for you.'

Gesturing that she should enter the light and spacious

room ahead of him, Ludo was quiet as Natalie endeavoured to take in her luxurious surroundings. Her heart raced when her gaze fell on the imposing carved bed in front of her. With its sash curtaining of sumptuous gold silk and matching counterpane scattered with an array of scarlet and gold-braided cushions, it was a bed fit for a princess. More than that, Natalie thought, it was a bed created for the perfect *seduction*...

Realising that Ludo was intimately observing her reaction, she didn't let her gaze linger a moment longer than necessary on the imposing bed. Frowning, she examined the art on the walls instead. It didn't help matters when she saw that the framed scenes depicted some of the most sensually charged stories in Greek mythology. There was an elegant print of *The Awakening of Adonis* by John Waterhouse, and two skilfully executed oil paintings of the beautiful Aphrodite and Andromeda. Andromeda was depicted in the part of the legend where she was chained to the rocks before Perseus came to rescue her from the sea monster.

Studying the pictures of the two bare-breasted women, Natalie felt the blood slow and thicken in her veins as though it were treacle. Ever since she'd first laid eyes on Ludo she seemed to have developed a heightened awareness of her womanhood—of needs that had lain dormant for too long without true opportunity for release. It was extremely disconcerting that they should come to the fore now.

She turned away and a far less provocative scene met her gaze, utterly stilling the anxious thoughts dominating her mind just then. Emitting a heartfelt sigh of pure pleasure, she stared transfixed at the awe-inspiring vista presented before her. The generously proportioned French windows stood open to reveal the most breath-taking view of the sparkling, still aquamarine sea. An exquisite breeze imbued with the arresting tones of bougainvillaea and pine in drifted intoxicatingly just at that very moment. Overwhelmed at her good fortune in being able to experience such beautiful natural delights, Natalie turned round to share her joy with her host.

'I'm almost speechless. This is one of the most incredible views I've ever seen. I feel so lucky.' She smiled, then added quickly, 'To be here, I mean.' Her smile started to slide off of her face when she saw the knowing look in Ludo's arresting blue eyes.

'Because you are here with me or because you have fallen in love with my country?' he teased.

'I've always been in love with Greece,' she murmured, crossing her arms over the soft linen bodice of her dress. 'This is my mother's country too, remember?'

'I did not forget, my angel. Did you think I had?'

He had gradually been moving towards her as he spoke, and now he stood in front of her with a scorching glance hot enough to melt her innermost core. Nervously, Natalie smoothed a less than steady hand down the front of her dress. 'You said—you told me that this was my room? I have to ask…do you intend to share it?'

'No, Natalie, I do not.' His flawless blue eyes glinted enigmatically. 'The only room you will share with me— and then only if you invite yourself—is *mine*. It is right next door to this one and the door will always be open during the night, should you feel inclined to visit me, *glykia mou.*'

It wasn't what she had expected him to say at all. For a long moment, even though her mind teemed with all the possible reasons she could think of as to why he didn't simply announce he was expecting her to act like his fiancée from day one and sleep with him—especially after their explosive kiss downstairs—Ludo's matter-of-fact answer perturbed her.

'That's fine,' she answered tetchily, immediately on the defensive. 'As long as you don't take it for granted that I *will* visit you.' Two hot flags of searing heat scorched her cheeks. 'We are only *pretending* to be engaged after all.'

Chuckling softly, Ludo lightly pushed back the slightly waving strand of hair that glanced against her cheekbone, and the movement reacquainted her with the tantalising drift of his provocative cologne.

'What a charming young woman you are, *glykia mou.* Yet, charming as you are, I hasten to remind you that we made a bargain, did we not?'

Lifting her chin, Natalie scowled, even as her heart thundered at her own daring. 'Yes, we did. But as far as I can recall our bargain didn't involve casual sex. We only agreed that I would come to Greece with you and *pretend* to be your fiancée. There was nothing said about our having intimate relations.'

'Are you saying that you are not attracted to me?'

'Clearly, after the kiss we shared downstairs, that would be a lie. But just because I find you attractive it doesn't mean I'm going to sleep with you at the drop of a hat!'

'No...?'

Even as he sardonically uttered the word Ludo overpowered her with an ardent embrace and once again captured her lips. As her mouth opened to receive the hot invasion of his tongue and his arms possessively encircled her narrow waist Natalie couldn't help whimpering with pleasure. Immediately his action acquainted her with the intoxicating heat radiating through his linen shirt, as well as the steely hardness of his strong, hard-muscled body. If he continued to drug her into submission with his arousing kisses, much as she secretly revelled in the seductive attention, she realised she wouldn't have a prayer of denying him that nocturnal visit—and the implications of such an action *terrified* her.

Dragging her lips determinedly away, she tried to shape what she hoped was a blasé smile. 'Do you think I might have some time to myself to unpack? Perhaps when I'm done I could join you for that cool drink your housekeeper said was out on the terrace?'

'You certainly know how to drive a hard bargain, angel. Was that your intention? To drive me crazy with desire so that I will give you anything you ask for?'

'You make it sound like I have some kind of plan. I definitely don't. The only reason I'm here at all is because you agreed to pay my father a fairer price for his business. You kept your end of the bargain before we left England and now I'm keeping mine. Other than that

I have no expectations…except perhaps to enjoy a holiday. It's been a long time since I've had a proper break.'

The stunning Adonis in front of her threw up his hands in frustration. 'Then go and unpack your things and meet me out on the terrace as soon as you can. Just so that you know—my own intention is to monopolise every moment of your time while you are here, Natalie…so much so that when the time comes for you to leave the very notion of parting from me and my country will break your heart!'

Striding to the door, he didn't spare her a single glance before angrily departing. Staring after him, Natalie moved over to the sumptuous silk-covered bed and sank down onto it, clutching her hands over her chest in bewilderment and shock.

He was not a man to be easily subdued when frustrated. When a long cold shower didn't help temper his thwarted desire, Ludo strode out onto the private balcony adjacent to his bedroom in an attempt to lose himself in the breathtaking Mediterranean view that for the past three years he had denied himself. Vying with the tantalising images of Natalie he had in his mind, memories of his childhood and youth inevitably came flooding back.

Inhaling a deep breath, he endeavoured to get a better grip on his emotions. He had just started to relax a little when on the horizon glinting in the sunshine he glimpsed a small white sailing vessel. It was about the same size and proportion of the boat that Ludo's brother had used whilst staying on Margaritari. *Why didn't I*

insist on providing him with a bigger and sturdier ves-
sel? If I had it would have had a much better chance of
staying afloat in those gusting winds than the one Theo
used...the one Theo drowned beneath...

But even as his heart pounded with renewed sorrow and regret Ludo couldn't help remembering his big
brother's amused voice saying, 'You need more than one
sailor to handle a bigger boat, little brother, and I want to
be by myself on this holiday. I'm surrounded by people
every working day of my life, and often during the night
too if I'm on call. A small boat will do me just fine!'

Rubbing his chest with the heel of his hand, Ludo
freed a heartfelt sigh. Some way, somehow, he was
going to have to come to terms with what had happened to his brother properly, or the crowd of 'what ifs'
and 'if onlys' would burden him for the rest of his life.
He couldn't let that happen. If he did, then Theo's inspirational and admirable example of how to live a good
and useful life would be buried along with his memory.

Once again he sought to divert his troubling thoughts
with the memory of the honeyed heat of Natalie's sexy
mouth and the feel of her slim, shapely body in his arms.
Allowing himself a brief smile of anticipation, he wondered if tonight would be the night when she paid that
visit to his room. The hope that she would made him realise that it had been at least an hour since he'd left her
to her own devices—ostensibly to unpack and maybe
to take a reviving shower after their travels, like he had.
Surely she must be finished by now?

He'd noted that all she'd brought with her was one
small suitcase and a tote. Women in Ludo's experience

usually brought far more than that when going on holiday with him—but then he already intuitively knew that Natalie was unlike most of the women he was acquainted with. She was neither self-centred nor vain, and if he was right she wasn't trying to impress anybody either.

When he knocked on her door a couple of times and she didn't appear, he immediately turned on his heel and hurried downstairs to see where she had got to.

CHAPTER SEVEN

WITH HER INSIDES churning at the prospect of facing Ludo again after he'd stormed from the room, Natalie made herself unpack and hang up her clothes. This wasn't the way she'd envisaged her stay in Greece starting out.

In the streamlined, beautifully accessorised marble bathroom she took a quick cooling shower and then, in a bid to lift her spirits, selected one of her favourite dresses to wear. It was a burnt orange halter-neck in a flatteringly soft fabric that trailed elegantly down to her feet, and she teamed it with some pretty Indian bangles and flat Roman-style sandals. With the timeless Mediterranean glinting in the sun behind her, wearing the dress helped her feel as though she really *was* on holiday…at least so long as she didn't think about Ludo being angry with her, or the myriad of potentially difficult connotations of agreeing to pose as his fiancée.

What had he meant by his declaration that by the time she came to leave the very idea would break her heart? It had sounded as though he was furious that she would dare to deny him *anything*. It had already occurred to Natalie that he was probably a man who used physical gratification as a way to soothe deep private pain. Having been denied his chosen way of gaining some relief, it wasn't hard to understand why he'd reacted so furiously. The death of his brother and his own self-imposed exile from his home had to be weighing heavily on him. But, whatever Ludo's meaning, Natalie had heard pain and longing in his voice and that alone already had the power to break her heart.

Turning into the cavernous arched hallway that led to the dining room, kitchen and the herb garden so lovingly attended by Allena and her husband, Ludo discovered exactly where his guest had gone. She was immersed in animated conversation with Christos, and he saw with a start of pleasure that she was wearing the most beautiful burnt orange-coloured gown. Her long hair was arranged in a loose fashion on the top of her head, so that a few silken tendrils drifted free to frame her face, and the halter-necked design of the dress revealed her long slim neck and slender shoulders. The flowing material was the perfect foil for her stunning womanly form.

As if intuiting his presence Natalie turned, and the rose-tinted blush that heated her cheeks rendered her pretty as a picture. Ludo's lips shaped a deliberately slow and appreciative smile. 'So this is where you are. And I see that you have dressed for dinner. You look as lovely as Aphrodite herself. Come…let me look at you.'

Catching hold of her hand, he made her pivot slowly so that he could study every facet of the gown and her lovely, lissom shape. Behind them, Christos discreetly made his way out into the garden with a knowing smile.

'You remind me of a beautiful water-nymph in that

dress,' he commented, the timbre of his voice turning unwittingly husky.

'Aren't they supposed to be graceful, ephemeral creatures?' Her luminous grey eyes teasingly sparkled. 'You can't be comparing me to one of those, surely? When I was a child my dad always told me I was about as graceful as an elephant with two left feet.'

'I'd ask you if he was blind but, having met him, I know that he isn't.'

'No…I suppose he was just being realistic.'

'And you have carried the belief that you are not graceful around with you since you were a child?'

'It was just playful family banter. It doesn't mean that he didn't love me.'

As Natalie once again managed to bewitch him with her beautiful smile and sparkling eyes Ludo impetuously drew her against him, suddenly needing to hold her so he could once more experience the pleasure of having her in his arms, her exquisite feminine curves pressed up close to his body. It seemed that every time he touched her, every time he so much as *glanced* at her, a fire spread throughout his blood that wouldn't easily be extinguished. At least not until he made her his. Then and only then, when she gazed up at him with the same fever of longing and lust that he now experienced, would he attest to feeling remotely satisfied.

'He should have told you every day how beautiful, how precious you were to him,' he murmured, brushing a gentle kiss to the side of her velvet-soft cheek.

'He might never have said those exact words,' Natalie demurred, 'but I knew he felt the sentiment behind them. I'd hate you to get the wrong impression about him. Honestly, behind his bluff, confident exterior is a man who cares deeply about his loved ones.'

Happy to stay right where he was, with his hands resting lightly on the gentle flare of her slender and yet pleasingly curvaceous hips, Ludo stared hungrily back into the soft grey eyes and thoughtfully reflected on her comment.

'I seem to remember when we first met you questioned whether you were a kind and devoted daughter. In my opinion, from what I've observed so far Natalie, you most definitely *are*. But I think you take on far too much responsibility for your father. Is it your fault that he acquired the destructive habits that resulted in him being forced to sell his business?'

'Of course it isn't.'

Frowning, Natalie abruptly stepped away, and Ludo couldn't help regretting the impulse that had made him mention her father's debts. But he honestly felt aggrieved on her behalf. It was one thing being a good son or daughter, but quite another feeling responsible for every mistake a parent made. He sighed, and then, because she looked so enchanting, immediately found a smile.

'Please don't believe I am telling you how to think or feel. I am only concerned that you do not regard yourself enough. Also, it has been a lifelong habit of mine to be frank, and I know my earlier display of temper must have upset you.'

Moving nearer, he gently curled one of the long loose tendrils of hair that glanced against her cheek behind her ear. At first her answering smile was tentative and uncertain. But then, like the sun emerging from behind a rain cloud, the warm curve of her lips became quite simply exquisite.

'I'm not upset. The tensions of any journey can make a person snappy and on edge. But I'd like to be frank too, Ludo. I'm a firm believer that a worry shared is a worry halved. I know that you're still grieving for your brother, and you're worried about facing your parents after not seeing them for so long, but might it help you to talk about your concerns with me? Whatever you say, I promise I would never betray a confidence. I'd just listen and hopefully give you some support.'

'Of course you would.' His expression was sombre. 'It's probably what you do for all the waifs and strays and wounded hearts that come your way, isn't it? The bed and breakfast that you run with your mother is probably like a local, more comfortable branch of the Samaritans.' His lips twisted for a moment. 'And who wouldn't welcome a vision like you to talk to?'

He didn't mean to be cruel, but he couldn't quell the bitterness that suddenly surfaced in him. Why couldn't there have been someone like Natalie around when he'd heard the news that Theo had died? Someone he would have felt safe breaking his heart in front of? Someone who wouldn't judge him or see a chance to advance themselves in some way by their association with him?

He shook his head. 'I'm sorry, Natalie. But now is not the time for me to bare my soul. I am not saying I've completely closed the door on the possibility, but just not right now.'

She treated him to another understanding smile, and for a few captivating moments Ludo allowed himself simply to bask in it, as though it were warm rain after a cold, dry spell.

'Anyway,' she said, 'Christos was telling me about your garden—that it's full of orange and lemon trees. Can I see it?'

'It will be my pleasure to show you the garden, *glykia mou.*'

Cupping her elbow, Ludo couldn't help the glow of pride that swept through him that Natalie should be interested in the garden. The beauty and bounty of nature had always been one of his passions, right from when he was a boy, but apart from his mother, who had often talked about the healing power of it, he had rarely encountered women who felt the same way as he did.

Outside, Christos touched the tip of his straw hat in acknowledgement as Ludo and Natalie appeared. Speaking in Greek, he commented, 'You came at the right time to enjoy the oranges and lemons, Mr Petrakis. If you had left it much later the fruit would not have been at its best.'

'I know. And, by the way, thank you for all your hard work tending the gardens, Christos. I am convinced it is your magic touch that makes everything grow so abundantly.'

'It is my pleasure to be of service.'

Ludo was gratified to know that his devoted and respected employee was still happy to be working for him. When Christos and his wife retired he would make sure to provide them with a lovely home and garden so that he could continue enjoying his craft. Moving on, still cupping Natalie's elbow, Ludo guided her onto the meandering red stone path that led to the verdant green where the trees and fruit flourished so abundantly. Even before the trees came into view the air was drenched with the intoxicating scent of ripened fruit.

Breaking away from him, the woman by his side enthusiastically clapped her hands. 'This scent is incredible!' Her bright shining eyes and joyful enthusiasm were so engaging that for a moment Ludo was struck dumb.

'Walk on,' he invited smilingly, 'and you will see the fruit that is responsible.'

It was like walking into the Garden of Eden. Both the perfume and the sight of lush oranges and lemons hanging heavily from slim branches amid a bejewelled floral carpet of emerald-green was nothing less than wondrous. What added to her wonderment and pleasure was that her handsome companion seemed so much more relaxed than he had been earlier. It had given her heart when he'd told her he hadn't completely closed the door on baring his soul to her. A passing warm breeze lifted the gold lock of hair that glanced against his forehead, and in that instant he suddenly looked so carefree and young that she could imagine him in a gentler time, long before the unbearable tragedy of losing his beloved brother and separation from his homeland had etched indelible scars on his heart that likely would never be erased.

'It takes my breath away.' Shaking her head, she spontaneously held the palm of her hand over her heart.

'It makes me wonder what on earth I could have done to deserve being treated to such a sight.'

Without comment, Ludo walked over and took her by the hand. Unsure of what he was going to do, Natalie felt her heart drum hard as he led her across the grass to a fulsome lemon tree, plucked a plump yellow fruit from one of the branches, then tugged her hand towards him.

'Open your palm,' he instructed.

She obeyed, and he gave the lemon a hard squeeze so that the skin split and ripe juice spilled out into her hand like sparkling nectar, filling her nostrils with the sharp fresh scent of the sun-kissed fruit. As Ludo took his hand away Natalie moved her hand back and forth beneath her nose. 'It's glorious!' She smiled. 'It must be the freshest scent in the world.'

'If you add a teaspoon of sugar to the juice and rub your hands together I'm assured you'll have the best method of softening your skin that you could find.'

'How do you know that?'

With his sky-blue eyes squinting against the sunlight, Ludo grinned with pleasure.

'I heard about it from my mother. I used to watch her apply lemon juice and sugar to her hands after she'd washed the dishes. All I can tell you is that her hands were always soft as a child's. Don't take my word for it. When you get the chance give it a try.'

'I will.'

'Now, let's go over to the fountain and you can rinse your hands.'

At a magnificent solid-stone fountain, with its crystal-clear waters gushing from the upturned sculpted jug of a young shepherdess, Natalie rinsed her hands, bringing them up to her face to cool her sun-kissed cheeks. She knew it wasn't just the sun that had warmed them. Ludo Petrakis had cast the most mesmerising spell over her. A spell that right then she had no desire to ever be free of... 'That's better.' She smiled.

'Then I think we should go in to eat. Allena has prepared us something special, and if my guess is right it will probably be my favourite *moussaka,* followed by some *baklava.* I hope you have a sweet tooth, Natalie?'

'I do have a sweet tooth, and *baklava* happens to be a favourite of mine.'

Ludo's glance was slow and assessing, and in the ensuing momentary silence Natalie almost held her breath, wondering what he was thinking. She soon found out.

'It is very gratifying to know that you can yield to temptation, *glykia mou,*' he drawled. 'Because right now the temptation of *you* is sorely testing me.'

When he reached for her hand once again she let him clasp it without hesitation, loving the reassuring warmth of his touch and realising she could very easily become addicted to it.

Turning, Ludo led her back down the stone path and into the house...

After enjoying the superb moussaka and fresh three-bean salad that Allena had served them, also the delicious syrup-drenched baklava, they took their coffee out onto the terrace, where Ludo had first taken Natalie on their arrival. It was now almost full dusk, and the glass-like surface of the Mediterranean gleamed not with sunlight but with the bewitching, serene light of the moon.

Natalie leaned back in her rattan chair and sighed contentedly. About to share her thoughts on the beautiful scene with her companion, she saw that his eyelids were closed, and didn't know if he'd fallen into a light doze or was simply lost in thought. The journey on the plane had certainly been fraught with tension for him, knowing he was going back home for the first time since his brother's funeral. For now, she decided to keep her thoughts to herself so as not to disturb him.

It was certainly no hardship to relax with all the breathtaking beauty on display, and Natalie couldn't help but include Ludo in that description. More and more she was starting to believe that he was right. It *would* break her heart to leave this place…to leave *him*. The thought made her sit up with a jolt. The impulse she'd followed in accepting his deal to come with him was dangerously beginning to backfire on her. And tomorrow he was going to introduce her to his parents as his *fiancée*. As much as she was enamoured of this wonderful country, and longed to have the time to explore some of it, Natalie wondered if she really could go through with the pretence Ludo had suggested after all.

The sudden unexpected movement of his hand over a hard-muscled thigh in his cream-coloured chinos alerted her to the fact that he wasn't dozing at all, but just sitting quietly.

Reaching forward to collect her cup of coffee from the table, she ventured, 'Ludo? Are you all right?'

'Of course I'm all right. Why do you ask?'

'I was just concerned about how you were feeling. Ever since I told you that my mum had heard about what happened to your brother I've had the sense you've been retreating little by little. You hardly talked at all on the journey here. I didn't mean to upset you by telling you what she said.'

Lifting his hand to his forehead, Ludo rubbed a little, his blue eyes glinting warily as a cat's when confronted by some potential sudden danger.

'I sometimes think that Greek people round the world have an uncanny sense of knowing what's going on with each other even if they've never met. I shouldn't have been surprised that your mother had heard of the tragedy, but I was. If I seem to have shut down a little it's because any reference to my brother inevitably brings back great sadness and regret for me. I am also going to have to face my parents tomorrow and explain to them why I ran away after the funeral.'

Natalie swallowed hard. 'Ran away?'

'Yes. I packed my bags and left straight after the funeral without giving them any real explanation. I couldn't deal with their grief. It cut me like a knife to see them so heartbroken…not knowing what to do anymore. They had always been just like my brother Theo—steady and dependable. As if nothing, not even an earthquake, could shake their unified solidity.' He shook his head, agitatedly combing his fingers through his golden sun-streaked hair. 'And instead of supporting them through that terrible time and providing solace I chose to escape. I wanted to try and blot out the past and all that had happened by losing myself in my work and trying my damndest not to think about it.'

'And did that help?'

'Of course it didn't help!' Furious with himself, with Natalie, and perhaps with the whole world too, Ludo shot up from his chair, breathing hard. 'I discovered you can run away as far as you like—even to the remotest place on the planet—but you can't leave your sorrow and grief behind. Wherever you go, the pain travels with you. All running away did for me was add to my already unbearable sense of guilt and inadequacy. The realisation that as a son I had totally failed my parents— the people I love the most. They devoted their lives to raising me and Theo and look how I repaid them. It's unforgivable.'

The anguish in his voice immediately made Natalie get to her feet. 'You didn't do it deliberately, Ludo. It wasn't planned. You were hurting too, remember? It was a totally understandable reaction.'

Dropping his hands to his lean straight hips, he trapped her gaze with the sheer desolation in his eyes. 'The only way I can make it up to them is by introducing you as my fiancée, Natalie. That's why you have to do this for me. It is not enough that I return home by myself.'

'Why?' She stepped round the table to face him. 'Why isn't it enough? You're their beloved son, Ludo. A son any parents would be proud of. And people forgive those they love. Even when they've done the so-called "unforgivable".'

'Do they indeed?' His burning blue eyes gleamed

cynically. 'I wonder how you have become such an optimist. It is my experience that forgiving someone who has hurt you, and hurt you badly, is the hardest thing of all.'

'But if you see that you only hurt yourself more by not forgiving them, then maybe it's not so hard. For instance, when my dad walked out on my mum and me, I felt so heartbroken and betrayed that I thought I'd never trust him again. How could he do such a thing to us? I thought he was a liar and a cheat and deserved never to be happy again! For a long time I didn't even want to see him. But through it all my mum wouldn't hear one bad word said about him and she urged me to forgive him. Trust me, it wasn't easy… But it had to be done if I was ever to have any peace, because it was killing me holding all that blame and hurt in my heart. Then, when he had his heart attack, the decision to forgive him for everything was easy. I'm so glad I realised it, because now our relationship is closer than ever.'

Her heart was galloping as she came to the end of her impassioned speech—a speech that had asserted feelings she hadn't expressed to anyone before. Not even her mum.

Combing her fingers shakily through her hair, Natalie was appalled at herself. 'I'm sorry' she murmured, 'We were talking about your parents. I only wanted to illustrate that I believe if you really love someone that love never dies. I don't doubt for one second that your parents have already forgiven you, Ludo. My mother once told me that the love for your child surpasses any other and lives on even when a parent dies.'

Now her face was burning. The man in front of her had neither moved nor tried to interrupt her. Instead, the long, considered glance he was giving her suggested he was thinking hard, hopefully finding some solace in her assertion that a parent's love never died, no matter what their offspring had done. Natalie could only pray that it was true.

Beneath the white linen shirt he was wearing Ludo's broad athletic shoulders lifted in an enigmatic shrug that revealed very little about what he felt, and her anxiety skyrocketed—she had blundered in where maybe she shouldn't have.

'Whether my parents forgive me or not, we will find out tomorrow. But right now I intend to go for a very long walk so I can reflect on our reunion.'

'Would you like me to go with you?'

One corner of his mouth lifted slightly towards a high bronzed cheekbone. 'No. This is one walk that I must take on my own. If you want some entertainment ask Allena to show you what we have available. And if you think of anything else you need, just ask her. If you feel that you want an early night, go ahead. Don't trouble to wait up for me. We can talk again in the morning over breakfast. *Kalinihta,* Natalie. Sleep well.'

Stepping closer, Ludo almost absentmindedly brushed her cheek with his warm lips, and as he turned and walked away the warmth from his body stirred the air, mingling with the scent of bougainvillaea draped heavily over the terrace walls, as if the flowers too registered his leaving and couldn't help but be saddened by it.

CHAPTER EIGHT

HE LIKED THE night. Even more, he liked the night air of his country. No matter where a person went on the island, they breathed in air that was drenched with an eclectic variety of sensual aromas. Some of the most pervading scents were of olives and pine, bougainvillaea and jasmine, crusty bread baked in traditional fire ovens. And wherever people ate the delicious aroma of roasted meats and the freshest fish imaginable would tempt even the most jaded of appetites. But more than the tempting food and scents that lured tourists to the country time and time again Ludo loved the sight and sound of the Mediterranean and the Aegean best of all. It had always calmed and centred him, no matter what worry might be plaguing him at the time.

But the day he'd heard that Theo had drowned in the waters off Margaritari was the day that Ludo had come to *despise* the sea. How could he ever take pleasure in it again after it had so cruelly taken his brother from him?

Walking along the near deserted beach, he stopped to gaze up at the bewitching crescent moon that hung in the inky dome above him.

'Make a wish on the crescent moon,' his mother had

often told him and his brother when they were boys. 'If you do, it is bound to come true, my children.'

Well, Ludo had wished to be as rich as Croesus. No doubt Theo had made a much more humanitarian plea to be of service to those less fortunate than himself. Even as a young boy he had exhibited uncommon kindness and patience. But, no matter how wealthy or powerful he became, Ludo knew he would instantly give up every single euro he had if he could have his brother back.

Once again, a familiar arrow of grief pierced him as though he were on fire and, rubbing his chest in a bid to try and ease the pain, he made himself walk farther on down the beach. One or two tourists greeted him, and after reluctantly acknowledging them he quickly moved on. He wasn't in the mood to be sociable tonight.

Having removed his canvas shoes as soon as he'd stepped onto the sand, and despite the sorrow and regret that weighed him down, he briefly luxuriated in the sensation of sun-baked golden grains on the soles of his feet. The thought came to him that he should have brought Natalie. Why had he turned down her offer to accompany him? He should know by now that her presence soothed him. Soothed him and *aroused* him.

He suddenly felt a strong urge to hear her voice, to listen to the encouraging advice that seemed to come to her so naturally. What if he let down his guard and admitted he no longer wanted to endure the fears and concerns that plagued him on his own? What if he asked Natalie to *share* them? Would she be willing to do that for him?

But even as he mulled the idea over in his head Ludo

remembered how she had urged him to believe that his parents had already forgiven him for his negligence. It had dangerously raised hopes that would be cruelly dashed if they had not. Then where would he be? His so-called success meant nothing if he didn't have their unconditional love and respect.

His thoughts returned to Natalie. Would she have taken up his suggestion and had an early night? During their meal that evening she'd shielded a yawn from him more than once. She was probably looking forward to a good night's sleep—while he undoubtedly faced another torturous night wrestling with his fears about how tomorrow would go.

Damn it all to hell! Why couldn't he have engineered a simpler existence than the one he'd chosen? Instead of obsessively working himself into the ground and trying to accumulate even more wealth, what he wouldn't give right now to be wooing the love of his life—as his father had done when he'd met his mother—to be anticipating building a home and family together and perhaps living a good part of the year on Margaritari as he'd once dreamed he would? It hit him how tired he'd grown of the endless travelling that filled most of his year. What he really wanted to do was to spend some proper time with family and friends, to immerse himself again in the simple but solid values that shone like a beacon of goodness and common sense in a world that frequently moved too fast, where people restlessly went from one meaningless pleasure to the next in search of that most elusive goal of all…*happiness.*

The truth was that, for Ludo, the dog-eat-dog business world that he'd so eagerly embraced had all but lost its appeal since Theo died. He might have sought refuge in it when he'd exiled himself from his parents, but the exercise had failed miserably. All it had shown him was how emotionally barren his life had become. He was just kidding himself that he wanted to keep on travelling down the same soulless path. In truth, Ludo had missed his home and country much more than he'd realised.

Unbidden, a mental vision stole into his mind of Natalie holding out her hand beneath the lemon tree, so that Ludo might demonstrate the ripeness of the fruit. There was a strangely alluring innocence about her that grew more and more compelling every time he saw her. But it was playing merry havoc with his libido. Just thinking about her graceful slender figure, her river of shining hair and big grey eyes, made him feel near *desperate* to take her between his sheets and passionately seduce her.

Would she ever feel inclined, or indeed brave enough, to invite herself into his room one of these nights, as he'd suggested? Ludo didn't know why, but despite their almost instantaneous connection he'd intuited that he shouldn't seduce Natalie just to fulfil his own hungry desire for gratification. He should give her time to realise that her own needs were just as great as his. When she came round to the fact of her own free will, the heat between them would be nothing less than *explosive,* he was sure.

But it didn't help to dwell on the tantalising prospect. Kicking at the sand with another frustrated sigh, he found himself ambling towards the seashore.

He wasn't the only one to be won over by Natalie's charms. During dinner her genteel manners and ready smile had clearly formed a bond between her and Allena. Given the opportunity, would a similar bond ever be forged between Natalie and his own mother? Irritably reminding himself that their engagement was nothing but a bittersweet ruse, born of a desire to convince his parents to see him in a better light, Ludo emitted a furious curse. Reaching down, he picked up a small jagged rock that was half buried beneath the sand and threw it into the foaming moonlit waves lapping onto the shore.

Natalie had been so tired that she'd fallen asleep on the bed fully dressed. She'd tried hard to wait up for Ludo, but when the evening had worn on and he still hadn't shown she'd regretfully made her way upstairs to the bedroom.

After staring out at the moonlit sea from the terrace for what seemed like an eternity, thinking how tragic it was that the revered and beloved Theo had perished there beneath the waves, she'd found herself overwhelmed by a sense of sadness she hadn't been able to dispel easily. Lost in her poignant daydream, she'd experienced a moment of real panic, imagining Ludo walking alone by the seashore, with nothing but sorrow and regret accompanying him. She should have insisted that she join him, even if he'd got angry. It would have been worth the risk to make sure he was all right.

Finally, unable to fight what felt like sheer exhaustion, Natalie had crossed the room to the lavish bed, sat down to remove her sandals and before she knew it, had lain down curled up in a foetal position and fallen fast asleep.

She didn't have a clue what time it was when she woke the next morning, but the sun beaming in through the open patio doors was glorious. When she sat up and saw that she still wore the pretty orange dress she'd had on last night she shook her head in disbelief. That had never happened before. But then yesterday had been full-on, with all the travelling and its accompanying tension—that tension increasing when Ludo had chosen to go for a moonlit walk on his own last night and she hadn't seen him return.

Hurriedly stripping off the colourful dress, Natalie headed straight into the bathroom. But not before nervously wondering if Ludo thought her ungracious or rude for not waiting up for him. After all, it was hardly the behaviour of the supposedly devoted fiancée his parents were expecting to meet today, was it? The realisation of what she had pledged to do hit her again like a head-on collision. But the shock that eddied through her also acted as a spur for her to hurry up and present herself to her host. She realised she had a lot of questions to ask about their proposed visit to his family home.

A smiling Allena informed Natalie that Ludo was out on the terrace, waiting for her to join him for breakfast. Drawing in a long, deep breath, she hovered in an arched doorway that was draped with blossom, silently observing him as he lounged in a cane chair with his knees drawn up against his chest and his arms loosely wrapped round them.

His attire today consisted of a casual white linen shirt and rust-coloured chinos. His feet were bare. With the stunning vista of the sparkling ocean glinting in the sun before him, his sun-kissed golden hair and long limbs made him resemble a beautiful dancer in repose, and her heartbeat skittered nervously. She was utterly mesmerised by the breathtaking picture he made.

Turning suddenly, he took her completely by surprise with his greeting. How long had he known she was standing there?

'*Kalimera,* Natalie. I trust you slept well?' he drawled, smiling.

The stunning sapphire eyes that crinkled at the corners when he utilised his smile rendered her temporarily speechless.

Quickly gathering her wits, she replied, 'I slept like a log, thanks. In fact I was so tired last night that I fell asleep fully clothed and didn't wake up until about half an hour ago. I hope I haven't kept you waiting too long?'

'I was expecting you to arrive at any moment—so, no. You didn't keep me waiting too long. And even if you did it was worth the wait. You look very lovely in that dress.'

The simply-cut cornflower-blue dress that Natalie wore had short sleeves and a pretty sweetheart neckline, embroidered with the tiniest of white daisies, and the folds of the skirt draped softly down to her knees. She loved it because her mother had bought it for her trip to Greece, professing it to be modestly respectable but pretty enough to win her the 'right' kind of attention. There was only one man whose attention she wanted to win, Natalie privately acknowledged, and that was the real-life Adonis sitting in front of her.

'Thanks. My mum bought it for me.'

'Ahh… Now I see why you chose to wear it today. It's exactly the kind of dress that a Greek mother would buy for her young and beautiful daughter. A dress she can confidently wear to a family gathering with friends and relations. It is suitably virginal and will definitely make the right impression,' he teased. 'Now, why don't you come to the table and help yourself to some yogurt and honey for breakfast?'

Still reeling from his comment that her dress was 'suitably virginal', Natalie hurriedly pulled out a chair opposite him and sat down—anything to stop Ludo seeing that she was blushing painfully. As she scooped some yogurt into a cereal bowl from the generous ceramic dish in front of her she was in no hurry to meet his omniscient gaze.

'I waited up for you for quite some time last night,' she told him. 'What time did you get in?'

'About one or two in the morning.' He shrugged. 'Who knows? I was hardly keeping track of the time.'

'Did it help to clear your head, going for such a long walk?'

'Perhaps.' His reply was painfully non-committal.

'It's a tremendously brave thing that you're doing, Ludo—coming back home after three years and facing what happened,' she told him encouragingly. 'Your parents must be so happy at the prospect of seeing you again.'

'You are an eternal optimist, I think.'

'Maybe I am.' Natalie frowned. 'But I'd rather believe in hope and resolution than be cynical.'

'You should try some honey with your yogurt. I am sure you know it is traditional.'

Suddenly his piercing blue eyes were boring into hers and she forgot what she'd been going to say.

'Here…'

Leaning towards her, he scooped up a teaspoon of the richly golden nectar. Just when Natalie expected him to stir it into her helping of yogurt he touched the spoon to her lips for her to sample it instead. Her body tightened and the tips of her breasts tingled fiercely at the sensual nature of the gesture. Obediently and self-consciously she licked the honey off the spoon. The whole time she was hotly aware that Ludo was staring at her.

'Hmm,' she responded, emitting a soft sigh. 'It's delicious.'

Her expression was no longer self-conscious but laced with helpless invitation. The man was driving her crazy! Natalie might not be experienced in the art of seduction, but she was getting close to desperate for Ludo to seduce *her*. In turn, he gave her an amused slow smile that made her want to rip off his shirt, discard the pretty blue dress that he'd declared 'suitably virginal' and all but drag him across the table and insist he make love to her…

The thought made her bite her lip to prevent herself from giggling because it was so outrageous. It was also diametrically opposed to anything she'd ever contemplated in her life before.

'You're such a goody-two-shoes when it comes to

men, Nat,' a friend had once teased her. 'Haven't you ever met a man you simply just *had* to have?'

Not until she'd set eyes on Ludo Petrakis, she hadn't...

'You looked like you were about to laugh. What was so funny?' Ludo asked, depositing the spoon he'd used for the honey on a saucer.

'A crazy thought came into my mind, that's all,' she admitted warily.

'Want to share it with me?'

'No.' Tucking her hair behind her ear, she shrugged carelessly in a bid to deflect his curiosity. 'At least not right now. Can you tell me a little bit more about your parents before I meet them? And is it possible to stop off somewhere on the way to buy your mother a gift? I'd really like to get her something. Does she like flowers?'

'Of course—but she has a large garden full of flowers. You don't have to worry about getting her a gift. Your presence as my fiancée will be gift enough, Natalie.'

Feeling suddenly deflated, she frowned. Her brow puckered. 'But I'm not your fiancée, am I? We're only pretending that I am.'

The muscle that flinched in the side of his smooth tanned cheekbone indicated his annoyance. 'I know that.'

'At any rate, it's polite to take a gift when someone invites you into their home for the first time, isn't it?'

He sighed. 'If it means that much to you, angel, then we will stop off at a place I know and purchase a nice vase that she might put her own flowers in. Will that suffice?'

Feeling marginally better, Natalie somehow found a smile. 'Thank you. It does. Will you tell me a bit about what your mother is like? I'd really like to know.'

Ludo's expression instantly relaxed, as though the topic couldn't help but fill him with pleasure.

'She is a beautiful woman and a wonderful mother and she loves to put people at ease when they visit her. What else can I tell you?' His blue eyes twinkled in amusement. 'She is an incredible cook and an accomplished seamstress—she was a dressmaker before she met my father. He utterly relies on her, you know? But he wouldn't thank me for telling you that. He is a typical "man's man" and proud of it. Now, can you do something for me before we talk further?'

'What would that be?'

Her heart jumped a mile high as her gaze fell into his dazzling blue irises. She was still aroused. It was surely an impossible challenge to hold his glance for long and not reveal her desire? With his elbows resting on the table, Ludo leaned in a little closer—so close that she could count every single long golden lash that fringed his eyelids.

'Can you try not to look so adorable when you smile?' he asked huskily. 'It makes me want to wipe the smile clean off your face with a hot, languorous kiss that would very likely lead me into removing that pretty virginal dress your mother bought you and more besides.'

Just in time Natalie suppressed a groan. 'I don't think— I mean, I think we should—we should—'

'Give it a try?'

Swallowing hard, she reached for a white paper napkin and touched it to her lips, lightly dabbing at them. 'I think we should stay on a safer subject, don't you?'

'Even if it's nearly killing me to have you look at me with those innocent grey eyes and not tell you in graphic detail what I'd like us to do together in bed?'

'That's how I make you feel?' Her voice had dropped to a shocked whisper.

'You have no idea,' he growled, then abruptly got to his feet and drove his long fingers through his hair. 'But no doubt it will keep. We have to make the journey to see my parents very soon, and I suppose we should concentrate on getting ready.'

'How long will it take us to get there?'

'About an hour.'

'Where exactly do they live?'

'About four kilometres from Lindos, but the area is quite rural in comparison to the town. Thankfully, it's also close to the beach.'

'And that's where you grew up?'

Once again Natalie registered wariness in Ludo's eyes. He was still apprehensive about seeing his parents, and probably fearing the worst about their reception of him. She wished she knew a way to help put him more at ease.

He turned away to gaze out at the sea. 'Yes…it is where my brother Theo and I grew up. We had a truly magical childhood, living there. We were so free— which should be the right of all children, in my view. Most days we ran down to the beach to play before school. Then we'd run home in anticipation of our breakfast.'

'You had breakfast? I know that many Greeks don't… apart from drinking coffee, I mean.'

'My mother believed it was important for children to start the day with some food in their bellies.' With a wryly arched brow, he turned back towards her. 'She gave us soft cheese spread on sesame-seeded *psomi* to eat.'

'I love that bread. My mum still makes it now and then, especially when we have friends to dinner.'

Joining him, Natalie was mindful of not disturbing his poignant and unexpectedly heart-warming train of thought and couldn't deny the warmth it instigated in her own heart that he would share the memory with her.

'You will have to tell my mother. She is sure to want to know all about it.' Lifting his palm, Ludo briefly pressed it to her cheek, as if he didn't trust himself to let it linger. 'I think it's time that we went. If there is anything else you wish to ask me you can ask it on the journey.'

In the next instant he'd moved swiftly away to the open patio doors, and before she could reply he disappeared inside.

CHAPTER NINE

THE TRADITIONALLY BUILT white house that was so familiar to Ludo loomed up before them minutes before the Range Rover reached the end of the rutted undulating track they'd been travelling on. Although the architecture was typical of many homes in the locale, it was unusually tall and imposing. Built on the crest of a hill, it could be seen for miles.

The unmade track was very soon replaced by a smooth driveway lined with fig trees that led directly to the house's white-stone arched terrace. Behind the dwelling the deceptively calm waters of the Aegean created the most stunning iridescent backdrop, and even though he knew the house and the view well, it still made Ludo draw breath at the beauty of it.

But he didn't contemplate the scene for very long. Parking the car, he felt his stomach churn at the prospect of his first encounter with his parents after three long years. Was it possible that they would ever forgive him for his desertion at a time when they'd most needed him…particularly his mother? If they didn't, then he would simply just have to wish them well and walk away again—even if it broke his heart.

'Ludo?'

Beside him, Natalie's soft voice halted his painful reflection, reminding him he wasn't going to have to do this on his own. He remembered thinking about the possibility of sharing his worries with her last night and the tension in the pit of his belly eased a little.

'It's going to be all right.'

She smiled, and he reached out for her small hand and squeezed it in gratitude. It struck him afresh how pretty and innocent she looked today in the simple blue dress her mother had bought her. The conservative sweetheart neckline revealed not the slightest décolletage, yet in his opinion a sexy black cocktail dress couldn't have been nearly as alluring or beguiling.

'I'm sure you are right. If anyone has the ability to convince me of that it is you, *agapiti mou*. Let's do this, shall we?' His voice was gruffer than he'd meant it to be, but the relinquishing of his guard had left him feeling curiously vulnerable.

As he stepped down from the Range Rover onto the patterned marble drive he glanced towards the entrance of the house. With his heart beating double time he saw his parents walking towards them. Wearing an elegant blue tunic over white palazzo pants, her dark blonde hair shorter than he'd seen her wear it before, his mother Eva looked as effortlessly elegant as ever, if a little thinner. She was holding on to his father's strong muscled arm.

Unusually, his father was wearing a suit, as if to instigate some formality into the proceedings and perhaps to remind his errant son that he was a long way from being forgiven and accepted…at least by *him*.

Acutely aware that emotions were probably running high in all of them, Ludo returned his gaze to his mother and saw her smile tentatively, as if unsure how he was going to receive her. That uncertain look on her beautiful face twisted his heart. Yet because his father's expression was so serious he hesitated to throw his arms round her as he longed to.

He needn't have worried. Releasing her husband's arm, Eva Petrakis stepped onto the mosaic tiles where Ludo stood and wholeheartedly embraced him. Her still slender body trembled as he hugged her back without hesitation, his senses awash in a sea of childhood memories of her unstinting love and affection for him and his brother. Oh, how he had missed her!

With her hands resting lightly but firmly on his arms, as if she was reluctant to let him go, she stood back to scan his features. In Greek, she told him how worried she'd been about him, and that every night when she went to bed she'd prayed he was safe and well and planning on coming home soon…home where he belonged.

In return, Ludo murmured his sincere apology and regret. She smiled, gently touching his face. Then she told him that she knew far more of how he felt than he'd realised. There was no need for him ever to feel sorry about his actions again. She understood and had never blamed him for them, so neither should he blame himself. As hard as it had been for her and Alekos to accept, they had now reconciled themselves to the fact that it had been Theo's time. It was their profound belief that he was home with God now…

Leaning towards him, she planted a warmly affectionate kiss on Ludo's cheek and, lowering her voice, told him that he should give his father a little more time to realise what a great gift it was for them to have him home again. 'Be patient,' she advised sagely.

Observing his father across her shoulder, Ludo saw that sorrow and time had indeed taken their toll on him. There were deep grooves in the forehead of his handsome face, and his curling dark hair was more liberally sprinkled with salt and pepper strands than it had been three years ago. But without a doubt he still emitted the same formidable energy that Theo had envied so much.

'If I live to be my father's age and still have the strength and energy to accomplish as much in one day as he can,' he'd often declared, *'then I'll know the Petrakis gene pool hasn't failed me!'*

Swallowing down the lump that swelled in his throat at the bittersweet memory, Ludo moved away from his mother and determinedly went to stand in front of the man who had been responsible for raising him.

'Hello, Father,' he greeted him. 'It has been too long, yes?'

Even though he was absolutely sincere—because events and the passage of time had rendered the already considerable distance between them a veritable chasm—his words couldn't help but sound awkward and strained. Instead of embracing the older man, as he might normally have done, he held out his hand. Alekos Petrakis didn't take it. Ludo's tentative hopes for a reconciliation splintered like shattered glass.

'So you have deigned to come home at long last?' his father remarked coldly. 'I had hoped you would grow into a man to equal your brother Theo in conduct and character, but your absence these past three years has demonstrated to me that I hoped in vain. I do not recognise you, Ludovic, and it grieves me sorely that I do not.'

Ludo reeled. It felt as though he'd been punched hard. 'I am sorry you feel like that, Father. But Theo has his path and I have mine.'

The shame-filled break in his voice catapulted him back to being the small boy who'd longed to have his father regard him as highly as he did his big brother, and he couldn't help flinching in embarrassment as well as pain. The older man's admission had all but floored him. Didn't he see *any* good in him at all? Were the only people who had any kind of belief in his worth the two women who stood patiently waiting for him to join them?

'Had,' his father corrected him. 'You said Theo "has" his path. Your brother is no longer with us, remember?'

Ludo silently cursed the unfortunate blunder. The accusing look in his father's brown eyes cut him to the quick. Hardly able to bear it, he turned away, seeing with a jolt of surprise that his mother Eva had moved up close to Natalie and was exchanging a reassuring smile with her. Natalie held out the slim glass vase she had insisted on buying as a gift and his mother graciously accepted it. Remembering that she'd advised him to be patient with regard to his father, he determinedly quashed any further thoughts of failure and remorse and returned to the women.

'He doesn't want to know me,' he murmured, glancing ruefully at his mother, then at Natalie.

'He just needs a little more time, my son,' she answered in English. 'You both do. Time to get to know each other again.' Carefully setting down the delicate vase on a wrought-iron table behind them, Eva reached for his hand and gently squeezed it. 'Now, we have all been dreadfully remiss. You have not introduced us to your beautiful fiancée, Ludo, and I'd like you to remedy that. She has just given me the most beautiful vase as a gift and I am taken aback by her generosity.'

Without hesitation Ludo caught hold of Natalie's hand and gripped it firmly. An instantaneous bolt of electricity flashed between them and for a long moment his glance cleaved to hers. He wished they were somewhere more private, so he could show her *exactly* how she made him feel. It was a revelation that he seemed to need her so much. At the same time he knew it was important to make the proper introductions.

'Mother, this is Natalie Carr—and Natalie…this is my mother, Eva Petrakis.'

'*Kalos orises,* Natalie. Although I'm told that you are half-Greek, I will speak to you in English because my son tells me you do not speak Greek at home with your mother. It is a shame you do not speak it, but I'm sure that will change given time. I cannot tell you how long I have waited for the moment when I would welcome my soon-to-be daughter to our home, and it comes as no surprise to me to find that you are so beautiful. My son has always had the most exquisite taste.'

Natalie found herself affectionately hugged by the elegant and friendly Eva in a waft of classic Arpège perfume. She smiled because it was the same fragrance

that her mother wore, and it made her feel immediately
at home.

'Yia sas.' Using one of the few greetings in Greek
she *did* know, she said hello. 'It's so nice to meet you,
Mrs Petrakis. Ludo always talks about you with such
affection.'

She stole a glance at the man standing silently by her
side, quite aware that he'd become even more uneasy
since that short conversation just now with his father.
The older man seemed formidably stern to her. She
would dearly love to know what had transpired between
them, and guessed it wasn't good.

His mother, on the other hand, was clearly a different proposition. She seemed much more forgiving and
approachable. And even though Natalie wasn't really
the 'soon-to-be daughter' she'd longed for, strangely
she wasn't embarrassed that it wasn't the truth. All she
could think right then was that Ludo needed her help.
More than that, she'd made a contract with him that
she was bound to follow through on. He'd kept his part
of the bargain by giving her father a better deal for his
business, and now she had to act the part of his fiancée convincingly…at least until the time came for her
to return to the UK.

The thought was a harsh and sobering one.

'Ludo has always been my baby.' Eva smiled, her
gaze lovingly meeting her son's. 'He was always such
a mischievous little boy, but I loved that he was so playful and liked to have fun. Our friends and neighbours
adored him. They called him the golden-haired Petrakis angel.'

Beneath his lightly tanned chiselled features Ludo reddened a little. The realisation that his mother's tender little speech had embarrassed him made Natalie warm to him even more, because she guessed how much the fond declaration must secretly please him. After what had happened three years ago he must be all but *starving* for a demonstration of his parents' love and affection—along with their forgiveness.

'Come with me, Natalie.' Firmly grasping her hand, Eva started to walk Natalie over to the man who stood silently and a little broodingly, observing them all. 'I want to introduce you to my husband—Ludo's father—Alekos Petrakis.'

'*Yia sas.* It's a pleasure to meet you, Mr Petrakis.'

She tried hard to inject some confidence into her tone but it wasn't easy. Not when she had the distinct feeling that the man with the unflinchingly direct brown eyes was not an easy man to fool. But to Natalie's surprise he warmly captured her hand between his much larger palms and his pleased smile seemed utterly genuine.

'*Kalos orises,* Natalie. So you are the woman who is brave enough to take on my son Ludovic?'

Her heart thumped hard as she started to reply. 'You never know, Mr Petrakis—maybe Ludo is the brave one? We haven't known each other for very long. When he gets to know me a little better he might discover that I have a few unappealing traits that can't help but irritate him.'

To her surprise, Alekos threw back his leonine head and laughed heartily. But before he could make a comment, Ludo usurped him.

'I doubt that very much, my angel. You have too many traits that please me to counteract my being irritated by any less appealing ones. Plus, you are very easy on the eye…do you not agree, Father?'

Natalie hardly dared to breathe. What was clear to her was that Ludo was holding out an olive branch to his stern parent…trying to disperse some of the tension between them with light humour. She prayed his father would recognise that was what he intended. The older man gave a slight downward nod of his head to indicate yes, and the dark eyes flicked appreciatively over Natalie's face.

'Your wife-to-be is certainly bewitching.' He smiled, and Eva Petrakis' coral-painted mouth curved with a delighted smile of her own. Linking her arm with her husband's, she looked searchingly at Natalie and frowned. 'Why are you not wearing an engagement ring? Has my charming son not purchased one for you yet?'

Touching his hand to Natalie's back, Ludo let it slide downwards so that he could encircle her waist. His fingers firmed against her ribcage beneath her dress, and she couldn't deny that his warm touch helped her feel more secure.

'We were waiting until we arrived in Greece to select one.'

His dazzling blue eyes emitted a silent signal for her to agree with him.

'In fact I intend to call a jeweller friend of mine in Lindos about it tomorrow.'

'And I presume you have asked Natalie's father for

her hand in marriage?' Alekos challenged with a frown. 'You know it is the custom.'

Ludo pulled her closer into his side. Had he sensed her tremble just then? Suddenly their pretence at being engaged was presenting more problems than she'd anticipated. Out of the blue, Natalie recalled her mother's stories of her childhood in Crete. An engaged couple's parents also had to have a period of getting to know one another before their children were wed. Why hadn't she remembered that when she'd agreed with Ludo to masquerade as his fiancée? More importantly, why hadn't *he*?

'It all happened so suddenly…what we feel for each other, I mean.'

Incredibly, Ludo was gazing into her eyes as though he meant every word he was saying. Her heart galloped as hard as a racehorse out of the starting gates and her mouth turned dry as sand. It was as though she'd suddenly been plunged into some fantastical dream.

'We have barely had time to think about anything other than the fact we want to be together,' he explained. 'When we return to the UK I will be formally asking Natalie's father for her hand, just as soon as we can arrange a meeting.'

'And afterwards you must come back to us, so that we may have an engagement party for you. If Natalie's parents would like to be there—as I am sure they will— you must ring me straight away so that we can organise things, my son.' His mother's voice was both happy and eager. Her beaming glance fell on Natalie. 'I know it has all been rather sudden for you, my dear, but do you have any idea at all about a date for the wedding?'

'We were thinking that later on in the year might be better. Perhaps autumn,' Ludo interjected smoothly, robbing her of the chance to reply.

It was just as well, Natalie thought. She was far too stunned that he should be anywhere near mentioning a date when in reality they both knew that the event wasn't even going to take place. Just as soon as they were alone again they were going to have to have a very serious talk, because right now events were taking on all the urgency and speed of an ambulance crew racing hell for leather to an emergency, and she wasn't confident she could halt them.

The deceit was making her feel intensely uncomfortable…not to mention *guilty*. Yet despite her unease, Natalie felt a sense of heartfelt disappointment that she *wasn't* engaged to Ludo, wasn't going to marry him. The undeniable revelation that she was head over heels in love with him made it hard to project even the most temporary appearance of composure.

'So you are going to adhere to the traditional time for a marriage, when the olive harvest is gathered in?' Ludo's father was nodding his approval of the idea. 'I think that is a very wise choice. It will help people see that you are a man of principle, Ludovic…a man to whom family values are still important.'

He might almost have added *after all* to that statement, Natalie thought, tensing anxiously. The immediate sight of a muscle jerking in the side of Ludo's sculpted cheekbone told her he had read his father's declaration in the same way and vehemently resented it. In the next instant he confirmed it.

'So you do not believe I was a man who had principles and family values before, Father?' he ground out tersely.

Natalie's stomach plunged at the sudden potential for familial disaster.

'I speak as I find,' Alekos answered stiffly. 'If you ever indeed had both those qualities, then you clearly lost them when your brother died.'

With a furious curse Ludo spun away from Natalie to stand in front of his father. She flinched. His pain at being so cruelly judged by his own flesh and blood was agonisingly tangible.

'Why?' he demanded, glaring. 'Because you conclude I left without reason? Did you never ask yourself *why* I needed to put so much distance between us? Did you not guess how much I was hurting, too? When Theo died I would have given anything for the accident to have happened to *me,* not him! *He* was the one everyone regarded as a good man—a son to be proud of—and he was! He was amazing, and the work that he did was of benefit to hundreds…maybe thousands of families. Whereas I—'

Suddenly he was staring down at the ground, shaking his head in bewilderment and rage. 'I directed my talents to making money…a *lot* of money. It's almost like a dirty word to you, Father, isn't it? I'm not worthy enough to be thought of as good, even if I *can* help people by creating jobs. And you know what? I learned how to become rich from *you.* It takes blood, sweat and tears to make it in this world—you taught me that. Work hard and the world will be your oyster—then you can have anything you want. That was your mantra all through our childhood. But when Theo became a doctor you decided to make a distinction between what was good and what was bad. And you did it because you liked the kudos and admiration you got from your friends due to your son being a renowned doctor.'

Breathing hard, Ludo scraped his fingers through his hair. 'Well, I am what I am, and it hardly matters what you think of me now. But you should know that Theo was the best friend I could ever have wished for. He was my ally, too. I'll always remember him not just for being my brother but for the love and support he gave me throughout our time together. *He* was the wise man who told me it would only cause me more pain if I fought against your prejudice when you always made it clear that you preferred him to me. "Just be yourself," he told me. "Follow your heart wherever that may lead you. You need no one's approval...not even Father's." I only came back here to see my mother. I truly regret that I added to her suffering after Theo went, and if there is anything I can do to make it up to her it is my solemn promise that I will.'

'I never sought compensation from you, Ludo. But you have already lifted my heart and my spirits by coming back to me and bringing me a soon-to-be beloved daughter.'

Eva Petrakis pulled him into her arms and hugged him fiercely. Then she moved across to Natalie and gently touched coral-painted fingertips to her cheek. Her pretty blue eyes were moist with tears.

'Not only has my dear son returned to me, but he has brought me the daughter that I have long prayed for. One day I hope she will grant my dearest wish and present me with my first grandchild.'

The sound of birdsong, and in the distance of the waves crashing onto the seashore, faded out to be replaced by an almost dizzying white noise in Natalie's head. She didn't seem to have the ability to feel anything but shock and distress after Ludo's poignant outburst. And now, after what his mother had just said, she hardly trusted herself to string a coherent sentence together. All she knew was that the woman standing in front of her with such hope and trust in her eyes didn't deserve any more heartache or pain. But then neither did her son…

'I think we have stood out here in the midday sun for long enough.' Eva smiled. 'We should all go inside for a while, and I will see to some refreshments for us. I assume you are staying for lunch? But of *course* you are! We have so much to celebrate. This is turning out to be a very good day indeed.' Frowning at her husband, who hadn't moved so much as an inch since his son had publically berated him, she said, 'Come with me, Alekos. I think we should have a little talk before we join the children.'

As they moved towards the open patio doors that led inside the house Ludo gripped Natalie's hand hard— as though it were a lifeline in the choppiest of stormy seas. He made a point of deliberately ignoring his father's gaze completely.

CHAPTER TEN

LUDO HAD STAYED ominously quiet so far on the return journey to his villa, and Natalie knew why. Although his mother had tried hard to get the two men to make peace with each other during a delicious prolonged lunch they had both stubbornly resisted her efforts. Ludo was angry with his father for not understanding or forgiving his need to escape after his brother's funeral, and in Natalie's opinion Alekos was holding on to an old perception of his son that he either couldn't or *wouldn't* change.

At any rate, the conversation that had taken place had mostly been between herself and Eva Petrakis, and by the time it had come for the two couples to say their goodbyes father and son were barely even making eye contact.

The situation couldn't have been sadder. After Ludo's impassioned outburst, confessing his feelings, there should have been some resolution between him and his father—or at least a willingness on both their parts to forgive what had happened between them so that they could make some headway into forging a better relationship in the future.

But in spite of her compassion, and her concern for

Ludo's dilemma, Natalie found she couldn't ignore her own needs. She wanted to make it clear to him that she wasn't blindly going to go along with whatever he wanted to make his life easier just because he'd paid her father more for his business. He'd asserted he was no blackmailer, but he *did* have a reputation for ruthlessly winning deals, and she didn't want to end up feeling a fool.

As they drove on towards the villa, Natalie couldn't remain silent any longer. 'I know that the situation at your parents' was very difficult for you,' she told him, nervously clutching her hands together in her lap, 'but it wasn't easy for me either. I can see now why you brought me with you and made that deal with me. It's easier to confront a situation like you have with your father when you have someone else in your corner—someone to help act as a sort of buffer between you. But my big concern is that you're thinking of me purely as one of your business deals, and all you want is the outcome you desire without taking into account *my* feelings.'

She saw Ludo's shoulders tense immediately and his hands firmed on the steering wheel. He momentarily took his eyes off the road to consider her bleakly.

'Is that really the impression you have of me, Natalie? That I only think of you as a business deal I want to win at all costs and don't regard you as a person with needs of your own?'

The surprised and hurt tone in his voice made her anxious that she'd got his motives completely wrong. Her face coloured hotly.

'You *do* regard me, then?' Her voice dropped to a near whisper even as her eyes filled with tears. 'I mean…you do care about what I feel?'

'The fact that you have to ask tells me that you do not think I do. I think it is probably best if we finish this conversation back at the house.'

Scowling, he trained his gaze firmly back on the road, and Natalie turned hers away to stare forlornly out of the window.

It was dusk when they reached the villa. Still quiet, Ludo held the door open for her to precede him. As they entered the spacious open-plan lounge with its sea of marble flooring she was about to speak when he abruptly brushed past her and swept up the marble staircase.

'Ludo, where are you going?'

Because of their conversation in the car, Natalie's felt almost sick with fear that he was going to tell her to go home…that he no longer required her help. She made a snap decision to pursue him, seeing with surprise that he was ripping open the buttons of his linen shirt and taking it off as he went. The arresting sight of his bare, taut, tanned musculature and athletic shoulders sent her heart bumping not only in alarm but with a dizzying sense of excitement too. What on earth was he doing?

Not quick enough to reach him, she saw him get to his bedroom and stride inside without even turning to see if she followed. Taking a deep breath, she cautiously rapped her knuckles against the door. Even though it was partially open she wouldn't risk walking in unannounced.

'Ludo? I know you're probably not in the mood for talking, but you're starting to worry me. I don't want the conversation we had in the car just now to come between us and make us stop communicating. Can I come in?'

'Of course. Unless you want us to converse with each other from either side of the door.'

Smoothing a nervous hand down the front of the blue dress he had professed to like so much, Natalie pushed the door wider and walked inside. Ludo was standing in front of the large silk-canopied bed that dominated the room and seemed to be making a deliberate point of tracking every step of her cautious approach.

'Why did you take off your shirt?' It hadn't been the first thing she wanted to ask him, but she asked anyway because she was curious.

'I wanted to get rid of the taint of disapproval from my father. Unfortunately it's apt to cling and cast a shadow if I keep it on. I didn't want that.'

Even as he discarded the crumpled garment onto the bedspread he glanced at Natalie with a provocative smile. His magnificent sculpted torso was bare, and his rust-coloured chinos were riding low enough on his well-defined lean hips for her to glimpse the column of darker hair that led even lower down. She forced herself not to be so swayed by his arresting male beauty that she wouldn't be able to discuss things sensibly.

'So it's not because I made you angry by asking if you regarded our arrangement as purely a business deal you had to win?'

'It didn't make me angry, but it did upset me coupled with the fact that our reunion lunch with my parents was spoilt by my father glaring at me across the table like I was public enemy number one. It's not hard to understand why I'm on edge and would prefer to just forget about the whole thing.'

'But it won't help if you simply put what happened to the back of your mind.' Natalie sighed. 'It won't be as easy to discard as your shirt, Ludo. The memory will surface again and again if you don't try and deal with it properly. If you want to talk about it then I'm a good listener.'

'So you would still listen to my troubles even though you are suspicious of my motives?'

Her heart twisted with regret that she'd expressed that. 'I've just had to contend with you telling your parents that you're buying me an engagement ring tomorrow and there will be a wedding in the autumn, when none of that is remotely true. But now that I've met your parents and seen how much they mean to you I think I'm astute enough to know that you mean no harm by the deception. If you want to talk to me about things I really am willing to listen and try and help if I can.'

'It might not be true that we're getting married in the autumn, but I still intend to buy you an engagement ring. Our engagement will hardly be convincing if I don't. I take it even if you don't agree you will still keep your part of the deal?'

Pursing her lips at the suggestion of doubt in his tone, Natalie nodded her head. 'I will. But right now I'd like you to open up to me a little and tell me how you *really* feel about things.'

Ludo scowled. 'You think I'll feel better if I get

things off my chest? Is that what you're saying? Don't you think I've done enough of that today? You saw how my father dealt with it. It only made things even worse between us.'

'He's probably feeling just like you are right now. Instead of feeling justified that he was so stubborn, I bet he wishes he could turn back the clock and have the time over again to make things right. You're his *son*, Ludo. I'm sure he loves you very much.'

The man in front of her was still wearing a mistrustful scowl. 'I don't want to discuss this any further. What I want to do is have a drink. Preferably a *strong* one.' Feeling uncomfortably cornered, he rubbed an irritable hand round his jaw.

'And that's going to solve everything, is it?' Shaking her head in dismay, Natalie frowned. It was quite unbelievable how stubborn he could be. Clearly he must have inherited the trait from his father.

'No. It's not. But it's going to help me feel a hell of a lot better than I do right now after that debacle of a family reunion!'

He dragged the heel of his hand across his chest and his riveting sapphire eyes glistened furiously. But the anger that had appeared as suddenly as a flash flood out of a clear blue sky dispersed just as quickly, and this time his gaze transfixed her for an entirely different reason. It was smouldering with unmistakable *lust*.

'That is,' he drawled, 'unless you can think of another way of making me feel better, Natalie....'

She swore she could count every single beat of her heart as she stood there. In the past few seconds her ability to hear every sound that echoed round that stylish and spacious bedroom, right down to the waves breaking onto the shore outside, had somehow become preternaturally sharp, as had the rest of her senses.

Lifting her hair off the back of her neck to help cool her heated skin, she murmured, 'I can't. But that doesn't mean I want you to drink. Alcohol is what my father resorted to when he couldn't deal with his despair—and take it from me, it only made things worse. Is that what you want, Ludo? To feel worse than you do already? Much better to talk things out than to let your feelings fester and make you ill.'

'It must have been a great boon to your father to have a daughter like you. So wise for someone so young… and so forgiving.'

Natalie felt the heat rising in her cheeks, because she didn't know if he was being sincere or sardonic. 'When you love somebody you naturally want to do everything you can to help them when they need it.'

'I agree. But what if sometimes you need *their* help even more? Do you think that makes you a bad person?'

'Of course not.' Tucking her hair behind her ear with a less than steady hand, she realised that Ludo might have taken her well-meant reply about helping someone you love as a criticism of his own actions when he'd departed after his brother's funeral instead of staying behind to help his parents deal with their grief. She'd be mortified if he believed that. 'Ludo, I hope you don't think I was being insensitive. I was only trying to explain what motivated me to help *my* dad.'

'Is it even possible that someone like you could be insensitive? I don't think so. Come over here.'

'Why?'

He shrugged a shoulder. 'I want to talk to you. I also want to apologise for making you think I don't regard your feelings.'

Gesturing for her to move closer, he gave her a smile that was indisputably slow and seductive. Natalie did as he asked—she couldn't resist him. But her legs were shaking so badly she hardly knew how she managed it.

When they were face to face Ludo lifted his hand and slid it beneath the heavy silken weight of her long hair, letting his palm curve warmly against her nape. His touch and the intimate closeness of his body electrified her into stillness. So much so that her nipples stung with an almost unholy ache for him to touch them. Never before, in all her twenty-four years, had she experienced such wanton, primitive desire for a man—and the force of it shook her hard.

'I said I would only expect you to share my bed if you invited yourself into my room,' he reminded her huskily, his burning blue gaze shamelessly scorching her.

'Is that why you said you wanted to talk to me?' She found herself mesmerised by the alluring sculpted shape of his lips and the heat that reached out to her from his half-naked body. It was impossible to keep her nerves steady.

'Do you know how long I've waited for a girl like you to come into my life?' he asked.

'What do you mean by that? Do you mean you hoped

to meet someone ordinary who doesn't move in the same exalted circles as you do?'

'You are far from ordinary, *glykia mou*…and I don't care where you come from or what kind of circles you move in. I'm simply telling you that I want you.'

'Why?' She barely knew why she even asked, because the answer was shockingly apparent as his eager hands shaped her bottom through her dress and brought her body flush against his. Behind the button fly of his chinos she sensed his heat and his hardness—and he didn't try to hide it to spare her blushes.

'I think there's been enough talking. I'm sure you knew that when you knocked on my door and asked if you could come in…'

A shuddering sigh of need left Natalie's throat as Ludo reached for the zip at the back of her dress, dragged it downwards and stripped the garment off her shoulders. Just when she thought he might be going to kiss her he slid his fingers beneath the straps of the daring black lace bra that she'd bought for this trip, hardly knowing why she should select such an uncharacteristically impractical item. It was a million miles away from her usual safe utilitarian style.

Ludo yanked down the delicate silk and lace to bare her breasts. With a bold glance that challenged her to deny him he cupped her and brought his mouth firmly down onto a stinging erect nipple. His hot wet tongue caressed her flesh and his teeth bit, sending shooting spears of molten lightning straight to her womb. The pleasure-pain was so intense that she grabbed on to his head with a groan. A few sizzling seconds later he looked up and with a devil-may-care glance dragged the rest of her dress down to her feet and helped her step out of it. As Natalie tremblingly kicked off her shoes he kept her steady by holding firmly on to her hips. When she was done, he deftly unhooked her bra and let it fall to the floor.

'Do you know how beautiful you are? You are like a goddess,' he declared, sweeping his gaze appreciatively up and down her semi-nude figure. 'So beautiful that it hurts me to look at you.'

Ludo meant every word. She had the most exquisite shape, highlighted by an impossibly tiny waist and gently flaring hips. And with her river of shining hair cascading down over her pert breasts she reminded him again of mythological depictions of Athena and Andromeda. His attempt to make peace with his father earlier had been anything *but* a success, but being here with Natalie like this, fulfilling the fantasy that he'd been gripped by since first seeing her on the train to London, was going a long way to helping him set aside his personal pain.

Her luminous grey eyes widened as he stooped to position one arm beneath her thighs and the other round her back. The texture of her matchless smooth skin was like the softest velvet, and the experience of holding her semi-naked body in his arms was one of the keenest pleasures he had ever known. With her luxuriant hair brushing tantalisingly against his forearm and the scent of her perfume saturating his senses like a hot and thirsty sirocco, she was a woman to weave serious sexual fantasies about.

But it wasn't just Natalie's looks that made her appeal to him more than any other woman he'd been attracted to before. There was an air of innocence about her that was utterly refreshing after the parade of hard-nosed businesswomen, models and gold-diggers he'd dated from time to time. He'd known his parents would love her…how could they not? She was just the kind of girl they'd always hoped he would meet. And behind his desire, behind the hope he dared not give a name to, there was a nagging sensation of being jealous of any other man who had known her intimately. Had they realised at the time what a prize they'd won for themselves?

Pushing his jealousy aside, he tipped Natalie back and carefully lowered her onto the opulent silk counterpane. As he stood beside the bed, taking the opportunity to survey her loveliness, she returned the compliment by letting her gaze avidly roam him. The hunger in her eyes was unmistakable, and it hardened Ludo even more.

Natalie caught her breath. The well-defined biceps beneath Ludo's naturally bronzed skin intensified the desire that had been building in her blood all day. She was suddenly impatient for him to join her, so that she might know first-hand the raw power that his strong, fit body exuded so effortlessly. The man was temptation personified, and it never failed to strike her how perfectly proportioned and beautiful he was.

As soon as her glance fell into that sea of sapphire-blue once more he gave her a dazzling and knowing smile and dropped down next to her on the bed. The need for conversation redundant, he moved over her with graceful fluidity and straddled her hips with his strong, long-boned thighs. When he sat back on his haunches to undo his chinos her ability to think clearly utterly fled. All Natalie knew was that she wanted Ludo as much as he wanted her—if not *more*. Yet she momentarily closed her eyes when he dispensed with his trousers and the navy silk boxers that he wore underneath simply because she couldn't stem her anxiety over not being able to please him as much as a man of his experience might be expecting her to...

How could she when she'd never gone all the way with a man before?

Would he be furious with her when he found out? She'd long realised she must be in quite a minority to be still a virgin at twenty-four.

Her nervousness immediately evaporated the instant Ludo touched his lips to hers. The man's deliciously expert kisses were to *die* for. When she responded eagerly, her own lack of expertise didn't seem to matter one iota. Winding her arms about his strong neck, she gave herself up to the passionate embrace with all her heart, and didn't tense when he caught the sides of her lace panties and rolled them down over her thighs. The only feelings that washed though her right then were excitement and lust, and when he returned to claim her mouth in another avaricious kiss Natalie couldn't help but wind her long slender legs round his hard, lean waist. It all seemed so natural and so right.

'Let me love you,' he entreated against her ear, murmuring low.

With her hands resting on the strong banks of his

shoulders, she gave him a tremulous smile. 'There is nothing I want more,' she admitted softly.

Somewhere along the line he had retrieved a foil packet from his trouser pocket and he briefly sat back on his haunches to deal with protection. But not before Natalie allowed herself a curious glimpse. With a contented sigh she rested her head back on the sumptuous silk pillow and readied herself to receive him.

She bit down hard on her lip at his first eager invasion, and couldn't deny the initial sting of pain that she experienced—but when Ludo's muscular body suddenly stilled in surprise she pulled him against her to encourage him to continue, kissing him. There would be plenty of time for that particular awkward discussion later, she thought. Right now all Natalie wanted was to be made love to by the man she now knew without a doubt was the thief of her heart. A man who on the surface appeared to have everything that was supposed to signal success in the world…wealth, property, business acumen second to none, as well as movie-star good looks.

But in truth, she reflected, he was clearly lacking the one thing he perhaps craved above all else—the thing most people yearned for. Unconditional love and acceptance. From family, friends and colleagues, and—given time—*the person they fell in love with*. Even though that last part of her realisation made her pulse race, Natalie knew she wouldn't deny her lover anything. Not now, when she'd just surrendered her most precious gift to him.

Pressing himself deeper and deeper inside her, Ludo wound his fingers through hers as they began to move as one, his breathing becoming more and more laboured as he succumbed fully to the passion that drove him so hungrily to seek release.

For Natalie, the tide of molten heat that had consumed her from the moment he'd welcomed her into his room was now at its peak, and the power of it was like a ferocious drowning sea, sweeping her away to a heart-pounding place of no return...

Wrapping her in his arms as he lay spent beside her, Ludo felt his mind teeming with questions. His heart thudding, he lightly twined a long strand of her silken hair round his fingers and asked, 'Why didn't you tell me that this would be your first time?'

Meeting his glance with her big grey eyes, Natalie gave him a long, considered look. 'Would you have still made love to me if I'd admitted it?'

'You are far too irresistible for me *not* to have. But I would have tried to be a little more gentle...more considerate.'

'I loved it that you were so passionate, Ludo. I may not have much experience, but even so I have desires— just like you.'

His heart thudded a little less hard but he was still confounded by her frank response. Confounded and enthralled. He'd never met a woman like her. 'What made you wait so long to give yourself to someone?'

She blushed, and because she looked so adorable Ludo couldn't help planting a light kiss on her forehead.

'My mother always told me to wait until the time was right...until I was sure that the man I gave my virginity to was worthy of it. Well, today was the day I knew the time was right and the man more than worthy.'

'See what you've done, my angel?'

'What do you mean? What have I done?'

'You have made me want you all over again.'

With a shameless grin, Ludo impelled her firmly onto his aroused manhood, proud and pleased that she fitted him like the most exquisite satin glove.

'Except this time, although I will be no less passionate, I will endeavour to go more slowly…to take my time and savour you more so that you may experience the utmost pleasure.'

Her long hair cascaded down over her naked breasts like a waterfall and her beautiful eyes widened to saucers. 'Like lessons in love, you mean?'

With a throaty laugh of sheer delight, he stilled any further inclination she might have to talk by capturing her lips in a long and sexy, heartfelt kiss…

CHAPTER ELEVEN

EVEN THOUGH THE afternoon at his parents' had not gone as well as he might have dared to hope, it had been one of the most wonderful evenings of his life. Natalie had Ludo in a spin. The air of innocence that he'd sensed about her from the beginning had been proved to be right. But he was stunned at just how far that innocence had extended. More than that, at the fact that she would willingly surrender that innocence to *him*. In spite of the upsetting altercation with his father earlier, he was walking on air—and predisposed to take his lover out to dinner.

He no longer cared that the locals would see him and know that he'd returned, or indeed if they made private unflattering judgements about him. It was strange, but with Natalie by his side Ludo felt as if he could deal with just about *anything*—even the painful realisation that he would probably never have his father's love and regard.

His favourite local restaurant overlooking the moonlit bay was heaving with tourists and locals alike tonight, and as soon as he and Natalie walked in heads turned to observe them. Deciding it was because his partner looked so ravishing in her mint-coloured dress and the cream pashmina that she'd draped round her shoulders, Ludo felt a strong glow of pride eddy through him.

'*Kopiaste*…welcome. Come in and join us,' the restaurant staff eagerly greeted them. Accustomed to getting a table wherever he went, whether he'd booked ahead or not, Ludo decided not to go elsewhere when he was told they were fully booked tonight but would not dream of turning him and his beautiful partner away. He smilingly kept hold of Natalie's hand and waited patiently while a space in one of the most attractive parts of the restaurant was hastily made available and an extra table was laid. The friendly *maître d'*, whose family Ludo had known for years, attended them personally, and on his instruction a young waiter and waitress brought appetising plates of *mezes* and some complimentary *ouzo* to their table in celebration of his return home.

But although the staff behaved impeccably Ludo could see in their eyes that they were having difficulty containing their curiosity. He had read the speculation in the Greek press three years ago about why he'd left the country so abruptly following his brother's funeral. The picture they'd painted of him had not been a good one…

'Everybody seems so pleased to see you,' Natalie commented, her grey eyes shining.

'Of course.' Ludo couldn't help being wry. 'Money talks.'

'Please don't be cynical. Not tonight. I'm feeling so happy and I want to stay feeling that way…at least until the evening is over.'

Reaching for her small elegant hand, he could have bitten off his tongue for bringing that wounded look to her eyes. 'I fear my cynicism about people has become a habit. But it doesn't mean that can't change,' he added, smiling.

'No, it doesn't,' she agreed and, lifting his hand, brushed her soft lips across his knuckles.

'You are a dangerous woman, Natalie Carr,' he responded, deliberately lowering his voice. 'A small kiss and one approving glance from your bewitching grey eyes and I'm undone. All I really want to do now is take you home and teach you some more lessons in love.'

Her pretty cheeks coloured, just as Ludo had known they would.

'Well…I know I have a lot to learn. But, as tempting as that sounds, I'd really like something to eat first. What do you recommend?'

He didn't even bother to glance at the leather-bound menu he'd been given. He knew it like the back of his hand. There had been many occasions in the past when he and his brother Theo had dined here. He deliberately set the heartrending memory aside to concentrate on Natalie.

'Leave it to me.' He smiled, and immediately signalled for the *maître d',* who had made sure to stay close by in readiness to take his order.

That night Natalie fell asleep in Ludo's arms, with the sweet scent of night-blooming jasmine drifting in through the open windows of the bedroom. It seemed that everything that had happened was taking on the magical qualities of a dream, and she wished that life might imitate that dream forever.

When she woke early the next morning, with her head on Ludo's chest, Natalie couldn't resist spending several minutes just breathing in his unique warm scent and observing the handsome features that looked more peaceful and vulnerable than she'd ever seen them. There was nothing remotely threatening or untrustworthy about him, she concluded. He had a good heart. Why couldn't his father see that? She refused to believe her perception was coloured rose just because she only saw the good in Ludo, and because she was head over heels in love with him.

Hugging herself at the reason why she suddenly felt so light and free, she planted the softest kiss on the blade of his chiselled jaw and regretfully left the lavish warm bed. Leaving him to sleep on, she dressed in a pair of light blue denims and a white cotton shirt, then made her way downstairs in search of some coffee and perhaps some delicious Greek bread to go with it. Making love certainly built up an appetite, she thought. She was absolutely starving!

She was drinking her second cup of coffee, courtesy of Allena, when Ludo walked out onto the patio to find her. He too was wearing jeans, but with an ice-blue shirt that emphasised the stunning hue of his incredible eyes. She noticed that he hadn't had a shave, and his jaw was shadowed with bristles. There was no question that it suited him. The less groomed look made him appear dangerous and sexy as hell, Natalie decided, the tips of

her breasts tingling fiercely at the delicious memory of
his ardent lovemaking last night…

'Good morning,' she said with a smile, her hands
curved round her still steaming cup of coffee.

'Kalimera.' He strode round the table and with a grin
removed the cup of coffee and put it down on the table.
Then he gently but firmly hauled her to her feet. 'I was
worried when I woke up and found you gone,' he in-
toned huskily, moving her body intimately close to his.

'There was no need. I only came down here for a cup
of coffee and some bread. My appetite is at its sharp-
est in the morning.'

'Really? Then why did you desert me? I would have
willingly satisfied your hunger if you'd stayed in bed
with me.'

Feeling as though she'd strayed to the edge of a cliff
and was about to plunge headlong over the precipice,
Natalie dug her fingers into Ludo's hard lean waist as
if her life depended on it. 'You're a very bad boy,' she
said softly, unable to help the slight quaver in her voice.

He lifted an amused eyebrow. 'If I'm bad, it's because you're always tempting me, Miss Carr. Promise me you'll never stop being the one temptation I can
never resist?'

He kissed her hard, angling her jaw so that he could
deepen the scalding contact even more. Natalie was
dizzy with desire and longing for him. Her blood
pounded hotly through her veins as though she was on
fire. When he laid his hand over her breast beneath her
shirt she couldn't help wishing with all her heart that

she had indeed stayed in bed with him this morning, instead of leaving him to go in search of coffee.

'Excuse me, Mr Petrakis, your father is here to see you.'

Allena's slightly nervous but respectful voice had them both turning abruptly in shock and surprise. Ludo's features suddenly turned unnaturally pale. With his blue eyes briefly conveying a silent apology, he moved away from Natalie to go and stand in front of his house-keeper.

'Where is he?' he asked her.

Allena told him that she'd taken him into the living room and was about to make him some coffee.

'Tell him I'll join him in a minute.'

When Allena had returned inside Natalie went straight over to Ludo and instinctively reached for his hand. He flinched as though abruptly woken from a dream. It was easy to see that this unexpected turn of events had caught him on the raw, and she wondered what he was thinking.

'Are you all right?'

'Not really.' He freed his hand from hers to drag his fingers through the already mussed golden strands of his hair. 'Whatever he wants to say to me, it can't be good.'

'You don't know that yet. Why don't you just go in and talk to him, help put your mind at rest, instead of standing out here worrying?'

He scowled, already turning away from her. 'Like I said, whatever he has to say to me, it can't be good. It never is. Go and finish your coffee, Natalie. No doubt I'll be back soon.'

She watched him go as though he were about to present himself in front of a firing squad, and silently prayed that whatever Alekos Petrakis had to say to his son it wouldn't make him despise himself even more than he already did over the tragic events of three years ago.

His father had his back to him when Ludo entered the living room, and he realised that he was twisting and turning a long string of tasselled orange marble worry beads known as *komboloi* that had been passed on to him by his own father when he was young. The sight jolted him into stillness for a moment. It had been a long time since he'd seen him use them. The last time had been at his brother's funeral.

Sucking in a deep breath to steady himself, he announced his arrival with, 'Hello, Father. You want to see me?'

The older man hastily slid the beads into the pocket of his immaculate suit jacket and turned round. Once again it shocked Ludo to see the deep new lines of worry that furrowed his brow.

'Ludovic. You were not about to go out, I trust?'

'Not immediately, no.' Ludo did indeed have plans for himself and Natalie that morning, but it wouldn't hurt to delay them.

'Good. Shall we sit down? I believe that your excellent housekeeper is bringing some coffee.'

They moved across the room to the two lavish gold couches positioned either side of a carved mahogany table. Almost right on cue Allena appeared with a tray of coffee and a dish of small *baklavas*. Thanking her,

Ludo reached forward to hand his father a cup and saucer and poured him his beverage. It was such a simple,
commonplace gesture, but somehow he had a sense that
it had more significance than he perhaps realised.

Stirring a generous spoonful of sugar into his coffee, Alekos asked, 'Where is your charming fiancée
this morning?'

'She's waiting for me outside on the patio.'

'As much as it would please me to have her join us,
I think it best that she does not. At least not until we
have had some private time together…do you agree?'

Taken aback that his father would even *consider* his
opinion, Ludo lightly shrugged a shoulder. 'I agree.
There is no point in including her in our conversation
if things are going to be unpleasant.'

Alekos Petrakis gravely shook his head, as if he
couldn't quite believe what he had just heard. 'Am I
such an ogre that you automatically expect things to
be *unpleasant* between us? If you do, then all I can tell
you is that I truly regret that.'

Stunned into silence, Ludo watched him wipe away
the tear that had trickled down over his weathered
bronzed cheek. Never before had he known his father
to weep, or indeed to be sentimental in any way. What
on earth was going on?

'You had better tell me what you want to say, Father.
I'm sure you must have some particular reason for coming here to see me today.'

Returning his cup and saucer to the table, Alekos
Petrakis sighed heavily and linked his hands together
across his lap. 'I came here to tell you that I love you,

my son. And to express my deep regret that for all these years you did not know it. Your mother and I had a long talk last night after your visit, and she made me see how foolish and stubborn I have been…how *blind* I have been about you. It was fear that made me that way. Fear of losing you.'

His mouth drying, Ludo stared. 'What do you mean, fear of losing me?'

Alekos's dark eyes met and cleaved to his. 'We have never told you, but you were born premature and we nearly lost you. The doctors worked day and night to save your life. One day our hopes would be high that you were going to survive, and the next…' After a helpless catch in his voice he made himself continue. 'The next day we'd prepare ourselves to bury you. We were told by the doctors that even if you lived you would never be strong. When you did survive, and we brought you home, your poor mother watched over you day and night like a hawk, and I somehow convinced myself that it was *my* fault you were so weak…that I had in me bad seed. What other reason could there be? Theo was big and strong—why weren't you?'

Rising to his feet, Alekos pulled out a handkerchief to mop his brow. 'My logic was ridiculous. I see that now. Your mother always told me that Theo might be the big and strong son but you—*you* were the handsome and clever one. I wish I had seen that when you were a boy, Ludovic, because your mother turned out to be absolutely right. But whether you are handsome and clever, or big and strong, it does not matter. What matters is that you know I am proud of you and love you as deeply and strongly as I loved your dear brother. Can you forgive a very foolish old man for the stupidity of the past so that he may build a happier relationship with his beloved son in the future?'

Already on his feet, Ludo strode round the table and embraced his father hard. It was as though the dam that had been closed against the forceful sea of emotion behind the gates of his heart had suddenly burst open, and the relief it brought made him feel as if he could breathe freely again.

'There is nothing to forgive, Father. I too have made a grave mistake in believing that you didn't care for me as much as you did my brother. I also have a stubborn streak, and sometimes believe I am right when I am wrong. I deeply regret walking away after Theo died. I convinced myself that you had no time for me, that my achievements were not as worthy of regard as his were, and that if I stayed it would be like rubbing salt into the wound of losing him.'

'He would be cross with us both for being so stubborn and wasting so much time in feeling aggrieved, no?'

Grinning, Ludo stepped out of the embrace and slapped his father on the back. 'He would. But he'd also be happy that we have at last made amends. So will my mother when you tell her. Nothing would make me happier than knowing that she feels more at peace about our relationship.'

'I have a question for you,' said Ludo's father.

'What's that?' Old habits died hard, and Ludo

couldn't help tensing a little in anticipation of what he was going to ask.

'I wanted to ask you about Margaritari…your island. What do you intend to do about it now? It has been a long time since you have allowed people to stay on it, and it seems such a shame to leave such a beautiful place to lay in waste when it could bring people pleasure. Nor should you let what happened to Theo destroy your own pleasure in it, Ludo.'

'I admit that I've missed visiting the island. It is like no other place on earth. When we visited it as children Theo and I knew it was special. That's why as soon as I had the chance I bought it.'

His father looked thoughtful. 'Then go and visit it again. Take Natalie and go and create some happy memories there to alleviate the sorrowful ones. For what it's worth, my son, I really think you should take my advice.'

Ludo thought he should, too. But first there was something important he had to do…something that involved purchasing an engagement ring.

As if reading his mind, Alekos put his arm round his shoulders and said, 'Now, let us go and find your beautiful fiancée. I want to reassure her that you and I no longer bear any grudges. I also want to tell her that I am proud my son has been guided by his heart and not his head in choosing such a lovely woman to be his wife. Which reminds me—weren't you two supposed to be getting an engagement ring today?'

Not missing a beat, Ludo replied, 'We were—we *are*.'

'Good. Then later on tonight we must meet up again,

so that your mother and I can see the ring, and then go out to dinner and celebrate.'

Natalie was over the moon when Ludo appeared with his father and they told her that all previous tensions or grudges between them were no more. Following the wonderful revelation that both men were now willing to forgive and forget, she made the discovery over more coffee and *baklava* that Alekos Petrakis had a wicked sense of humour as he regaled her with illuminating tales from his boyhood and the mischief he had got up to.

'I was not always the upstanding citizen you see before you today!' he confessed laughingly.

But even as she enjoyed his jokes and stories Natalie couldn't help feeling a little down. It was clear that Alekos was regarding her as his son's *bona fide* wife-to-be, and yet again she couldn't help feeling hurt because it wasn't true. How would he and his charming wife Eva react when they found out that her engagement to Ludo was nothing but a sham? That as soon as they left Greece in all probability she'd be going back to work in the bed and breakfast she ran with her mother, never to see their charismatic son again…even though in secret she loved him with all her heart?

When Alekos had bade them goodbye, making them promise they would drive over that evening to show them the engagement ring they had chosen, Natalie felt almost sick with guilt and regret.

In complete contrast to the blues that had descended on *her*, Ludo was uncharacteristically relaxed and happy. 'Will you do something for me?' he asked, impelling her into his arms as they returned inside the house after waving his father goodbye.

Her nerves jangled a little and her mouth dried. Her gaze was wary. 'What's that?'

His blue eyes sparkling, as though nothing was amiss or possibly *could* be, he replied, 'I want you to go upstairs and find something pretty to wear. Perhaps the beautiful dress you wore on our first night here? I'd like to get some photographs of us together when we buy the engagement ring.'

Natalie blinked and stared. 'Don't you think this charade has gone far enough, Ludo?'

'I don't know what you mean.'

'Are you honestly saying you want to keep up the pretence that we're engaged? It's going to break your father's heart when he learns that it's not true, and, personally, I *really* don't want to be responsible for that. He's a good man, and you've just made up with him after years of hardly speaking to each other. How do you think he's going to feel when he finds out you've been playing him for a fool?'

His hands dropping away from her waist as if he'd been mortally stung, Ludo flashed her a piercing blue gaze like the precursor to an all-out thunderstorm.

'Again I have to ask you—have you forgotten the deal we made before we flew out here?'

Her heart knocking painfully against her ribs, Natalie shook her head sadly. 'I've forgotten nothing, Ludo... including giving you my word that I'd pretend to be your fiancée unless things became too difficult or untenable.

I have to tell you that that's exactly what they've become. *Untenable.*'

With her head held high and her heart pierced by unbearable sorrow, she headed for the marble staircase without sparing him a second glance.

CHAPTER TWELVE

THE BEDROOM DOOR was flung open just as Natalie was hauling her suitcase onto the bed in order to pack. With the heel of her hand she hastily scrubbed away the scalding tears that had been blurring her vision and spun round to find Ludo standing in the doorway, with his arms crossed over his chest and an enigmatic smile hitching his lips.

She was immediately incensed. 'I can't believe you think the situation is remotely amusing! The fact that you do tells me you're not the man I thought you were.'

'I am far from amused that you think my father too good a man to be deceived about our engagement. Anything *but*.'

'Then what are you smiling about?'

Inside her chest Natalie's heart ached with distress. All she wanted to do right now was board the next plane back to the UK and spend some time reflecting on what she could do to prevent herself from ever being so gullible again.

Slowly, Ludo started to walk across the room towards her. When he was almost a foot away Natalie caught the familiar sensuous drift of his cologne and her insides cartwheeled. How would she ever come to terms with not seeing him again? Her feelings for him were no five-minute wonder, here today and gone tomorrow, she was crazy about him—despite his using her to help achieve his own ends. It didn't matter that he'd made a deal with her, or that he'd followed through on his part of the bargain—she now found she couldn't meet hers. How could she when even contemplating such a painful idea had suddenly become impossible?

'You've been crying,' he observed.

There was a look in his eyes that momentarily stole her breath.

'Yes, I've been crying.' Sniffing, she pulled out a crumpled tissue from her jeans pocket and blew her nose.

'Why?'

'Can't you guess? I'm crying because you were right, Ludo…it *is* going to break my heart to leave you. I also don't want to leave Greece. I didn't want to go home so soon, but now I'm going to have to. I thought I could do this but I can't…not after learning how much it means to your mother that you've met someone special and are engaged, and not after listening to your father today and seeing how much he loves you. I can't do it because I'm not mercenary and I don't want to hurt people. If you want to sue me for reneging on our deal then go ahead. There's nothing I can do about that.'

'You said that it would break your heart to leave me. Did you mean it?'

Sounding amazed, Ludo moved in a little closer and

smiled. Feeling heat pour into her face, Natalie swallowed hard and stared.

'Yes. I'm not trying to put you in an awkward position, but I mean it.'

'How does telling me such an incredible thing put me in an awkward position?

'I don't want you to feel you have to do anything about it. It's bad enough that people are going to be hurt because I'm not going to be able to continue to carry out my part of our bargain.'

'You mean my parents?' His expression was grave.

'Of course I mean your parents'

'What about me, Natalie? Do you not consider that I might be hurt if you don't adhere to our bargain and agree to be my fiancée?'

'You mean if I don't *pretend* to be your fiancée?'

'I no longer want you to pretend.'

He moved in even closer—so close that his warm breath fanned her face. Every plane and facet of the handsome features that were so dear to her made her heart ache anew, because after today she might never see them again.

Then, suddenly registering what he had just said, she turned rigid with shock. 'What did you say?'

'I said I no longer want you to pretend to be my fiancée. I want us to get engaged for real.'

'You're joking.'

'No, I'm not. I want us to become officially engaged with a view to getting married. I'm deadly serious.'

At the end of this declaration he tenderly gathered Natalie's face between his hands and brought his lips passionately down on hers. There was nothing she could do but eagerly respond. The lessons in love that he had given her had made her an addict for his touch, for the slow, tantalising kisses that rendered her so weak with need that she couldn't think straight…couldn't even remember her own name when he made love to her.

She was so glad his arms were round her waist when she could finally bear to tear her lips away from his or she might have stumbled.

'This really isn't some kind of a joke, is it?' she asked huskily, staring up into the incandescent sea of blue that never failed to mesmerise her.

'No. It isn't a joke. I would never be so cruel. I mean every word I've said. I don't want a pretend engagement, Natalie, I want a real one. So there is no longer any need for you to worry about deceiving my parents. I genuinely want you to be my wife, *agape mou*. When I buy an engagement ring for you today I want it to be for real.'

'But why would you want that?'

'Do you really need to ask? Have you not already guessed?' He exhaled a wry breath, then, smiling warmly down into her eyes, said, 'I love you Natalie… I love you with all my heart and soul and I don't think I can even bear the thought of living without you. That's why I want to marry you.'

For several heart-pounding seconds his passionate declaration stunned her into silence. Then, gathering her wits, she tenderly touched her palm to his cheek and smiled back.

'I love you too, Ludo. I wouldn't consider marrying

you if I didn't. You swept into my life like a whirlwind and turned everything I thought about myself and what I wanted upside down. I know it might sound ridiculous, but I had more or less resigned myself to being single for the rest of my life, because I couldn't imagine marrying anyone for anything less than true love.'

'That is what I thought, too. I longed to find someone real and true who would be my friend and my companion as well as my lover... The idea that a woman might only marry me for my money was a genuine fear of mine.'

'I would never marry you for your money, Ludo.' Natalie frowned. 'I'm an old-fashioned girl who believes that there's someone for everyone—that when two people fall in love it's written in stars.' Her cheeks reddened self-consciously. 'And I believe it was written in the stars that day we met on the train and you paid for my ticket. Especially when you turned out to be the man who was buying my father's business! People sometimes read me wrong because I have a side to me that's very pragmatic, but I've had to be. When my dad left I had to be a support and friend to my mother, as well as help her to get a business up and running so that we had an income. But I'm still an incurable romantic. Anyway, I learned early on in my life, from what happened with my parents, that money is no guarantee of living happily ever after with someone. Not unless their love for each other is more important than anything material.'

Tipping up her chin, Ludo stole a brief, hungry kiss. When he lifted his head to gauge her reaction, he seemed delighted by the fact that she was blushing again.

'I told you once that you have a very sexy voice, remember? As much as I would love to listen to you talk some more, *glykia mou*, we have a special appointment at my friend's jewellers in Lindos. He is closing the shop for the afternoon so that we might take our time in choosing a ring. He is the most sought-after designer and will create something utterly exquisite for you. That may take a few weeks, and we will have to wait for it to be made, but my intention is to buy you a beautiful ring that we can take with us today, so that the world knows we intend to marry. That being the case—we should be making our way over there now.'

'That seems awfully expensive, Ludo. Surely just one ring will do?'

He stole another kiss and playfully pinched her cheek. 'In the circles I've moved in you are unlike any other woman I have ever known, my love. Most of those women have their eye on a man who can keep them in the style they believe they deserve, and they do not much care if he is a good person or even if they really like him…as long as he is rich. But with you, Natalie, I already know you love me for myself and not for the material things I may provide. Therefore I'd be pleased if you indulge me in this matter today.'

'If it means that much to you, then I will.'

'Good.'

'Ludo, can I ask you something? Something we haven't really talked about?'

His hands resting lightly on her hips, he gave her a briefly wary nod. 'What's on your mind?'

Because it wasn't an easy question to ask, and she was slightly dreading hearing the answer, Natalie grimaced. 'Have you—have you had many lovers before me?'

'No. Not many. So few, in fact, that none of them are even memorable. They weren't exactly good choices. But I'm not interested in revisiting my past, Natalie.' He sighed. 'I'm much more interested in what's going on right now and the lovely woman who is standing in front of me…the woman who has so miraculously told me that she loves me and that it would break her heart to leave me.'

'It's true.' It was her turn to reach up and plant a soft kiss on his bristled cheekbone. 'She *does* love you, Ludo…with all her heart. And if you really want a photograph of us to mark the occasion of our engagement I'll go and put on that dress you like so much and tidy my hair.'

'Natalie?'

'Yes?'

'Do you mind going into the bathroom to dress instead of staying in here? Because if you stand here and disrobe I might not be able to resist the temptation to help you.'

'If you do that we'll never get to the jewellers today.'

'You are right. We had better focus on the matter in hand. I'm sure there'll be plenty of time later for the other things I'd like to focus on.'

With a boldly lascivious gleam in the sapphire eyes

she had so come to love, Ludo reluctantly freed her from his embrace, turned her round and gave her a little push in the small of her back. He was still chuckling when she hurried into the bathroom and shut the door.

The heavily perfumed air was just as hypnotic and spell-binding as Ludo remembered, and it throbbed with the soporific sound of bees and insects. Blessedly devoid of the noise of traffic—there was none on the island, and the only means of reaching it was by boat—if there was one place in all the world where a person couldn't help but relax and unwind from day-to-day stresses then Margaritari was that place.

He'd taken his father's advice about returning to the island and creating some happier memories, and had brought Natalie with him to do just that. He had also shared with his father his conviction that he felt he'd be-come a better man for having met and fallen in love with her, and hoped with all his heart that they would enjoy a marriage as long and as happy as Eva's and Alekos's.

Barefoot, he started to follow the crescent-shaped arc of lush golden sand, thoughtfully gazing out at the calm blue waters gently rippling beside it and sending up a silent prayer of thanks for his good fortune. He had made his peace with his father and he was in love with the kindest, most beautiful girl in the world. And he didn't care who knew it.

Right now Natalie was back in the simple but elegant stone cottage he'd had built for his own use, telephoning her father. He hadn't forgotten that his cultural tradition demanded that he ask him for her hand in marriage, but first Natalie wanted to talk to Bill Carr in private and tell him why she wanted to marry Ludo. They were madly in love…it was as simple as that.

He hoped her father would not try and talk her out of it in the belief that he was leading her on…that he might not follow through on his declaration to marry her…that he was untrustworthy. Snapping himself out of the old habit of fearing he was not as well regarded as others, he stopped walking and stood quietly staring out to sea at the vast incandescent horizon that stretched out before him. Sadly he remembered his brother Theo. Even though he had died too young, and so tragically, somehow Ludo knew that he was pleased he had made up with their father and had met Natalie and fallen in love with her. He had a strong sense that his beloved brother wished them well…

'Ludo!'

He turned at the sound of the voice that thrilled him like no other, his heart thrumming in anticipation of what she might be going to tell him. He prayed the news was good.

Natalie was running towards him across the sand, barefoot and beautiful in the mint-coloured sarong he had bought her at the market in Lindos, her lovely long hair cascading over her shoulders like a shining waterfall. In her hand she was carrying a small bunch of oleander and lavender. As she drew level he made himself resist taking her into his arms and gave her the chance to get her breath back first.

'He gives us both his blessing, and says that you can ring him when we get back to the cottage.' Her grey eyes shining, she grinned. 'He also said I'm to tell you that you're a lucky man…a *very* lucky man.'

'Does he think I don't know that already?' Impatient to hold her, Ludo hauled his wife-to-be against his chest, the heady scent of the small floral bouquet she held drifting hypnotically beneath his nose. 'So, he gives us his blessing and does not mind that you are to become Mrs Ludo Petrakis?'

'As long as it's what I want, then he's more than happy. In fact he's going round to my mum's tomorrow to tell her the news himself. Apparently she's invited him to stay for dinner.' Natalie's brow furrowed a little. 'I suppose it's good that they're talking properly… Anyway, my dad says it's only right that if he gives us his blessing to be married he should be the one to tell her.'

'He sounds to be in good spirits. Is his health any better?'

'Much. You have no idea how much it helped him when you agreed to pay him that extra sum for the business. He says he's buzzing with ideas for a new one. I just hope he doesn't get too carried away and overdo it.'

'And why have you brought these flowers to the beach, *agape mou?* If you want to admire them they are all around us in the coves and by the rock pools… the garden is also full of them.'

'I know. That's where I picked these from. To tell you the truth, I wanted us to say a little prayer for your brother and cast them out to sea in his memory,' Natalie answered softly. 'Do you mind…?'

'Do I *mind*?' Ludo shook his head from side to side in wonderment. 'It is so like you to think of something like this. I'm so proud to know you, Natalie…and prouder still that you are soon to be my wife.'

'Let's do it, then.' Gazing lovingly up into his eyes, she gently stepped out of their embrace and crouched down beside the seashore.

He willingly dropped down beside her. 'Let us remember Theo Petrakis…'

Quietly murmuring a prayer in Greek, Ludo repeated it for Natalie afterwards in English. When he was done, he gestured to her to let her know, and one by one she let the delicate flowers float out into the ocean.…

Being on the island was like being on honeymoon. Every night, after making passionate love with the man she loved, Natalie would fall into a blissful sleep in his arms, and every morning, soon after waking, she'd run down to the sea to take a refreshing dip in cool tranquil waters not yet warmed by the sun. Then she'd hurry back to the cottage to have breakfast with Ludo out on the terrace.

They had been on the island for almost a week now, and he had lost that wary look that conveyed his cynicism about the world—a look he'd seemed to wear habitually when they'd first met. He was looking younger every day. Even his brow was less furrowed, as if all his cares had fallen away. Natalie couldn't help but sigh contentedly.

Sitting opposite her at the rattan table, Ludo lowered his aviator sunglasses and his sublime sapphire eyes couldn't help but dazzle her.

'What is it?' he wanted to know.

'I was just thinking how much more relaxed you look than you did when we first met. It must be this place. It's magical, isn't it?'

'There is definitely a touch of paradise about it. I almost have to pinch myself when I remember that I own it.' Straightening in his chair, he tunnelled his fingers through his hair, as if coming to some momentous decision. 'In fact, it is so like paradise that I have decided it's not right to keep it just for myself and family and friends. I've been thinking about building some more accommodation, so that the families of sick children on the surrounding islands might come here for a rest or a holiday when they need it. Of course they wouldn't have to pay for the privilege. I thought I could set up a foundation in Theo's name. What do you think?'

'What do I *think*?' Natalie's heart was racing with excitement and pride. 'I think it's a wonderful idea. Could I help you set it up? If I'm not going to be working at the bed and breakfast any more after we're married I'd like something useful to do…something that I could believe in.'

'Of course you can help. That is…until we have our first child. I'm a strong believer in a mother being there for her children as they are growing up if she can be. How do you feel about that, *glykia mou*?'

'I agree.' Reaching across the table, she smilingly squeezed his hand. 'I want to be there for *all* our children as they grow up. As long as their father is there for them as much as possible, too.'

With a delighted smile, Ludo raised her hand and turned it over to plant a lingering warm kiss in the centre of her palm. 'We very definitely have an agreement. You said *all* our children? That implies we will have more than one or two?'

Natalie dimpled. 'I was thinking maybe three or four?'

'And I'm thinking I'm going to be a very busy man for the next few years if you are planning *that* kind of agenda, my angel. In which case I suppose there's no time like the present to get started on carrying it out!'

* * * * *

THE COUNT'S PRIZE

BY
CHRISTINA HOLLIS

Christina Hollis was born in Somerset, and now lives in the idyllic Wye valley. She was born reading and her childhood dream was to become a writer. This was realised when she became a successful journalist and lecturer in organic horticulture. Then she gave it all up to become a full-time mother of two and run half an acre of productive country garden.

Writing Mills & Boon romances is another ambition realised. It fills most of her time, in between complicated rural school runs. The rest of her life is divided among garden and kitchen, either growing fruit and vegetables or cooking with them. Her daughter's cat always closely supervises everything she does around the home, from typing to picking strawberries!

You can learn more about Christina and her writing at www.christinahollis.com.

To Martyn,
for all your invaluable help and understanding.

CHAPTER ONE

JOSIE couldn't help herself. Trying to pretend that this was going to be just another job was impossible. Bouncing forward in her seat, she rapped on the glass partition separating her from the di Sirena family's impeccably dressed chauffeur.

'Stop! Please stop!'

The man immediately stamped on the brakes and whipped around to look at her, his face full of concern. 'Is there something wrong, Dr Street?'

'No, no, sorry, nothing's wrong. I didn't mean to alarm you. It's just that I was told the Castello Sirena is very beautiful, so I want to be sure of getting a good look at it,' Josie confided, sinking back into the sumptuous leather upholstery.

Her chauffeur nodded in agreement. 'That's quite understandable, *signorina*. This castle has been called the most beautiful Italian property still in private hands. But, as you will be staying for a month, surely you will have plenty of opportunities for sightseeing?'

'I don't know—I've got so much to do while I'm here. I might not have that much spare time to just…admire it,' she said, smiling. Her excitement at the prospect of

new archaeological discoveries was shadowed slightly
by the thought of talking about her work in front of
students next term, but that worry could wait. She had
lots of lovely research to do before then. 'I'm preparing
my first course, and I want to bring some of my undergraduate study trips to this part of Italy.'

One look at the surrounding countryside, glowing
gold in the sunshine, and Josie knew that seeing the
Castello Sirena just as part of a research project was
going to be difficult. The place oozed distraction. However, the ink was barely dry on her PhD and contract
of employment at the university, so she didn't want to
smudge either by not making the absolute most of this
opportunity. It had taken endless persuading and pre-
sentations to get any funding at all for this trip and she'd
been so lucky that her best friend, Antonia, had invited
her to investigate their family estate in such a way—
the Castello Sirena was usually closed to researchers.
Without that cherry, she didn't think her office would
have given her the money to travel, and as it was they'd
only funded her for a couple of weeks at most.

As a child, she had driven her mother mad by filling
their tiny house with muddy bits of 'buried treasure'
found in the garden. Mrs Street had sacrificed a lot over
the years to see her daughter through university, so Josie
was determined to build herself a professional reputation for always putting her job first—at least, that was
what she kept telling herself.

She whipped her camera out of her bag.

'Can you spare a minute while I take some photos?'
she asked the driver. 'My mum back home in England

is never likely to see a place like this for herself. I want to give her some proof I'm actually going to be staying in a castle!'

She had hardly finished speaking before the driver got out and opened the car door for her.

'Oh, that's so kind of you! I didn't mean to put you to any trouble…'

'It's no trouble, *signorina*, as I told you when I took charge of your bags.'

His words made Josie go hot with horror all over again. The summer day was warm enough already, without an embarrassing reminder of that scene at the airport. She was so used to fending for herself, being greeted there by a stranger in a sharp suit and totally black sunglasses had made her instantly suspicious. She had refused to hand over her things until she'd checked his ID.

'Then thank you.'

Josie stepped out of the car and into the furnace that was Tuscany in July. She took a few quick snaps along the tree-lined drive towards the great castle on the hill, then dived back into the luxury of the di Sirena limousine as soon as she could. Its air-conditioning was a wonderful treat on a day like today.

'What was that lovely smell?' she asked as they set off down a cool green corridor formed by trees planted on either side of the mile-long drive.

'This lime avenue is in flower.' Her driver waved his hand towards the leafy green canopy overhead as they cruised along. 'Insects love them. You can hear them buzzing from a long way away. Count Dario once told me there could easily be several million bees working away on the flowers at any one time.'

Josie thought that was a very fitting image. Count Dario was the brother of her friend Antonia. Josie had never met him but, from the tales Antonia told about him, the man sounded a real drone. He partied every night and loafed around his estates during the day while everyone else did the actual work. It was no wonder he knew all about bees.

'Stroll beneath these trees when the sun is high above the old *campanile*, Dr Street, and you'll hear them purring like a Rolls-Royce engine.'

Josie sighed. 'It sounds lovely.'

'You should make the most of this place while you have it all to yourself,' the driver said. 'It was another late one last night, so everyone is still asleep. We've already been told the current crop of house guests won't be taking lunch today. Signora Costa, the housekeeper, will be making arrangements for you to eat alone, Dr Street.'

Josie shut her eyes in relief and thanked her lucky stars. The *castello* might be a new experience for her, but she had holidayed at Antonia's apartment in Rome and the di Sirena family villa in Rimini several times. In both places, her best friend's neighbours were all seriously grand. They were lovely people, but that didn't stop Josie feeling as out of place as a sardine in a tank full of angel-fish. She always enjoyed playing with little Fabio while his mother, Antonia, went shopping; it was the evenings spent listening to people she didn't know talking about spending three months skiing and visiting places she had only seen in colour supplements that Josie found hard work. Making small talk was her idea of hell. She was taking it for granted that Antonia's older brother would be nocturnal because of his notoriously wild social life. That suited her. It meant she would be free to work in and around the ancient splendour of the Castello Sirena all day and be fast asleep before he surfaced, ready for another night on the tiles. With the limited amount of time available to her, she didn't think she could afford to waste a single day.

At the thought of what Count Dario would be doing in the evenings, it was impossible not to feel a twinge of envy. She looked around at the sun-drenched acres of the Castello Sirena. Although she loved her work, Josie sometimes felt like a hamster on a wheel. She had to keep forging ahead just to pay her bills, while people like Count Dario had everything handed to them on solid silver ancestral platters.

When she'd first started sharing rooms with Antonia at university, she'd wondered if their wildly differing backgrounds would poison their friendship. Instead, it was a source of endless amusement. And when either of them hit rough times, the other was there with support.

Loyalty was important to Josie. She'd thought she had found it in her ex-fiancé, but she had been proved as wrong about him as Antonia had been about her own partner, Rick. When Antonia got pregnant, Rick had abandoned the poor girl instantly. Josie helped her best friend to pick up the pieces, but secretly she thought Antonia was better off without the guy.

After her own experiences, Josie was developing a

very jaundiced outlook when it came to men. When her friend decided that she wanted to stay at home with her baby, rather than getting back to her studies, it was a blow to Josie. Her work just wasn't the same without her friend. That was why she was so looking forward to this project. It gave her a great chance to work, with the prospect of catching up with Antonia and little Fabio when they got home from Rimini.

Josie had to admit that a bit of her envied her friend's freedom to choose…

'Right, here we are.'

The chauffeur broke into her thoughts as he pulled up at the great front entrance to the *castello*. Josie got out of the car, pulling her skirt straight. As she looked up at the rambling old building she fiddled with some unruly strands of brown hair that had escaped from her ponytail. Imagine living in a place like this. The high stone walls and towering fairy-tale turrets were so beautiful. She wondered how many warriors had cantered up to this awe-inspiring entrance over the centuries. Its great oak door was studded with huge iron nails and bleached by hundreds of bright summer days like this one. In the centre, the figure of an iron mermaid, copied from the di Sirena family's crest, looked down on her with scorn.

Behind her, the chauffeur drove off to deliver her luggage to the back of the house. Conscious of being the latest in an endless line of visitors over the years, Josie advanced, caught hold of the great iron bell pull on one side of the door and got ready to pin on her best public smile.

* * *

Count Dario di Sirena was bored. As usual, he had entertained his guests lavishly the night before, but that meant there was no one up and about to entertain *him* yet. The yachting club members had been busy into the early hours, sampling the wide range of wines in the *castello*'s cellars. Alcohol had no particular attraction for Dario any more, so he was letting his guests sleep it off this morning while he made his usual early start. That was fine for them, but it left him short of a tennis partner. Hitting balls pitched at him by a machine was no substitute for a proper match. Not that many visitors to the castle ever seemed keen on sport, although they never refused his hospitality. His guests' interest in him only as a name to drop was beginning to irritate Dario.

Just for once I'd like to find someone willing to forget my rank and give me a good hard game, he thought, scything the heads off a dozen innocent moon daisies with the head of his racket. He opened a green swathe through the sea of calm white flowers. Seeing it, he took another pass, sending florets spinning through the sunshine. As he was idly wondering if it might be satisfying to try scything the whole meadow like that, he heard one of his cars.

Shading his eyes against the relentless sunlight, he watched it stop briefly outside the house while a girl got out. Dario quickly tried to remember who this new visitor could be. Surely it wasn't Antonia's friend? She wasn't supposed to be arriving until the twelfth. He checked the date on his watch, and grimaced. Today *was* the twelfth. He sighed. Since he'd inherited his title, he found time passed so quickly that all the days merged into one another. Time slipped away like water through his hands, and what did he have to show for it? A golf handicap that was fast approaching zero, and enough frequent flyer miles to circumnavigate the solar system.

Anything Dario wanted, he could have.

Except a good reason for getting up early, he thought.

Shouldering his racket, he strode over to introduce himself to the new visitor with a smile.

Antonia had told him that her best friend was here to work and was not to be…distracted. The way his sister described Dr Josie Street, Dario half expected to be playing host to an eccentric nun. The woman he now saw trying to raise the alarm outside his house was far more appealing than that.

Although… he considered, looking her over with a practised eye, *she's doing her best to hide it.* Josie's tightly drawn-back hair, concentrated frown and shapeless clothes all indicated a woman fighting her natural good looks as hard as she could. She certainly fitted his image of an English academic. *Hmm…maybe someone should tell her that there's more to life than study,* he thought in passing as he drew closer to her.

Years spent toiling on archaeological digs as a student meant Josie was no weakling, but the bell pull defeated her. She tried knocking on the door, but its six inches of solid oak deadened all sound. The chauffeur was bound to have warned the other staff that she was on her way, but Josie suspected it would be some time before they came to check. When one final haul couldn't

dislodge the bell pull she stood back, brushing flakes
of rust from her hands in disgust.

'*Buon giorno.*'

She jumped at the intrusion, and swung around. A
man was walking towards her out of the sun, and the
mere sight of him made her stand and stare. Towering
head and shoulders over her, he was all toned limbs
and easy grace. His unruly black hair and flashing
eyes were teamed with a golden tan and immaculate
tennis whites. It was a breathtaking combination, and
she suspected he knew that only too well. In contrast
to Josie's dusty travelling clothes, everything he wore
seemed brand new. The state-of-the art tennis racket he
bounced against the palm of his left hand as he drew
closer didn't look as if it had ever been used in anger.
It even had daisies woven into its strings.

I wonder if they were threaded there by some girl?
Josie thought, glancing around to see if this vision was
making his way over to someone glamorous who might
be standing nearby. The courtyard was otherwise deserted so, wonder of wonders, he must be heading
straight for her.

She didn't need to be told who it was. Those soft
brown eyes and dense dark lashes were instantly familiar. This must be her host, Antonia's brother. To Josie's
eyes, he looked even more wayward than his reputation.

'Allow me to introduce myself. I am Count Dario
di Sirena.'

The vision confirmed her suspicions with a voice like
warm honey. In a grand gesture he reached for her hand
and swept it up to his lips for a formal kiss.

Josie's immediate reaction was shock. 'Why aren't you in bed?' she blurted out.

Dario raised his eyebrows. 'I assume that isn't an invitation?'

Josie snatched back her hand and retreated, blushing furiously. She had got off on the wrong foot in spectacular style, even for her.

Dario smiled, ignoring her awkwardness. 'You must be Josie.'

'Dr Josephine Street, yes,' she muttered, ignoring the little voice inside her telling her off for sounding so sullen. Meeting new people had never been easy for her, and it was ten times harder when they were this gorgeous.

'That's very formal, Dr Josephine Street!' Dario teased, but Josie was too flustered to smile back at him and flirt like he was no doubt expecting.

'I'm a very formal person.'

'Then allow me to say that it gives me the greatest pleasure to welcome you into my humble home,' he announced with mock gravity. As he spoke, he inclined in a semi-formal bow. When Josie pointedly refused his unspoken invitation to join in the joke he straightened up again, but he was still smiling.

Josie knew that hiding her shyness behind a brave face often worked, so she fell back on that. She lifted her chin and returned his gaze boldly. This was a man who was at ease in every situation—she had learned that much from Antonia's stories. The same stories that had led her to surreptitiously search for him on Google the other night. Neither the gossip columns nor Antonia had exaggerated. His aristocratic bearing made those anecdotes all too believable, and one look at Count Dario di Sirena showed that his charm ran deep. He was as gorgeous as he was imposing, and radiated an inner assurance that all the wealth and power in the world couldn't buy. Dario in the living, breathing flesh was a different prospect altogether from his sister—Josie's cheerful, chubby friend. Without a doubt, he was the best-looking man she had ever seen. The way he looked at her was its own distraction: it set her firmly at the centre of his universe.

It took a supreme act of will on Josie's part to remember that most men had the attention span of fruit flies. She took it for granted that when she failed to massage his ego Dario would soon lose interest and disappear. That tactic had worked only too well for her in the past, even though she hadn't done it deliberately. Men seemed to vanish, whether she wanted them to or not. An experienced charmer like Dario wouldn't waste his time in trying to pursue her.

'I'm surprised you chose to come straight here instead of staying at Rimini with Antonia and little Fabio first, Dr Street,' he said conversationally, trying to penetrate her awkward silence.

The spotlight of his attention paralysed Josie. Somehow he seemed to be blinding her, even though his face was in shadow. She moved uncomfortably, trying to persuade herself it was the sun that was sending her temperature off the scale.

'You can call me Josie,' she mumbled. 'I've stayed at your villa there before, and felt that I rather cramped

Antonia's style. She always tried to include me in her
entertaining, but all those posh neighbours with their
stories about people and places I didn't know were…'
She groped for a way to put it politely.

'Not quite your cup of tea?'

Dario's words were slow, but the merriment in his
eyes was quicksilver. Hearing his beautiful Italian accent caress such a typically English phrase, Josie felt
it melt the veneer of sophistication she had tried to put
on. The fierce heat of embarrassment rushed up over
her breasts and stained her face with a blush again.

'The chauffeur took my luggage away with him and
left me here on my own. I was trying to work out how
to attract someone's attention.'

'You've got my attention now,' Dario said with calm
assurance, and something deep inside Josie flared to
life, wishing that were true. Impervious to Josie's internal turmoil, Dario reached out to the bell pull and
flicked aside a small catch that Josie hadn't noticed. It
was keeping the iron rod clamped in place.

'Ah—of course. Thank you.'

She put out her hand automatically, but he caught it
before she could connect with the heavy iron ring. For
a split second she experienced the grip of his strong
brown fingers again, then his touch fell away.

'I wouldn't. That's the *castello*'s original fire alarm,
and this is the assembly point. It operates a big bell that
gathers everyone within earshot and I don't think either
of us would want that, would we?'

Josie shuddered. The idea of being the centre of attention horrified her—unless her audience was as warm

and friendly as this man. With a smile that told her he knew exactly what she was thinking, Dario flicked the safety catch back on.

'To ring the bell, you need to get up close and personal with Stella Maris here,' he said, nodding towards the iron mermaid. 'One of my forebears had a wicked sense of humour.'

Dario seemed to have inherited it. Sticking out his index finger, he pressed the mermaid firmly in the tummy button. An astonishingly loud ring drilled into the interior of the house.

'Ah! Was this one of the inventions of the eighth Count? When Toni suggested I came here, I read everything I could find about the *castello*,' Josie gabbled to cover her embarrassment.

Dario looked bemused, then shrugged. 'If you say so. I have no idea, I'm afraid. Whoever thought of it must have wanted to deter honest women.' Dario gave her a wickedly expressive look.

Josie blushed again. Beside Dario, she felt like a hedge sparrow matched against a peregrine falcon. He was totally at ease in his sunny surroundings, and dressed to enjoy them. Josie wasn't. Her shoes were comfortable but clumpy, while her chain-store skirt suit was totally out of place beyond her university's lecture theatre.

Within seconds, the great main door creaked open and a servant showed them into Dario's home.

The *castello*'s entrance hall was dominated by a huge stone hearth. The fire back was a copy of the di Sirena family crest, with more mermaids like the ones Josie had seen discreetly stamped on Antonia's luggage.

'There go your things,' Dario observed as a member of his staff swept past carrying a suitcase in each hand. 'They'll have put you in the West tower. That means you won't be disturbed by any of the yachting club who stayed here last night. They're all in the East wing. Come on, I'll show you up to your suite.'

While Josie stared in wonder at the entrance hall's carved ceilings and wooden panelling, he was taking the marble staircase two at a time. When he called to her, she had to run to catch up.

'I'm sure you must have better things to do, Count Dario. Don't let me put you to any trouble.' Her voice echoed through the foyer.

He looked down at her sharply from his vantage point on the first landing. 'You're already a friend of the family, Josie, so to you I'm Antonia's brother. Just call me Dario. It really would be my pleasure to show you to your suite,' he finished firmly.

Josie followed him, although she had her reservations.

'Are you sure you can find it?' she said drily as they walked through a warren of corridors. All the flawless white plaster and polished woodwork made them look alike to her.

'I have been rattling around inside this place all my life. Hasn't Antonia told you why these floors are so shiny?'

Josie shook her head, smiling at the incongruous image of Dario with floor polish in hand.

'I'd tie dusters to her feet and push her up and down, along all these miles of corridors. No matter how upset she was, that could always make her laugh.'

'It's hard to think of anyone being unhappy in a place as beautiful as this,' she murmured.

'People forget—there is more to life than just a life-style.' Dario sighed, pushing open the nearest door. They were in the oldest part of the castle, where a huge lookout tower had been built within the shelter of its thick stone walls. It had been completely modernised, with a circular staircase leading up to a self-contained suite arranged on three floors. The first floor was laid out for dining and relaxing, while the second contained a bedroom and en suite bathroom.

'—and finally,' Dario announced as he led her up beyond the second floor doorway, 'there's something I call the solar...'

They had reached the top floor and he stepped out into a large circular room with windows facing in every direction. There were glass panels set into the roof too, so the whole space was flooded with light. It felt almost as free as being outside, but with the benefit of a so-phisticated air-conditioning system.

'Wow...' Josie breathed, but couldn't say anything more. She walked around the sunlit interior, taking in its panoramic views of the Tuscan countryside. The atmosphere outside was as clear as vodka. Pencil-slim cypress stood out like exclamation marks against roll-ing fields of arid grass, sunflowers and the green cor-rugations of the estate's vineyards.

'You should see it after nightfall,' Dario told her,

waiting until she paused before strolling slowly over to stand beside her. 'It's a scene of black velvet, full of possibilities. Headlights streaking along the Florence road…is it a triumph or a tragedy, a baby arriving or a lover departing? It'll be hard for you to pick out the little farmhouses scattered across my land until you know the area better, but by night Luigi's house, Enrico's olive grove and Federico's farmhouse will all be recognisable.' His voice dropped to a wistful note. 'I come up here sometimes to sit in the silence and wonder what they're all doing.'

He was standing so close to her, Josie could feel his presence as well as catch the delicious drift of his aromatic aftershave. It gave her a tremulous feeling deep inside her body.

What's happening to me? I've come here to work, she thought in alarm, glancing up at him.

Dario was gazing out across the view, lost in thought. At that moment, as though feeling her gaze fall on him, he turned his head and their eyes met. Another sensuous ripple thrilled straight through her.

And, as if knowing what was on her mind, Dario granted her a slow, sweet, irresistible smile.

CHAPTER TWO

JOSIE's mind and body churned as she almost drowned in Dario's gaze.

It must have been like this with Andy and that woman at the university, she thought with a shiver. *I can't risk getting between this man and the girlfriend he's bound to have hidden away somewhere.*

After what felt like an eternity, she managed to regain enough control to step away from him, as if to take a tour around the room.

'This suite is wonderful, Dario, but it's way out of my league. Don't you have anything smaller?' she asked, desperately trying to bring them both back to earth.

He looked startled for a moment, then laughed.

'This isn't a hotel! As I kept telling Antonia, you don't have to pay anything at all for your visit, Josie. As her friend, you have a standing invitation to stay here whenever you like, for as long as you like. Surely she passed on my message?'

'She did, but I always pay my own way.'

'And the local hospital fund was very grateful when I forwarded your contribution.' Dario grinned. 'So why don't we pretend your generosity qualified you for a complimentary upgrade?'

Josie hesitated, but decided that she had made her point.

'In which case, thank you, Dario. But I'm afraid you won't get much chance to look out of these windows while I'm staying here,' she told him, and herself, briskly. 'This looks like the perfect place for me to spread out my finds and paperwork. It's well away from everyone else, so we won't disturb each other. Thank you for bringing me up here.'

Dario gave her a smile of silent amusement. The meaning in her clipped words was only too obvious. She wanted to be alone, so he slowly headed back towards the door.

'You're trying so hard not to let yourself go, aren't you?' he murmured, just loud enough for her to hear.

'I don't know what you mean.'

He turned to face her, and then grinned again. 'That blush tells me you've been taking too much notice of Antonia's stories, Josie.' He chuckled, his rich Florentine accent making her name sound incredibly beautiful. 'Be assured that, as my sister's best friend, you are quite safe. From me, at least.'

'Anyone coming on to me would be making a mistake, Dario,' she said firmly, 'and I'd be making an even bigger mistake if I fell for it,' she added. Her voice stopped his smile in an instant.

'I suppose that's understandable, when you've seen what has happened to Antonia.'

'And to me.'

His eyes flashed dangerously. 'You don't mean that waster Rick tried it on with you, too?'

'No—no! I just assumed Antonia had told you about—' Josie stopped, and mentally hugged her friend. Antonia must have been very discreet. 'That is…I mean…I had a similar experience, though it was nothing compared to what Toni's been through. At the time I tried to warn her, but it was hard when she was so happy.'

His expression turned into one she couldn't quite identify. 'Knowing Antonia, trying to warn her off was a rash move. And yet you're still friends?'

'Of course.'

Dario's dark, finely arched eyebrows shot up. 'Weren't you afraid she would dump you for trying to make her see sense?'

'Oh, yes, but I felt I had no choice. I couldn't bear to stand back and watch her throw away all her hard work for a man who was nothing but a lightweight—if you know what I mean.'

Her glance flicked around the palatial surroundings of her suite. She hoped he wouldn't take her words personally. Seeing all the brand new luxury decorating the age-old splendour of the Castello Sirena, Josie decided she was going to like staying here, despite its attractively distracting Count.

'I most certainly do know. I get plenty of gold diggers prospecting around me,' he said grimly.

Josie laughed. 'The only digging I'm interested in is the historical sort. So if you've got any ancestral skeletons hidden in your wardrobe, I'm the one to find out where their bodies are buried. *Your* dark secrets are your own affair, though!'

She was still glancing idly around the room as she spoke. When he didn't reply, she looked back at him quizzically. For a second, there was such a depth of feeling in his irresistible dark eyes that not even Dario could hide it. The instant she trapped his gaze, the look vanished. His expression was left as bland as any first-time house guest could wish for, but Josie wasn't fooled for a second.

In that instant she had seen a genuine reaction from a man who must be as used to putting on a public face as she was. Somehow, Josie knew, she had touched Dario di Sirena on a raw nerve. The man was hiding something. She had no idea what it was, or what she had done to provoke him.

All she knew was that she would have to be on the alert from that moment on.

Dario rarely allowed himself to be anything *but* alert. He had been born an aristocrat, and now fell back on the full force of his upbringing. He kissed her hand again and covered his momentary lapse with his most charming smile, which usually distracted even the most stubborn woman. Except…it didn't have that effect on Dr Josie Street. Right now her green eyes were as bright and hard as emeralds, and her long silky lashes could do nothing to soften her curious, intelligent gaze. For a moment, she'd forgotten to be shy. Then a lock of hair dared to escape from the band that was holding her severe ponytail in place and she snatched back her hand. The wayward strand was scraped irritably behind her ear and she turned her back on him to fuss with her suitcases.

Dario chose to take the hint. 'Goodbye, Josie. I hope you enjoy your stay here.'

'I'm sure I shall, Dario. Especially when Toni and Fabio get back here next week.'

'You could still join them both in Rimini now, if you like.' Dario lifted his tennis racket again and began idly spinning it over his palm. 'I could arrange transport for you right away.' For some reason, the thought of Josie and her all-too-perceptive gaze staying here for the week made him uneasy.

'No, thank you.' She glanced over her shoulder at him with a glint of green ice. 'As I said before, I'd rather work here than gossip with the beautiful people of Rimini.'

He raised his eyebrows again. 'It's a rare woman who would choose that.'

'Not rare, just honest,' she countered.

Dario tipped his head in salute. 'That quality is in short supply in the circles I move in. I can see why you would have difficulty fitting in.'

She shrugged. 'Research demands honesty, and it gets to be a habit. That's all.'

'I'll bear that in mind,' Dario said as he left, wondering what it would take to make Dr Josephine Street loosen up.

Josie couldn't wait to plunge out into the estate and start exploring. She unpacked as fast as she could, intending to get busy straight away, but her suite was as distracting as Count Dario di Sirena himself. It seemed odd to hang up her cheap white T-shirts on beautiful hand-made padded hangers filled with lavender. The marble wet room that was part of her en suite bathroom was an irresistible temptation as the sun climbed higher outside. Tearing off her shoes and tights, she padded around in it barefoot for a while.

By the time she had changed and finished exploring the three floors of her hideaway in the tower, Dario's other guests were in a holding pattern down in the courtyard. Watching all those chauffeur-driven limousines and prestige sports cars jockeying for position was an entertainment in itself. Josie spent much more time than she meant to with her elbows on her windowsill, staring down at the magnificent procession.

It was only when the Count himself came into view that she dodged back from the window. She moved as though she had been burned, not wanting Dario to think that her claim to be busy was just empty waffle.

Work first, play later, she kept reminding herself, although, for her, *later* never quite seemed to arrive.

Antonia was always joking that no one would ever catch Josie idling. Josie wasn't sure she liked what that said about her, but she really did have a lot of work that had to be done before the new academic year started.

Italy and its history had fascinated Josie since she was a child. Pottering about in her back garden, she was always unearthing things and taking them in to school. One piece had turned out to be a broken Roman brooch, lost by a woman over two thousand years ago. That single piece, and an inspirational teacher, had really fired

Josie's imagination. Now, twenty years later, she was here in the land of the Romans preparing to inspire others, allowed to design a whole new course! She was acutely conscious of her luck, and grateful for the sacrifices her mother had made. The downside was the extra pressure she felt to make the best of all her chances.

That was why watching Dario walk across the courtyard was bound to disrupt her plans. Something about him drew her back to the window again like a flower to sunlight. He had swapped his tennis kit for taupe jodhpurs, a white shirt and a pair of highly polished riding boots. The pale clothes showed off his exotic colouring perfectly. Josie could hardly believe her luck. Hard work had brought her here to Italy, and now she was staring down at a drop-dead gorgeous guy from a tower that would have made Rapunzel sick with envy. Dario strolled across the forecourt, heading for the shade of the lime avenue like an emperor inspecting his lands. His leisurely strides were deceptive. They ate up the distance so quickly that soon the canopy of lush green leaves would hide him from view.

Then Count Dario di Sirena stopped, turned and looked quite deliberately straight up at where Josie was watching him from her window. She was transfixed. Something made her raise her right hand to wave, but another impulse snapped it straight back down to her side. She could imagine how her mother would sigh if she knew about this little tableau. Mrs Street would go all misty-eyed and lose herself again in the story of how she had met Josie's father. Josie hated that. Her mother was the sad proof of how easy it was to misjudge a man, and it always dragged her own personal error of judgement out into the light again.

Dario continued to look up at her thoughtfully for a moment, then nodded a salute and turned to disappear into the trees. In a burst of embarrassment, Josie ducked away from the window and scrabbled around to find her notebooks and camera. This was a working trip, with a lot to do and not much time in which to do it. She had to build her reputation as a serious academic. Gawping at Dario di Sirena wouldn't help *that* at all! Packing her things into a messenger bag, she slung it over her shoulder and headed down to the castle's entrance hall.

Once out in the sunshine again with a map provided by the resident housekeeper, Josie was careful to turn her back on the lime avenue. She set off in an entirely different direction from Dario, in case he got the impression she was following him. Heading out to the far side of the estate, she passed through shady groves of ancient olive trees and fragrant citrus, soaking up the sun. She wanted to reach the point where the di Sirena estate's grand gated drive met the twisting country road that idled past on its way to Florence.

She had spotted two men working on a stone wall there. In her experience, boundary walls were magical things. All through history, people had haggled over them and changed them, climbed over them and dropped things in the process, or hidden special little items in between their stones or under their foundations. She set off towards the workmen in a hurry, but the intense heat soon sapped her energy. Strolling along was the only way to travel on a beautiful day like this. A skylark lifted off from right under her feet, while corn buntings and yellowhammers rattled away from every thicket she passed.

She had drunk almost a whole bottle of water by the time she'd toiled all the way over to the workmen. One of them had already left in search of his dinner. The other was clearing up ready to disappear, too. Luckily he was a fund of stories, with a keen eye for what he called 'little bits of something and nothing'. She was listening to him intently when she felt, rather than heard, a drumming sound reverberating through the parched grassland beneath her feet.

It was Dario. Mounted on a magnificent bay horse, he was cantering towards where she stood.

Josie planned to call out a casual, carefree hello, as though his appearance didn't make her pulse immediately speed up. However, as she watched him ride towards her like a prince, come out of a storybook to claim her for his own, the words somehow caught in her throat and she was silent as he drew up in front of her.

He grinned. 'I've had friendlier greetings!'

Josie swallowed and managed to force words out of her suddenly dry mouth. 'Oh…I'm sorry, Dario. I was engrossed in what Signor Costa had to say, and you caught me by surprise.'

'As I see. What's keeping you so busy?' Bringing his horse to a halt, he circled it around while sharing a few words with his estate worker.

'You want to know about the history of this boundary wall?' he asked Josie when he had finished his conversation.

She nodded, but looking at Dario made it difficult to remember what she *did* want. He looked magnificent, mounted high above her, the reins of his horse in one hand while the other rested loosely on the muscular plane of his thigh.

'Yes—can you help?'

He laughed. 'Not directly. I came over to see if you needed a translator.'

Josie's heart turned a somersault, but she managed to keep her voice under control.

'Thank you, but I can manage,' she replied confidently. Then, afraid of sounding rude, she added, 'I find I can concentrate better without distractions. I…I mean on my own…'

'That's a shame. I was looking forward to watching you at work. It makes a refreshing change. People don't normally come here to do anything constructive. It's a place built for pleasure.'

Josie stifled an involuntary moan. The chances of getting any work done with Count Dario around were minimal. She would be spending all her time trying not to look at the scenery—and she wasn't thinking about the Tuscan hills…

What's the matter with me? She struggled with her conscience. It won in the end—but only just.

'Th…thank you for the offer, Dario, but at the moment I'm just fact-finding for the course I'm designing. I'm sure you'd find it very boring.'

He looked at her, his eyes amused, as though he could see straight through her flimsy defences.

'OK, then. I need to check up on something on the

other side of the village anyway, so I'll leave you alone to get on with your work—for the moment, at least.'

He backed his horse to leave. Josie couldn't decide whether she was relieved to be left alone or sorry that he was going.

'Since you've taken the trouble to come all this way to stay in my home, I'll ask around to see if anyone else has some stories about the boundary wall. And come to me when you're ready to see some more of the Castello Sirena's secrets.'

He sounded completely genuine, but the smile she gave him in return was apprehensive.

'That would be great. Thanks.'

Josie had never known herself to be so easily distracted before—*ever*.

This sort of thing happens to other women, not to me! she thought. It made her feel weak, which in turn made her feel cross with herself and she scowled.

'Are you sure you're OK?' Dario asked.

'It's the heat, that's all,' she told him abruptly. 'Sun like this is so rare in England, I'm not used to it.'

'Then take care of yourself.' Suddenly his voice was unexpectedly firm. 'Keep to the shade, and always wear a hat. When I see you again, I don't want it to be as a sunstroke victim in the local casualty unit.'

Raising one hand in a salute, he rode away. Josie found herself staring after him and had to apologise to Giacomo, the workman. She didn't need a translation of the workman's reply. His knowing chuckle was enough to give her a pretty good idea of what he was thinking. Blushing furiously, she made a point of turning back to her study of the ancient stones that were being used to repair the wall rather than watch Dario.

Work first, play later, she repeated to herself—but for once her usual mantra didn't seem quite so comforting.

Dario couldn't quite put his finger on it, but there was something about Dr Josie Street that unsettled him. He kept thinking about her pale face and tense movements on and off for the rest of the day. She was socially awkward and dressed to disappear into the background rather than make a fashion statement. All the same, he could see why his sister had taken to her—Josie had a charm all of her own. She was delightfully easy to tease, and her innocence was irresistible for someone whose social palate had felt somewhat jaded of late. She had been so animated in her conversation with Giacomo. Dario had seen her gestures from a hundred yards away and automatically assumed she needed a translator. It was only as he rode nearer he saw she was simply engrossed in her subject. He liked that. He hadn't been nearly so keen on the way she seemed to lose all her self-confidence when she saw him.

She went out of her way to communicate with Giacomo, but she could barely string two sentences together once I appeared, he thought.

For a moment, Dario was reminded of Arietta. He had no idea why, because she had been the complete opposite of Josie—talkative with him, but almost silent in company. Forcibly dismissing the image of his late fiancée, he tried to think of something else. It should have been easy enough. After all, he had lived without Arietta for far longer than they had been together.

But to find her loss could still hurt him acted as a powerful warning.

Arietta's memory will not *be allowed to come back to haunt me again tonight,* Dario thought firmly as he got ready to go out for dinner that evening. As he fastened a pair of solid gold cufflinks into his white dress shirt, he heard the rapid crunch of gravel from outside. Looking out of a window, he saw Josie striding away into the distance, so he strolled out onto his balcony.

'Where are you off to in such a hurry?' he called down to her. 'Can I give you a lift?'

She stopped and turned in a clatter of falling equipment. She was carrying a shuttle tray but it was piled far too high with trowels, brushes and other tools. Now half of them were slithering to the ground.

'Thanks…' she put a hand across her chest as though trying to hide her practical but dull overalls '…but I couldn't put you to all that trouble…'

'It's no trouble.' He swung back into his suite but, by the time he had pulled on his jacket and made his way down to the courtyard, she was gone.

Dario kept a lookout for Josie as he drove towards the main gates of his estate a little while later. When he spotted her, she was already hard at work beside the old boundary wall. They waved to each other in passing. That was something; but Dario knew she must have virtually run like a rabbit to have got there so fast. He wondered why. There could be nothing scary about him.

Little scenes with Josie kept edging their way into his mind all that evening, despite the attentions of several female guests. Unlike Josie, they were all dressed in the finest clothes that Milan, Paris and New York had to offer. Everything—all their glamour, all their charm—was aimed straight at him. Dario got the same treatment at every party he attended, so he was used to it and hardly noticed. Occasionally he allowed himself to succumb to the flattery, but for some reason his heart wasn't in it tonight and his mind started to wander. What sort of dresses might his new house guest have brought with her? He looked around the assembly, idly imagining Josie dressed in purple silk or black satin. At that point his mind veered off on a very interesting tangent.

I've got sheets that colour, he thought. *I wonder what Josie would look like between them.*

Just then a waiter materialised silently at his side. The man was holding a chilled bottle of champagne wrapped in stiff folds of linen.

'No, thanks, I'm driving.' Dario waved him away regretfully, but the interlude put a mischievous thought in his head. He always enjoyed champagne, and kept a good selection of vintages back at the castle.

I'm sure a glass or two of that would help Josie celebrate her first day at the rock face, he thought.

Making his excuses to his host, he left and made a rapid escape.

* * *

By the end of the day Josie was so tired she could barely put one foot in front of the other, but she could not have been happier. For most of the time she had been alone, which for her made work more relaxing than any holiday. However, in spite of her determination, her mind had kept wandering in the direction of Dario and she needed a rest.

Dragging herself off to bed, she set her alarm very early so she could write up her notes first thing and still be outside before sunrise. The last thing she remembered was the low drone of a powerful engine, cutting through the velvet darkness outside. As she closed her eyes, she remembered the way Dario had described the view from the solar by night and the beautiful turbulence of his expression when he'd looked at her. It was enough to send every other thought clean out of her mind. Drifting off to sleep in her sumptuous empress-sized bed, she smiled. This was a wonderful place, but Dario was full of dangerous temptation for her. The only safe place for an encounter with him would be in her dreams.

By the time his car swung into the courtyard, she was fast asleep.

Dario leapt out of his car but, before he called for a chauffeur to take it away, he glanced up at the West wing tower. It was in total darkness. That was a blow. Hoping Josie had simply switched off her lights to enjoy the view from the windows as he had suggested, he fetched a bottle of champagne and a couple of glasses. Then he went up and tapped on the door of her suite.

Never mind. She can still have the full Castello Sirena treatment, he thought, ignoring his disappointment that he wouldn't be there to share it with her. Scribbling a quick note on the bottle's label, he stood it outside her door.

For some reason he couldn't quite fathom, he wanted to tempt Josie into having a little fun, more than he'd wanted anything for a while. His interrupted dinner party was proof enough. Maybe her resistance was simply a new challenge? Whatever the reason, clearly he wasn't going to be able to get her out of his mind until he'd won her over.

A long, leisurely lunch should kick things off nicely, he decided.

Josie was so polite, Dario knew she would never be able to refuse his invitation.

He smiled as he strolled off to bed. It would be deliciously ironic to use her typical English reserve to build bridges between them...

CHAPTER THREE

NEXT morning, Josie's alarm woke her before dawn had tinted the sky. The temptation to roll over and snuggle down for another couple of hours was almost overwhelming, but there were a thousand acres of the di Sirena estate waiting to be explored, and she couldn't resist that. Getting ready in double quick time, she flung open the door of her suite, ready to run out and get started—and almost tripped over a bottle of champagne waiting just outside.

It must have been left over from Dario's wild night out! She smiled, putting it aside.

Josie hadn't spent a night out—wild or otherwise—for ages. With a twinge of faint embarrassment, she remembered how painful social events like that could be for her.

She slipped out of the castle while the day was still dim and the air cool. For the next few hours she crisscrossed the di Sirena estate and was soon cursing herself for not bringing a hat. She used pools of shadow wherever she could, but the sun burned hotter by the second.

At first she was so absorbed by her work she had no

time to think about anything else. Then she became aware that she was not alone. Wherever she went, Count Dario di Sirena was never far away. She spotted his horse tethered beside the olive press just after she left, then later she saw him approaching the dairy as she was heading away into the hills.

It's nothing but coincidence, she thought.

Although coincidence couldn't quite explain the sudden shiver she got every time their paths crossed.

Dario thought that going out for a ride would give him some much needed space and time in his schedule to think. It worked—but not in the way he expected. The still, silent images of Josie observing him from her window, or waving to him as he left home the night before, kept creeping into his mind. He couldn't puzzle out exactly what it was about her that attracted him, but it wasn't for want of opportunity. It seemed that wherever he went today, there she was. She popped up in the most unlikely places, from the hay store to the olive press. After a while it began to make Dario feel slightly uncomfortable. He might have thought he was being stalked, but for one thing. Instead of following him, Josie always managed to be one step ahead. It was as though she was reading his mind and anticipating his movements. He snorted with derision. The idea was ridiculous—but it didn't stop him thinking about it. Usually he was never in any doubt about anything, but Josie was definitely having an effect on him.

From her tightly drawn ponytail right down to the steel toecaps of her sensible work boots, Dr Josie

Street meant business. That made her almost unique, in Dario's experience. Her furious blush when he'd explained about the champagne was the closest he got to an unguarded moment, and she barely said a thing even then. It was such a refreshing change from the endless, meaningless chatter poured into his ears at parties every night. Unless something was worth saying Josie kept quiet. Everything about her felt so calm, so stable and so right. So why did she always manage to put him on edge? Dario shook such thoughts away and decided it was definitely time to take command of the situation.

When Josie found herself drawn to a shady glade, she didn't consider there was anything mysterious about it—to begin with. It was simply her desperate need to get out of the heat and dazzling sun. Spotting the glitter of water in a forested depression overlooking the *castello*, she headed straight for it. There wasn't time to enjoy the view as she slithered down a steep rough bank, desperate to reach the cool green depths of the woodland below. Only when she plunged between the gnarled sweet chestnuts, ash trees and birches could she catch her breath and take stock of her surroundings.

As her eyes became accustomed to the cool gloom, a voice drifted through the trees towards her.

'Ciao, Josie.'

Dario had looped the reins of his horse over the low branch of a tree and was crouched beside it. He looked like a magnificent animal poised to spring—but in his hand he held a delicate, wide-brimmed straw hat.

'You made me jump!'

'I intended to.' He grinned. 'You didn't take any notice of my warning about sunstroke, so I've come to make you see sense.'

'You seem to appear everywhere I go today,' she said suspiciously.

He stood up and walked towards her, offering the hat.

'I could say the same thing about you. Everywhere I go, you're there ahead of me. I got my staff to look out one of Antonia's hats for you. She won't mind—but I would be very disappointed if you refused this as well as my champagne, Josie.' He smiled.

The sight of Dario dominating the glade was almost enough to rob her of the power of speech. Although he was so tall and well built, he moved almost silently across the forest floor towards her. With his raven dark hair and beautifully honed body accentuated by his white shirt and dark trousers, Josie was reminded again of a panther stalking its prey. Realising what was likely to happen to her resolve if she didn't keep Dario at a distance, she tried to put up a strong defence.

'I notice you're not wearing a hat yourself.' Her voice was uncertain with nerves.

'I'm used to the sun—although you're quite right. Experience isn't a licence to take risks. I make sure I keep to the shade wherever possible, as much for Ferrari's sake as mine.' He tipped his head towards where his bay horse was quietly pulling at some succulent undergrowth. 'I've been exploring these hills all my life, so I know the best places,' he said with a gleam in his eyes. 'For instance, did you know this pool has a secret? We're being watched.'

Crooking his index finger, he beckoned her towards the water's edge.

'When we were children, Antonia used to love being scared by the monster that lives behind that curtain of leaves up there.' He pointed to where greenery hung down over the source of a waterfall tumbling into the pool. 'She used to dare me to pull it back, then she'd run away screaming when I did.'

Josie watched the water splashing down from beneath heavy curtains of fern and ivy. It escaped over bare wet rocks to send ripples dancing out over the clean, clear water.

'There doesn't look to be anything to be scared of.'

Dario chuckled. 'You say that now, but when you're six years old an ancient carved face hidden among the rocks can seem very scary. Local legend says it's Etruscan, but an expert like you would need to check it out to make certain. Antonia has never got around to it.'

Josie's eyes lit up. 'Now you've got me interested.'

'I knew I would.' His smile widened mischievously. 'So—what do you say? Would you dare to come with me now and take a look?'

Josie couldn't answer. She was studying the pool. It had been edged with wide stones, but everything was now worn with age and green with algae. It looked treacherous. Dario was already striding around the perimeter to the other side and calling across the water to her.

'I'll go first. Look, it's perfectly safe—but, if you're nervous, you'll get a better view if you stand over there, beside that nearest alder...'

Josie had dropped her bag and reached his side before he finished speaking. Her fear of being thought not up to a task was greater than her fear of the water, until she saw where she would have to walk. The path to the spring's source was narrow and cut into solid rock. In places, water splashed and played over it as though from a hose.

Edging along, she followed as close behind Dario as she dared. As he crossed the wettest place she took a step forward, felt her foot slip and caught her breath in a tiny cry of panic. Instantly, he grabbed her hand but she had already fought and won the battle to retain her footing. Once again she pulled herself from his grasp.

'I'm fine, thank you.'

Dario wasn't convinced, but grudgingly gave her the benefit of the doubt. 'As long as you're sure.'

'I didn't mean to alarm you. Water just isn't my thing, that's all,' she said, gritting her teeth.

'Does that mean you won't be using the swimming pool down at the *castello* during your stay?' he murmured as they pressed on.

She steeled herself to ignore the interesting tone in his voice.

'Not if I can help it.'

'A shame. Though I, too, much prefer the fun that can be had on dry land.' His words were suggestive, but when Josie glanced at him suspiciously he met her gaze innocently, belying the wickedness she could see in his smile.

'At a time like this I'm inclined to agree with you,' she answered with grim determination as she concen-

trated on keeping her balance and ignoring the butterflies in her stomach. 'Can you hurry up and show me
whatever it is? This is turning into some kind of en-
durance test!'

'As someone who is in the business of teaching, you
should know that nothing good comes without effort.'

'The benefits of hard work can be overstated,' Josie
said quietly before she could stop herself.

She had to concentrate grimly on her footwork, but
Dario could afford to look at her quizzically.

'What do you mean?'

Josie cursed the twin distractions of Etruscan art and
the slippery surface. She had said too much. Furious
with herself for accidentally bringing up such a sensitive subject, she tried to laugh it off.

'Oh…while I was studying, my boyfriend found
someone else to catalogue his artefacts for him. You
know how it is,' she finished lamely, expecting him
to laugh.

He didn't. Instead, he looked at her for a quiet moment, while Josie shivered under his leisurely, assessing gaze.

'What a foolish man, not to see what he had,' he said
quietly, before turning away as if the compliment had
never happened. Josie took a deep breath, trying to control the adrenalin suddenly fizzing through her veins.

'Here we are…careful…now look at this…'

Reaching out, Dario pushed aside the curtain of
young hart's tongue fronds. Nourished by the run off
from the slopes above, they were easily two feet long
and covered the source of the waterfall with thick green

ripples. As he moved the leaves apart, Josie saw that the water poured out from the mouth of a hideous grinning mask. It must have truly terrified Antonia when she'd played here as a child, more than twenty years before.

'Wow!' she breathed.

In her excitement she forgot all her fears about the slippery surface. Squeezing in front of Dario, she leaned forward for a closer look. At that moment a wren burst out indignantly from its hiding place behind the stone head. Whirring past Josie's face, it missed her by inches and gave her such a fright she jumped, lost her footing—and toppled straight into the pool.

Her world exploded in a mass of bubbles. Before she had time to realise what was happening, she was grabbed and pulled above the surface again. Half drowned and spluttering, she found herself held tightly in Dario's arms. She felt his body shaking and heard his laughter, but her indignation died as she discovered how incredible it felt to be pressed against his hard, unyielding body.

She stopped struggling. For one glorious moment the glade fell still and silent. All she could hear was the sound of her own heartbeat and feel Dario's pulse beating in time with hers. It was intoxicating, and such a primal feeling. His beautiful face was so close, she felt her lips part in anticipation of something so wonderful she dared not give it a name.

Then she remembered what it felt like when temptation led to betrayal. Panic engulfed her. In a surge of desperation, she tried to wriggle from his grasp, flailing the water into a maelstrom.

'Hold still!'

Josie stopped splashing. Her feet floated down and she found her toes brushing the floor of the pool.

'Oh…' she moaned, feeling a complete fool.

'You're quite safe with me,' he said reassuringly, and Josie wanted to believe it.

She tipped her head back to look at him properly. Water trickling over the carved intensity of his face sparkled in golden streaks of sunlight flickering through the trees.

'Oh, dear—you seem to have got a faceful of water!' She blushed. 'I'm so sorry.'

Dario said nothing. His white shirt was plastered against his chest, showing dark shadows of hair beneath. Feeling his body, so hot and vital in the cool seductive depths of the pool, Josie unconsciously relaxed against him. Her whole body felt as liquid as the water, ready to absorb him and flow around him for ever. His eyes feasted on her face, and it was the ultimate aphrodisiac. When his hands began to move, she held her breath in an agony of expectation. As he gently brushed a lock of wet hair away from the corner of her mouth, she closed her eyes again. Unable to resist, she parted her lips and this time she knew exactly what she wanted. Her breathing quickened in desperate anticipation of his kiss.

Then, at the last moment, either her common sense returned or her nerve failed her—she never knew which it was. Opening her eyes, she shook her head so quickly and violently that droplets of water flew through the air like shards of glass. Letting go of his supportive hand, she waded away from him and towards the edge of the pool. There, she hauled herself out of the water and began to walk away, back to where her things lay scattered on the forest floor. She had never felt so tempted by a man before in her life. She knew she had to put some distance between them as soon as possible, for the sake of her own sanity.

Still waist-deep in the water, Dario surveyed her like Neptune.

'You should be more careful.'

'I know—that's why I got out of there as soon as I could,' Josie snapped. 'I'll be keeping well away from the edge from now on, believe me.'

In every sense of the word, she added silently.

The thought of Dario leaping in to save her again if she got into difficulties was doing very strange things to her body.

Dario hardly heard what she said. Josie amazed him. Not many people were prepared to stand up to him. Now, soaked to the skin and with her wet white T-shirt clinging to her body in almost transparent folds, she was a breathtaking sight.

Acutely aware of his scrutiny, Josie kept on walking away from him, trying to wring the water out of her clothes and ponytail as she did so.

'And please don't look at me like that.'

'Have you got eyes in the back of your head?'

'I don't need them, where you're concerned. I can feel you looking at me.'

'It's meant as a compliment,' he mused.

'Then thank you, but please stop,' she said sharply.

'I'd like to get a photograph of that spring. It's exactly the sort of thing I'm interested in. If you really do want to help me, Dario, you could tell me if there are any more hidden treasures like that one on your estate.'

She could already feel the heat of the day pulling the moisture out of her cheap, thin clothes. If she blushed much more, they would be drying out from the inside as well as the outside. Trying to ignore the sounds behind her of Dario stripping off his sodden shirt, she knelt on the forest floor. Emptying the contents of her messenger bag onto the soft green moss surrounding the pool, she picked out her camera.

'You should come out here in the sunshine with me. You'll get dry quicker,' Dario called.

Before she could stop herself, Josie looked up and saw him in magnificent silhouette. He was rubbing some still-dry parts of his shirt over his wet body before sliding his arms into its damp embrace again. 'It's a great way to cool off, but when I decided to treat you to lunch out here I never expected to need towels as well.'

'Lunch?'

'You don't think I'd come out to find you without being fully prepared?' He strolled across the glade, doing up the buttons of his shirt as he walked. Josie purposely avoided watching the way his fingers moved, as it brought back all too clearly the memory of their potent strength. Instead, she looked him straight in the face—but that laid her wide open to the devastating effect of his smile.

* * *

Holding Josie powerless in his arms had aroused all
sorts of feelings in Dario. Now, he couldn't stop thinking about the best use for secluded glades—and that
was seduction. When he had ridden out here to surprise
her with an impromptu picnic, he hadn't expected to
end up holding her so tightly against his body, even in
the role of lifeguard. Dario was a typical red-blooded
Italian male and found it difficult to ignore temptation.
Especially when it came in the form of a voluptuous
woman in thin, wet clothing.

As Dario raised his arm to unstrap the picnic basket
from his horse's saddle, his white sleeve flickered
brightly against the mysterious depths of the wood. It
was as good as a signal to Josie. She tensed as he walked
back to join her.

'Hmm…as I thought—the staff have only packed
hand towels, although if I put this picnic rug around
your shoulders—'

The rug was folded up so tightly he needed both
hands to shake it free. Unfurling it, he moved forward
to swirl it around Josie's shoulders, but when he touched
her she drew in her breath and backed away.

'I can manage, thank you.' Reaching out, she snatched
the picnic rug from his fingers.

'You're shivering. Let's go and sit in that patch of
sunshine over there.'

Picking up the picnic basket, he went over to the
far side of the clearing. When he looked back she was
following, but slowly and at a distance. Dario smiled
to himself; he had enough experience to know when a

woman was nearly his. He started to unpack the things he had brought, then sat back on his heels as she came towards him cautiously.

'The archaeology isn't suddenly going to disappear before you can get to it, and I'm hardly going to eat you when my kitchen has provided us with all *this*.' He spread a hand towards the tempting display he was setting out. 'Why not take the time actually to enjoy yourself for once, Josie? Are you too sensible to relax? Give it a try over lunch—there's no one here to see!'

Unable to resist his challenge, as he'd known she would be, she sat down, but several feet away from him. When Dario went back to his work without comment, she eventually leaned forward to help. Without moving his head, he saw her hands moving in and out of his peripheral vision, arranging pristine white crockery like clouds against the sky-blue picnic cloth.

'There. What could be better than that?' He turned to her.

For a split second they looked into each other's eyes, then her glance slipped away to the half a dozen tempting types of antipasto the *castello*'s kitchen had packed for them. As the pool of sunlight gilded her wet brown hair, Dario opened a bottle of limoncello and poured a shot of it into each of two crystal glasses. Topping them up with chilled mineral water, he handed one to Josie. Then, touching his glass lightly against hers, he said softly, *'Salute!'*

She gazed at him, then at the food on display, and then at the drink in her hand.

'You did all this for me?' Her tone was one of sheer disbelief.

'Where I come from, picnics are a couple of rounds of sandwiches grabbed from a supermarket. I don't know what to say…or where to start…' she began, but Dario didn't need to be told—the look in her eyes said it all. He moved around, away from the sudden rush of emotion he felt at her obvious pleasure, until he was on the far side of their feast. From there, safely back in seduction mode, he started to offer her little dishes of *caponata* and pasta salad, smiling as she gave in to temptation.

Josie chose some roasted tomatoes and peppers, gleaming with the estate's own olive oil, mozzarella and a slice of fragrant focaccia spiked with rosemary and crystals of sea salt. While Dario loaded his plate with a little of everything on display, she watched him covertly. His movements had the smooth assurance of a man born to lead. With another shiver, she noticed the strength in his smooth brown forearms. The sleeves of his shirt were turned back, showing off his taut muscles. That provoked a reaction deeper than anything her ex-fiancé had ever sown in her. Unexpected sensations simmered within her, and they were scary—not because Dario felt threatening, but because of the way her body responded so easily to his. She could remember every nuance of feeling aroused by his capable hands as they rescued her from the water. Her body had been without the touch of a man for so long, she had forgotten how exciting the slightest contact could be.

'Is there anything else you'd like, Josie?'

In her heightened state, his voice was a purr of encouragement as seductive as the sound of the golden orioles warbling deep in the woodland around them. She felt her mouth go dry. Her whole body began to melt under the warmth of his gaze. To hide her growing arousal, she took a long, slow sip of her limoncello. Nothing in her life so far had prepared her for the sensuous promise she heard in Dario's voice—or the primitive reactions of her body. The lilt of his rich accent cast a magical spell over her every time he spoke her name.

This is seduction by telepathy, she thought.

Dario seemed perfectly attuned to her, and her physical response to his confident masculinity. Her body turned to water beneath his gaze, ebbing and flowing like the warm flush that threatened to engulf her entirely. It was a struggle to conceal the effect he was having on her. Before they met, she had assumed any contact with this man would be brief and boring. Now his silent temptation threatened to undermine all her good intentions to concentrate on her work while she had the chance.

'Let me guess. Before you got here, you had already assumed you would dislike me on sight. Now you find I'm not the man you expected. Isn't that so?' he said quietly.

Josie swallowed her reply. It would only incriminate her, when her expression alone was enough to set the light of amusement dancing in his amazing eyes.

'And now you are wondering how I know that! It's

because I thought exactly the same about you, Josie. To begin with.'

She picked up her cutlery, pretending to be more interested in her meal than she was in Dario. It was a mistake. She might be able to ignore the tremors of excitement powering through her body but it was impossible to suppress the way her hands were trembling. Sunlight filtering between the leaves high above flickered and danced over her silver fork, betraying her.

'You're making me nervous,' she announced in her defence.

'Really? I don't know why. It's never been my intention to scare you.'

'I didn't say I was scared. It's more a kind of… passive intimidation…' she managed. The past histories of her mother, her best friend and her own broken engagement were powerful reminders of what could happen when a man didn't get things his own way, but right now defiance was the last thing on Josie's mind.

Dario's beautifully sculpted mouth lifted in a smile. 'I imagine my forebears would be pleased to hear you say that. They ruled by the sword. But, speaking for myself, I've never liked to think I make people nervous. I want you to enjoy yourself, Josie. So…what more can I do to please you?'

The tempting lilt in his voice was deliberately ambiguous. She could see it in his eloquent dark eyes.

'I think this lovely lunch is enough for the time being, thank you,' she told him unsteadily.

He nodded, and turned his attention to his own plate.

Josie felt a sudden stab of disappointment that he had taken her words as a hint to back off.

'What keeps a man like you buried out here in the countryside?' she said, desperate to steer the topic of conversation away from herself. As she moved, a mischievous little breeze cooled the damp T-shirt beneath the blanket around her shoulders. It clung to the smooth curves of her breasts, sharpening her nipples into almost painful points. They were tingling in a way that made her want to learn a whole lot more about Dario, despite all her reservations.

'I can't tear myself away from the place.' He raised both his hands in a gesture of resignation. 'This estate, these people—they are my duty but, beyond that, this countryside is part of me. Although I couldn't expect a modern woman to understand this.'

Josie stiffened. '*Modern?* What's that supposed to mean? Are you making fun of me?'

Dario turned his attention to a pile of fruit that stood between them. Selecting a perfect peach, he cupped it in one hand, feeling its mass and appreciating its weight.

'The meaning I had in mind was *intellectual*,' he said idly. 'You're used to using your mind instead of taking simple pleasure from your surroundings. You've come here from a place where learning is prized above emotion, and so that has coloured your attitude.'

'I sometimes wish it hadn't,' she said wistfully.

He smiled. It was a slow, seductive gesture that reached right out to her.

'Good…because here at the Castello Sirena, emotions run deep; deeper even than the spring that feeds our ancient pool. It is a place made for pleasure, not for relentless work. Let me show you.' His voice was a warm caress of desire. 'In my world, even the simple acting of eating can be transformed into a beautiful experience.'

Taking a silver fruit knife, he cut a neat segment from the fruit in his other hand. Reaching across their picnic, he held the slice out to her.

Josie's mind went to pieces completely.

Work later, play now...

The gentle sounds of nature receded as her head filled with clouds of cotton wool. She seemed to be looking at herself from outside. Instead of taking the piece of fruit from Dario's fingers with her own, she watched herself lean forward to take it directly into her mouth. Through a warm mist of arousal, she heard herself gasp as the peach's rich nectar ran down her chin.

Dario had never expected her to do something so spontaneous. His shock and surprise seamlessly turned to raw lust, ready to overwhelm him. No one could expect a man like Count Dario di Sirena to refuse such an invitation. Swiftly and silently, he took Josie's hands and moved in to taste her.

CHAPTER FOUR

FOR endless moments Josie was powerless to resist Dario's sudden onslaught. The tip of his tongue traced delicately over her skin until she willed him to pull her into his arms and make mad passionate love to her…

…Then a sudden breeze rustling through the trees startled her out of her paralysis. Shrinking away from him, she stood up, but he followed. Josie had been so completely lost in the moment, she was still holding his hand. There was no point in trying to let go now—her body wouldn't allow it. When he took a step forward to claim her again, she succumbed to the magic of his mouth a second time.

Josie knew she should resist, but it was as though their kisses were always meant to be. As his arms enfolded her, she melted under their firm pressure. The touch of his fingers as they glided over her back pressed her wet T-shirt against her naked skin. When she shivered he held her closer, but she wasn't cold. The heat of desire kept rising and building within her until she twined her arms around his neck. This was it—she was ready to be released from her long and painful sentence of self-denial. All the years of loneliness would slip away, forgotten, in this single supreme act. She pressed her body against his, feeling the scarily exciting kick of his manhood against her belly. When that happened he drew back, and for the first time in what felt like heady hours of excitement their lips parted.

Dario's chest rose and fell rapidly as he snatched at steadying breaths. Josie fought the urge to lean forward and kiss him again—and for one desperate moment she saw him struggle with that same primitive need. Then he closed his eyes and his head sank until his forehead rested against hers. For one heart-stopping moment she thought he was going to take her lips again.

'Yes…' she breathed in reply, not wanting him to stop. His response was a sigh almost absorbed by the silence. 'Please, Dario…'

After all, as he had said, there was no one about to see…and no one but Josie's conscience to know what happened out here among the trees. Her mind had tortured her for too long already. Rising on tiptoe, she searched for his lips with her own and tasted his skin.

All the time her hands roamed over his body, he stood as still as stone. It was only when her hands slid around his waist that he stirred and gave a wordless moan of longing and regret. Then he reached around and grasped her wrists. That one simple movement woke Josie from her trance. With a spasm of alarm, she realised how close she had come to total surrender. She stood back and stared at him, shocked.

Dario's expression was a mask of regret, his eyes squeezed shut as he whispered, 'No…I can't… I'm sorry…*Arietta…*'

Josie's longing drained away, replaced by the old, familiar mix of anger, shame and humiliation.

'You could at least call me by the right name!' she spat.

That broke the spell.

'I should never have done anything at all,' he said grimly, dropping her hands and striding away across the glade towards his horse.

Josie watched him go in silent horror. If only she had trusted her instincts. For years, she had been careful to stay out of harm's way. On that principle, she should have kept right away from Dario. She had suspected there must be a girl in his life, and now she knew—*and no wonder,* she added, *he's irresistible!*

Instantly, she regretted the terrible thought. It catapulted her straight back to the dark, awful moment when she'd discovered Andy had been cheating on her. Back then, she hadn't been able to understand how any woman could inflict such agony on another and here she was, guilty of almost exactly the same thing.

I've always said I couldn't bear to put anyone through what I've suffered, she thought. *Not even for a man with kisses like that...*

She had to get away. Snatching up her bag and camera, she plunged out of the glade and into the sunshine. The thought of investigating that fountainhead now made her feel sick with guilt. It would always be linked in her mind with the first time Dario had touched her, and where that wonderful sensation had led.

If I hadn't succumbed to him, hadn't encouraged *him, if he hadn't moved in on me...*

Desperate for distraction, she scrambled back up the slope, away from that seductively shady woodland glade. The sun beat down mercilessly and she had left the sun hat behind. Tough, dry grasses scratched at her hands and the dusty hot air kept catching in her throat. By the time she reached the crest of the hill, her breath was tearing holes in her chest but she still couldn't forget the feel of Dario's hands and the exciting insistence of his lips.

Dropping to the ground in the meagre shade of a juniper, she looked down on the scene she had left behind. Dario had returned to the woodland edge. He was half in shadow, half in sunlight. Shielding her eyes against the sun, she studied him. His hands were on his hips and he was staring up the hill towards her. As she watched, waiting for him to jeer at her, he did something quite unexpected. His head dropped, he rubbed his hands over his face as if trying to scrub off something dirty—and then he turned away.

It was an indignity too far.

Josie was only too aware that she used work as an excuse to retreat from real life. *And this is why!* she thought furiously. *Is it any wonder I keep myself to myself when there are men like Dario about?*

She took out her notebook and looked around for something new to study, determined to try to carry on as normal. It was hopeless. She could only think of one thing, and it wasn't work.

It seemed to Josie that whenever she tried to taste life as other people lived it, she came unstuck. She had started off her adult life by using hard work as the measure of her success. By the time she had realised her fiancé was more interested in his own prospects than their future together, he was already having an affair with one of her colleagues. That betrayal had been awful, and public. But there was another, darker side to her disappointment. The idea that sex with Andy had never set her on fire had been a private worry, which made today ten times more painful. In a few seconds Dario had blown away all her fears of being frigid, and released the animal inside her. Now she found herself wanting more. A man who could surely have any woman he wanted had managed to unravel all her self-control simply by holding her in his arms. In the seductive shadows, that scared her. Out here in the brutal light of day, it stoked her anger. It took the sight of Dario's reaction to provoke an emotion in her more powerful than the fear of her own needs.

No one turns their back on me any more! she thought, getting to her feet and brushing her hands free from dust in a gesture dramatic enough for him to see. Shaking out the folds of her damp T-shirt and jabbing all the escaped strands of soggy hair behind her ears, she took a deep breath. Then she marched down the slope again. In a few frantic moments she had learned a little about Dario di Sirena—but a whole lot more about herself.

It was time to start being ruthlessly honest. He had kissed her only after she had first accepted his offer of a picnic in a secluded spot.

So what else did I expect to happen, after that clinch in the pool?

The man had acted completely in character. In contrast, she had sent her common sense back home to England!

A simple 'no thank you' to the picnic would probably have done the trick. I should have tried that first, she told herself, but knew it would have been impossible. Well, now she had to face up to the consequences of her actions.

The sun pounded down on her head almost as fiercely as the blood pulsed in her ears. Josie now realised she had been secretly wondering what it would be like to be kissed by Dario since first setting eyes on his sensuous mouth and those wonderfully dark, expressive eyes.

It was time to put her willpower to the test. Officially she was here to work, and that would be so much easier with Dario's goodwill rather than his contempt.

I'm bigger than my shame, master of my anger, even stronger than the lust that's still running through me—and this will prove it! she thought, stamping the seal on her determination with every step. The slope gave her a bit more momentum than she expected.

Dario was adjusting the harness of his horse, ready to leave the scene of the disaster. When he heard a noise and turned back to see what was happening, Josie was half-jogging down the hill in order to keep her balance.

'I hope you don't think I'm running back to you,' she said with all the dignity she could scrape together.

'No. But I do hope you have come back to accept my apology,' he said gravely, picking up her discarded sun hat and holding it out to her.

Josie hesitated, unable to decide whether he was being sincere or simply laughing at her. Stiffening her resolve, she grabbed the hat. To show how mad she was at him, she jammed it firmly onto her head. It was only then she realised Antonia's head must be bigger than her own. The sun hat came right down over her eyes, only stopping when it lodged on her ears.

Before she could do anything about it, lean brown fingers intruded into her restricted field of vision. Dario tilted the brim so he could look straight down into her eyes.

'That's better. As I said, you should never go without a hat in this sun.'

His tone was as cool as a mountain stream, in stark contrast to the liquid heat of his kisses only moments ago. There was no trace of emotion visible in him now, either good or bad. Angry though she was, Josie felt her knees turn to jelly again beneath his penetrating gaze.

'I shouldn't have behaved like that,' she said, hotly conscious of his scrutiny.

'Neither should I.'

He took a couple of careful steps back, putting a discreet distance between them again, before continuing unevenly, 'And then I made things worse by calling you by the wrong name. I apologise.' He cleared his throat, then continued with obvious reluctance. 'Arietta was my fiancée. She died some time ago. There was an accident—'

He stopped. She saw him take a deep breath and steady himself.

'I thought I had put the episode behind me, but apparently not.'

Josie stared at him, making her face a mask. She had to—her whole body was alive with uncertainty again. She knew all about loss, but it seemed Dario had suffered a far worse disaster than her own.

'I...I understand. I'm sorry, too. It was just as much my fault as yours. I shouldn't have led you on, Dario. We both got carried away. That's all.'

He nodded his appreciation, then cleared his throat again. 'It took a lot of courage to come back here after what happened, Josie.'

He was right, but she had never expected him to acknowledge that.

'I learned a long time ago that running away never solved anything, so now I just try to learn from my mistakes. I won't make the same one twice,' she said, trying to defuse the situation.

'No, I can't imagine you would,' he said drily.

From the far side of the glade came the sound of his horse, which had wandered off and was now fretting with its bit.

I must be mad, she thought. *Straight after kissing him like some sort of harlot, I've swung back to acting like a boring old maid!*

His kiss had made her feel like a woman again for the first time in years. She had forgotten how good that sensation could be, and she wanted to experience it again. Soon. She dithered, blushing, and not knowing what to say.

If I told you what I was really thinking, it would be 'goodbye research, hello disaster!' she thought.

'In which case, I'll leave you to get on with your work and say *arrivederci*—for now.'

As Dario turned to walk away, Josie felt a powerful urge to call him back. He anticipated her. Swinging himself up into his saddle, he turned his horse in a wide arc, passing very close to where she stood. He treated her to a long, lingering view of his tight breeches and enviable seat as he circled the glade.

Lifting the corners of his mouth in a smile, he acknowledged their new intimacy. 'But the next time your schedule allows you some room to do something scarily spontaneous again, Josie, be sure to let me know.'

Nudging his horse into a canter, he headed out of the glade and off across the grassy hillside.

Josie was left to stare after him. The way Dario had coaxed her into baring her soul to him was uncanny. She might have expected to feel angry that he found her so easy to read. Instead, she felt let down and strangely empty inside. The wonderful warmth of arousal he had coaxed into life deep within her body threatened to fade as she watched him ride away.

But it didn't die completely—and, since tasting the temptation of his kiss, Josie knew it never would.

CHAPTER FIVE

DARIO didn't look back. He rode fast, straight back to
the stables. There he leapt off his horse and let the stal-
lion find his own way to the nearest stable lad. Dario's
favourite refuge in times of crisis was his art. Striding
straight for his studio in the *castello* grounds, he went
in and slammed the door. Leaning back heavily against
it, he tried to think. Since Arietta died, he had roamed
from woman to woman, picking, choosing, but never
staying with anyone for long. To do anything else was
unthinkable. He always slipped away before emotion
could coil him in its oily grasp. Other people might
envy him, but they only saw his free and easy attitude.
Casual charm was his mask of choice.

Until now, he had never cared what other people
thought. He had gone out each day with a smile on
his face, and that was enough to reassure most people
that he was happy. Now the sunlight had shone into
more than that secluded glade. It had thrown back the
shadows from the most private place inside him. It was
somewhere so dark, not even Dario was aware of how
deep its secrets went. All he knew was that this morn-

ing he had let his nonchalant shield slip. So what was different about today?

Dr Josie Street, he thought.

Their kisses had torn away everything; he'd been captured by the simple pleasure of that moment, of that woman, in a way he hadn't experienced in years. Raw, naked lust had risen up, overwhelming all his finer feelings and making him almost lose control. Shame burnt through him—for a moment he'd forgotten Arietta.

When Josie had stormed away after their spectacular kiss, Dario had found himself unable to follow her. Instead, he had let out a stream of curses. He had enjoyed many women since losing Arietta, so what had happened today to make him say *her* name out loud?

Maybe it was because Josie was so different from all those other women. She had something they lacked. For a start, she might appear composed and serious, but he sensed that deeper down there was a core of fire. The women who usually competed for his attention never hid their passion. They tried to use it as bait. Josie fought to hide hers every inch of the way.

In that respect we're alike, he thought with a jolt of recognition. Most of the time she coped by staying silent, but that would never work on him again—not after he had felt the heat of her response and the passion of her kisses. Those few incendiary moments had unleashed the tigress in her, but instinctively Dario knew that if he casually took advantage of her awakened passion then Josie would never forgive herself. Or him.

There was another reason why he held back, too. Time had dimmed Arietta's memory but, for some reason, it had burst back into life when he'd responded to Josie. She attracted him in a way that no other woman had since Arietta, but he had no desire to go through that much pain again. And he suspected that if he pursued Josie, that was exactly what would happen.

For the rest of the day, Josie could think of nothing but Dario's kiss and the feel of his body. As she worked her way around the grounds of the Castello Sirena, her senses were tuned to detect him. Every moment she spent practising her Italian with the farm workers and villagers, she was secretly wondering about Dario— where he was and what he was doing.

Later, when she retreated to her room to write up her notes, she finally found out. As the shadows lengthened, the growl of a high-performance engine passed beneath her window. Looking out, she saw a beautiful royal-blue sports car accelerate away down the lime avenue.

That told her Dario's take on their encounter was very different from her own.

He must have put her out of his mind already. He was going back out on the town.

The next few days were a horrible mixture of routine and denial for Josie. Her mind kept telling her to forget about Dario. Her body had different ideas. Each time she thought of him, her pulse ran riot. She coped in the only way she knew how, by drawing up a punishing schedule of surveying and study for every day of her projected stay. She ticked tasks off that 'to do' list like a metronome. Every evening she fell into her dreamily comfortable bed, satisfied with what she had achieved. It was a routine that had got her top marks for as long as she could remember. It also shielded her bruised heart and kept a tight lid on her newly discovered libido. But soon her emotions fought against being confined any longer. The moment she closed her eyes, images of Dario filled her mind. The sound of his sports car roaring away as he set off on another night of pleasure made her pictures of him still more vivid. She could almost feel his hands around her waist, his cheek brushing her hair and his long, lingering kisses setting her senses on fire all over again...

She tried to tell herself he was a distraction she couldn't afford. That might have worked for her after Andy left, but it sure as hell didn't work with Dario.

Although their paths had somehow stopped crossing after their encounter in the wood, Josie wanted Dario to know it was because she was working, and not just hiding away from him. Whenever she was out on the estate she tried to forget him, but spent half her time looking over her shoulder. She was as wary as a gazelle on the African plains, on the alert for the lion that might pounce at any time.

As time went on and he didn't appear, she began to settle back into her normal routine, managing, for the most part, to push her frustrated desires back into hiding—and then one evening Dario rode out of the sunset while she was busy brushing the fine, dry soil away from her latest find. From being lost in her thoughts, Josie was thrown into confusion. With desperate movements she stood up, shoving her hair behind her ears and brushing the worst of the dust from the legs of her overalls. Then she rubbed her sleeve over her brow, before realising it was as grimy as her knees had been. Desperately she grabbed the towel from the table where she washed her finds. Without a mirror, she had to hope it made any smudges better and not worse. Trying to look absorbed in her work for the agonising minutes it took him to ride up to her was impossible. It was only when she stopped trying that he smiled.

'Dario,' she greeted him quietly.

'Josie,' he replied in kind as he jumped down from his horse.

Despite her apprehension, she couldn't help checking his saddle for another picnic basket. There wasn't one.

'I wondered what you were doing here,' she said to cover her embarrassment when he noticed what she was looking at.

'I live here, remember?'

'When you aren't roaring around the countryside by night,' she said before she could stop herself.

He raised his eyebrows, strolling past her to investigate her finds table. 'You noticed?'

'I can't help it…er…because the sound of your engine disturbs my work every night, that is.'

'But your suite is always in darkness,' he said casually, picking up one of her site sketches. 'I'm here to deliver a message, by the way. I thought you'd like to know that Antonia rang—she's coming home tomorrow. Hmm…I like this drawing. It's artistic as well as being accurate. You're clearly a woman of many talents.'

Josie tried not to feel smug, but it didn't work. In the face of his obvious appreciation, she felt horribly tongue-tied.

'You learn to be a jack of all trades in this job,' she muttered. 'Art used to be a bit of a hobby of mine. Not that I ever get a chance to do anything about it these days, apart from site sketches,' she said wistfully.

He made a disapproving noise. 'Have you ever thought of working some of these drawings up into full-sized paintings? They would add something unique to your coursework.'

'It's tempting…' she said, stealing a long look at his beautiful profile as he studied her work, '…but there's no point. Effort like that would be wasted on the academics who read my stuff.'

'Come on, Josie—don't be so defeatist! You're a highly qualified woman with a lot of talent, both inside and outside of your usual sphere. Why be content with such a small market for your skills?'

'You sound very sure of yourself. Who's to say anybody else would share your opinion?'

'I've studied art for long enough to know good work when I see it—you should have more confidence in yourself!'

His voice tailed off, as though he'd just heard his own enthusiasm. Josie glanced at him, but he looked away at almost the same instant. She almost caught herself smiling. According to Antonia, her brother Dario was a famous seducer but, standing in front of her now, he looked completely lost for words.

His uncomfortable silence didn't last long; he seemed

to gather himself and carried on in a more practical manner. 'With artistic talent like this, you could draw in a much wider audience. Quality artwork would attract people who wouldn't normally think of picking up an archaeology textbook. Me, for one.'

Josie chewed her lip. 'Do you really think so?'

'Definitely. I'm certain others would think that way, too.'

He sounded genuine, and smiled to drive the point straight into her heart. The memory of their eventful picnic made Josie break eye contact and move away from him. She started to tap a pile of already tidy papers into a meticulously rectangular block.

'Oh, I don't know. I don't have the time, or the equipment...'

'You should *make* time. It counts as work, so you wouldn't have to feel it's being wasted,' Dario said in a voice that gave her no option. 'And, as for equipment, that's no excuse either. I keep a well-stocked studio. Anything you want, you can get from me. In a purely artistic sense, of course,' he added hurriedly, seeing her frown.

'It's very kind, Dario, but I really can't spare the time...'

She looked over towards the Roman hearth she was uncovering, stone by stone. It was long, knee-numbing stuff.

He dropped his voice to a conspiratorial whisper. 'Come on...you know you want to! That floor has waited two thousand years for you to come along with your trowel and brush. Light and landscape is something that must be captured when it happens, and while it lasts. Like happiness, and laughter,' he added.

When she smiled, he suddenly reached out to her. She flinched, and his fingers stopped short of making contact with her cheek. She took a step back, leaving his hand to fall back to his side.

'I can see you've fully recovered from…the heat,' he said with a brittle smile. 'In which case, as I've done what I came to do, I'll leave you to your work. Goodbye, Josie, but don't forget what I said. Capture the moment. If you wait too long, it will slip through your fingers. And you'll always regret missing out.'

'You sound very sure about that!' She chuckled, but all signs of amusement had vanished from his expression.

'I am. Life can deal anyone a bad hand, Josie. Work is a great refuge, but you need to keep it in proportion. Look at me—running this estate and making sure I can pass it on to little Fabio in good heart takes up a lot of time, and it used to be that I'd focus only on that—but it's no way to live.'

'Fabio? But he's not your son.' Josie picked up on the name but then put her hand to her mouth. 'I'm sorry; it's none of my business.'

He looked startled, but hid it quickly. 'You're so close to Antonia, I assumed you knew all about that already.'

'We spend most of our time chatting about work,' Josie said. 'At least we did, until Fabio came along. We hardly ever talk about our families.'

He shrugged. 'I simply assumed she would have filled you in.'

'Dario, I don't need to be told anything more about you than I know already, unless you'd like me to know something,' she said, while secretly hoping he would insist on revealing more.

He was silent, seeming to struggle with his thoughts for a moment before the mask came down and, to Josie's disappointment, he was once again the suave, charming playboy.

'You're right. We both have work to do, so I'll let you get back into your trench,' he said smoothly, before mounting his horse and cantering quickly back the way he had come.

From then on, Josie couldn't stop wondering why Dario had made his little nephew his heir. Dario was only a few years older than she was. What made him so sure, so young, that he would never have children of his own? Was it something to do with his mysterious dead fiancée? Josie wasn't sure she wanted to find out the answer, but his words nagged at her like a puzzle begging to be solved.

She was tortured with curiosity for the rest of the day, but her worst moment came that night as she was drifting off to sleep, when the sound of his high-powered car dragged her awake again. Every night it took him away, leaving her sleepless and alone.

Dario and the memory of his kisses had awoken a need in Josie that would not let her rest. She got out of bed and went over to the window to watch the tail-lights of his car speeding away down the long lime avenue. Dario was heading off towards the city, with all its temptations and distractions. He had a million friends. His social life was so full he need never be alone, but something about him made Josie think that, secretly, he might be as lonely as she was.

Josie's curiosity kept her awake until she heard Dario return in the early hours. Her lack of sleep meant she woke up late the next morning, which put her in a foul mood from the beginning. She knew from experience that she would never catch up on the lost time. She was also half-afraid Dario might have taken her words to heart and brought a conquest home to prove a point. She found herself angry for caring so much about it, but she needn't have worried. The *castello* and its estate were both practically deserted as she walked the half mile to her excavation beside the old olive press. She worked away at uncovering the ancient flagstone hearth until the sun was high in the sky. Then she heard the sound of a car. It was one of the di Sirena limousines, and it sighed to a halt at the junction between the main drive and the drove road.

'Josie! Look what we've got for you!' a familiar voice called out.

Josie stood up to see her friend Antonia erupting from the car's back seat and galloping along the track towards her, swinging several paper carrier bags. Plump and pretty, Toni had the enthusiasm of a puppy but was out of breath in seconds. Jumping out of her trench, Josie ran to meet her. Taking the bag, she peered inside.

'An orange bikini?' She goggled. 'That's the very last thing I would have guessed!'

'Dario said you needed one.' Antonia was grinning from ear to ear. 'He says you've got to learn to swim.'

'If I got into a swimming pool with your brother while I was wearing this, I think drowning would be the least of my worries,' Josie said drily.

'You're all right. You'd be perfectly safe.'

Josie laughed. 'Oh, dear. And people say *I'm* unworldly! Hey—it looks like your mothering skills have gone a bit haywire…' she said, craning past Antonia to check the deserted back seat of the limousine. 'You've *never* left Fabio back in Rimini?'

'Of course not, silly! Dario was waiting for us by the gate on his horse, Ferrari. He had brought one of Fabio's ponies out with him so they could ride home together.'

'*One* of his ponies? How many does that child have?' Josie asked in astonishment.

Antonia rolled her big brown eyes in a gesture so reminiscent of Dario, Josie was touched. She smiled.

'I have no idea. Dario likes him to have the right size, so we have a selection here.' Antonia smiled a bit guiltily. 'Money might not buy happiness, but it makes most problems go away.' She hesitated for a moment, as if lost in thought. After a pause, she shook herself and elbowed Josie in the ribs again, grinning. 'So you're still on speaking terms with Dario, then? He never said.'

'Why would he? I'm just a guest here.' Josie laughed, but jumped back into her trench before Antonia could see her expression.

'Then you can have a great time getting to know him better at the party tomorrow,' Antonia replied airily. 'Dario's decided he's going to use it as an excuse to celebrate our safe return from Rimini. He's invited everyone we know and a few more besides, so it'll be brilliant. But then, Dario's parties always are.'

'Thank goodness I shall be safely tucked up in bed long before that.'

Antonia frowned. 'Oh, come on, Josie! I know you aren't the sociable type, but couldn't you make an exception just this once? It'll be fun. There are usually all sorts of things going on—an auction of promises, and games—'

Josie grimaced.

'Don't look like that. It's all in aid of charity and you'll love it, really! Besides, the food's always fabulous here, even though I do say it myself—' She had been hovering near the finds table and now peered into Josie's lunch-box with interest. The castle kitchens provided Josie with a mini-feast to go each day, and she could never finish it all.

'Have some,' she told her friend, who didn't need to be asked twice.

'You can't possibly miss one of Dario's parties!' Antonia insisted, choosing some mini-calzone.

'I shouldn't think I'm invited. I haven't heard anything about it.'

'Josie, you're a friend of the family—just walk in!'

'I don't think so,' Josie said uncomfortably. 'That's not how parties work where I come from. In any case, I'll have more than enough to do, cataloguing all the finds from this little spot. Work and an early night. You know that's what I'm here for, after all.'

...Although now I can't help wishing that Dario himself might come and sweep me away from all this, she thought wistfully.

CHAPTER SIX

ANTONIA promised to return and help Josie catalogue her finds, once she had put Fabio down for an afternoon nap. When a brand new four-by-four painted with the di Sirena logo came rolling along the drove road towards her excavation, Josie assumed Antonia had managed to get away at last, but it wasn't her friend who had come to find her. When the vehicle stopped, a member of the castle staff climbed out of the driving seat. The man carried a large transparent box, so Josie could see before he handed it to her that it was full of artist's materials.

'Oh, wow!' she said in delight. 'Thank Count Dario very much for me. This is perfect!' she called after the driver as he got back into his vehicle and drove away.

Opening the container, she breathed in the wonderful, very particular aroma of brand new pencils, brushes and paper. Her fingers itched to start work.

Why not? she thought, filled with devilment at the idea of trying something that wasn't on her written list of things to do. There was no one to see. Dario himself had encouraged it, *and if he thinks I'm good enough...* she thought, unable to remember anyone praising her artwork before. That made her feel good in a way that was somehow more satisfying, more *personal* than praise for her academic work had ever been. When she spotted a formal white envelope tucked in between a sketchbook and a watercolour pan, she began to feel really special.

Her heart beating faster by the second, Josie picked up the letter. She could hardly wait to rip it open and find out what it said, but the envelope alone was unique. It was faintly watermarked with the di Sirena mermaids, and addressed in fountain pen with bold copperplate handwriting. That was another reason to stop and stare.

Dr J. L. Street, she read.

She turned the letter over to find a red blob of glisteningly official sealing wax. It had been impressed with the magnificent crest of the di Sirena family. She let out her breath in a whistle. It was almost as grand as a medieval manuscript! Easing it open, she found that the envelope was lined with fine grey tissue paper. It contained a single sheet of deckle-edged notepaper folded neatly around a large, thick white card. Looking at the letter first, she found a couple of exquisitely written lines:

> *Dear Josie, here are a few things I selected for you at random. If you need anything more, let me know.*

It was signed with the single word 'Dario', which flowed across the page like the faint but distinctive tang of his aftershave.

His note had enclosed an invitation like nothing she had ever seen in her life before:

The pleasure of your company is requested at a grand charity ball on the 18th July, hosted by Count Dario di Sirena. Evening dress to be worn.

She read from the stiff card, embellished with gold tracery, and, wide-eyed with astonishment, she shook her head in disbelief.

This is amazing! she thought. *Fancy getting an official invitation to something like that! I can't believe it...and my mum certainly never will...it almost makes me wish I had the nerve to go...*

She let out a long drawn-out moan of disappointment. The thought of seeing Dario formally dressed again was almost enough to make her accept the invitation, even though she was sure Antonia was behind it. She knew Dario must look truly magnificent in his natural surroundings of a glittering formal party, wearing a tuxedo and strolling around with a glass of champagne in his hand. It made him all the more alluring, and it made Josie certain that she had to turn down his invitation.

She was tongue-tied enough in his presence. His party would be filled with people she didn't know, and with whom she had nothing in common. That would be bad enough, but to feel like that while she was in Dario's company would be unbearable. He had all the social skills and charm, while she had none. Though Josie was honest enough to admit that wasn't the whole reason. If her heart had felt at risk from their kiss by the pool, what would happen when she was at a party, where Dario was in his element? It felt as though this invitation tempted her further away from the world she knew—from where it was safe.

Josie stared at the wonderful invitation for a long time. Then she slid it back into its envelope and tucked it away in her bag with real regret. There was nothing for it. She sat down at her table to write a polite refusal—but didn't even get as far as 'Dear Dario'. That was no way to reply to an invitation like this. She would have to do it face to face. Standing up, she took two steps towards the *castello*, then went and sat down again. It was hard enough looking Dario in the eyes, without having to resist the temptation to throw caution to the wind and go to the ball.

She picked up her phone, but it took a while before she could press the right keys in the right order. When one of Dario's staff answered instead of him, she almost laughed with relief.

'I'm just ringing to let Count Dario know that I'm not able to attend his party,' she said in a sparkling rush, then ran out of words. The PA merely thanked her politely, and put down the phone. Josie stared at her handset. Turning down Dario's invitation was bad enough. Having her refusal accepted as a matter of course was worse.

Dario frowned at the slip of paper he had been handed by his PA. Its message presented him with another novelty. As always seemed to happen these days, Josie was

at the bottom of it. People had been known to crawl
from their sickbeds to attend one of his parties, but she
had looked perfectly fit and well when he last saw her.
He smiled, lingering over that image of her lithe, toned
body. It didn't seem right that she should deny herself
the chance of an evening's entertainment. She ought to
make the most of every opportunity the Castello Sirena
could offer while she was here.

Picking up his phone, he got her number and rang
her in person.

'Everyone else jumps at the chance of attending a
Castello Sirena party,' he said without bothering to introduce himself.

'I'm sorry, Dario. Parties aren't really my thing.'

She sounded uncertain, and he wasn't so easily deterred. 'I know you said you weren't wild about the
social life in Rimini, but this will be different.'

'No, it won't. Not unless your social circle has magi-
cally shrunk away to nothing, or is composed solely of
archaeologists.'

'*Dannazione!* Now why didn't *I* think of that before I
had all those invitations sent out? I could have included
the staff of the National Museum!' he drawled with lilting amusement. He added, 'Don't forget there will be at
least one other archaeologist there—Antonia.'

'And I'm sure she'll love the chance to play the part
of hostess again—I don't want to get in her way. I'm
sorry, Dario, but I won't be there. Better luck next time.'

'And would you really be more likely to attend "next
time"?'

'Er…' she hesitated, but knew lying was impossible;

Dario was bound to know she wasn't telling the truth
'...probably not, no.'

'Is that your final decision?'

'I'm afraid so. It was really kind of you to invite me,
Dario. I'd better leave the partying to those who can
appreciate it,' she said, unable to suppress the note of
wistfulness in her words.

'OK...' he said, then went silent.

'Are you still there?' she said after a pause.

'I was waiting for you to change your mind.'

She had to laugh at that. 'Well, I'll give you ten out of
ten for persistence, but it's not going to happen, Dario!'

'Fine,' he said, and then he was gone.

In the years since Arietta's death, Dario had replayed
their final, fatal row a million times in his mind. He
had vowed long ago that he would never make the same
mistakes again and, so far, he hadn't. If a woman decided to go her own way, that was fine by him. If she
wanted to leave, he would open the door, thank her for
her time and show her out.

*But Josie actually sounded sorry that she couldn't
come,* he thought. Letting out a curse, he jumped up
and decided he needed a distraction.

'I'm going out for a ride,' he called out to anyone
who could hear, uncharacteristically leaving his staff
to worry about his appointments for the rest of the day.

Heading straight for Ferrari's stable, he pulled his
saddle off its tree but, after a moment's consideration,
dropped it back down again. Vaulting onto the stal-
lion's broad back, he rode out of the stable yard and into

the estate. His mood was so black, it transmitted itself straight to his horse. Pointing him in the direction of the far hills, Dario gave Ferrari his head. He was so deep in thought it was only as he reined in the horse after their pipe-opener that he realised how far their gallop had taken them. The silvery streak in the far distance was the drove road. He was heading towards the old olive press—and Josie's dig.

Things had got right out of control. Now he couldn't even take an innocent ride in the country without winding up on her doorstep.

Why can't I take what she says at face value? he thought irritably. *Why can't I get her out of my mind?*

Dr Josie Street's problem is that she can't see further than her next intellectual puzzle, Dario decided. Her life was so lacking in fun, she hardly knew what the word meant. She not only refused to go to his party, she would rather use a telephone to tell him, rather than come out with it face to face. There must be something wrong, something lurking behind her stubborn single-mindedness. Grimly determined to find out what it was, he came to a decision. Josie would learn to relax and enjoy her stay at the *castello* if he had to stand over her and supervise her every moment.

And her every movement, he thought, suddenly struck by a vision of Josie in that wet white T-shirt.

Coming back to reality, he had two choices. He could let well alone, turn right and head straight back to his studio. There, he could take out his frustrations on a new canvas.

Or he could turn left and give Dr Josie Street an experience she would never forget.

The result was a foregone conclusion. Dario pulled out his mobile and made one short, succinct phone call to Antonia. Then he turned Ferrari's head in the direction of the old olive press and rode out like the last in a long line of conquering heroes.

At first, the sound was only the smallest disturbance in the summer day. The continuous scratchy songs of grasshoppers under the hot Tuscan sun absorbed the unusual sound until it was close enough to resolve itself into the regular rhythm of a walking horse.

Josie dropped her trowel. Every nerve in her body went on high alert. When the jingle of harness joined the steady reverberation of hoof beats, she got out of her trench. The sun reflected off the glittering white dust of the drove road, making her raise one arm to shade her eyes against the glare. There was nothing to see— yet. The approaching horseman was hidden by a dip in the track, but Josie didn't need to see him to know who it was. Something deep within her soul told her it was Dario, and he was coming for her.

Time stood still for her the second she saw that dark tousled head, contrasting so vividly with his golden skin and dazzling white shirt. It was revealed with tantalising slowness as he made his way relentlessly towards her. Flashes of painful brilliance seared her retinas as his horse's bridle glinted in the sunlight. She hardly noticed. When he drew so close she could smell the rich mixture of saddle soap and leather, she wondered if the power of speech had deserted her completely. Now was the time to find out.

'Dario.'

His name sizzled on her lips as it hit the dry air.

'Josie.'

Thickened by the heat, his accent made her name sound more foreign and exotic than ever.

'Are you here because I turned down your invitation?'

He straightened his back, becoming every inch the dignified aristocrat. 'No. That was your decision. This has nothing to do with the invitation, but it does have everything to do with you, Josie.'

The chill in his voice sent her backing into the canopy pole. She was like the figurehead of a ship, clutching at the last point of stability as her universe rolled and bucked around her.

'I've come to take you home with me, Josie.'

She moistened her dry lips with the tip of her tongue, very slowly.

'What? *Why?*' Her voice was barely a whisper, but his explanation was strong and sure.

'Antonia needs your help,' he announced.

Primed for him to admit that he wanted her, Josie deflated with sudden, sharp disappointment. She felt her fingers release their grip on the aluminium pole. Her hands fell to her sides and she walked forward onto the drove road. When Dario didn't automatically move his horse to fall in step beside her, she stopped and looked back at him quizzically.

'I came to give you a lift.'

He ran his hand down Ferrari's mane to make the point that they were a team, and for the moment Josie was the odd one out.

'You're not serious?'

The thought of being carried home was more frightening than Josie wanted to let on. Her gaze ran over the sleek sides of the horse but fell short of the powerful, brooding form of its rider. Her silence told Dario more than she wanted to put into words.

'Don't tell me you can neither swim nor ride?' He was incredulous.

'There isn't much call for either, down in a trench.'

'That doesn't matter. There's nothing to it. And, in any case, I shall be the one doing the riding—all you have to do is put your arms around my waist.'

Josie's gaze rose almost shyly to include Dario as well as Ferrari.

'So I'd be sitting behind you?' she said slowly.

'Yes.'

'Oh…' she said eventually. Her voice was little more than a whisper, but the heat of excitement powering through her veins was more fierce than the summer sun. Dario was wrong. If he had ridden up and swept her into his arms without a word she wouldn't have been able to utter a single complaint. She would have been stunned into silence, and an all too willing and dangerous surrender.

Dario's immense self-confidence transmitted itself to Ferrari, who paced obediently over to the shade of an ancient, almost horizontal olive tree growing at the wayside. Horse and rider were infused with the arrogant pride of centuries, and all Josie could do was obey.

'The trunk of this tree slopes gently enough to make a perfect mounting block.'

Josie looked at it speculatively. As there was no alternative, she hopped up onto the lowest point of the sun-warmed tree. While she tentatively edged her way along its trunk, Dario backed his horse in close.

Josie was scared, but couldn't bear to say so. She looked at Dario, and he saw the fear in her eyes.

'Don't think—put your hands on my shoulders and just do it.'

She thought back to the pool, and remembered that moment of exhilaration just after she fell into the water. Dario had caught her up and saved her from drowning, only to flood her with a bewitching torrent of feelings that had tortured her from that moment on.

And it's starting all over again, she realised as the heat of his gaze raked over her body.

Sitting astride his horse, he looked and sounded supremely confident. There was no hint of threat about him, merely the majesty of a man on his own land.

He must be right. This will be perfectly OK, she persuaded herself.

Taking her courage in both hands, she did as Dario told her and found herself sitting behind him, astride Ferrari. She was so scared her lungs almost stopped working. All she could get were little panting breaths of the hot dry air.

'Relax, Josie! This is the perfect way to travel.'

Dario's voice was a purr of reassurance, but she was far too tense to appreciate it.

'Only when you're used to it,' she said in a thin, strained voice. It sounded at least an octave higher than normal.

'You will feel safer if you put your arms around my waist rather than gripping my shoulders.'

'Will I?' The doubt in her voice was so obvious she felt his laughter rumble up from beneath his ribs before she heard it.

'Try it.'

Josie had to summon up a lot more nerve before she could loosen her hands, one at a time, to take a terrifyingly light grip around his ribcage.

'I won't break.' He chuckled, and she felt the movement dance though his whole body.

'Why is your horse called Ferrari?' She looked down with apprehension. The ground seemed a horribly long way away.

There was a pause. 'Because he is very fast, and dangerous in the wrong hands,' Dario said in a voice rich with meaning.

Josie made a conscious effort to keep her hands loose on Dario's sides, but it was almost impossible. The warmth of him begged to be experienced skin to skin, without the bother of fear, clothes or anything else.

'Do you feel safe?'

'Compared with what?' she asked in a small, quavering voice. The horse's back felt very warm and tense beneath her. 'Does it get any worse than this?'

'I won't let it. Loosen up, Josie. I'll keep you safe.'

Dario's deep brown voice persuaded her to try to relax. His confidence was infectious. Gradually she felt it loosen her limbs, and so did Ferrari. The surface she was sitting on became mobile in several different directions at once as Dario directed his horse back onto the drove road.

'How does that feel? Better?'

'Ask me after I've got off at the other end. It's probably one of those experiences that's better viewed in hindsight,' she croaked.

'A simple OK would do. Or *suffice*, if you like, Dr Street.'

'Now you're laughing at me again,' she accused.

'No…never. I'm trying to get you to relax, and maybe distract you a little. You'll enjoy the experience much more if you do. Listen to that—' He pointed to one of the resident skylarks swinging up towards the heavens. 'You'd never hear that from inside a car.'

'No, but I can enjoy the same sounds while I'm safely down in my trench.'

'Only with the little bit of your brain that isn't wrapped up in your work. Where is your sense of adventure, Josie? This way you get to enjoy everything my home has to offer, so much more intimately.' He paused, and she felt his ribcage expand as he drew in a long breath. 'Mind you, I normally race around at top speed myself, travelling between appointments or chasing deadlines. Taking it this slowly is making me appreciate it more, too.'

'Don't you already know every inch of this estate? You and Antonia have both told me how you used to spend most of your time out here when you were children.'

'Yes, because it was safer than staying inside the castle,' Dario said quietly. 'If our parents were in residence, their fighting could easily spill over onto us. If they were away, on the yacht or at the ski lodge, say, Antonia and I had to run the gauntlet of the staff they'd bussed in to keep us clean and fed. That was always a bit of a lottery. The good ones left when they got fed up with living in chaos, and the bad ones got fired—eventually. We were left to run riot, roaming the hills when it was dry and dodging from house to house around the estate when the weather was bad. They say it takes a whole village to raise a child. That was certainly true in our case.'

Dario stopped suddenly, and Josie realised he'd said more than he'd meant to. In spite of desperately wanting to know more, she managed to act as if he'd simply carried on with small talk and, keeping a firm grip around his waist, looked out across the undulating countryside as he changed the subject and pointed out some of his old haunts.

'I've been invited into quite a few of those places already,' she told him. 'Everyone around here is really friendly. They always stop and chat.'

He laughed. 'I thought you hated being interrupted when you were working?'

'Yes…but there's something about this place that makes me want to learn more about the people living here today, rather than being buried in the past all the time.'

'That's good.' In a spontaneous movement, Dario dropped one hand and reached back. He touched her thigh, and patted it briefly. It was only a tiny movement, but it sent powerful messages surging through her body. With a sigh she felt herself submit to the waves of warmth travelling from his body to hers. Gradually she softened towards the experience. As she relaxed against him, her arms closed in around the reassuring solidity of his body. Before she knew what was happening, her cheek brushed his shoulder. It was just for a moment, but long enough to appreciate the clean soap and cologne fragrance of him.

She drew in a long, lingering breath of it. 'This is wonderful…' she murmured.

'Are you enjoying it, Josie?'

As always, his beautiful voice filled her name with colours she had never noticed before.

'I am. This is lovely.'

'Good. That's exactly as it should be. After all your hard work, you deserve a little treat or two. Some time off, and a few hours of indulgence.'

Josie thought about the party. She had so wanted to say yes to that invitation, she wished he would ask her again. Now she felt so safe in his presence, she would have been tempted to accept—but Dario was lost in thought. For some time, the only sounds were the skylarks, the jingle of harness and the regular dull thud of Ferrari's hooves on the dusty white track.

'You're right. I'm a lucky man. This place is wonderful,' he said at length.

CHAPTER SEVEN

JOSIE was in heaven. Once she got used to the gentle
rhythm of Ferrari's gait, she could think of nothing
but the sensation of having her arms around Dario's
waist. His body was so warm and vital. She could feel
the play of his muscles as they moved beneath the thin
white fabric of his shirt. It brought back all the bittersweet memories of their picnic in the wood, her fear…
and his kisses… She closed her eyes. With each measured step they took, her breasts nudged tantalisingly
against Dario's back. That made the growing fire inside
her burn even brighter.

'You can lean against me all you like,' he said softly.
'If it will make you feel better.'

After a moment's hesitation, she did. It was hypnotically wonderful. Only the change in sound of Ferrari's
hooves as they moved from the drove road to the gravel
outside the stable yard persuaded her to open her eyes
again and sit up straight.

'Wait. I'll lift you down,' Dario told her as a stable
lad ran to take Ferrari's reins.

Wide awake now, Josie fizzed with excitement. Dropping lightly to the ground, Dario reached up and put

his hands around her waist to lift her from the horse's back. When her feet touched the gravel she discovered exactly how much the experience had taken from her.

'My legs have gone to jelly!' she whispered, frantically grabbing at him. He put his arms around her to steady her and a shockwave pulsed through her body. Suddenly she was greedy for his touch and didn't want him to let her go.

'That's natural. And I'm in no hurry to go anywhere.'

'B…but you've always got another appointment somewhere or other…'

'That can wait for a few moments. I would never abandon you out here with jelly legs.'

Josie looked at him and it was well worth it. He was smiling.

He's going to ask me about the party again and there's no way I can refuse! she thought, breathless with panic and anticipation. *There's no way I can refuse him anything!*

But she had misjudged him.

A moment later, his fingers closed on her upper arms and he gently pushed her away. In that instant she felt the electric charge flowing through her body falter and fail as he broke the circuit.

'Goodbye, Josie,' he said in a husky voice.

And then he was gone.

All Josie's fantasies about being able to attend Dario's party shattered like a Ming vase. She tried to convince herself it didn't matter, but it did. Putting on a brave face, she walked into the castle to meet Antonia, although thoughts of what might have been were a permanent loop of regret running through her mind. *Couldn't she have said yes? Been brave, just for once? What was she going to do with her carefully protected heart anyway—keep it in a museum?*

'Now Fabio's asleep we can hit the town,' Antonia said confidently as she skipped downstairs from the nursery. 'What are you going to wear tomorrow night?'

'I'm not going.'

'Oh…still not? Why not?'

'I've got too much to do. You know how it is,' Josie said with a nonchalance that fooled neither of them.

'Well, *you* might be able to pass up the chance of a night of glamour and romance tomorrow, Jo, but that doesn't mean *I* have to. I want you to come and help me choose a dress for the party, and we can talk about your project at the old olive press while we do it. I told you there was plenty to discover here, didn't I?'

'You did—and you were absolutely right.' Josie wasn't just thinking of archaeology. She gazed through the open *castello* door at the sun-drenched forecourt outside. Dario would have to cross it on his way to or from the stables and garage complex, but the forecourt stayed deserted.

Despite the bright day, it felt as though her life had lost some of its sparkle. 'I'd love to come with you,' she said brightly, trying to summon up some genuine enthusiasm.

'Good. The chauffeur will have the limo here in a couple of minutes,' her friend said, grinning.

* * *

Shopping with Antonia on her home ground was a new experience for Josie. It couldn't have been more different from her everyday life back in England. Instead of dragging around crowded chain stores getting hotter and more frustrated by the second, this was an expedition into another world.

An air-conditioned di Sirena limousine swept them almost silently to Florence. They were dropped off within sauntering distance of the designer quarter. The streets were shady, with chic little cafés every few yards for the tired of spending. Before they could get too hot, Antonia paused outside her favourite designer's showroom. To Josie's amazement, they didn't even need to open the door for themselves. An assistant threw it back on its hinges at the mere sight of Antonia. They were greeted like royalty, and ushered into cool splendour. Josie decided this must have been what it was like to be shown into an ancient Roman temple, only this building was on a *much* more opulent scale. She stopped and stared, completely overawed by all the gold leaf and pink marble columns until Antonia took her in hand.

'Come and meet Madame, Jo. She makes all my clothes when I'm at home.'

Madame was a tiny Parisian in towering black stilettos, a chic little black dress and jet-black hair scraped back into a neat bun. She was the consummate European, flourishing her scarlet nails like a matador's cape to hypnotise and tempt. When they were formally introduced, Josie was so starstruck she almost bowed.

'Oh, lighten up, Jo!' Antonia laughed. 'The staff are here to serve *us*, not the other way around. Take a seat, dunk your biscotti, do whatever you want. They won't care!'

Cautiously, Josie let herself be shown to a seat. When Antonia ordered a latte, she did exactly the same, although she would rather have had a cup of tea. Then her friend was shown the finished dresses she had previously ordered from Madame's autumn collection, together with samples of a dozen new designs in a rainbow of colours. Once she knew she was safely out of the spotlight, Josie began to relax. Soon she was lounging in her comfortable armchair and offering her opinion to Antonia as confidently as Madame.

Then one of the covey of assistants emerged from a room at the back of the salon carrying a single dress reverently in her hands. It was a fluid length of shimmering silk in the most beautiful shade of green Josie had ever seen. She was vaguely aware of Antonia standing up for a closer look, but nothing could distract her from that stunning vision.

'You've got to try that on, Toni,' she said with longing. 'With your dark colouring, it would make you look really exotic.'

'You think?' Antonia took the ravishing cocktail dress from the assistant, turning its hanger so that light danced over its discreet detail of gold threads. 'I don't know…bias cut is awfully unforgiving to a tummy like mine.' She chewed the inside of her cheek, then appeared to have a sudden inspiration.

'Tell you what, Jo—why don't *you* try it on? It would be a brilliant match for your eyes.'

'I don't know…' she said slowly, although deep down

she did. They all did. There was no way any woman alive could have refused such an offer.

'Oh, come on—it'll look gorgeous!' Antonia smiled. 'You know you want to…'

Josie laughed in spite of herself, and gave in. 'All right,' she decided, struggling out of the depths of her comfy armchair before she could change her mind. 'I'll do it!'

Swishing the dress from Antonia's hands, she strode off to where an assistant was waiting to help her change. The changing room was nothing like the tiny curtained cubicles she was used to. It was larger than her flat back in England, and the surroundings made taking her clothes off in front of a complete stranger almost feel natural.

Almost, but not quite! she thought, blushing.

Unable to look at her reflection while she stripped, she concentrated on the lacy wisps of sweet-pea-coloured lingerie draped artistically around the room. Seeing all those lovely things made her ache to attend the party. For once in her life she would have given anything to dress up and strut her stuff, to show gorgeous Dario a completely different side of her. If only the single decent dress she had brought to Italy wasn't so old and enormous. She had bought it for her engagement party, but Andy's subsequent betrayal and her retreat into overwork had seen the weight fall off her. She had thought it would be good enough to wear for private dinners at the *castello*, but that was before she'd actually met Dario. Nothing would have persuaded her to wear it now.

Suddenly shy at dressing up in the lovely green silk dress, she pulled it on hurriedly, half afraid to look. The assistant's gasp horrified her.

'Oh, no—don't say I've wrecked it?'

Hideous scenes of split seams or gashed silk filled her mind as she glanced at the mirrored wall beside her.

One glimpse and she stopped, awestruck. The dress was perfect.

And so am I! she thought before modesty caught up with her. She turned pink at the thought.

The assistant was first to come to her senses. She flung open the changing room door and stood back, motioning for Josie to walk out into the showroom.

The collective intake of breath from Antonia, Madame and all her assistants was worth every second of self-doubt Josie had ever suffered in her life. She instantly felt taller, more self-confident and...

'*Wow*, Josie!' Antonia breathed reverently. 'You're *beautiful*!'

'Yes,' she said shakily, managing to agree with a compliment for the first time in her life. It gave her a little shiver of shock. She was amazed to find that was another sensation she liked.

'What do you think they'd say if I walked into the university Christmas ball wearing this, Toni?'

'They wouldn't say anything,' her friend sighed. 'They wouldn't be able to.'

Madame was not amused. 'That dress might have been made with you in mind. You simply must have it, Dr Street.'

With those words, Josie stopped looking delighted

and started looking worried. She discreetly mouthed a desperate question across at her friend. *'How much is it?'*

'Oh, you don't need to worry about that,' Antonia said airily.

'But I do!' Josie said aloud.

'Think of it as a birthday present. Happy birthday,' Antonia said.

'But it's not my birthday.'

Antonia smiled more enigmatically than the Mona Lisa. 'I know,' she said mysteriously.

Although she couldn't wait to get back to the *castello* to try on her new dress again, Josie got her generous friend to take her from the salon to a chain store, where she felt happier and could spend her own money. Now she was discovering how much fun it was to be spontaneous, there was no stopping her.

As she was indulging herself with satin and lace, Dario's words about wanting to know when she felt like doing something scarily spontaneous came back to her with a guilty rush of excitement.

I wonder exactly how spontaneous I can be? she thought to herself with a sudden burst of bravado. *I might surprise you yet, Count Dario di Sirena!*

'I could gatecrash…' she said, not realising that she had said it out loud.

'Do what?' Antonia replied absently, her attention on some ankle bracelets.

Josie blushed, but then went for broke. 'The party. Antonia, can I come to the party after all?'

Antonia looked around at Josie with a broad smile. 'Yes! I thought you'd never ask!' she said, throwing her arms around her friend.

'But I've already refused Dario's invitation, not once, but twice!' Josie frowned.

'He won't mind, but if you're going to worry you can come as my guest. Everyone's allowed a "plus one", so tell yourself you're mine,' Antonia said, as quick as a flash.

'You have an answer for everything.' Josie shook her head in awe.

Antonia smiled a wicked smile. 'Of course. It's called native cunning.'

Dario was in his studio, trying to plan a new painting. He couldn't settle to anything and had tried to find some way of filling the time while Antonia and Josie were in Florence. First, he'd gone out on Ferrari again. That had been unsettling. Every step of the way recalled Josie's arms around his waist, her body pressed tight against his. Before he'd known it, he had accidentally reached the old olive press where her boxes of finds and tools stood neatly packed away beneath the awning that protected her work. It was his own land and he had visited the place a hundred times over the years, but it felt like an intrusion to be there alone today. He'd seen the box he had sent her and, looking more closely, noticed she had already unpacked a sketchbook and made a start.

Unused to feeling uncomfortable on his home ground, Dario had turned Ferrari's head away from the place so full of Josie's presence. He thought it would be cooler to ride up through the trees. Instead, his temperature rose as he drew closer to the place in that woodland glade where he had kissed her. Not for the first time, her spirit disrupted his plans.

I've only known her a few days, and yet she's on my mind all the time. I can taste the sweetness of her lips and feel the warmth of her body, even when she's miles away. What's the matter with me? he thought restlessly. He couldn't concentrate on his work. He decided to try to replace all his thoughts of her with something else, and fast.

That was when he had abandoned the wide expanse of his estate for the contained luxury of his studio. Hoping to lose himself in his art, Dario soon found another of his usually perfect cures wasn't up to the task. In a complete change of direction, he started to paint a portrait. Things went wrong from the beginning. The subject of his portrait was supposed to be Arietta. To Dario's irritation, his preliminary sketches kept turning into someone else entirely—and that 'someone' looked uncannily like Dr Josephine Street.

When a flash of sunlight danced around the room, he was glad of the distraction. Then he saw it was reflecting off a sleek black car as it slid along the lime avenue towards the front door.

It's Josie! He threw down his stick of charcoal, then snatched it up again.

No. It's Antonia. And...her friend, he corrected himself carefully, resisting the temptation to go out and welcome them home.

* * *

Josie hurried straight up to her own suite. The moment she was safely inside, she started unpacking all the carrier bags she had brought back from Florence. Reverently, she put the beautiful dress Antonia had bought her on one of the padded hangers. Then she carried it up to the top floor of her suite and hung it up in the room Dario had called the solar. That way, she could see it while she worked. At least, that was the theory. Once the dress was displayed in sunlit glory, it was all Josie could do to tear herself away and unpack everything else she had bought. Antonia had exploited her temporary brainstorm by suggesting another indulgence, which had prompted a real spending spree.

Now you're coming to the party tomorrow night, Jo, we can have some real fun. I've arranged for a masseuse and my usual team of beauticians to visit the castle. You and I can make a real day of it.

From that moment on, Josie's work had to take a back seat, although, happily, in her attempts to drive Dario from her mind, she was far ahead with her research. She spent far more time admiring her new dress from every angle and counting down the minutes until her makeover. Whenever she thought about the party, she felt sick with nerves and excited at the same time. She took the tops off all the bottles of gel and bubbles and oils she had bought for the occasion and inhaled until she was high on a cocktail of jasmine and adrenalin.

When she finished what passed for work that day, she took the green silk down into her bedroom so she could carry on admiring it. When a maid came in to turn down her bed, Josie didn't have to ask if she liked the dress.

'You'll be the centre of attention at tomorrow night's party, *signorina*!' the girl whispered with awe.

Josie couldn't answer. All her worries about the celebrity guest list were coming back in force. She thought of the evening ahead and privately planned to spend the whole evening hiding behind a pillar if necessary, nice and close to the buffet.

Next day, Josie's work rate plummeted to zero but she hardly cared. Her worries about it were reduced to a tiny cloud hovering on the extreme edge of a much larger storm. Happily, the makeover took up nearly all her time, and it was heavenly. Every moment brought her closer to the party, the dress…and Dario. That thought made her so nervous she could barely touch the little party savouries that Antonia kept ordering from the kitchens.

After a long soak in scented water right up to her neck, Josie had an aromatherapy massage with rose oil. While she was trapped beneath a hairdresser's skilful fingers and with a manicurist at work on each hand, Antonia seized her moment.

'I'm so pleased you decided to come to the party, Jo. You never know. It might be an introduction to that tall, dark, handsome man who'll sweep you off your feet.'

Josie could only think of one person who fitted that description: Dario. She had been thinking about nobody else, and was suddenly afraid she might give herself away. She tried to distract Antonia with a careless laugh.

'Hah! The last time that happened, my heart got kicked down the road like a tin can,' she said, trying to sound as though it didn't matter.

'Andy Dutton was neither tall, nor dark, nor handsome,' Antonia huffed.

Josie recoiled from the memory of the biggest romantic disaster of her life. 'That's why I've come to a decision. I've decided it's time to put that whole horrible business behind me and move on,' Josie announced bravely, and immediately felt better for saying it. Once she had put her feelings into words, things suddenly felt so much clearer in her mind. 'I'm only sorry I couldn't have realised it sooner,' she sighed.

'So you've finally come around to my way of thinking? That it's time to forget him?' Antonia grinned, delighted.

'Yes—and no. I may have recovered from getting my feelings burned by Andy, but it's made me determined never to get so close to that particular kind of fire again,' she said, but as she spoke, the memory of Dario's kisses flooded through her. How could she say such things, yet still feel like this? Thoughts of his hard, hot body beneath her hands filled her with a longing that all the massage oils in the world could never relieve—and the sensation was spectacular.

'Fine—so tonight you're not looking for trouble, you're just there to enjoy yourself,' Antonia said airily. 'What can possibly go wrong with that?'

'I'm not looking for anything,' Josie announced, trying hard to convince herself that it was true.

Her mind was too full of Dario for safety. Dealing with that would be more than enough for her to handle.

As the day went on, time slowed down to a snail's pace. First, Josie's hair was piled up like a Roman princess. Then, when her fingers and toes had been thoroughly pampered, her nails were painted the colour of mother-of-pearl, making them shimmer with her slightest movement. Then she got the chance to choose some diamond earrings from Antonia's collection of jewellery, and a pair of equally sparkly stilettos from her friend's huge collection of shoes. After that, time crawled by until there was barely half an hour to go before the party. Then Antonia started fluttering around her like a demented butterfly.

'I don't know how you can stay so calm, Jo!'

'I do all my panicking inside. Inside, I'm running about like a mad thing!' she added with a thrill of excitement, checking her watch for the fifth time. They stood together in Josie's drawing room, while Antonia fussed around her and they both waited for the staff to announce that the guests were arriving.

Finally, Antonia stood back to admire her handiwork. Josie couldn't resist glancing at herself in the full-length mirror the staff had set up for the occasion. It was incredible. Antonia was right—she was almost unrecognisable. A smile was the only thing she needed to make the picture absolutely perfect. Blushing with an unusual rush of pride, she looked away from her reflection quickly.

'Not even Dario would know it's you.' Antonia giggled as they got the call from the staff and went downstairs through the cool corridors of the great castle.

'Here's hoping,' Josie said as her heart began to accelerate. After everything she had told Dario about being determined not to come to his party, here she was. All it had taken was this beautiful dress, and the need to prove to him that she *could* enjoy herself when she wanted. Despite her nerves, she felt as if she were living in a fairy tale. She put a hand to her forehead. Was she delirious? Would she wake up to find she had been dreaming?

Antonia gently led her towards the great marble staircase. The sound of restrained small talk rose from the crowd of guests down in the foyer, each receiving their first glass of champagne.

If I could lose myself in this mob, maybe I would feel less like a human sacrifice, she thought, trying to feel relieved. As she came downstairs, her embarrassment level rose as a wave of silence spread through the crowd below. In the seconds before they remembered their manners and greeted their hostess, Josie felt the eyes of every person in the place trained on her. She and Antonia joined the straggle of other people heading away through the portrait gallery towards the castle's grand banqueting hall. They were all marvelling at the grand di Sirena ancestors, but Josie's attention was turned in a quite different direction. The portrait gallery ran around three sides of a glazed quadrangle which was open to the skies. There, the leaves of a big old apricot tree stirred in the sultry dusk.

She nudged Antonia. 'I think I might have changed my mind about this—I wish I was out there rather than in here!' she whispered.

'Rubbish. You'll love it once the party's started. Look how you dithered about coming to work here in the first place. I don't hear you worrying about putting anyone to any trouble now!'

No, thought Josie. *That's because all my other worries have faded in comparison, from the moment I met Dario.*

She sighed and tried to look on the bright side. She looked around at the flash and dazzle of diamonds and military medals worn by all the other guests. Why would he even look at her? Getting on well with his sister hardly counted in stellar company like this. Suddenly, her reckless giggle returned.

Dario felt pretty impressed with me when we kissed! she thought, and blushed. What would all these people think if they knew what was going through her mind?

The double doors to the great banqueting hall were open wide, so it would have been easy to slip inside unnoticed. Josie looked around. People had been smiling appreciatively at her from the moment she'd appeared at the top of the stairs. Trying to sneak in wouldn't stop them doing that. She might as well make the most of her few moments in the spotlight. If nothing else, it would be good practice for the university's Christmas ball. Taking a deep breath, she pulled herself up straight and tall and strode bravely into the room.

The banqueting hall was already bright with people, but the first and only thing she saw was Dario. He was standing in front of a cold marble fireplace, talking to a languid blonde in scarlet satin.

As Josie entered, there was a lull in the conversation. Dario's gaze was already raking the room, but at the sudden silence it swooped over to her, then back to his slender companion. A split second later, he executed the perfect double take. Looking across at Josie again, he trapped her in his gaze. It killed his conversation stone dead, and Josie froze. All the polite, charming, witty things she'd planned to say to him fled from her mind. She was left staring at him across the room, speechless with amazement.

Dario looked every bit as wonderful as she had known he would, each night when she'd heard him drive away into town. He was resplendent in a formal black dinner jacket and trousers with a plain white shirt and black bow-tie. His crisp shirt accentuated the pale gold of his colouring and the dark allure of his eyes—and that was where she got the biggest reward of all. His gaze was totally absorbed by her. He smiled suddenly, in such a genuine gesture of pleasure that Josie was lost. In that moment all her worries about gatecrashing his party dissolved. The naked desire in his expression sent her senses spinning. Her own burning need for him made her want to stride forward, push her fingers through his unruly tousle of curls and kiss him again and again, no questions asked.

Instead, she blushed, dropped her gaze and shuffled uncertainly on the spot.

Dario abandoned his companion without a backward glance and crossed the room in a few strides. Taking Josie's hand, he lifted it to his lips.

'Josie…tonight, you could tempt a saint,' he breathed.

Speechless, she raised her eyes as his kiss connected with her fingers. Dario's gaze pinned her to the spot. She relished the feel of his skin against hers, and the touch of his fingers as they curled around her palm. He held her in a grasp that was strong, yet cool. At any other time, or in the hands of any other man, Josie would have pulled away. This perfect man, on this special night, was different.

I'm going to enjoy every moment of this party, she told herself, staggered by the realisation.

She looked around nervously. An appreciative crowd was smiling at the little scene being acted out in front of them. By the time her eyes flicked back to Dario, he had resumed his usual suave, unflappable charm.

'Thank you for coming, Dr Street. I know how much you dislike gatherings like this, and I'm flattered you chose to make an exception for mine.' He smiled, then added a compliment that sent shivers of anticipation dancing up and down Josie's spine.

'I've never seen a more lovely woman. Or one so beautifully dressed,' he said simply. 'You are without doubt the most beautiful guest here this evening.'

CHAPTER EIGHT

JOSIE opened her mouth to say something, but every sensible thought in her mind had evaporated. She closed it again, and tried another smile. Luckily, those muscles were still working, despite the effect Dario was having on the rest of her body. She could only hope her expression spoke for her.

No one has ever called me beautiful before. I've always been just ordinary old Jo, or Dr Street, she thought.

'Now, I shall introduce you to some of my charming friends. They will take good care of you for me while I am doing my duty as host.'

Dario drew her away from the throng and towards a stout, cheerful-looking couple. Despite their expensive designer clothes, they had open, weather-beaten faces and expressions that Josie took to instantly.

'This is Signor and Signora Bocca. They own a neighbouring estate and their son—Beniamino—went off to university very recently. Dr Street will be able to put your minds at rest about undergraduate life,' he told them, giving Josie a wicked wink.

The couple chuckled, shamefaced.

'He's gone to the USA on a scholarship, and Antonia told me you worked in Iowa for a while last summer, Josie. Maybe you could tell them all about it?' He smiled.

'It'll be my pleasure, Dario,' she said, and it was true. Dario squeezed her hand in parting, and it felt as though he knew exactly what she was thinking.

Despite his affable smile, Dario was uneasy. Something strange was going on inside his head, and his body wanted its own way, too. Once again, it was all down to Josie. He tried to think, but it was difficult to do that while keeping a buoyant conversation going with the lovely Tamara. Dario felt duty-bound to keep a discreet eye on Josie, now she was here. He knew enough of her shyness to realise that attending his party after all must have taken a lot of courage. He was impressed and relieved at the same time. Although he enjoyed socialising, for the first time in his life he had felt like getting his staff to cancel a party at the last moment. Now Josie had arrived, he could admit her rejection had weighed on his mind like a lead weight. The second she'd walked in, everything had changed. Simply seeing her made him ready to relax and enjoy himself.

After a few more minutes of idly seductive chit-chat with Tamara, he realised something still wasn't right. The thought of spiriting this long-legged lovely away from the party left him cold. Tamara might be clever and charming, but suddenly that was no longer enough for him. She would be a meaningless conquest, and their conversation had lost all its attraction for him.

Tamara was twinkling as she tried to win back Dario's attention, but his gaze took every opportunity to escape. He tried dragging it back to her as she told him some long and complicated story about her PA having to courier lost documents from one side of the EU to the other. He attempted to smile at all the right moments, but his heart wasn't in it. Tamara had everything—except his attention. He wished he could see straight through her and out the other side.

The only thing that could hold his gaze was a knot of local businessmen and dignitaries over in the far corner of the room.

It has come to something when a girl like Tamara has fewer attractions for me than a bunch of men I speak to every day, he thought, trying to ignore the obvious fact that it wasn't them holding his attention captive. It was the bright shining star at the centre of their universe.

Dario put a hand up to his neck and felt the muscles as tight as steel hawsers. He had hoped this party would help him to let off some steam, relax a little. Right now he was feeling more tense than he had done in years. What had changed? His guests were all enjoying themselves hugely—Josie included.

What's wrong with that? he rebuked himself. *That's what parties are for, for God's sake—so people can come out and forget themselves for a while!*

That day in the glade, he had teased Josie about being unable to enjoy herself. As he watched her tonight, nothing looked further from the truth. She was revelling in all the attention, but Dario knew he had one big advantage over the men surrounding her. So far, he was the only one in the place who had taken his interest in her any further. With a flash of relief, he finally realised what had been torturing him for so long.

I want to keep it that way.

Josie was special. Her particular brand of intelligence and charm—not to mention her breathtaking appearance tonight—promised delights far beyond anything Tamara and his other coterie of lovelies could offer him. All he had to do was cross the room to where she stood. The other men were bound to defer to him at once.

Don't disrupt her moment in the sun, Dario! he growled to himself. *She's enjoying herself.*

He took a deep breath and tried to act on his own advice. Then he realised Tamara was reaching out to worm her long slender arms around his waist like over-cooked vermicelli.

Dodging neatly out of her reach, he made some noises of regret and moved Tamara by the hand to-wards a gaggle of women discussing interior design with Antonia. Kissing her freshly powdered cheek as consolation, he abandoned her and began to work his way around the room.

Dario purposely set off to charm the guests furthest away from where Josie was holding court. It was a care-fully calculated move. He was always scrupulous about observing the social niceties. As the host, he had a duty to all his guests, not just to his favourite ones. But, all the time, every fibre of his being ached for Josie, her company, her laughter, her...*everything.* Finally, after the longest hour of his life, hers was the last little clique on his circuit. With one hand, he lifted a glass of champagne from a nearby tray, then stuck the other into his trouser pocket and sauntered casually to the edge of her group.

'Josie…'

He spoke, and she smiled.

Dario took that as his cue to advance and stand beside her. Instead of lifting her fingers to his lips as he had done the first time they'd met, on impulse, his hand went straight to her waist as he kissed her lightly on the cheek. She didn't flinch from either gesture, he noticed with a delicious kick of pleasure.

'How are you enjoying the party?'

'I didn't think you'd recognise me,' she said apprehensively.

'I would know you anywhere,' he said, and it was true. She was so lovely, he couldn't bear to leave her alone for a moment. No one knew more than he did how every single second in the company of a beautiful woman should be cherished. One wrong word, one thoughtless gesture and happiness could be snatched away for ever. Nothing could have persuaded him to risk going through the pain he'd endured in losing Arietta— but he wasn't prepared to see Josie fall prey to one of his guests. The idea of a treasure like her in the clutches of another man was unthinkable.

'I really am so glad you felt able to come,' he said before she had time to think. His fingers were still resting just below her ribcage. When she didn't automatically pull away, he let them linger, but only fractionally longer than good manners should have allowed. However, Josie seemed uneasy and her eyes flicked away, in the direction of another group of guests. He waited, puzzled. She did it again. Then he realised she was looking at the woman he had abandoned when he'd blazed a trail around the room to her.

'Oh, that's just Tamara,' Dario said casually, stepping back.

On the other side of the room, the blonde raised one hand and blew him a kiss.

'Hmm. It doesn't look as though she's saying, "Oh, that's just Dario," to those other people,' Josie said stiffly.

Dario felt a surge of purely male satisfaction. She was jealous—tonight she was as good as his.

'Would you like me to introduce you to her?' he said innocently. 'We've been friends—just friends—for years.' He smiled, and her lovely face lit up with a promise that was reflected all through her body. He saw her tension vanish. She took two languid steps towards him like a gentle breeze, and the effect was instantaneous. Dario forgot all about keeping control or seducing her slowly. All he wanted to do was take possession of her.

'I meant what I said, Josie. I'm really glad you decided to come after all,' he murmured.

'After you kept telling me that I should relax more? How could I do anything else?'

His dark eyes sparkled with amusement. 'You're the very last person I'd expect to find a party relaxing. I assumed you'd take up residence in my library tonight, as it's the least likely place to find other guests. Have you seen my library yet?'

'Yes. It was all very...*interesting*,' Josie said tactfully.

He smiled. 'That's a good answer. One of my forebears bought a lot of those books by the yard, back in the nineteenth century.'

She nodded. 'That explains the strange order they're in.'

'Not necessarily. My staff don't always bother to put things back in the proper place after I've read something.'

'You actually read those books?' she marvelled.

Dario took a sip of champagne. 'I'd invite you to come and look at them again with me sometime, but I know what your reaction to that would be.'

'You never know.'

'After our picnic the other day?'

'I've changed my usual clothes for this evening, and my appearance. How do you know I haven't changed in other ways?' she teased him back.

'Because a mermaid can never forsake the sea.'

Josie giggled, and lifted her glass to scrutinise its contents. 'This must be very good champagne. I'm not entirely sure I understood that!'

'In that stunning outfit, you would make the perfect mermaid.' His hand went to her hair, delicately lifting a strand back into place.

'Josie...in honour of this special occasion I should like to offer you a little memento.'

She was so carried away by the look of appreciation in his eyes that he might have been offering her the moon. Nodding wordlessly, she saw him signal to one of his staff. The man disappeared, only to hurry up to them a few seconds later, holding a spray of white cymbidiums, their throats flecked with pink and cream spots.

Dario took the flowers with a nod of thanks and smiled. 'The most beautiful flowers, for my most beautiful guest. May I?'

'Yes, please,' Josie breathed.

Dario took another step closer to her, so that his smart black shoes were toe to toe with the sparkly little stilettos she had borrowed from Antonia. Then he slid the fingers of one hand between her dress and the pale skin of her breast. Lifting the fine material away, he pinned the orchids safely to her shoulder.

'There,' he said, taking his time to remove his fingers. They trailed gracefully over her skin, making her delicate tan seem pale in contrast to his nut-brown fingers. She shivered at the delicious friction of their touch, but made no move to stop him or pull away, not even when she saw him take the opportunity to admire the swell of her breasts beneath the fabric of her dress and the delicate line of her throat.

His gaze moved back to her face and he smiled down at her. 'I also suspect that your adoring fans will soon block your way to the buffet. Let me act as your pilot.'

Without waiting for Josie's reply, he slid his arm lightly around her waist and swept her around the vast room with flair. Everyone turned to watch as they passed. They were all smiling and with satisfaction Dario saw that Josie was, too.

The buffet had been set up on a long row of polished tables in an anteroom. It was a feast for all the senses.

Flower arrangements in the di Sirena colours of blue and gold, pyramids of tropical fruit and baskets of hand-made bread rolls in every shape and variety all gave off a wonderful fragrance. Light from the chandeliers dazzled over silver trays and crystal bowls of titbits. Dario knew the glorious sight and the polite murmur of conversation surrounding it would make both her work and England seem a very long way off for Josie—and that was exactly what he wanted.

Dismissing a footman who offered to help, he lifted a plate from the nearest stack of delicate china and handed it to her himself.

'You've barely touched your champagne. Shall I get you a soft drink instead?'

'No, this is wonderful.' Josie took a sip, but he could tell it was just for the look of the thing. Her attention was riveted on him.

She is making real progress, he thought, watching her expand beneath the warmth of his gaze like a beautiful butterfly emerging from a chrysalis. There was a glow of confidence about her tonight that she usually only wore while working. Dario had never given much thought to her hair before, but now he had to fight the urge to reach out and touch it all the time. Instead of being scraped back in a formidably efficient ponytail, it was arranged in a glorious confection which seemed spun from barley sugar. Her lovely dress left her arms and most of her shoulders bare, and he could see the tan line left by the short sleeves of the simple tops she usually wore. Wherever her skin had been exposed to the Tuscan sun, the past few days had toasted it to light gold. He found the contrast delicious. Her legs never normally saw the light of day when hidden by her working uniform of white T-shirt and overalls, and he looked down to see if they were pale, too. The room was warm and, as far as Dario was concerned, it was getting warmer by the second.

'I'm so sorry I messed you about over your invitation, Dario,' she murmured. 'I haven't enjoyed a party so much for...well, *ever*!'

Dario smiled away her apology. He liked the way her breath was coming in nervous little laughs tonight. The chandeliers high above threw dancing shadows as she moved, accentuating the tempting depths of her cleavage. The fine material of her dress showed him something else. The rise of her nipples was so blatantly obvious through the silk of her bodice, Dario could forgive her anything. And, now she was with him, he felt more relaxed than he could remember.

In contrast, Josie couldn't stand still. Once she had made up her mind to think only of enjoying herself, it was as if her body had woken up from a long hibernation. The nearness of Dario sent sparks fizzing up and down her spine. Although more guests were arriving at the buffet all the time, she was only aware of him and every movement he made—offering her first choice of all the delicious dishes on display, or half turning to talk to someone beside him. She felt almost too shy to look at him directly, but that hardly mattered. His slightest movement sent the delicate notes of his vanilla and spice aftershave wandering through the air between them. His fine, capable hands moved briefly

into her line of vision now and again as he reached for
something to pass to one of his guests. Polite and attentive, he kept every conversation light and easy. Josie
was glad—she could hardly think of a thing to say. The
sound of his voice was like deep water, tempting her to
go closer than might be safe. And then...

And then, in the crush of people around the buffet
table, they were jostled together. Josie felt his hand go
to her bare shoulder, steadying her. Her head jerked
around, but she found her automatic challenge calmed
by one of Dario's special smiles. The feel of his body
pressed against hers made Josie blush, and not in anger.

'I always assumed that life in a grand *castello* like
this would be very prim and proper,' she managed to
say, then gasped as he slyly glided his hand down over
her back until it found a resting place at her waist. At
the loss of his touch, it was all Josie could do to suppress a moan of disappointment.

Desire left her feeling light-headed. The room suddenly felt very hot. She rode this wave of warmth and
waited to be engulfed by another embarrassing blush.
Then she realised something else was happening to her
body. Heat wasn't only travelling upwards. It was circling in a liquid coil of excitement, centred on a part of
her body that had always been more trouble than it was
worth in the past. Tonight, it made her feel spectacular.
There was barely a whisper of a gap between her body
and Dario's. Only the decency of their clothes stood between the subtle friction of his skin against hers. Josie's
lips parted. She felt a little gasp escape. It wasn't loud
enough for anyone else to hear, but Dario noticed. She

smiled at him—a tentative look from beneath her eyelashes, but he understood. His bland expression dissolved and his eyes blazed with desire before he smiled, slowly.

'You sound hot, Josie,' he said in a low voice. 'When we've chosen our food, why don't we take it somewhere a little cooler?' *...and more private*, was the assumption.

This was about much more than simply relaxing. Josie knew it would be so easy to say yes to Dario—but so dangerous. She could hardly wait to experience the luxury of his kisses again, although she knew that would be just the beginning. She could not expect a man like him to be satisfied with a single kiss—and, with a certainty that scared her, Josie knew she wanted more than that, too. Since Andy had abandoned her she had resisted every other attempt to sweet-talk her into bed, but tonight was different. Dario was unique.

'That would be good,' she said slowly.

He raised his eyebrows. 'Is that all?'

'For the moment.' She adjusted her corsage of orchids. 'You have all your other guests to satisfy first, don't forget.' The double meaning was deliberate, and both she and Dario knew it.

'I've spoken to everyone else already and they're mingling quite happily. So, as it's my special night, it's time I found something to satisfy *me*.' The blatant hunger in his eyes made her mouth go dry and her breath catch. Suddenly it was impossible to tear her eyes from his and for a long moment they simply stood, gazes locked, while the rest of the world seemed to melt away.

Josie felt as though she were falling down Alice's rabbit hole, as though after tonight she'd emerge a whole new person. Feeling suddenly overwhelmed at what that might mean, she wrenched her eyes away and concentrated on the canapés, helping herself to a couple of tiny lobster crostini. She took a deep breath, determined to change the subject.

'This really is the most wonderful party, Dario.'

'I thought you weren't keen on parties,' he said slyly.

'True, yet I've never in my life been to something as opulent as this.'

'Then you're glad you came?'

'Definitely. It's the best party I've ever been to. Well, unless you count my birthdays!'

'Oh, so you do indulge yourself sometimes, then?'

She laughed. 'Not really. It's just something my mum has always done for me, every year for as long as I can remember. She makes a cake just big enough for the two of us, supposedly in secret, and we splash out on a takeaway—someone else does the cooking, and there's no washing-up. A bit like this—only about a thousand times smaller!' she joked.

'It must be wonderful to have someone think so much of you that they do that for you every year.'

'You'd swap all this for that?' She laughed.

'Yes. I would.'

She looked at him, incredulous, and noticed a trace of wistfulness in his expression.

'You're not telling me you've never been given a birthday party?'

'No, I never have.'

'Not even when you were tiny?'

He shook his head.

'Dario, that's awful!'

'It was the same for Antonia.' He shrugged off her concern.

'No wonder she used to love to party all night, every chance she got.'

He smiled wryly. 'I think it was certainly part of it. How did you cope, sharing a flat?'

'When I'd had enough, I used to go and stay at Andy's—when he was my fiancé. Obviously, that stopped when...' Josie paused in surprise. The normal dull stab of pain hadn't come when she'd mentioned Andy's name. Perhaps, on this glittering evening, with this beautiful man, she could leave the past behind. She remembered what Dario had said: *foolish man, not to see what he had.* Just for a moment, she felt it might have been true.

'Don't think of him now.' Dario reached out and brushed a strand of shining hair behind her ear.

'No! I want to tell you.'

Suddenly, she wanted Dario to know her sad little story, as though in saying it, she would be free.

'Andy didn't just cheat, you see. He'd been having an affair for a while, and it turned out quite a few members of the faculty had known all about it. I found out he had been putting it around that I was... That he wasn't getting...' She blushed and went silent.

'I'm sorry. I had no idea,' Dario said grimly.

'I'm still surprised Antonia hasn't told you all about

this,' she said, looking at him acutely as she moved away from the table. Dario shadowed her closely.

'I may have practically raised my little sister single-handed, but that doesn't mean we discuss each other's friends.' He guided Josie away from the crowds.

She twitched a shoulder, relieved. 'Maybe I've now just become too suspicious of everyone's motives!'

'Suspicious? How could *anyone* ever be suspicious of me?' Dario rocked back on his heels with mock-injured innocence. 'I have no secrets. Everything I do is completely transparent. With me, what you see is what you get.' The corner of his mouth twitched wryly, belying his words.

'I'm not so sure about that,' said Josie, remembering the way he had clammed up on her that first day, when she'd suggested there might be skeletons in his past.

'Then take my word for it. Work aside, are you enjoying your stay here?' he said as they strolled along.

'I'm loving every minute,' Josie said. Walking along beside Dario, through a beautiful Italian castle, she was living her most exotic fantasy. 'It's all wonderful—far beyond anything I've experienced before.' She shook her head in wonder until the diamond drops of her borrowed earrings tinkled.

Dario looked down at her, his eyes dark and thoughtful. He knew he could take her, that tonight she was his. Yet suddenly he found himself wanting more from her than just her body. He wanted her to know more of him, to show her something of himself—something more intimate even than the kisses they'd shared. Impulsively, he said, 'Let me show you what I've been working on today.'

Lifting her plate and glass from her hands, he put them on the nearest wide stone windowsill. Then he gravely offered her his arm. With a thrill of daring, Josie put her hand into the crook of his elbow. With a smile of triumph, he led her out through the quadrangle, beneath the boughs of the ancient apricot tree towards the privacy of his artist's studio.

CHAPTER NINE

'Wow! So this is what you get up to!' Josie breathed as Dario opened the door to a small modern office unit, discreetly sited away from the *castello*.

Dario had real artistic skill. She could see that before she crossed the threshold of the building. His work was everywhere. Bright abstracts and stylized still-life studies hung from the walls, stood on easels or leaned against shelves neatly lined with equipment. His eye for composition was obvious, he had a free and easy way with media of all types and a real feeling for colour.

'You'll never see it all from there.'

He put his arm lightly around her shoulder to draw her inside. At first Josie was distracted by the warmth of his touch, but then her curiosity got the better of her. She moved away to inspect a Rothko-inspired piece waiting to be finished off.

'You could do this professionally, Dario.'

'Yes, but I'm not going to. You, on the other hand, really could do something with your talent.'

'And the equipment you sent me. In all the excitement, I forgot to thank you for it.' Turning to him, she rose on tiptoe and spontaneously kissed him on the cheek. 'Thank you, Dario.'

'You're very welcome,' he said warmly. This evening was turning out to be a revelation on so many levels. Not even Tamara or other women like her, in his bed or out of it, could make him feel so alive. Josie had attracted him from the first moment he'd seen her. Those reckless moments in the clearing had been wonderful while they'd lasted, but coming out with Arietta's name had wrecked everything. He had been working through an emotional hangover since then, unable to expose himself again. And then Josie had appeared at his party. Not only that, but she had made it very clear that she was here to enjoy everything he had to offer. *Everything.*

His chest tightened and his breathing became shallow. His heart was pounding, but this time it was more measured than at the picnic. When he looked at Josie tonight, he felt no trace of betraying his past. Arietta would never leave him, but he wouldn't allow her memory to intrude this time. Tonight, he felt transformed. A weight he hadn't realised he had been carrying fell away from his shoulders. It freed him to enjoy Josie's company, and anything else that she might suggest.

'It's a beautiful evening,' he said, his voice husky with anticipation. 'We don't want to waste it stuck in here. Why don't we take advantage of it?'

And each other, he thought as they stepped out into the warm, dark night. She looked so lovely he was almost afraid to touch her, for fear she might break.

He took her hand and squeezed it. In response, she moved in close to him. The evening was so peaceful, he could hear his own pulse and knew Arietta was slipping away from him with every heartbeat. He could not forget her completely—but she would never again cast such a long shadow over his life. With a pang of guilt mixed with relief, he realised that was a good thing. It was something else he could celebrate with Josie tonight.

She was gazing up at the night sky. He escorted her away from his studio, taking care to make his movements casual and unforced so as not to alarm her and break the spell.

The evening was alive as they strolled across the *castello*'s inner courtyard. Crickets chirruped and the breeze brought the fragrance of wild honeysuckle whispering in from beyond the high walls surrounding them. Then the sounds of an orchestra filtered through the warm evening air.

'You have a band?'

'Not personally.' Dario smiled. 'They're hired for the evening. Listen—I love this tune, don't you?'

Before Josie knew it, she was in his arms.

Words weren't needed. The feel of his hand spreading protectively over the small of her back and his fingers lacing into hers was enough. Rocking gently, he danced her slowly around the courtyard. Taut with nerves, Josie followed his lead.

'Relax.'

He dropped his head so that it nestled against her shoulder. She could feel his breath moving in delicate ripples over her bare skin. The feel of it and the softness of his hair brushing her cheek was enough to release a shudder of longing from her body.

'I knew you'd like this song.'

'It's…incredible.'

'You deserve nothing less, Josie,' he murmured.

'I don't know about that.'

'Stop it—you always do yourself down! You've already achieved so much in your life, climbed so high, and all on your own. Tonight, you should enjoy being the most beautiful star of them all.'

Josie giggled nervously. He leaned back a little so he could search her expression.

'Why laugh? There's nothing funny about that.'

'You're right. I shouldn't have done it. It's just that… it's been a very long time since anyone said anything like that to me.'

'Then "anyone" has been most remiss.'

'There hasn't been an "anyone". Not since Andy left me,' she murmured, adding silently to herself, *and I won't want anyone else now I've had your arms around me, Dario.*

She couldn't say that out loud. It would sound too lonely and needy.

'It sounds like your Andy was a bastard.'

Josie shook her head ruefully. 'No. He was just a man with ambition. We met on the same course at university and found we had the same aims and the same dreams. At first we shared everything with each other, and planned for the future. I blamed him so much for cheating on me, but maybe…maybe we never loved each other properly. Not like—' *Not like how I'm starting to feel about you,* she almost said, before snapping her mouth closed to block the words. This giddy feeling wasn't love! It was probably just sheer relief that she was forgiving Andy, and happiness at the beauty of the night.

'You're a loyal woman not to bad-mouth him in public.'

'Oh, don't talk to me about loyalty.' She groaned. 'My mother still cooks Sunday lunch for two every weekend, just in case my father walks back through the door. I tell her that's hardly likely after ten years, but she brings a whole new meaning to the word "faithful".'

Dario's arm tightened around her. 'So your father walked out, and your fiancé abandoned you...?' His voice sounded light, but underneath he was seething with anger at the two men who had dared to treat Josie so callously. 'It's a wonder you trust any men at all.'

'I don't—which is why I'm not harbouring any illusions about *you*, Dario!'

She forced a laugh. In response, he drew her so closely in to the shelter of his body she felt a chuckle emanate from deep within him. It felt so wonderful the last remnants of her self-control began shredding away beneath the gentle movements of their dance. She stopped still, knowing she had to stop now if she was ever going to, and pulled away from his embrace, but as slowly as possible. She couldn't bear to lose contact with him until the very last moment. Knowing she was about to lose control, she made a last effort to resist.

'Thank you for a truly magical evening, Dario.'

'The pleasure was all mine.' He trailed his hands down her bare arms, reluctant to finally let her go until the last moment. Gazing at her through the dusky light, he suddenly noticed something and tutted. 'I'm afraid our dance didn't do your corsage much good.'

Josie looked down. The fleshy white sepals of her flowers had been crushed against his broad chest. They were bruised and brown. Hoping they weren't a sign that he would leave her heart just as crushed, Josie sighed. 'That's such a shame. I was going to get them preserved as a souvenir of this wonderful evening. They won't keep now.'

Dario's hand moved again, but this time to take her arm. 'Then you'll need a replacement. There are plenty of flowers out in the rose garden.'

He drew her gently in the direction of a door set into the high stone wall surrounding the courtyard. Opening it, the first thing she experienced was a wave of birdsong, rising up from the distance. Then the overwhelming perfume of a thousand roses swept her away.

At her gasp, he smiled. 'Nightingale Valley is living up to its name tonight.'

'My goodness,' she breathed. Dario looked at her, admiring the purity of her profile in the moonlight, her eyes alight with joy. The flowers forgotten, he linked his hands around her waist and drew her near again.

'I have a confession to make, Josie.'

She looked up at him questioningly.

'The fact is, I had a very selfish reason for holding this party. And, as a man who has become used to having anything he wants, I couldn't deny myself.'

She looked up. He was smiling.

'So? What was the reason?' *Surely not just to seduce me!* she thought breathlessly.

'You'll think it's really stupid.'

She clapped her hands flat to his chest. 'Try me.'

He gave a humourless laugh. 'Remember what I said about birthdays, and how Antonia and I were always forgotten? Well, when I inherited the *castello* I swore to make every birthday really special. I'm beyond the age when I make the date public, but that doesn't mean I have to deny myself a party. And today's the day.'

Josie was enchanted. 'Oh, Dario! Happy birthday! But why didn't you or Toni tell me? I would have got you a present and a card—instead, I've got nothing…'

Somewhere, in the back of her mind, the penny dropped. It had been tossed across that designer's salon by Antonia and now bounced around inside her brain, but Josie was far more concerned with the look on Dario's face.

He grimaced again. 'That's another reason why I don't broadcast the date. As you've said yourself, anything I want, I already have. Why should I put my friends to the trouble and expense of buying me things?'

Josie was shocked and couldn't help showing it. 'Birthdays have got nothing to do with money. That's not what presents are about!'

He stared at her, genuinely intrigued. 'Isn't it?'

'No!' Josie pulled away from him emphatically. 'They're a way of reminding people that their friends care enough about them to give them something in honour of the day.'

He gave her a look, as though he was waiting for further explanation.

'I would have taken the time to choose something

you really wanted. Something for your studio, maybe. I'm sure there are all sorts of little things you need—new colours, brushes…the sort of thing that it would be too much of a bother for you to break off and go out and buy for yourself.'

'That's what the Internet is for—and why I employ staff.'

Josie sighed with annoyance. 'It's the gesture that matters, not the thing itself.'

His mouth moved, but then he must have thought better of saying anything and stayed silent. She thought of all the gestures they had shared, the looks, the touches and those kisses…

'Sometimes the greatest gifts cost nothing at all,' she added thoughtfully.

Dario waved his hand, as if brushing away the subject. 'We're not here to talk about me. Come and experience the di Sirena night, Josie.'

Taking her by the hand, he led her into the fragrance-drenched air of Nightingale Valley. One deep breath filled her full of enchantment.

'Dario…it's wonderful…' she whispered.

He chuckled. 'I thought you'd done a grand tour of the estate and would know all about this place.'

'Yes, but that was during the day, while I was working. It has taken you to open my eyes to its natural wonders. *All* of them,' she said, a thoughtful look on her face.

'It's a pleasure—and I would love to give you more,' he said, drawing her gently towards his body again. Unable to wait a moment longer, he lowered his head and kissed her full on the lips. It was a long, lingering explosion of sensations that sapped her last ounce of resistance. When their lips finally parted she leaned against him, suddenly as weak as water and trying to catch her breath.

'Did you know that kisses get lonely?' Dario's voice was as soft as the touch of his lips against hers as he kissed her again.

It was exquisite, a perfect melding of sensations that coursed through Josie's veins like warm chocolate. A shocking, daring idea had been forming in her mind. Dario had lit the fuse and now it exploded into her brain. All the same, she had to steel herself before the words would come out.

'I know exactly what I'd like to give you for your birthday, Dario. It's something you don't have—and something no money in the world could buy.' She swallowed hard before whispering, 'Can you guess what it is?'

His dark eyes glittering in the moonlight, he looked down at her and shook his head.

'It's me,' she whispered.

He continued looking down at her, almost expressionless. Only a muscle flickering in his cheek showed the control he was exerting over his reactions. Before she knew what was happening, he was leading her across to the far side of the rose garden. There, a wooden gate opened out into the estate proper. Before letting her through it, he stopped and turned to her.

'Are you sure this is really what you want, Josie?' he asked seriously.

She smiled and nodded, not wanting to interrupt the wonderful flow of birdsong rising from the valley below them. Dario suddenly smiled at her, the tension seeming to leave his body. With one hand, he loosened his tie and undid the top button of his shirt. In the half-light, the contrast of the black velvet against the bright white of his shirt was dazzling. Taking her by the hand again, he led her down a wide woodland track, following the contours of the hillside.

'There's a lake at the bottom with a gazebo overlooking the water. You'll like it there.'

Josie knew she would like it anywhere if Dario was with her.

'I'm so glad I came to your party after all,' she whispered.

Dario paused and looked back at her. All the shades of evening couldn't disguise the flash of his beautiful white teeth.

'I couldn't agree more.'

When they reached the lake, the gentle susurration of insects was punctuated by the plop of something small diving into the water.

'A frog,' he reassured her as she drew closer. Taking her gently in his arms, Dario's kiss was long, slow and sweet.

'You made such a spectacular entrance this evening,' he breathed at last.

'But I didn't do anything.'

'You didn't have to. A woman so poised, and looking like an angel...you took my breath away.' Always uncomfortable with praise, Josie shook her head and blushed.

'No—don't deny it. Be proud! Every woman and every man in the place couldn't take their eyes off you. You were the star—my star—and I had to spirit you away before anyone else could.'

In the breathless hush that followed his words, a nightingale burst into song from a hazel thicket within a few feet of where they stood. Josie smiled and, as Dario's touch tingled around the outline of her face to lift it for another kiss, a second bird joined in.

'Rivals for the same prize,' she whispered.

Dario's kisses made thinking about anything but him impossible. The insistent presence of his body completely enthralled her. The firm ridge of his arousal pushed against her as he held her close, cradling her in his arms. The tip of his tongue sensitised the entire curve of her neck. Josie shivered in wild anticipation and instantly he pulled off his jacket and enveloped her in it.

'I'm not cold.'

'I want to make sure you don't get that way.'

Curving an arm lightly around her shoulders, he led her towards a clearing in the trees. The full moon was just rising above the south-eastern horizon, its silvery light sending rippling reflections across the lake that slept peacefully in its cool shadows. Flag irises and sweet rush stood sentinel around a palatial summer-house, complete with its own little jetty. Josie looked nervously at a small rowing boat and oars that were tied to it.

'I know you'll be happier on dry land.' Dario's low laughter lit up her face as he opened the gazebo. The small house was the perfect place for romance. Its cedar-wood walls retained the day's warmth, while beeswax polish and swags of lavender hanging from the rafters perfumed the air with the memories of summers long past.

'I want you.' Dario's voice was husky with testos-terone.

When he kissed her now it was with more urgency. A slow burning fire had been kindled from the moment their eyes had first met. Now it burst into flames of unquenchable passion. When his hands began to move over her, Josie could do nothing to stop him. As he reached the voluptuous curves of her body, she gasped, throwing back her head in anticipation. Dario was quick to act, kissing the cool pale column of her throat from the tip of her chin to the hollow at its base. As his hands cupped her breasts she remembered the way his sen-sitive fingers had enclosed that ripe peach on the day of their picnic. A little moan of anticipation left her lips, encouraging Dario to dip his head and move his lips over the thin silk of her dress. It was so delicate, the small nubs of her erect nipples were clearly vis-ible. They were too much of a temptation for Dario. He tried his teeth against one, gently testing its sensi-tivity. The effect of his teasing sent Josie into parox-ysms of desire. Her fingers drove into his midnight-dark hair, pulling his head closer. Moonlight glittered over its tousled luxuriance, and Josie couldn't help herself.

Sliding her hands over his shoulders, she cupped his face and brought it up level with her own.

'Take me,' she moaned in a voice barely recognisable as her own.

Dario engulfed her in his arms, plundering kiss after kiss from her willing mouth. Josie shrugged off his jacket and let her hands work their way beneath the cool white fabric of his shirt to find the red-hot elemental man inside. Soon they were both naked in the moonlight. Dario filled her senses so completely, she was barely aware of her surroundings as he laid her on the soft down-filled cushions of the summer-house sofa. His outline was sleek and hard as he towered over her, ready, willing and more than able to claim his ultimate prize. As he swooped down to cover her body, she twined her legs around his narrow waist, desperate to bring him closer to the core of her being. As he glided over her in the darkness, her body was torn with a cry of need that echoed into the night.

Long, long afterwards, Josie lay gazing out along the length of the lake. She had no idea of the time, but it must be so late it was now early. The summer night had never darkened completely. A single bright star was left in the sky. It stood high above the water, its pinpoint of light dancing on surface ripples stirred by a light breeze. The nightingales were still singing, but they had been joined by one or two sleepy robins. Dario lay with his head nestled against her neck, quite still apart from the gentle rise and fall of his breathing. Josie should have been in heaven. Instead, her mind churned over and over what had happened during the spectacular hours they had shared. Dario had stripped away all her inhibitions, taken her to paradise and kept her there. Josie thought back, exhausted and overwhelmed by the wild passion he unleashed in her. She glowed at the memory…but now she knew she couldn't get enough of him. From this moment on, nothing life could give her had a chance of competing with the night she had just spent— unless it included Dario.

And that thought was what tortured her now. This man was a playboy—a party animal to his capable, dexterous fingertips. Josie wanted his body, but knew she couldn't bear to have it without his love and loyalty as well. But that was a greedy, impossible dream. Dario was no more capable of giving her a lifelong commitment than Andy had been. Josie had finally realised just how little her ex-fiancé now meant to her, but Dario was an entirely different prospect. She wanted him with every fibre of her being—but she would never be able to keep him. No woman could hope to do that.

When he stirred, Josie knew she had to brace herself and resist him. One more encounter, one fleeting touch, one smile and she would be heading for disaster again. When his hand began to glide sleepily over her naked thigh, she took a deep breath, slipped out of his grasp and stood up.

'Dario, I…' There were no words. 'I have to go.'

To hide her expression, she turned away from him quickly and pretended to be more interested in gathering up her scattered clothes than watching him wake.

'Where are you going? It's still early—let's start

all over again...' His drowsy words simmered with promise.

Josie looked back at him. She knew it was a mistake, but she was unable to stop herself. He looked magnificent, as ever. The early sunlight played over his golden muscles, and she felt desire tighten its grip on her body again. She had to escape while she still could. One hand pressed tight against her belly, trying to restrain her desperate need for him, she looked away.

'Last night, I had the most wonderful time of my life, Dario, but I shouldn't have let it happen.'

'Why ever not? I thought it was one of your very best ideas,' he said, smiling.

Josie began to pull on her clothes anyhow.

'What I mean is, I don't want you to think that I'm asking for more than you've already given me. I don't want to force you into anything, Dario.'

Dario's smile faded. 'What are you saying?' He sat up, looking suddenly angry.

Josie struggled with her feelings. All she wanted to do was drop everything and lean into his powerful embrace again. The only thing stopping her was the knowledge that Dario had done this dozens of times in the past, and had cast off those other girls as easily as he had thrown off his clothes the night before. She was worth more than that, and she knew it. He'd helped her know it. She would remember his searing looks scorching straight across the party towards her for as long as she lived. The only thing that could spoil that memory would be the devastation of his abandonment.

If I end it now I can remember all the good things,

without the horror that pursued me after Andy's betrayal, she thought. *It will be so hard to let Dario go, but he would only cheat on me eventually, and that would wreck every special thing we've had.*

'I've already given you everything, Dario.'

'You say that, but I know you have much more to offer me, *tesoro*,' he said with gruff exasperation. He reached out to her, but she sidestepped before his hand could connect with her arm. 'What do you want me to say? Did you think that I was going to offer a lifelong commitment on the basis of a single night? You must know me—or at least my reputation—better than that, Josie.'

She hurriedly pulled on her beautiful dress. 'I don't want you to say anything, Dario, especially about the future. But...well, actually I...I suppose I don't know what I mean...'

He watched her for a few seconds and she saw his expression rapidly closing down. With a chill of recognition, she saw him retreating from her and the intimacy they had shared through the warm, still hours of darkness.

'I do. I've often had to say the same thing. It's a novelty to be on the receiving end, I'll admit, but I think I can help you.' He spoke the words in a way that made Josie want to run. Dario's reputation scared her enough, without needing details.

'It goes something like this: "That was a fantastic night, so let's remember it fondly and move on." That's what you're trying to tell me, isn't it?' he announced, getting up without warning and turning his back on her.

Josie stared at him. Secretly, she had been expecting, no, *hoping*, that Dario would put up at least some token resistance in the face of her brush-off. Instead, he concentrated on rescuing his clothes, which had been scattered during their reckless night of passion. She felt her insides contract with the loss of him.

Please don't end it here—not now, not yet! she thought. *Let me have a little more pleasure—an hour, a day, a week...*

It was no good. She knew only too well what would happen if she went down that route. One more kiss from Dario was sure to lead straight to heartbreak. Now she had tasted everything he had to give, she was too greedy to trust herself with him ever again.

Because when my heart and mind is full of him, that's when I'll discover he's 'entertaining' someone else and betraying me like Andy did.

'You're right, Dario,' she said unsteadily. 'It was wonderful...but that's it. We'll put this down to experience. I'll be gone soon, so it would be silly to try and make anything more out of it,' she said in an offhand way, puncturing their awkward silence as she tried to get a better response from him.

'Good. You're being very sensible, as usual. It's what I've come to expect from you, Josie.' He gave that lovely hint of the exotic to her name again, and it made her cry inside.

'You shouldn't get mixed up in casual flings. You aren't the type,' he went on, strolling over to lift a skein of her hair over her shoulder. It was a gesture that was more patronising than romantic. 'But I must thank you again for your most wonderful birthday present. It was a miraculous treat—like nothing I have ever been given before.'

He rapped out his words in an oddly emotionless way and didn't look at her as he moved away again. Josie was totally deflated. They might as well have shared an evening's carp fishing.

Snapping on his watch, he checked its display. 'I'm afraid I must go—I've promised to take Antonia into town this morning. She wants my help in selecting a nursery for Fabio.'

His voice was still gritty with testosterone. That thought added a terrible twist to Josie's almost unbearable longing. She had wielded such power over his body during the hours of darkness. Then, she could have made him stay by her side with a single touch. She was desperately tempted to try again now, but it was too great a risk. His face was unreadable, but the bright searching light of day would leave her no hiding place if he rejected her. Josie was determined to learn from all the mistakes she had made in the past and not make any new ones.

When they were both dressed, Dario escorted her all the way back to the *castello*, but neither spoke.

Josie couldn't help thinking he had been silenced by regret, and that idea struck her dumb with despair.

CHAPTER TEN

DARIO sat in his estate office later, tapping the end of a pencil against his teeth and staring at the Monet he had bought last time he was in New York. He would remember the night of his thirty-third birthday for the rest of his life, but not with pride.

He rubbed his chin thoughtfully, wincing slightly over the place where he had caught himself with the razor earlier that morning. It had been very difficult to look his reflection in the eye. Josie was affecting him in an unusual way. He always aimed to love women and leave them before either of them got hurt. He winced again. The mere thought of that four letter word 'love' made him cringe inwardly whenever he thought of Josie, and he had been thinking about her a lot over the past few hours. She was different in every way from the girls he usually dated. They weren't afraid to show their feelings. Instinctively, he had always known Josie wasn't like that. She wasn't the sort to make a fuss. She had stood up for her ex-fiancé after all, even though he had cheated on her and then walked away. Dario grimaced. He had waved goodbye to any number of women over the years, but this was his first experience of a girl waving to him first.

He checked his diary. With a lurch of concern he saw that Josie was due to leave within a week. He thought of her beautiful sunlit face that morning, and frowned. She had looked so preoccupied. What could possibly be worrying her? A surge of lust powered through his groin and he laughed at himself. Concern for a woman's state of mind hadn't troubled him for years. Wanting to experience her body again was a much more familiar urge.

For some reason he couldn't get Josie's words out of his mind.

I'll be gone soon.

They were true enough. Both she and Dario had known the date of her departure from the time this visit was arranged. So why had she kept mentioning it? Their exchanges in that awkwardly formal 'morning after' moment kept assaulting him in flashback.

We'll put this down to experience.

That agreement should have made him feel happier—after all, he had said it so many times to so many women over the years.

Why isn't it working this time? He ran his thumb back and forth across his lower lip. *Why not?*

He winced yet again, but not at the thought of what they had done last night. That still kept his body alight with desire. He puzzled on, gnawing at the problem like a wolf in a snare until the answer came to him in a single word.

We.

That word was the stumbling block. He hadn't used

it since Arietta was alive—the last time he had felt part
of a couple. And Josie had used it as well.

Suddenly he realised the truth—the clue to this
whole problem. Josie had thought of them as a couple,
not as simply a one-night stand. She didn't really want
it to end yet, any more than he did. At that thought, his
pulse started to race. His body tightened with an instinctive roar of possession at the very thought of her
walking to another man. The strength of his reaction
surprised him…terrified him.

He grasped suddenly for an image of Arietta. For a
panicked moment, he couldn't recall her face. He concentrated fiercely, feeling how much he'd loved her, how
he was responsible for her loss, and soon felt calmer.
Josie had been right to leave. He couldn't offer her anything more than a fling, even if she wanted it. Ruthlessly
ignoring the small voice which continued to protest
against never holding her in his arms again, he forced
his attention back to the estate.

A day later, head down, Josie marched towards her
camp beside the old olive press. Not even work had
been able to do anything about her burning sense of
shame and self-loathing since the party. *How could I
have been so stupid? Dad and Andy both promised me
the world, but they still walked away. If I think a rich
playboy is going to be any different, then I really am
fooling myself…*

Work had been such a safe haven for her until now;
she had convinced herself that it was all she ever
needed. Then one look at Dario and her defences had

crumbled. The moment he'd taken her hand at the party, Josie had known there could be no other man for her, not even if she lived to be a hundred. But she had to face facts. Dario had a reputation as a Casanova, and no man would give that up lightly. He might have played the part of honourable Count to perfection while he'd escorted her back to the *castello*, but that would be the end of it. Josie knew only too well how easily men could change and turn away.

Dario's lifestyle keeps admirers circling him like reef sharks. He never lingers with anyone for long, so why did I think I was any different? she thought furiously. *I had to finish it before he got the chance to break my heart. By this time next week, he won't remember what happened between us. In a month's time, he won't even remember my name. But his effect on me will last for ever...*

There was nothing for it but to retreat into her work once more. With only a week left of her stay, the best she could do was keep her head down and try to be invisible. She desperately wanted to confide in someone, but it was impossible. Antonia was watchful and understanding but, caught between her brother and her best friend, she didn't pry and Josie couldn't bear to drag her into the situation. Instead, she spent her time working as far away from Dario's haunts as she could, but his influence ran deep. Although determined to protect her poor battered heart from any further damage, Josie couldn't stop thinking about him.

When lack of concentration caused her to chip a second piece off the stonework she was uncovering, she threw her trowel down in disgust. For as long as she was here, Dario was going to dominate her thoughts and distract her from her work. There were only two solutions to that problem, and it was decision time. She could either finish her trip early and go home right now, or she could come to terms with her feelings for Dario.

I'm supposed to be a rational adult, so why can't I decide and stop drooping about like a love-struck schoolgirl? she asked herself.

The answer to that was all too obvious. She wanted Dario—but she was scared. Giving him so much power over her emotions was a step too far.

If only I could be strong enough to say goodbye... but not just yet...

A desperate remedy swam into her overheated brain. Perhaps she could simply let down her guard long enough to enjoy Dario for a little while longer. Just until the end of her stay at the *castello*. She could indulge herself for a few more days, but there would be a fixed time limit and they would both know it. She could experience Dario's charm and incredible love-making all over again, but walk away before he broke her heart. No one would have to make promises they couldn't keep. It would be nothing more than a wonderful footnote to her stay.

Other people have holiday romances all the time and no one dies of disappointment, do they? she reassured herself. *Why can't I, as long as I keep to the rules? If Dario can do it, then so can I. It's not as though anyone expects a fling to last. That's all I'll have to remember.*

Having convinced herself, Josie shut out her remaining doubts and packed up her tools. Then she set off to find Dario before she changed her mind.

Dario was in his studio, studying the painting he had been working on. His charcoal sketches hadn't caught the right mood at all. As an act of desperation, he had tried to commit directly to canvas, hoping to be inspired all over again. But this portrait refused to work well, even after his third attempt. Sighing, he turned away to pick up a turpentine-soaked rag, ready for another try. Then a figure in the doorway caught his eye. He stopped in mid-movement. It was Josie. For a moment, he felt his expression transformed by guilt but managed to turn it into a smile.

'Come in! This is an unexpected pleasure. I was beginning to think you were avoiding me.'

Josie blushed and hesitated, and he guessed that was exactly what she had been doing. But then he saw her stiffen her resolve—obviously and beautifully. She lifted her head and straightened her shoulders. Then she stepped into the studio, but looking around more warily than she had done on their glorious evening together. He knew that must be because this was his territory—his special place, with its atmosphere thick with the perfume of media in all their forms: linseed oil, paint and new canvas. It was a place he felt safe, but Josie clearly didn't.

'Why don't you come over here and see what I'm working on?'

She walked over to him, but without the self-confident stride she used to approach her own work. When she saw the image he was about to erase, there was a definite hesitation. Although she tried to hide it, he saw her shoulders droop and her mouth turn down. Even half-finished, his work in progress was clearly a beautiful dark-haired young woman.

'Is this Arietta?' Her voice hardly disturbed the atmosphere between them.

She must know the answer to that question already, Dario thought. Her gaze was so direct, it made him uncomfortable. He set his jaw and hardened his expression.

'It was supposed to be her, yes.' He anticipated her question. 'I thought she deserved her place in the di Sirena portrait gallery. After all, if things had worked out differently, she would have been my *Contessa*.'

Josie neither moved nor spoke, so Dario fixed her with a penetrating stare.

'Aren't you going to ask me about her?'

'You'll tell me if you want to,' she said quietly. 'I don't like talking about my own past. I can hardly expect you to be any different.'

He tipped his head in brief acknowledgement. 'We met when I was in my final year at university…' He couldn't find the words to frame what had happened. How they'd fallen in love almost from the first moment. It had been magical, perfect, unlike anything he'd ever known, until real life began to intrude. Looking back, he wondered how they'd have coped after university, when their idealism would have had to have changed to meet the practicalities of the world. 'We had a row one evening. Of all the stupid things, it was because I was spending too much time painting and not enough with her. She drove off into a storm. I went after her, but she was determined to get away from me. We were both travelling much too fast. She skidded into a flooded ditch.'

He waited for the usual spasm of pain to pass through his body. It always did when he thought about that terrible evening. Always—until today. He frowned, puzzled. Josie said nothing.

On top of everything else, she's a good listener! he thought, and tried saying more.

'She died on the way to hospital.'

'I'm so sorry, Dario.'

'Yes.'

She looked surprised at his automatic response, and Dario realised such a quick reply might have sounded heartless.

She's probably expecting me to sound more traumatised. I used to...but not now...

The revelation came to him easily, but he guessed it would be difficult to live with. He wondered if saying more could distance him from his past still further.

'It nearly destroyed me,' he began hesitantly, but there was no need. Telling Josie seemed so right, it felt good to unburden himself rather hold on to the pain. 'For years, no day passed without my thoughts turning to her. After all, meeting Arietta was a defining moment in my life. After she died, I tried to fill the void she left with partying. It has never worked. Nothing could compare with the simple enjoyment of spending time with a woman who understood me, for better or worse.'

A smile flickered across his face and was gone. 'But her memory has started to slip away from me. Little by little, day by day I have begun to feel I'm losing her. At first, inheriting the *castello* and its estate kept me so busy I didn't have time for memories. Now, when I try to recapture them, she is always retreating from me.'

He stopped. Josie watched him, unblinking. She was only a heartbeat away, and he could tell she was holding her breath. He knew, because he was doing exactly the same thing.

'I've fought it every inch of the way, Josie. I started to paint a portrait of Arietta as I remembered her, but it's not going well. I've worked and worked on this damned painting, but it's impossible. I can't catch her.'

He looked at the canvas for a second, then passed a hand quickly over his face to hide the fact that he no longer cared.

Josie couldn't help herself. She rushed forward and threw her arms around him.

'Dario, don't… I'm sure Arietta would hate to think you were unhappy…'

He dropped his hand abruptly. To her relief, she saw his eyes were dry, but their depths were full of a turbulence she had never seen before.

'How can you possibly know that?'

She let him go and backed away. That reassurance had been forced out of her in a moment of pure panic.

'I…I'm sorry. I have no idea. How can I? But I'm absolutely certain that she couldn't bear to think of you being upset and living a half life, full of regret.'

'That's exactly what Arietta said to me once, all those years ago.'

He was very still for a moment, and then reached for his wallet. Opening it, he pulled out a small well-worn photograph, which he showed to Josie. Then he held it next to his half-finished painting.

'Do you see the likeness?' he asked grimly.

Josie looked from the painting to the photograph, then back again.

'Well…' She hesitated, not wanting to say what she really thought.

'My painting doesn't look much like the girl in the photograph, does it?'

'You did say you were working from memory.'

'Yes. Exactly.'

Dario was staring at the picture with an unfathomable expression. Josie joined him. The photograph of Arietta was in black and white, but his painting was in glorious colour. Josie thought it would be an amazing coincidence for Arietta to have eyes exactly the same shade as her own and, as for that dress—in Dario's photo it looked white rather than the green shot with gold he had used for his portrait. Josie didn't know what to say. Something important was happening and she could only wonder what direction it was going to take. Finally, Dario placed the photograph down on the table beside him and turned towards her. To Josie's relief, he was smiling again.

'Well, now you've seen my problem—what's yours?'

Josie could hardly remember. A few minutes ago she had been completely absorbed in her own feelings. Now they were almost forgotten in the face of Dario's problems. They were far worse. He sounded so concerned about her, she could hardly bear to reply.

'It's nothing like as serious as the things you've been going through, but…to be honest, I've felt terrible since your birthday, Dario. I want to clear the air between us. I really did have a wonderful time at your party and… afterwards.'

She faltered, and couldn't help blushing. Dario grinned conspiratorially, bowing his head at the compliment.

'…But next morning I felt so awkward, I didn't know how to react. It was the first time I've ever done anything like that. All I knew was that I didn't want you to think you owed me anything, or that I expected any sort of commitment from you.'

'You made that perfectly clear at the time. I understood and respected your decision, and still do. I didn't have any difficulty with it then, or now.' He picked up the photograph of Arietta and put it carefully away in his wallet again. 'As far as I'm concerned, everything is fine between us.'

It didn't feel like that to Josie. She blushed even deeper.

'No… I know I was sending out mixed messages to you. It was all and then nothing…' Her voice trailed away. Living each day without Dario had been agony for her, yet he seemed so unmoved! If he didn't accept what she was about to say, the pain would be unspeakable, yet she knew she had to seize the moment and at least try, otherwise she'd never forgive herself for being a coward. 'There's no reason why we can't be...*friends* for the rest of my stay. Is there?' she added hurriedly.

Dario went absolutely still for a moment, then turned to clear up his brushes and paints. When he replied, his words were slow and considered.

'Josie, of course I want that. But let's be absolutely clear—I don't want any more misunderstandings. There must be no chance of anyone getting hurt by mistake.'

Josie didn't reply at once, but eventually, she stammered, 'W...we're both adults, aren't we?'

'All right, then. However, you'll have to take the lead. I don't want you to end up regretting anything.' The words seemed gentle, yet the tension around his jaw gave the impression of a lethal predator, barely held in check.

Josie couldn't speak, so she simply nodded. Dario turned away from the building tension, and began to scrub his canvas clean. She watched him, strangely relieved that Arietta's image would soon be erased.

'What are you going to paint now?'

He stopped to fold the cloth he held into a pad.

'I haven't decided yet,' he responded finally.

'Then...how about me?' Her voice was quiet, but clear.

Dario turned slowly towards her and smiled. It was like the sun coming out from behind a cloud that had lingered for far too long.

'Seriously?'

She hesitated for a moment, then nodded.

'Then yes—I'd love to do that. And...I think I'd like to paint you wearing the stunning dress you wore at the

party. The green silk wrapping that covered my wonderful present,' he said softly.

Looking out over the beautiful view from his studio window, Josie pretended to think. She couldn't. Her
mind was filled with images of a much more seductive
kind than mere landscape.

'The zip of that dress is rather tricky…it's not something I could manage on my own. I might need your
help to get it on and off,' she whispered, leaving no
doubt about who was taking the lead now.

Outside, the last swallows slipped through the sky
with the sound of roughened fingertips on silk. Then
Dario took the few steps that still separated them and
slid his arms around Josie's waist. She closed her eyes.

'So why not give in and let me help you for once?' he
whispered into the citrus-scented softness of her hair.

The touch of his breath on her neck sent shivers
over her skin. Lust flooded through her body with an
urgency that wouldn't wait for bed. When his hands
guided her into turning and facing him, she couldn't
resist. Their first kiss was a slow, haunting moment of
quiet bliss. Then Josie opened her eyes and found herself looking over his shoulder—straight at the unfinished portrait of Arietta. Her blood ran cold.

'You feel chilly,' Dario murmured, running his hands
over her bare arms with lingering appreciation.

'A breeze must have blown in from the garden. You'd
better close the blinds,' she whispered. He smiled and
did so, then turned to her, his eyes asking a question.
Josie gathered her courage for a final time and let herself speak the absolute truth. 'I want you, Dario. Now.'

He looked down at her, the smile lingering on his lips, but his dark eyes were hooded and intense. 'This is the last chance you have to change your mind.'

'I want you right now. It doesn't matter where we are,' she said huskily.

'That's exactly what I was thinking, *tesoro*.'

He pulled away from her, slowly and reluctantly. Still greedy for contact with her, his hand slid down from her shoulder to her hand and finally kissed each of her fingertips in turn before letting go of her. Then Josie took control as she had promised, her heightened state of arousal urging her on. Undressing Dario was a triumph of restraint over animal need. She forced herself to take her time, kissing every inch of skin she exposed. His hands roamed over her, wild and free. She could hear the hiss of his breath and knew he was struggling against his most basic urge to take command. Knowing that acted as a powerful aphrodisiac. Sliding his clothes off over the hard, hot planes of his body and hearing the swish of fine designer fabrics brushing against his skin was so exciting it lured Josie into trying things she had never been tempted to do before.

'All my experience counts for nothing,' he breathed into the still, warm air.

'You don't know what it means to hear you say that, Dario.' The thought of being able to please him made her actions feel all the more erotic. When he took hold of her now, she did nothing to stop him. She was bathed in a state of such high arousal, she wanted to be taken and possessed and to hell with the consequences.

'You are divine…' His words were as seductive as

the urgent pressure of his body against hers. '*Dio*, but you are everything I have ever wanted in a woman. I want you so much…'

She wanted him, too, with a passion more deep and urgent than anything she had ever known before. With a wordless sound of anticipation, he lifted her onto a low velvet-covered couch in the centre of the room. There, he took possession of her. They made love with a fast, fiery intensity that neither had experienced before— and Josie knew that from now on she would never find happiness with anyone but Dario. When he couldn't hold back any more, she enfolded him, holding him so close that she felt they were both part of one body. In response, he shouted his pleasure to the skies in one glorious burst of fulfilment.

CHAPTER ELEVEN

OVER the next few glorious days, Josie completely lost track of time. She was in Dario's arms, and it was the only thing that mattered to her in any way. She was completely absorbed by him, and her feelings were reflected and magnified in his fascination for her. The two of them became one in a delicious spell of seduction, but Josie was also acutely aware that there was a time limit on her happiness. She had to get back to the project that had first brought her into the charmed embrace of Dario's influence, before her time in Italy was over.

Catching her hand as she got out of bed one morning, he turned it over and kissed his way from the delicate skin on the inside of her wrist to the bend of her elbow. She gasped, barely resisting the temptation of Dario's husky 'Come back to bed?'

She forced herself to draw a line between the two parts of her life, pleasure and work.

He let her go, but when she bent to kiss him goodbye he almost persuaded her to stay. Returning her passion, he kissed her with such fire it drew all the breath from her body.

'No...stop, I must go, Dario!' she gasped, laughing—but her heart wanted her to stay for ever.

Watching Josie leave his room filled Dario with a cocktail of feelings. His body wanted her more than ever, but his mind had lost all sense of direction. Josie was so different from the other women who had populated his life so far. They always began to lose their appeal the moment he had satisfied his lust. That hadn't happened with Josie. Instead of becoming easier to resist over time, he was beginning to find it hard to decide where he stopped and she began. They had been inseparable since that moment she'd walked back into his studio. Their five-hour fling had now stretched into days, and Dario no longer had any idea of how it would end.

Gazing out of his bedroom window over his sunlit estate, he saw Federico's flock of doves circling over the courtyard. Josie must have thrown them some croissant crumbs as she left. As he smiled at the image, one downy feather detached itself from the flock and swung through the air. Caught by a little up-draught, it suddenly spiralled towards the blue sky again.

Funny, he thought as he decided to get up and follow Josie out to her work. *This whole business started because I wanted to keep her at arm's length. Now we might as well be riding on that feather, hovering between heaven and earth.*

It was a journey Josie assumed would be over by the following weekend. She already sighed softly each time Dario opened his appointments diary. His smile widened. Josie had given him the perfect birthday present, but he'd been planning for a few days and now he knew that she would be getting an even bigger surprise—from him!

Work was a constant thread running through Josie's life. She could never forsake it entirely, especially as she knew it would be the only thing left to comfort her when Dario was a painful memory, haunting her every moment.

Dario...

She softened at the mere thought of his name. She was almost powerless to resist him. She spent seductive nights wrapped in his arms, and was awakened by his kisses and passion each morning. He was encouraging her to take a more relaxed attitude to life. His influence over her was growing so much that she'd even dropped her famous independence long enough to let him take her visiting his friends. Dario had a formidable network of contacts. He introduced her to people whose private estates contained spectacular ruins, many of which had never been excavated before. Some were interested in hosting parts of Josie's intended field trips, so she arranged follow-up visits to survey the sites. This was where Dario sprang his biggest surprise of all. Instead of sitting on shady terraces sipping cocktails with his contacts, he was only interested in working at her side.

On days like today he was always there for her, but Josie was sure it wouldn't last. When her visit to the Castello Sirena ended she would leave, like the swallows. Dario couldn't follow her. Instead, he would forget her the moment autumn chills chased all thoughts of their shared summer days away...

The day before she was due to leave for England, Josie was out on site when her phone rang. Dario had been delayed back at the *castello* by paperwork, so she was waiting expectantly for his call. She answered on the first ring.

With luck, he's going to say he's on his way, she thought.

'Josie!'

It wasn't the voice she so wanted to hear, and her spirits sank.

'Bursar,' she replied evenly, managing to hide her disappointment. 'I didn't realise you knew my mobile number. I'm afraid I'm in Italy at the moment, so selling any more raffle tickets for university funds is out of the question,' she added, hoping he wouldn't ask her why until she'd had time to dream up some excuse.

'I know where you are, dear girl. That's why I'm ringing you. I have some good news.'

Josie racked her brain. She knew how this man worked. Money was everything to him: if he called her 'dear girl' she must have more of it than he did.

The chance would be a fine thing, she thought. *Unless—*

'Don't tell me the staff's syndicate numbers came up in the lottery last night?'

'Ah...no, but in a way you're on the right track. Remind me—how much money did you request to fund your research and field trips, dear girl?'

His cheery tone convinced Josie that he was building up to ask her some tremendous favour.

'That depends.'

'Well…why don't you think of a number and double it, say, to allow for inflation…wear and tear, that sort of thing?'

There was definitely something up, and there was only one way to flush this particular pigeon out of the undergrowth. Josie picked an enormous figure out of the air. 'Sixty thousand pounds.'

'Is that all?' The bursar sounded disappointed. 'Couldn't you make it a round hundred? Taking into account travelling costs, expenses, et cetera, et cetera?'

'Oh, *easily*,' Josie said with heavy sarcasm. 'It was the government's loss when I decided not to become a Member of Parliament.'

The bursar laughed like a drain.

He never *laughs at my jokes*, Josie thought. *The sun must really be shining out of me today.* Consumed with curiosity, she tried pushing the envelope a bit further to see if it came back stuffed with used notes.

'Why stop there? Why not make it two hundred thousand, to allow for shrinkage?'

'Oh, now, don't let's be greedy!' The bursar chuckled. 'Count Dario is being generous enough in letting you name your own price.'

Josie froze. 'What?'

'Count Dario di Sirena is so impressed with the work you've been doing on his estate, he wants to fund your plans to develop student field trips to the area. He thinks it will boost the local economy, so he's willing to finance your stay in Italy for as long as is necessary, and pay for all your research, too.'

Josie stiffened. 'Oh, he *is*, is he?'

'Yes. We've had some good long chats on the telephone. What a *very* nice chap he is!'

'Delightful.'

'He told me how much he enjoys seeing you working about the old place and bringing it to life. He's really interested in being of service to you, Josie.'

'Hmm.'

'Yes, he seemed extremely concerned that any financial constraints put on you by the university shouldn't curtail your ambitions.'

'Concerned? I'll bet he was. Hang on, Bursar. I need to discuss this matter with the Count myself, before we decide *anything*,' she announced, grimly determined that the only nice round figure she would accept from Dario would be a big fat zero.

Dario was sitting in his office, contemplating the di Sirena Monet that hung opposite his desk, when his peace was shattered by a whirlwind in human form. Josie was glowing from her half-mile hike across country and burning with righteous indignation.

'What the *hell* do you think you're doing?'

Dario could see from the way she slammed the door that 'Thinking of you' was obviously not the answer she wanted. He smiled instead, and gave her a chance to explain. It was a mistake.

'How dare you extend my stay without asking me? And how dare you pay off my department? I've had to grovel for every penny I've ever needed, yet I start sleeping with you and suddenly money is flowing in my direction faster than your flattery! How do you think that makes me feel, Dario?' she hissed.

Startled by her reaction but determined not to show it, he netted his fingers and watched her over them. 'Not grateful, that's for sure,' he drawled.

Her face changed. 'I won't be forced to rely on anyone else's…' she seemed about to say something else but then plumped for '…money. You're trying to make me dependent on you.'

'I thought you understood me better than that, Josie,' he replied in a more reasonable tone of voice. 'I think I understand *you* quite well. You're brilliant at your job and deserve to go as far as possible, yet I've heard you speak about how you have to beg for a share of the limited amount available, and you never get enough to use as you'd like on your projects. I have more money than I can possibly spend so, to me, the answer was obvious.'

Josie plonked her hands down on the edge of his table and leaned over to glare straight into his face. 'Maybe it is, to you. In fact you're just another hypocrite! And God knows what you've made me look like in front of my colleagues!'

Dario stood up sharply, making her jump back.

'What have they got to do with anything that goes on here? And as for calling me a hypocrite—*dannazione*! This funding for your project would mean you could stay here for longer. You don't want to leave here tomorrow any more than I want you to go—so what's hypocritical about trying to keep you here? I'm trying to help, Josie. Whatever is wrong with that?' Dario continued, exasperated. 'What *is* wrong with you?'

'Nothing!' she yelled—although he noticed she could no longer meet his gaze. 'Unless you call honesty and integrity faults!'

'It's a bit difficult holding a conversation with you when you're so far up on your high horse!' he retorted. 'Why don't you come down to earth so we can discuss this like adults?'

'Oh, would you *listen* to yourself?'

'No—you listen to *me*!' he snapped back. 'At first I thought you were too delicate a flower to get involved with me. Now you come bursting in here like poison ivy! If you really want the truth, I wanted to make up for the way you've been treated in the past. What's so bad about that?'

'Just about everything! Can't you see?'

'No!' Dario flopped back in his chair, throwing up his hands in disbelief. 'How can you say that?'

'*I* want to be in charge of what I feel and what I do and where I go, and by paying money to try and keep me here, you've made me feel like a…like a common…' Josie couldn't bring herself to say the word, but it was obvious which one she had in mind.

Dario's jaw dropped when he realised what she meant. 'How dare you? I would never dream of paying a woman to sleep with me,' he said coldly.

'You don't have to! You've got power, prestige, influence, social standing—what woman wouldn't want a part of that?' she yelled.

'Not you, obviously.'

She stared at him, hot and red and breathing very fast.

Making a supreme effort, Dario wrenched his attention back from her pulsating breasts to her face. It was funny how every tiny detail had fixed itself so firmly in his mind—the slight gap between her teeth, the way she kept brushing her hair behind her ears when she was angry—*or nervous*, he found himself thinking.

'This is it, Dario,' she said in a voice full of venom. 'I don't want to be your mistress any more.'

That was a shock. 'Really? I don't remember asking you to become my mistress in the first place. I didn't think that was the arrangement.'

Her angry flush became the nervous pink of embarrassment.

'S…stop it! You didn't have to ask me. N…not in so many words. You wanted my body and…and…and, I wanted yours…' She blushed even deeper at the admission. 'I was only going to be here for a little while. That's why we agreed to enjoy this while it lasted, and then put it all down to experience.'

'But we're both getting so much enjoyment, so much *pleasure* out of your stay. Why don't you like the idea of extending it?'

Because I can't stop wanting you!

'This isn't about the length of my stay, Dario! Can't you see what you've done? I've lobbied and argued and written and rung everyone I could think of for months and months, trying to get funding for my project, but nobody's taken me seriously. Then you push a pile of cash at them and *ecco*! *E*verything's fine and dandy.

But you can't see how this makes me feel—and, what's worse, you'll *never* understand—not in a million years!'

She burst into noisy tears of rage and frustration.

Dario stared at her. His sister was the only person he had seen cry real tears before. It was such a shocking sight, it took him a few seconds to react. Then in a flash of movement he was on his feet and pulling Josie into his arms. That made her howl all the louder. His arms full of weeping woman, Dario wondered how and why they were getting further and further away from the gentle dwindling of passion and eventual amicable parting he'd had in mind.

He heard her snivel something that might have been 'I'm a total failure…' and held her closer still.

'How can you say that?' he asked in a reply that could cover all sorts of eventualities. It seemed to work. There was an unsteady pause in her tears.

'I've always known it,' she said slowly, her words still stippled with tears, 'because every time I let anybody get under my skin, it all goes wrong. First my dad walked out, then my fiancé, and now you're trying to lead me into the same trap! Not even work can save me this time. I was happy here while there was a strict time limit. I could accept that, and it meant I didn't have to worry about our future. I knew we didn't have one. Now you've extended my stay here.'

'But that's a good thing! Isn't it?'

With a final sniff, she put her hands on his chest and levered herself back to look up at him. It was time to be honest.

'No, it isn't.' She closed her eyes and sighed heavily. 'You just don't get it, do you? This was supposed to be nothing more than a fling. I only allowed myself to sleep with you because I'd convinced myself that I could handle it on that basis. Now you've changed the rules, how is that supposed to make me feel? Guess!'

'Quite frankly, I can't.'

She gritted her teeth. 'It's setting me up for disaster. You'll find someone else, exactly like Andy did. The only difference is, this time I'll be expecting it. It'll be like sitting on a ticking time bomb. When it goes off and you leave me, I'll be convinced, once and for all, that I'm emotionally hopeless and ought to avoid any contact with other people ever again!'

'What?' He was incredulous. 'How can you say that? It's not true—and you can't simply shut yourself away! Everybody loves you!'

'No, they don't. *You* don't, for a start. And you never will.' Her eyes blazed, and he could see she was struggling very hard to control herself.

'But…think of all the goodwill there is for you, back in England,' he said, manfully hiding his desperation. This had started life as such a brilliant idea, but here was Josie, scattering his plans to the four winds. Dario was amazed to find that his usual caution had deserted him. Josie was hurting and he wanted to make her feel better, but he had no idea how. His own feelings had to be forgotten while he tried to salvage the situation.

'If they thought anything of me or my work at all, they would have given me enough money to do what I wanted in the first place. You wouldn't have had to go behind my back like this.'

'Josie! Try looking at this rationally. There's only one reason why they didn't give you all the money you needed—because it wasn't there to be given,' Dario said firmly. 'That's why the university was so delighted to accept my offer. All the people I spoke to there were full of praise for you. They would have loved to support you more, if only they'd been able to. In fact, before I stepped in they were worried that some other institution would head-hunt you.'

Hiccuping back her tears, Josie looked up at him suspiciously.

'You're making it up.'

He looked back at her with the smallest suspicion of a smile. 'Would a faithless playboy lie to you about something serious like that?'

'He might, if he thought it would get him back into my good books.'

'I think too much of you to lie, Josie.'

They both went very still—and then Dario frowned.

'…I mean as a friend of the family, of course. I didn't mean to upset you. All I wanted to do was to give you a nice surprise. It was nothing more than that.'

To his utter horror, Josie burst into floods of tears again.

'Whatever is the matter now?' Dario asked before a sudden flash of insight hit him. 'What's *really* upsetting you?'

'Don't you know?'

He shook his head, which only made her misery worse. He felt her pull in a huge shuddering breath before confronting him one last time.

'Thanks to you, I have to go back to England right now anyway because I love you and you couldn't care less about me and if I stay you'll dump me and it'll break my heart all over again and I won't be able to bear it!' she wailed in one long drawn-out howl of agony, before dragging herself from his sheltering arms and running straight out of the room.

Dario was so stunned he let her go. He had obviously read the situation all wrong, but he didn't have a clue how to put things right. He suppressed a desperate impulse to go chasing after her because he had no idea what to do or say. The awful suspicion that he would only make a terrible situation worse kept him trapped inside his office.

He thought about his portrait of Josie, wearing her lovely green dress. It was still incomplete because work on it had been interrupted so often by their desire for each other.

And now it will never be finished, he thought with a pang of realisation as the true scale of this disaster suddenly came home to him. *I've lost her just as surely as I lost Arietta.*

The name pierced him like an arrow, but in a way he didn't expect. It wasn't with the pain of sorrow, but with the shock of revelation.

For Arietta would *never* have spoken to him as Josie had done.

Storming back to her own rooms, Josie dressed, piled everything into her suitcases and scrawled a note asking for all her equipment to be packed up and sent back to England. The last thing she did was take her beautiful green cocktail dress from its padded hanger. She gazed at it for a long time before laying it down on a sheet of tissue paper and folding it reverently for its trip to England. Yet striking all her colleagues dumb at the university Christmas ball was the very last thing on her mind now.

All she wanted to do was get as far away from Dario as possible.

No, Arietta wouldn't have spoken to me like that, Dario thought with growing unease. *She would never have put up with me keeping a light alive for another woman in the first place.*

He remembered how he had fought with Arietta on the night she'd died. If he had let her come back in her own time, and not provoked her into going too fast as she went into that bend, his life would have turned out very differently.

And I wouldn't be standing here, resisting the temptation to go after Josie and tell her a few home truths, he thought bitterly. Knowing he was in the same building as she was, but separated from her by a huge gulf of misunderstanding, was unbearable. Abandoning his work, he strode out to his studio and turned her unfinished portrait to face the wall. Then he began methodically going through his tubes and pans of paint, and rinsing brushes. The only alternatives were to risk her dashing off for ever, or force a showdown that could have no winners.

Dario was the tenth Count di Sirena. Aristocrats didn't do that sort of thing. His ancestors had ruled by the sword and they were afraid of nothing. Josie knew that. He thought of her now in her new manifestation as a bouncing fireball of defiance and suddenly, strangely, he wanted to laugh.

She's brave, I'll give her that, he thought. *What a Contessa she would have made!*

That really did make him smile. It was an expression he couldn't sustain, because loving was something Dario had convinced himself he could live without. Letting another woman into his life would mean reliving all the agony he had suffered over Arietta, and he couldn't do it. *If I give in now then somehow, some day, I'd lose Josie too, and I couldn't bear to go through all that pain a second time.*

'As though living like *this* is any better!' he yelled, suddenly grabbing the nearest thing to hand and sending it flying across his studio.

It was a box of willow charcoal. It hit the wall and burst, sending brittle black shards in all directions. The sooty explosion brought Dario to his senses. Shocked, he went to retrieve what he could. As he did so, he passed the window and caught sight of the landscape he knew so well. It made him stop and think. For hundreds of years his forebears had fought and died for these glorious acres. If they had been afraid of what *might* happen, the di Sirena family would have died out long ago and Dario wouldn't now be enjoying the heady mix of joy and responsibility that made up his life. Those warriors had lived their lives to the full, and to hell with tomorrow.

Josie had been as brave as any of his sword-wielding ancestors and, in refusing to risk his heart a second time, Dario knew he had lost her.

Antonia was upset to see Josie leave, but she was too good a friend to pry. Everything was arranged with Castello Sirena efficiency, from a car to take Josie out to the *castello*'s airstrip, to her premature flight back to England. By the time everything was organised, the arid anger and despair that had forced Josie to storm away from Dario had faded. Now regret lodged in her throat like a cherry stone. She had been afraid this would happen, and sure enough her nightmare had come true. Why had she been stupid enough to let herself fall under Dario's spell?

Because I hoped history wouldn't repeat itself, she thought bitterly. *It's the same mistake every woman makes.*

She twisted her damp handkerchief between her hands, unable to believe that the man who made her feel like the only woman in the world could still end up hurting her so grievously. To take her mind off her pain, she checked her documents. Then she did it a second time. After that, she went through her handbag, over and over again. Counting change and flicking through her diary passed a few more minutes, but not enough. When a mutter of annoyance rippled through the di Sirena staff she looked up, glad of any distraction. Through the glass wall of their office, she could see someone on the phone. The ground crew were summoned. She watched them straggling into the room. They were some distance away, but the office door had been left open. Josie tried to hear enough without looking as though she was listening. She could only make out a few words, but that was all it took to throw her into a panic.

Dario was coming.

He must have given orders to delay her flight on the di Sirena jet. Josie had never felt so angry—or so alone.

At the worst possible moment, her phone announced an incoming text. With a distracted cry she grabbed it, then stopped and stared.

It was from Dario. The two short, simple words he'd sent her made no sense, but they still had the same effect as a blow to her head. Totally absorbed by his message, she stood up, but why, she didn't know. Then everything and everybody else in the aircraft hangar suddenly faded away from her consciousness. A little bubble of silence grew to envelop her. She glanced around wildly. Then she looked back at the display on her phone, as if by some miracle the characters had morphed into something more understandable. They still made no sense. Two words—after all the thousands of words she had wasted on Dario… It must be a mistake. It *had* to be. What else was she supposed to think? That he could be as cruel as he was unthinking?

A terrible rumbling sound echoed through the whole airstrip building. It was like thunder, but Josie knew thunder wouldn't reverberate up through her feet like that. And a storm would stop outside the main doors…

This one didn't. It was Dario. He was riding Ferrari,

galloping the horse so fast he couldn't stop. They hurtled straight into the hangar before he managed to pull up in a plunging, wheeling rattle of hooves.

'Well, Josie? What is your answer?'

She stared at him. He was pale, breathless and as focused on her as ever.

'No.'

He flung himself off his horse. Slapping it on the rump, he sent it back to the stables while he cornered Josie.

'No? What do you mean, *no*?'

'Exactly what I say. What are you trying to do to me, Dario? You mess up my life and then suddenly, out of the blue, you send me a text as though the past few hours had never happened. What do you think I am? A masochist, or simply insane?'

'Marry me.'

It had been a shock to read it as a message on her phone. Now it was more than that.

Josie looked at him and saw the truth. This was the last gamble of a desperate man. His expression was hunted, and his normally tidy hair windblown. She noticed a strange base note to the usually subtle fragrance of his aftershave. Later she realised it must be the tang of adrenalin, but at that moment all she could concentrate on was how she was going to get through the next few minutes. She breathed unevenly, trying to steady her nerves, but she found things had gone too far for that.

'That didn't make any sense when you sent it as a

text, Dario. Saying it out loud doesn't make it any more sensible.'

'It's what you want. *It must be what you want,*' he repeated, his voice rising.

From somewhere in the distance came the faint sound of the ground crew. They had an audience. For the first time in her life, Josie didn't care what anyone else saw, heard or thought. All she was interested in was Dario. She gazed at him, not knowing whether to laugh or cry.

'You sound like a man who is trying hard to convince himself.'

'I am convinced—because deep in my heart I know you want me, and I want you—'

Josie covered her face with her hands. 'No...you want my body, that's all. And yes, I want yours, too. But marriage is a partnership for life, Dario. I don't think you understand what that means,' she sighed.

'You're wrong—*wrong*, Josie! I know *exactly* how marriage works!' he growled through gritted teeth. 'I spent years watching my parents tearing each other apart. You think I've refused to commit before now simply because of Arietta? You don't know the half of it. There were times when I would have paid a king's ransom to get away from the unhappy life sentence that was my parents' marriage. They couldn't divorce: my father didn't want to be the first in his family line to break rank. My mother was too fond of his money and the position in society it gave her.'

Josie was shocked. 'Then why in the world do you

think that proposing marriage to me will be the answer to all your problems?'

'I don't.'

It was a clumsy, hurtful answer. Realising that, Dario swore under his breath and tried again.

'It's because I know nothing less than marriage will keep you here at my side.'

Josie looked at him narrowly. 'Go on.'

'What do you mean?'

'There must be more to it than that. You've told me your parents put you off marriage. Proposing to me must seem like running your head into a matrimonial noose! You don't need an heir, you've got Fabio, so it can't be because you've suddenly decided you require a legitimate son. Women flock around you. There must be something else.'

His eyes locked with hers. They were dark as jet as he said, 'I once told a woman I loved her, and she left me.'

'Arietta didn't leave you, she died.'

It was cruel, but Josie had long since stopped feeling kind when it came to Dario's relationships with other women.

'Yes.' He gazed at her with naked anguish. 'And I killed her. For years I've been telling myself I sent her car into that ditch as surely as if I had been driving it myself. I chased her away, Josie.'

'But it didn't stop you racing after me,' she said slowly.

She saw the colour drain away from his golden skin. He nodded.

'It was a risk I had to take. I couldn't bear the thought of you boarding that plane and flying out of my life. It wiped every other thought clean from my mind.'

He slumped down in the seat beside hers. Once again she saw him rub at his face as though trying to erase all his bad memories. Knowing what he must be going through but feeling powerless to help, Josie waited.

'When you first walked into my life, it brought back memories of how happy I had been—and how devastated I was when Arietta died,' he said eventually. 'I couldn't bear to lay myself open to that torture again. That's why, when Fabio was born, I made him my heir. I couldn't imagine letting any woman so far into my life that there could ever be the possibility of children. Until a few weeks ago it simply wasn't an option. Like you, I had learned that it was less painful to keep everyone at arm's length. That was why, when you stormed out on me this morning, I pretended I could leave you to come to your senses. I thought it was your loss, and that I didn't care. But it wasn't true. An awful fear began to crawl over me that one day I would forget you, the way I've forgotten Arietta. I don't want to do that, Josie. Not ever.'

It was too much. In the face of his confession, Josie's own injured feelings meant nothing. Forgetting all her resolutions, good and bad, she reached out and gently slipped her arms around him as he sat beside her. When he didn't resist, she leaned against him and laid her head against his chest.

'Does this mean you understand?'

'Maybe.' She nodded, and then felt him swallow hard.

Josie closed her eyes. Tears were very close, and she didn't want to weaken.

'I love you, Dario—more than you could ever imagine…but it won't work. I can't hope to compete for your love on the same level with Arietta. Don't you see? I've got all sorts of human failings, but she's an angel—*your* angel.'

'That's got nothing to do with the way I feel about you, Josie,' he said quietly. 'The pain of losing Arietta will never go away, but I don't feel the same about it now. My father was right when he asked me at the time what I knew about love. My answer then was "everything", but in truth it was less than nothing. *At the time.*'

'You weren't likely to learn much about love from him, by the sound of it,' Josie muttered, half to herself. She felt Dario's hand run over her back until it came to rest lightly on her shoulder.

'And it's why I think you should reconsider your proposal very carefully, Dario,' she continued with a sudden return of common sense. 'You've told me that the pain of losing Arietta stopped you risking your heart again, but falling in love is never going to be easy. Sometimes you just have to take a chance. I've been here before, so it's a scary place for me, too. I need to know I'll be getting all of you, not just tantalising glimpses of the loving, caring man you really are, deep down inside. How can you promise me this is for ever and not just until you get scared and back off?'

It was a long time before Dario could answer. 'A di Sirena is never scared.'

Josie lifted her chin and met his glittering black gaze with defiance. 'Then prove it to me.'

'No. I don't need to.' His voice rose dangerously, attracting the attention of everyone in the building. 'I've already done everything I can to prove how much I need you. There's only one thing left to say: Josie Street, I love you. I want you, body, heart, soul and spirit for as long as I live. Nothing else matters,' he said in a crescendo of passion that left her speechless and wide-eyed with wonder.

Their audience of ground crew erupted in noisy excitement, but Josie hardly noticed. She was at the still, small centre of a universe that consisted only of Dario. He was looking down at her with such intensity that nothing else mattered to her. Josie knew she wanted him more than any other man in the world, and always would. It was madness to hesitate even for a second, but she wanted to be too sensible to be bounced into a quick answer.

Suddenly it was all too much. The arguments, the worry, all the uncertainty… Her eyes filled with tears. That only added anger to her maelstrom of emotions. This was what she had wanted all along, wasn't it? For Dario to put her first and show that he loved her? Well, statements didn't come much more explicit than a public proposal of marriage.

'Dario, I'm scared…' she began, then saw he looked as stricken as she was. She wanted him with all her heart, but didn't know if she was brave enough to accept the challenge.

'This is all wrong! You told me you don't do meaningful relationships, and now I know why. You might think you want me now, but it won't last,' she said slowly, reliving the darkest days of her last betrayal.

'Do you think I care about other women, now I've met you?'

At the harsh sound of his words her thoughts fled and all she could do was gaze at him. The suave, sophisticated man who had charmed her from the instant they'd met had vanished. Dario was streaked with sweat from his desperate ride across country. He wouldn't have done that for any of the fragile beauties who had drifted around the *castello* at his last party—but he had done it for her.

'I...I don't know,' she said cautiously.

'No—and neither did I until the moment you tried to run out of my life, Josie. When Arietta died, it ripped all the heart from me. For years I managed to live without it. I simply existed, passing time. You changed all that. For the first time since losing Arietta, I started to enjoy the world around me. I began to anticipate the future, instead of merely looking forward to the next party. Isn't that enough? What we've found in each other is really good.'

'I know!' she burst out, unable to keep silent.

He pressed his lips together, trying to hold back the ultimate confession. 'I've given you far more of myself over these past few weeks than I've offered any other woman,' he admitted in a low voice. 'A little of me was more than enough for them.'

'Yes, but it isn't enough for me!' she blazed. 'I'm worth more than all of your other women put together!'

Horrified at her own outburst, she slapped her hands over her mouth, but it was too late. Stricken, she gazed at him.

He gave a silent whistle. 'That's quite an admission, coming from you. Shy, self-effacing Dr Josie Street.'

'I know. I'm sorry,' she said in a small voice.

'I didn't mean it as criticism. It was a compliment.'

Josie blinked. The effect was like rubbing sandpaper over her eyes. That could be the only reason her eyes started watering again.

'You were right about me, too, Josie. I've spent too long wallpapering over the cracks in my life. It took you to show me there's more to life than shallow pleasures. Without you, I'm nothing but an empty shell. I love you. Marry me. Will you?'

'Oh, Dario,' she breathed. 'Don't you know the answer?'

'I will never get used to this,' Josie murmured a few days later, as they watched workmen clambering over scaffolding set up along the lime avenue. The boughs of each tree were being spangled with fairy lights, ready for the grand party Dario had arranged to announce their engagement. Guests visiting the *castello* would have the best of both worlds. During the day, their arrival would be serenaded by bees and golden orioles. When they left, their way would be lit by a million coloured stars.

'Oh, I'm sure you will.' Dario's arm circled her waist and he drew her close to kiss her hair. It was flowing loose around her shoulders today, exactly as he liked it.

He enjoyed its clean, sweet fragrance for a while, then added, 'But just in case you need a little help, I've arranged something special for you. Your mother is coming over for our party this weekend.'

Josie looked up at him, her eyes alight.

'Dario, that's fantastic—but how did you manage that? I tried so hard to convince her, but she's always been too nervous to travel abroad before!'

He squeezed her playfully. 'I've arranged everything for her, from passport to transport, door to door. All she has to do is pack.'

'You really have thought of everything,' Josie said in wonder. 'And you did all this…for me?' It was impossible to keep a note of disbelief out of her voice.

'Of course. If it makes you happy, *cara*, then nothing is impossible. I would move the stars in the sky for you,' he said softly, and then kissed her until all her thoughts flew away.

* * * * *

MILLS & BOON®

MILLS & BOON®

Why not subscribe?
Never miss a title and save money too!

Here is what's available to you if you join the exclusive **Mills & Boon® Book Club** today:

* *Titles up to a month ahead of the shops*
* *Amazing discounts*
* *Free P&P*
* *Earn Bonus Book points that can be redeemed against other titles and gifts*
* *Choose from monthly or pre-paid plans*

Still want more?
Well, if you join today we'll even give you
50% OFF your first parcel!

So visit **www.millsandboon.co.uk/subscriptions**
or call **Customer Relations on 0844 844 1351***
to be a part of this exclusive Book Club!

**This call will cost you 7 pence per minute plus your
phone company's price per minute access charge.*